Nikolai's Revenge

Book 2 of The Savage Derangement Trilogy

Craig R Smith

Book Editor Kat Betts of Element Editing Services
Book Cover by C. C. Mickey

Edition Number 1 edition 2024

Prologue

A few families had settled into the silent place once known as the Sierra Nevada Complex; once a busy research laboratory owned and secretly operated by the Corporation. Soon after the nuclear holocoast erupted, the scientists and engineers abandoned the scientific complex and only a few chose to remain in what was now a deserted metal structure. The sealed complex kept the poison radiation out and kept those who had stayed safe. Most of the complex was far underground, but another poison would eventually lead to their doom. The faceless predator wouldn't kill those who had remained quickly like a living predator, but devour them from within. That was thirty seasons ago.

First the scientists and engineers would feel a scratchy throat and a slight fever; quite manageable for these individuals, but that would merely be the start of their eventual downfall. Before they knew it a violent fever struck them, which came with a raised temperature, hazy double vision, and a repugnant and repetitive cough that didn't seem to do anything. Gray substance began to run from their nostrils, ears and pores of their skin. It was like the poisoned air had infected those who remained with some type of parasite. The question remained: Could they survive this attack, or would they die a horrible death?

One by one each remaining inhabitant slowly expired like a low light in the night. But before the gray oozy substance could dissipate, two sets of metal feet approached the dying scientist with his glassed-over eyes, leaned over and inspected the dying man. In a digital voice, one of the visitors said, "Is the substance still useful, Master?"

The cyborg took a closer look at the dying man. "Even if it isn't, according to our sources, Cheeves, there is more of the gassy substance in the lower levels. If the human portion of my memory isn't too corrupted, I possess a detailed schematic of this complex and the Corporation always hid its secrets well."

"We can't fail Master Shadow Lord. It was clear on our mission here," echoed the mechanical helper.

A half smirk came from the cyborg's half-human, half-machine lips. "Yes, Shadow Lord is looking over our shoulders." The machine man looked at his metal body. "And we have so much to thank the agent of shadow, don't we?" Under his breath, he said, "What the Shadow Lord doesn't know, won't hurt him."

The cyborg motioned to his android aid to proceed. "Make sure you take enough of the substance for the Darkness and our own purposes, Cheeves."

Eighteen months ago

Doria and her family had traveled to the Sierra Nevada Complex, after hearing from a secondhand source that it was a safe place to settle, but no one could tell them who had secured the former corporate facility. The facility was massive in size, with several floors being built underground. The place was rustic, with few of the complex's gargantuan blast doors still working. Still, it was a place they could call home.

Resources were scarce and the surrounding environment inhospitable since the radiation poisoning had only started to dissipate, after the Corporation unleashed its Hell on Earth. The safety of the complex had become more important with the bombardment of every possible resource the Corporation's adversaries could utilize. Doria and her family had traveled a great distance, despite the continuous discouragement from her brother, Straus. Their family and a few others had traveled together, and they intended to create a community inside the complex.

The original fears of those they had left behind was that even if the complex was safe to inhabit, the air scrubbers and other electric devices would be rendered useless from the bombs' electric magnetic pulse signatures. What Doria and her followers didn't realize was that the complex had a tough titanium exterior that possessed a slight shielding; plus, the farther you went underground, the more the earth tended to insulate electronic devices. The facility also provided the settlers with more protection from the elements outside as long as they kept the massive blast door shut, or did the best they could. They were not aware of the horrors living inside the mausoleum complex.

Doria thought the place was older than the leaders of their community had thought, which included her husband. From the evidence found during previous expeditions upon arriving, the complex had been used as part of a research faculty, but other parts must have been storage for secret chemicals and other things the Corporation didn't want anyone to discover.

Life wasn't any easier living in the complex compared to living in the makeshift community where resources were scarce, where there was food poisoning caused by the radiation in the air, where children's growth was stunted. Water sources had either dried up or been poisoned by the fallout over the decades since the Corporation had unleashed hell on them. Doria was happy, or at least as happy as she could expect to be under the harsh conditions.

She was with her husband and their two children and that's all she needed to keep her sane. None of them had come down sick, unlike a few of the travelers, mostly the elderly who had too much exposure to the radiation in the air. Most of those who hunted or traveled in the open used special breathers and clothing that kept them safe, for the most part. If your gear broke while out exploring, time and the poisonous air would do you in.

The one thing none of the families ever did was venture too deep into the complex. There was a slight rank stench that lingered in the air, and it only intensified the farther in you ventured. That was the reason the community never camped too far into the complex's vast interior. Staying close to the complex's entrance also gave them an easy way to escape if it would ever be necessary. But the community never camped too close to the massive metal blast doors, since you could never tell what would stroll through from the outside.

Doria's followers had seen shadows outside the complex, but never came face to face with any of the mutated beasts that had survived the nuclear winter. She had come across a few of these mutilated carcasses when it was her turn to serve on the hunting posse; every adult who was able, did. Though occasional hunting parties, usual no less than four to five adults, had come across enormous prints in the ash-littered ground, but never deep enough to make out actual sizes of the creatures roaming in the night.

She had heard the tall tales, or at least what she perceived as overexaggeration; one time Doria found a gargantuan print herself. Normally, before the devastation of the environment, local guides could tell what species roamed the area with claw marks on tree trunks and patches of fur left behind. Now, with most indigenous trees bare, leafless and having no bark left, and none of the remaining species possessing anything remotely like fur, it was up to the individual's imagination what the creatures were like.

Doria reached down at the substantial print in the ashy surface and gently placed her hand inside. Her rebreather was doing its best to filter the toxic air out and provide breathable air. The foggy mask made it difficult to see the entire print, but she saw enough to be astonished. Her hand was dwarfed by the print. Whatever had made it would make quick work of her, if it ever got hold of her tiny frame.

A muffled voice came from behind. "Enormous, isn't it?"

Doria turned around as if the intruder had committed a heinous crime. There, standing directly to her right, was her spouse, Eric. She could only make out his smile through the environmental suit, none of his tall thin frame was noticeable. She relaxed as soon as she recognized her husband. "Are you trying to scare me to death?"

Eric's muffled chuckle danced in his suit helmet. "Just checking on you, can never be too careful outside the complex."

"I'm more than careful enough, you know that." She scoffed. "I'm just a little skittish being outside; that happens every time I'm on patrol."

There was one instance when one of the hunting members had wandered off and was eventually discovered. His face was mauled and his body full of lacerations through the torn environmental gear, guaranteeing the hunter wouldn't survive without aid. Could a protected human survive in the wild without a protective suit? These were savage times, but whatever had survived seemed to thrive. The mutation seemed to have toughened the beasts' hides, give them flesh-tearing maws and claws, and the ability to render environmental suits useless after they were through. The only creatures that the settlers were able to catch were less fortunate populations and the poisons had transformed them as well.

A call came from the distance. A mutilated creature lay dead, and the hunting party encircled the creature. It possessed extra antlers, receding gumlines and ridged teeth for cutting through the bare earth—that's what the complex settlers were forced to eat. This was a far cry from what they had in the small community Doria's brother had provided. Even with the low supplies, it seemed to each of the followers they'd had it better at the settlement than at their new home.

She looked from her husband to the leader of the hunting expedition. Her husband nodded and said, "This is a common mutation for most of the population, but its still unclear why in other places, notably in the Wasteland, this type of mutation doesn't exist."

The expedition leader returned. "It's because nothing can live for long out in the Wasteland, or that's the rumor at least."

The dead animal repulsed Doria, but she understood they had to eat and their stores didn't replenish themselves. "I think it's best we prepare the animal for transportation before whatever killed it comes back to claim its prize."

†

Doria observed her children play with some of the other children and it made her warm inside. She sighed with relief. *Finally, a place we can call home.* It wasn't like the place they lived with Straus and his family, this place was something Doria's family could consider their own and not an adopted home. Doria didn't really know much about the families they had chosen to live with. Even during the trip to the complex most of the families kept to themselves as much as possible.

Doria and her family left the small community her brother had built up because they desired a change of scenery. Life under Straus's leadership had become strained and several of those living in the makeshift community had ventured off on their own and were never heard from again. Even though she loved her brother, he had become more monarch than a quality leader. But she had thought about it hard and acknowledged that leading a dying species as theirs could be stressful and that could have led to Straus acting out. She and her older husband both agreed, despite the dangers the trip and living so far from her brother posed, this was the right move to make. She would work with the other adult females in whatever task was needed, but she wouldn't dare get too close to them. The thought of losing more people that were close to her brought back memories of her deceased parents and how they were slaughtered at the hands of an invective tyrant.

She hadn't seen them die firsthand, but their screams for mercy still haunted her nightly dreams. Just thinking of their demise was enough to send the mother of two into a hysterical frenzy. She had to stop what she was doing, because her body was shaking like a fir tree trying to get rid of its leaves. Her breathing came in short bursts and was difficult to control. Even her vison had temporarily doubled, a river of tears raining from her eyes. Doria wiped the tears away and hoped no one had seen the condition she was in. It took her quite a while to gain her composure, but once she did, she returned to preparing the family's meal.

That morning, Doria had been working on her routine daily chores, absorbing what morning breeze had rushed through the partially open blast door. Occasionally, she would look up from washing family clothes in the washbasin or crushing lima beans for dinner and watch children playing in the distance. The children were always in danger of disappearing in the dark shadows of the complex. In the distance, two women were working together; she only glanced at them for a second.

When she had awoken, Doria had a funning feeling that she couldn't pinpoint. It wasn't a warning or a tingling sensation; it was more like she had woken up and was living someone else's life. If she had to call it anything, maybe she would consider it an intuition. As she returned to her work, the emotional affliction intensified. Suddenly, Doria felt panic, but she wasn't sure why. Her heart began to race, her hands started to shake. It was almost like she was running from someone or something, but she wasn't.

It seemed like she, not one of children, was fleeing something horrific. This wasn't the first time she'd had this emotional feeling, she'd had it right before her parents died in the refugee camp, as the invaders kidnapped her and her brother. Both kin had felt the other's anxiety, even as one of them had been struck in the head and rendered unconscious. This was the first time Doria had experienced this with one of her children, and at first she thought it was some type of heart attack-until she was seeing through her oldest child's eyes and remembered back to her youth and her parents' deaths.

The fear struck her like a stone wall. She was experiencing someone fleeing from a certain danger, but she still didn't know how or whose emotions she was feeling.

A debilitating pain shot down her shoulder, forcing her to stop what she was doing. She couldn't even continue the washing. Doria's heart began to beat rapidly. She gripped at her chest, but that didn't alleviate her pain.

A cry for help echoed in Doria's mind, a voice that seemed too familiar. "Noah!" she whispered.

Noah was Doria's oldest child at the age of twelve. He had the knack of finding anything that could cause him or someone else harm, or even draw unwanted attention on them. It made sense to her now, the reason she felt these intense emotions. Her son was calling out to her, and she needed to come to his aid, but where was he? The panicked mother released the clothes she had been washing and searched around, but there was no sign of either of her children. Doria's heart pounded as her gaze darted, looking for her children like a meerkat searching for its young. Her neck craned swiftly from one end of the section they lived in with its shadow-laden steel bulkheads. She glanced over groups of females, some older than Doria, while others could have been daughters of the older women. The family's illumination lamps provided enough light to do chores and see group members from ten to fifteen feet away. Any farther encased individuals in shadows and they were hard to make out. The steel decking might have been cold to the touch, but it never felt as if it resided in a blizzard-like envirement.

Where had Doria seen them last? What had they been doing? Who had she seen them with? All questions the mother of two was struggling with and couldn't answer. Her anxiousness was keeping her from thinking correctly. Normally, Doria was fast on her feet and able to think quickly, making her a great leader.

"Noah!" she cried. "Amelia?" Doria called for her almost eight-year-old.

There was no response from either child. Never within earshot of their mother. The debilitating pain had temporarily subsided, and Doria began to search close to their makeshift home. Doria's ability to sense what Noah did was uncanny. Once, when the family still lived with her brother, Noah had fallen and injured his knee. Without consciously knowing or anyone coming to warn her, she knew her son had injured himself.

Each family tied the leathery living-quarter tents to the metal bulkhead, providing a little extra security, or at least they thought it did. The family dwelling was one of the larger ones, a section for Doria and her husband to sleep, one for Noah, and another for Amelia with a somewhat spacious section for the family to gather to eat or for entertainment. There was a tiny storage space. Most of the storage space sat at the western section of the camp, so there was no need for a lot of space. Other tent structures were smaller, even with families the size of Doria's, they were lucky that they had inherited a large tent from Straus.

The family's home was close to the center of the camp, and with Doria's position it made it easy for her and her husband to get to camp meetings, and for camp members to come to the family home for a scheduled meeting, when it was required. Other families were forced to live closer to the edge of camp, mostly arranged by seniority. But no family chose to live outside the camp, exposed to the unknowns of the rest of the steel ark complex.

Loud screaming came from the far end of the community, close to where receding shadows mapped out the outer perimeter of the camp. Two children rushed out from the shadows, waving their arms in the air and screaming at the top of their lungs. One of those children was Amelia.

Without any hesitation, Doria rushed to her youngest child, leaping past a food storage container and the two women she had originally ignored, and embraced her daughter. Amelia was covered in in dirt and blood. After fussing over her child, Doria discovered it wasn't Amelia's blood that covered the child. Doria turned Amelia towards her. "Whose blood is all over you, child?"

The little girl was sobbing, and it was apparent she was scared out of her wits. Amelia couldn't stop for one moment to explain to her mother what had happened. Tears ran down the little girl's cheeks and she was shaking. Her little friend was in a similar condition. It seemed all Doria wanted to do was comfort the child, but she had more pressing issues to deal with, ones that fueled her fear as a parent.

"Amelia, where is your brother? Where is Noah and why isn't he with you?"

In between sobs, the little girl managed to say, "Th . . . the mon . . . mon . . . ster . . . got . . . hhhimmm."

"What monster? You're not making any sense."

Amelia began to cry again.

†

Eventually, several adults, including Doria, were able to get enough out of the two children to search for Doria's son and two more missing children. Doria could always sense what her eldest was feeling and right now there was looming fear and apprehension. This wasn't normally like Noah, he was so adventurous, cautious about his surroundings and quick on his feet.

They had wandered off down two levels from where the community was. Doria, another adult female and two males joined the search party. The fear was if too many joined the party and more volunteered, others would be lost to the vast maze of stairwells and unknown levels below.

Doria's husband was one of the community's leaders, and he had to stay with the community to keep it calm during the intensive search. Too many adults threatened to go off in search of the so-called child-mutilator threat, yet Doria and her husband feared they didn't have enough evidence of such a tragedy or anything else to speak of. This would only worsen their search for the missing children. Whoever or whatever had attacked the children created another issue; it was proof that someone else besides the community was living in the deserted complex. Could it have been a survivor of one of the colonies they searched for when first arriving?

The deeper the search party got, the darker the hallways became. Each time they reached an end of a passageway, they were forced to climb down a set of metal gangway stairs. The sound of their shoes striking each metal step echoed into the dark shadows and each time they ascended or descended, it sent chills down Doria's spine.

As the search party descended into the depths of the complex, Doria could feel some gawking eyes observing them, but every time she looked around a dark corner or hallway, she found nothing. Her human eyes could not penetrate the pitch-blackness that consumed every inch of corridor down in the lower levels, not without her illumination device. The device cupped nicely into her feminine hand, not too bulky or heavy; allowing her to swing it one direction and back the other way with little resistance.

A scraping sound came from Doria's right, not too far from where she stood. As fast as she could, the mother of two shone her light down the empty corridor. All she could see was the reflection of light bouncing off the metal dividing wall, temporarily blinding her. It would take Doria several blinks to fight off the million or so spots that kept her blind. As she rubbed her eyes in the hopes of regaining her sight, a growl echoed down the direction she had just investigated. It sounded like a crazed wild dog, but with a deeper monotone. She swallowed hard, not knowing what she might encounter if she chose to investigate the sound.

A familiar sound followed in the same direction. A childlike cry, and the sound of her son calling out to her. "Mommy!" was all Doria heard in a faint voice, as if the voice's owner was struggling or gasping for breath. The sudden cry faded as quickly as it had started. She looked in the direction of the other members of the search party had traveled. She was alone, so she would have to do this on her own. Doria gathered all her willpower and moved down the empty hallway.

The hallway was as dark as the rest of the level. Doria could barely see her own shadow and without her lantern she would most likely be running into a hallway bulkhead at every turn. The only sound came from each footfall she made. The *stomp, stomp* of her boot heel was more than unnerving, keeping Doria on edge. There were no more cries for help or even the maleficent growl that had nearly scared her to death. She wasn't sure what was more nerve-racking, the demonic growl or the eerie silence.

"Noah," she called out in a half-whisper, half-shout, fearful of attracting any unwanted attention.

Doria still had the feeling that something was watching her.

She moved as if on eggshells or near a colossal beast fearful of awaking it. The one thing Doria had noticed since they had entered the lower levels was the musty smell of decay that lingered. This was the farthest any of them had dared to come.

The mother of two crept along, occasionally running her hand along the cold, dirty and at times rusted dividing wall to guide her. The darkness that reached beyond her lantern's array of illumination was a nothing but a sea of pitch-black darkness. The mother of two took a deep breath, her anxiety beginning to break down the wall of support she had built. *No time for an anxiety attack*, Doria thought.

Suddenly a scream that sounded like an adult male came from far down the other way. She thought about the rest of her search party. "Who else could it be?" Doria whispered. Now she was scared. Her senses were warning her that something was down here, but where and what did it want? Her heart began to pound a little faster, her hands were sweating and the aroma of rust filled her lungs. Even Doria's vision began to slowly blur. Something in the air was attacking her, and she fought the desire to flee the level completely.

Doria took a deep breath before she continued.

She held her lantern as far out in front of her as possible, but it only gave her field of vision another foot of visibility. She was taking tiny steps, dragging the soles of her boots along. Placing her hand against the dividing wall, she lost herself in the moment. Then a slurping, wet sound came from the dark plains of the hallway. That was followed by a low moaning that nearly released her from her panicked state, having her run the opposite way.

Doria swallowed her fear and raised her lantern slowly, shaking to the point she couldn't keep the lantern steady. The illumination bounced off the bulkhead, the metal floor and dark ceiling. Down the silent hallway was a dull light, like someone had left it on when they had left. Doria was receiving those anxious vibes once again. Whatever had growled at her before was in there, she just knew it. The only question was, was it the place her son had called out from?

She moved towards the yellow illumination, which seemed like a pinprick in the darkness. Her hand shook, and each step was like being a tightrope walker on a thin wire, high above everything else. Doria was forced to take deep, even breaths to avoid hyperventilating. The closer she came to the dull light the higher her overbearing emotions became.

"Relax, Doria. What is the worst that can happen? Death is such an overrated thing," she told herself. She laughed, knowing she was scared as hell no matter what happened. Something was in that room, and it could harm her or anyone else in their party. In fact, she was sure the thing was daring her, drawing her near. She could smell the looming death so strongly that it temporarily took her soul out of her body. The out-of-body experience was alien to her; she thought she was already dead.

Did the others come this way? she asked herself. *Or am I just trying to convince myself of it?*

A growling sound reverberated over and over again in her mind; she was hooked, and she and whatever made the noise were connected. The one advantage she had over whatever she was about to face was that it didn't know of her connection with her son.

That's how she knew Noah was with that thing, whatever it was. That was the scariest part of all. What had become of her son. The only thing she had was the notion his body was still with that thing. Her throat had become dry, and she couldn't call for Noah or scream for help. Something inside her told her that the people in the rescue party weren't the only ones in peril. The entire community was in danger, all of them. Doria couldn't explain how she knew this, like how she knew her son was in trouble, or how Noah was with that monstrosity of a thing, whatever it was. She just knew.

A vision of a decrepit thing with a humped back, a limp arm that hung to its side, with hairless, wrinkled skin. It could barely move. That vision surely wasn't aiding her or her nearly crapped-out nerves. Once again, she raised her arm and looked towards the dull light now only feet from her. She no longer had control of her breathing and she was shaking too much to hold the light well.

The entrance was doorless and the *thump, thump* noise was profound; it sounded like a pump continuously pumping but what and for what reason? The complex was as dead as a morgue. No matter how much she hesitated, she was being drawn into the room with the dull light and the thumping noise. A mashing sound, like flesh being ripped apart and something chewing—it was a wet and nauseating sound that almost made her vomit.

It was now or never, so Doria stepped through the doorway. The room was a mess. A pump or maintenance room, she wasn't sure. The dull light kept her next to blind, but at least she could make some things out. As she made her way into the room, Doria nearly fell over a corpse. As far as she could tell, one of the men in the search party, she was certain about that. Could he have been the one who screamed?

But she shook it off, thinking she was hallucinating. Her focus was finding her son and nothing else. Then she heard the same growl, but it was louder and sounded close; something moved swiftly past her sight, but it was too blurred in the light. As she made her way towards the rear of the room, there came the sound of mashing and flesh tearing. Something feasting on raw flesh.

Doria moved a step closer to the sound, and then another, that's when she saw the motion of the thing's gray back. She moved closer, despite her consciousness begging her to stop. With each step, more of the brute was exposed. The thing's skin was gray all over. It had long clawlike fingers and flesh-shredding teeth. Blood oozed from its maw as it fed on a corpse. The slush sound drove Doria nuts, but she had to find out. Was her son alive or dead?

She moved around the side of a tipped-over toolbox. The thing dug into its meal, ripping raw flesh. By this time Doria was merely feet away. It had a humanlike shape, but if it was ever human at all, it had lost that identity. The *crunch, crunch* continued, but somehow Doria knew the thing sensed her presence. At this point she could no longer feel the presence of her son. Was he dead? Faster and faster her heart raced, as if it would rip from her chest; it was racing faster than Doria ever thought capable.

The creature slowly turned its head towards her. Once it was ready, she could see it for what it really was. Its red, searing eyes, stared her down. It had stopped feeding. A piece of flesh dangled from its jagged maw with its claws were at the ready position. Doria didn't sense anger or hatred, not even anxiety from the thing before her. She looked down. Her husband lay on the floor, half eaten.

Half his face was missing, and his chest had been ripped open.

Doria wanted to cry, but nothing came out of her mouth. Her breathing had calmed, and she was no longer shaking. At that moment, she couldn't feel Noah; she understood that he was gone. These were her last moments. The thing growled at the mother and Doria stood there ready to take what was coming. The thing dropped her husband's flesh and lunged at Doria. She didn't feel what the thing would do to her, seconds later. No matter what, Doria had to find a way to escape—even if her soul was no longer moving with her physical body.

A small metal object, a spy, hidden in the shadows on the wall, recorded everything for its master and instantaneously transmitted the images back to the Merciless Reach.

Darkcloak was working diligently in his hidden cave in an undisclosed location within the Merciless Reach. A sensation in the shadow agent's head rang and Darkcloak opened a portal; the decrepit air split apart and one of the shadow agent's many spies appeared before him. The spy was a lanky, small thing with several eyes surrounding its oval-shaped head. Its limbs hung to the side like elastic straps and the being floated in the middle of the portal.

"Edogan," groaned Darkcloak. "What reason do I have for the privilege of your appearance?" Sarcasm dripped from his words.

The floating spy did what seemed like a bow in respect, but with the way its body was constructed—it had been created by Darkcloak—it was difficult to decipher if it was a bow or not. "Forgive me, Master Darkcloak, for interrupting you. I know how busy you are. Reports are coming back from the Sierra Nevada Complex on Earth…"

"I know where the complex is located," barked Darkcloak.

"Forgive me, Master."

"Continue, Edogan."

"Master, a human subject has been chosen at the complex for the biological agent."

An image of Doria popped up in front of Darkcloak.

Darkcloak had his own surprise for the rest of humanity that would upscale the Shadow Lord and the Darkness's own plans. Only Darkcloak was aware of his plan completely. "Has the mutant planted the biological agent on the subject?"

"Not yet, Master. We were waiting for your orders to do so."

Darkcloak growled at the spy. "Make it happen."

The spy bowed. "Yes, Master. And what of the Shadow Lord's cyborg; do we make contact with them as well, providing what we know?"

This was the problem with keeping his dark plan to himself, none of his spies understood the Darkness wouldn't know of their own plans. "Never say that name in my presence. We will be keeping our intel to ourselves and the subject chosen from the Shadow Empire."

Once the spy's image vanished, Darkcloak thought, *Now my real vengeance will begin.*

Chapter 1

Present Day

Clover slowly opened his eyes. The numbing residue left by the dream lingered. He didn't wonder about the dream itself or its meaning. It was like it had never happened, but this wasn't the first dream the bioengineered assassin had had. The difference between his dreams and humans was that he refused to give those dreams meaning. It wasn't something Clover could put a finger on, so instead of pondering the meaning, he brushed the dream aside as if it had never happened and got up.

Despite the darkness of the cavern he had made as his abode, Clover could see the rough, rocky texture of the cavern ceiling. The assassin could also see the tiniest things move in the darkness of the night. His nocturnal vision offered advantages that humans didn't have. He sat up and brushed himself off, freeing the rocks from the cavern floor from his back. The musty smell of the place didn't bother him one bit. In fact, Clover had gotten used to places such as this deserted cavern for a while now.

After the battle and destruction of Legion and his gang, Clover had returned to hibernating. Part self-exile and part rejuvenation from the events, it gave his body a chance to recover and his mind time to collect and put the pieces together. Legion was no longer alive to be his tormentor. Legion had been the physical manifestation that tormented Clover. Two restless bodies; one half, Clover the prototype of all mutations created by the Corporation and the ultimate assassin; and Legion, the perfect super soldier with an ego to match.

Legion was praised, before his fortunate demise, as the perfect soldier. The ideal leader of the super soldiers of the Corporation, which now lay in ruins like everything else humanity had touched. The super soldier's ego not only devastated the plans of the Corporation, he had murdered the one man he professed to love, General Reinhart, a father figure to the behemoth mutant. That displayed Legion's malcontent, his murderous rage, against all humans.

Even after the world ended in a cataclysmic thunderclap, the bioengineered assassin and the titanous super soldier continued their rift. Despite having an entire continent to roam, their genetic ties kept Legion inside Clover's mind for far too long. The assassin was glad his nemesis was dead, but Clover only seemed to replace one nightmare with another. Still, all that mattered at the moment was his new pursuit.

On one side, he had his design; a ruthless killer with predatorial instincts to hunt. The hunger for bloodshed had never left him. What had Nightshade, his mirror-image twin who he had encountered more times than he cared to, said about their bond? *Oh yes, now I remember,* Clover sighed. "We are the same, you see. No matter how you sugarcoat it, we are both contract killers, we just have different masters. If it smells like shit, tastes like shit, it must be shit, no matter what you do to disguise it."

Even now Clover felt Nightshade's presence, despite not knowing where the agent of darkness had fled. Even hearing Nightshade's voice, no matter how much it was manufactured from their last meeting, still ate away at Clover's mind. But he knew he wasn't the only one shielding his own existence from others. Nightshade was attempting to keep the Darkness, who or whatever it was, from discovering his current location.

"So maybe we do have something in common," mumbled Clover.

Clover swore that was the only thing the two of them had in common. Much like Legion, Nightshade detested humans altogether and the Darkness's favorite plaything would rather have Clover and himself annihilate what humans were left. Maybe it was instinctive, or there was a fear that humanity would regain its potency over time and the two assassins very existence would be in jeopardy. But Clover wasn't about to judge the humans so harshly. In fact, it was humankind that had nearly annihilated *itself* from existence; Clover's kind had little to do with it.

Clover's hibernation slumber was getting shorter each time he sank into a deep sleep. He never truly slept long— a couple of days max each time. He doubted if it would ever get any longer. The heat lingered too long after the sun set to rest. But Clover wondered, *Is it the nightmare keeping me from a deep slumber, or is something else at play?* The nightmarish dreams had changed. He no longer dreamed of the showdown with Legion and seeing his brother's face every time the assassin closed his eyes. Now there was something else taunting him, but Clover refused to acknowledge the lingering effects.

The longer he hibernated the farther Clover could travel from the place he utilized as a home base. Not that this location was a permanent place to call home, or any place as a matter of fact. He had been a nomadic hunter ever since the nuclear rain had ceased, but that was nearly twenty solar cycles ago. Clover was wary about his location being discovered, but by who he wasn't sure; the humans were still too low in numbers to threaten his own existence, let alone his own kind. Legion was gone and his loyal followers, those still alive, had scattered in every direction like field mice.

That only left nomads venturing into and from the Wasteland. Thinking of the Wasteland made Clover think of the Outland Rustlers. He had been scattering their clan, eliminating the ruthless killers here and there, when he got the chance. But eliminating their clans wasn't his high priority, Clover was after the Rustler elders. Legend said they were hybrids like himself, but Clover had his doubts. The assassin sensed that their concealed movements around the Wasteland were purposeful, and he hadn't gathered why, at least not yet.

Clover shook off the sleep and briefly pondered the nightmare. The residue of it still loomed in his head. It was the fifth time he'd had the dream in fifteen sleep cycles. It was the same dream, but each time something was different about it. Sometimes something small, something out of place, or someone's facial features had changed, but never the dark cloud face, no, it was always the same; dark and menacing.

Talking to himself, Clover said, "I will find you. And when I do, I will place fear into your heart no matter how many of your followers I must kill. I will uncover what you have been up to."

Clover doubted the Rustler elders really cared how many of their followers he murdered in cold blood. But didn't they all deserve it? The way the clans had raped, killed and kidnapped innocent travelers, didn't that justify retribution on them all?

Clover stretched and thought back to the dream. Nothing about the dream seemed familiar. With all the people he killed, including his own kind, why did he dream of a phantasm he didn't recognize or a woman he had never seen before? And what was up with the dark cloud? *Dreams*, thought Clover, *are meant for humans, not assassins.*

Clover had other fish to fry and had little time to pounder unusual dreams. He had stayed in the cavern about as long as he could and now it was time to continue his hunt. His pursuit for the elders was becoming too prolonged, and he had no doubt that he would encounter more of Legion's followers. He had come across several over the last six moon cycles. Some had fled his presence, others had pled for their lives, but most didn't mean much to him either way. He had only been forced to kill a handful. Those were the ones left of Legion's militia, and Clover couldn't afford to let them linger. He wasn't sure if they might attack him when he wasn't looking or try to track him into the Wasteland. The last thing Clover needed was to have a rogue agent looking to sell secrets to the first Outland Rustler they could find.

Clover took in a deep breath, strapped his dual katanas to his back and then put on his coat, raising the attached hood. With Clover's gear together, he made one more sweeping look before he headed for the exit. Just before he reached the opening, he looked back. Something was stalking him. Nothing was in the subterranean dwelling, but something was definitely tracking his movements, and Clover had a good idea of who it was.

"Nightshade, get out of my head," mumbled the assassin. "You won't like what you find in there."

Clover turned and exited the dark dwelling.

Clover reached the edge of the cliff. The wind had picked up and whipped his cloak wildly. He looked out over the desolate landscape. It appeared, from this elevation, that the human gods had drained a vast ocean and left the sandy basin behind. The difference was there wasn't any stranded ships left in the wake, only an occasional flash of light, which meant someone was moving across the surface below.

He always found the highest reaches to set up camp, and this one was no different. The height was calming, and it gave him a bird's-eye view, allowing the assassin to scan for potential targets. He would wait until the sun began to rise before setting out. The glare of the rising tangerine orb provided Clover just enough illumination to slip to the surface and begin tracking new prey. The only prey he preferred this day, like most, were the Outland Rustler type.

The sun hadn't begun its climb yet, but he could see and sense the things that hunted at night, and he admired their tenacious effort to scurry towards their inner sanctums before the sun exposed them in the open and cooked their frail bodies. Most predators that lurked so close to the Wasteland either did their hunting at night, or waited just below the surface, prepared to spring a deadly trap. Clover understood what to look for, since he was the alpha predator of these parts—and most others as well.

Clover proceeded to scan the open plain, as if he was searching for something quite specific, but he was doing it out of habit. If he was fortunate, he might find something that caught his interest, not so lucky for who or whatever that was. The assassin swept from left to right, high to low, but not much was stirring at this hour. Clover cleared his throat. He wouldn't get frustrated, he was used to being indefatigable. It was his best trait. It's how he had become such an efficient assassin and gained his looming reputation.

It was by his sensitive wolf's scent ability that he found the travelers in the dying night. Clover scanned back to his left, still nothing. Had his senses fooled him? He took a deep breath and rescanned the lower horizon. Out of the darkness, four small pinprick amber lights moved from the near bottom of the valley up towards the eastern horizon. Clover smiled at the discovery; he knew his sense of smell hadn't let him down.

Clover sniffed the humid air a second time.

"Human posse!" exclaimed the assassin under his breath. Like he was hissing at their ghastly appearance.

He could smell their perspiration in the southernly wind. By the scent, Clover could tell they had been moving through the desolate plains since before dawn. But they were moving slowly and were quite easy to track. Normally, he wouldn't bother with human groups tracking across the surface, but this one seemed to be headed straight for the Wasteland itself.

It's a human hunting party. Too large for a scouting expedition, but why are they moving towards the outer rim of the Wasteland? There are still too few of them to make a raiding run into Rustler territory . . . I guess it's perfectly good time to *take a look for myself, before the sun decides to bare its full self and makes it harder to track them.*

†

Near the outskirts of the devastated Metro City something moved in the waning shadows. A little mole creature scurried along, sending up small pockets of dust along its miniscule path. Nightshade watched the pathetic creature in his invisible state. The little rodent wiggled its fat stubby nose in the air, most likely to smell the air for any kind of food source. It used its tongue to keep its eyes moist. The air could dry them out and then it would only have its sense of smell for hunting. Nightshade thought the thing was much like another surviving rodent species—humanity, or what was left of it.

The chubby creature hopped from side to side, leaving tiny little footprints as it went. Nightshade made a game of following the poor creature, since he didn't have anything better to do. The assassin hopped as the rodent did, making sure he didn't let the creature know it was being followed. The wind whirled heavily on this day, sending sandy debris all over the outer streets of the devastated cityscape. Nightshade moved with stealth to stay within striking distance, like a viper preparing to strike.

In the rising sunlight, Nightshade's cloaked figure flickered behind the skeleton of a burned car. The wind whipped the torched fabric of the nearly destroyed front seat. The wind's howling got progressively louder as a strong wind gust blasted away at the empty field. The interior of an adjacent building swayed lightly in the wind as the pane-less glass window rattled. Nightshade made his move swiftly and pursued the tiny rodent.

First there was a flicker, then distortion of colors of the exterior brick wall that was nearly all incinerated from the war. Very few buildings stood erect with their exteriors intact. Those that did displayed what the nuclear blast had done to them, scarring the colors of their exteriors to a coal black, leaving no indication of what the original color had been. That was long ago and not his problem. A fuzzy flickering briefly exposed Nightshade for a moment, before he disappeared again under his cloaked veil.

The rodent looked back, sensing danger approaching, wiggling her stubby nose in the air. She discovered nothing and moved onwards. Nightshade's distortion moved within striking distance and when the cloaked figure felt the rodent couldn't get away, he pounced on her. Without any notice at all, the pudgy rodent was trapped under something she couldn't escape. She squealed loudly, and her escape seemed hopeless.

Nightshade chuckled. "Rodent on a stick, my favorite."

Now on her back, waving her tiny little paws skyward, something peered down at her. Nightshade's concealment shimmered in the rising sunlight. Then, slowly, he revealed himself. His pitch-black eyes stared down at his breakfast.

"Pipe down, you damn rodent."

He poked the little rodent's potbelly.

"Now, won't you make a tasty meal?"

The rodent squealed again, but Nightshade ignored it.

Then something caught the shadow assassin's undivided attention.

"Clover. It's about time you resurfaced. We have so much catching up to do. Shall I come to you or you to me?"

Nightshade's expression transformed from his mocking, joyful demeanor into a look of mortified shock.

"Now that was rude of him." The shadow assassin looked down at his meal. "Wasn't it, my portly little friend?" He shook off the disappointment. "No matter, we will meet soon enough, and we can conclude our Game of Death."

Nightshade began to chuckle softly.

Chapter 2

Present Day

The sun had risen to near its pinnacle, showering and antagonizing the barren landscape with its lethal radiation. A portal opened over what used to be the eastern border of California and western Nevada. The spacecraft was sleek and fast, and small enough to go unseen. Its reflective surface was shielded by the rays of the sun, making for perfect camouflage. The craft spun around and landed in an empty crevasse that used to be Lake Pyramid before the war of man broke out. Now it was just another empty watering hole that would serve to conceal the spacecraft's arrival.

The spacecraft hovered over the dry lake bed. Its landing thrusters kicked in, blaring ionized fumes, scorching the dry, parched land and flinging dust and earth away from the landing site. The main engines slowly reduced power as the landing thrusters controlled the ship's descent. The small craft wobbled side to side, as the immense resistance of the thrusters combating the planet's gravitational force. Then, finally, the small spacecraft slammed onto the ground, shaking.

Compressed gas hissed out of several vents aligned the bottom of the craft. There was no sign of movement. Nothing exited the craft for a long time, it just sat there, idle, as rays of sunshine reached its lean, concaved outer hull. Then from the side of the craft's hull, a humming sound emerged, like pistons and electromagnetic gadgets were in the process of working diligently. The exit ramp lowered like a drawbridge from a medieval bastion. Slowly the ramp exposed the innermost portions of the spacecraft and its occupants to the outside world.

At first only shadows could be seen moving within the interior of the spacecraft. They moved back and forth, like they were busy moving things about. A metal clank echoed from the top of the ramp, followed by a second one, like something was moving awkwardly. Two shadows emerged from the concealment of the craft and walked slowly down the concourse, one a human-sized figure followed by a much bulkier one that loomed mountainous over the one in front of it.

Both figures reached the surface and the smaller one turned to observe the bulkier figure. With his one human eye, since he was half-human, half-cyborg, the smaller figure nodded a response. The android carried a large metal case that seemed to make the metal creature appear slightly smaller than it was and it set the case down gently and looked up at the smaller figure, its blue digital eyes transfixed on the other. The all-metal figure stood up at attention, as if awaiting orders from its commanding officer. In a digital tone, the figure asked, "Is that significant placement, sir?"

The smaller figure looked at its servant and smiled. The cyborg nodded his response. "It will be fine, Cheeves."

The machine took a step back to let its master inspect the condition of the metal case. The half-cyborg ran his metal hand over the contour of the casing and stared at the casing with a sense of glee. "Soon, my lovely, we will have revenge on those that have wronged us," whispered the figure with a slight chuckle. The human eye of the hybrid figure looked up at his servant with a stern glance. "Isn't that right, Cheeves?"

Still at attention, the bulky android responded in a snap. "As you command, Master Volkov."

The hybrid figure was none other than former CEO of the Corporation, Nikolai Volkov, thought deceased before the War of Men. He had returned to seek revenge on those who had sidetracked his plans as CEO. He had planned his revenge carefully and with precision foresight. It had taken years to develop the plan and even longer to set up its parameters.

Nikolai looked up at the gloomy and cataclysmic sky, letting the warmth run down his face. His digital eye soaked in the solar rays, while his human eye squinted at the sun. *This is the beginning of the end for them all,* Nikolai thought. *My unimpeachable plan won't just take them down, it will make them watch each other die as they wallow in their own self-pity.*

Nikolai looked back at his android assistant. Its burly metal frame glistened in the sun. Its dark, digital eyes stared back at him. The bulky android didn't give any type of expression at all, it was just there to serve his every need. Nikolai stared back down at the metal case and gave a dreadful, sinister smile. The wind had picked back up and it Swirled around them.

Plain cyclones threw dry earth everywhere in the dried-up crevasse. They danced an odd dance, swinging in and out of one another. Nikolai ignored their nuisance presence as he squeezed his mechanical hand open and closed, as if a cramp had set in. The tiny mechanical pistons squealed in agony as they were forced to move. Nikolai remembered how he had become this monster he now was. The memory was fresh in his head, despite all the time that had passed.

"The one that did this to me will pay for his treachery. He will suffer the most for what he did to me. My vengeance on him will be the greatest," Nikolai mumbled.

Flashback: Ten years ago

There was a sinister giggle breaking through the darkness

Nikolai looked all around, but the darkness still enveloped most of his sight. His vision was blurred and he couldn't make out anything that wasn't directly in his path. Even his blurred vision didn't give him much information, it was like scurrying along his backyard semiblind. Nikolai huffed and puffed as he fled his attacker. He could feel his heartbeat increase and his lungs were losing breath rapidly.

Nikolai felt something wet near his midsection; he was bleeding immensely. Blood encased his hand, and he could still feel the wound spilling out his life's essence. His head began to spin, and his already blurred vision worsened. He still hadn't seen his attacker. He had been too preoccupied to bother glancing back.

I need to keep moving or whomever attacked me in the kitchen will catch me for sure, Nikolai thought.

The Corporation's CEO understood that he may be leaving a trail of blood for his assassin to follow, but he couldn't help any of that now. He had to just get away from whatever had wounded him. He was quite surprised he hadn't been captured or shot yet. *I'm way too tired to keep going on like this. I will have to face my assailant eventually if I'm going to survive.*

A bolt of pain shot up through the CEO and he stumbled and nearly wiped out.

Nikolai heard the assassin call out to him, but the words seemed faded and distorted. He could only make out every third word the invisible assassin said. "Keep fleeing, my friend. I can do this all day, but you have the sands of time running against you," the Shadow Agent called.

Nikolai stumbled into the assassin's view, holding something in his unbloodied hand. The CEO was breathing quite heavily.

Nightshade appeared right out of thin air. took a big gulp of air. *Why didn't the security sensors pick up on the intruder?* The CEO's stomach tightened as if he had been punched in the gut. "Where in the fuck did you come from?" Nikolai stared right into the assassin's dark void-filled eyes. The assassin had a disquieting, rigid grin planted on his face. The rest of Nightshade's garb seemed quite familiar to him. Everything down to the weapons on the assassin's back, which stood out over the assassin's six-foot-tall frame.

Even though he had never seen the assassin himself, he had seen digital photos given to him both by Reinhart and his own spies within Reinhart's project. He got the impression that this was one of Reinhart's deadly assassins, maybe even Clover himself, come to eliminate Nikolai personally. *That sleazy son of a bitch!* thought Nikolai Volkov. *The one person I thought I could count on has betrayed me. He has sent this assassin to tie up loose ends and take control of his subjects without the Corporation's interference.* Nikolai had to shake the thought off before he got caught in a daze by the assassin standing before him. *I'll deal with Reinhart's treachery later.* Nikolai looked back to Nightshade who hadn't made his killing move yet. *I have to get out of this dire situation before I can plan my vengeance.*

Nikolai vanished swiftly but gingerly behind a group of shrubs, but that didn't allow the CEO to escape Nightshade's enhanced senses. The assassin could smell the scared human and hear Volkov's heart beating a mile a second. "I can hear your heart racing and smell your stink. Don't think for a moment I don't know where you are hiding, Volkov. It's my job to hunt vermin like yourself, and a piece of vegetation won't conceal you from me."

The CEO made sure the assassin had busted through the shrubs yet, then he spoke into a metal device. "Initiate Protocol 75."

Protocol 75 was a security protocol in case any high-ranking member of the board was either assassinated or was threatened. Nikolai adjusted the protocol in case he lost control of the Corporation, or the rebels won the war against the Corporation's security assets. It was to save the Corporation from losing complete control.

A digital voice responded but the agent couldn't make out what it had said in response. Nikolai turned toward his pursuer. The CEO still held the area where his liver was, and he was still bleeding out. He whipped around with a snub-nosed .38 in his grasp. He held it tightly, aiming it directly at Nightshade.

"Go fuck yourself!"

Shots fired in rapid succession, but none of them found their target. Each of the bullets ran either too high over the head and shoulders of Nightshade, or they ran awry, not even threating to strike its target.

"That's the spirit I like to see," mocked Nightshade.

Nikolai leaned against an old well basin with half its wall missing. It was no longer used to retrieve water and had no pulley at its top. His blood had already coated the weather-stained stones that remained.

Nightshade threw a razor-sharp four-pronged weapon that whirled through the air at a wounded Nikolai. End over end the killing device flew in search of its victim. It moved quicker than Nikolai could flee. It was like Nikolai was frozen, his legs buried in concrete. He couldn't move.

A sharp pain ran up Nikolai Volkov's arm and into his right shoulder. The CEO let out a toe-curling scream, but Volkov he was about to pass out and never saw the attacking weapon return to the assassin, as Nightshade held out his hand and through a telepathic command had the weapon return to the assassin's hand. Nikolai's heart was beating too fast that the *thump, thump* echoed in his head.

His face contorted and he didn't notice as the assassin's aerial weapon struck him for a second time, slamming into his forearm. By then it was too late. Nikolai's pistol flew from his hand, and he became defenseless in the process. The CEO had only a moment to look down at part of the assassin weapon sunk into his arm with blood dripping from his flesh before the momentum of the attack sent the CEO rolling over into the empty well. He disappeared into its darkness.

Nightshade leaned over edge of the tiny well. He couldn't see or hear a thing.

"Nikolai, are you down there? Don't think this will end my pursuit of you," called the shadow assassin.

Nikolai lay at the bottom of the empty well. He hadn't died, but if he didn't receive medical attention immediately his mortal wound would kill him. He couldn't climb out of the well, his broken legs and one broken wrist would prevent any ascension. Nikolai could only lay there, helpless and unconscious.

Out of the cracks of the bottom of the well came microscopic nanobots making their way to the unconscious CEO. Some entered Nikolai's wound, while others began to stabilize the patient and work on the wound itself. All the bots had to do was prevent Nikolai from dying. A tiny portal ripped open inside the well, where the now semi-conscious corporate CEO seemed to be breathing his last breath. A voice owned by the Shadow Lord, which only seemed a distant memory to Nikolai ordered the human to be extracted. A group of carbons nanobots started to make the outer casing of a hull. The bots worked tirelessly to build the structure to transport the injured CEO. To the dying man, they were a gift from the heavens with their smooth minuscule bodies surrounding him. He had no idea if they were real or a hallucination of a dying man, but either way it made Nikolai smile. *At least I won't die alone*, he thought. In the blink of an eye the bots had constructed a vehicle sturdy enough to transport the CEO, with safety glass and a formfitting cockpit.

Nikolai never discovered who had sent the worker bots, but they saved his life.

A portal opened and the transport made of nanobots drifted through the portal and disappeared for ever.

Nikolai never knew what brought him to the hospital he had arrived at or who his benefactor had been, and even though he was a changed man afterwards, he was grateful for the help.

Nikolai grinded his teeth as he observed the plain cyclones move out of the dried-up crevasse.

"Fuckin Clover. That bastard will pay for his insolence."

A group of rebels on the planet of Dragonaria. That's where the former CEO discovered the identity of his assassin. Even with the help he had received, part of his muscle tissue, partly from his fall into the empty well and partly from the assassin's attack, had damaged muscle tissue, not to mention the liver damage that nearly took Nikolai's life. The crude equipment the rebels had to work with forced him to need the cyborg construction to salvage the rest of his physical body and save his mind from being lost as well.

Despite his hybrid form, Nikolai had never found out who his assassin was working for. The CEO had never learned that Nightshade was his assassin, and not Clover, so he kept a grudge against Reinhart's favorite.

Nikolai stared back at his android servant. *It's time to stop dreaming of vengeance and time for action.* He slapped his hands together like he was ready to open a birthday gift. "Well, Cheeves, it's time to start creating havoc."

Cheeves nodded its metal head. "Yes, sir."

"We have deceit to sow and people to corrupt and time is only wasting away. Let's begin."

Cheeves picked up the metal case and followed its master.

Present Day

The human party moved at a snail's pace.

The oncoming sun allowed the group to shed their torchlights and would allow them to move at a brisker pace. No matter though, the coarse terrain made travel tedious and slow, regardless of what the party's numbers were or how good a shape the members were in. The seven-member party moved along in a haphazard, single-file line.

Each member carried their own supply packs and had some form of sidearm weapon, with the front and rear members carrying the heavy artillery rifles. They had worn gear and attire; that's what the Wasteland did to gear—it frayed and ruined whatever you possessed. The men also carried breathing apparatuses, because humans, even ones that consistently traversed the Wastelands couldn't survive without them, especially in the deepest parts of the Wasteland were the air temperature and coarse sand would get into human lungs. Other species that had learned to adapt to the harsh conditions could move without such devices. Human lungs still hadn't had the chance to evolve thicker membrane walls and filtering systems, so they used the breathing masks to do it for them.

It was rare to see so many traveling party members so well armed, weapons of the sort were so scarce, and many were lost in the war. It took a monumental effort to find a gun in the first place, let alone finding so many in one location—the Outland Rustlers had seen to that with their raiding parties and unique ambush tactics.

Straus looked back to the rear of the party as if to make sure no one was being left behind. His goggles were covered with dust and gave off a golden tint in the looming sunlight. The leader's gear appeared worn and tired. Straus's lip curled.

"Let's tighten it up, gentlemen. And while we are at it, let's pick up the pace. We don't have all day."

Just as Straus had half turned back towards the direction they were heading, the sound of heavy boots passed right through the gap in the traveling group. The figure moved with such speed, none of the group members, either in the front of the place or behind them, knew the figure was present. They threw up sand as they passed and left a trail of footprints, easy enough to trace. It was like the person wanted the traveling party to know which direction it had gone.

"Rustlers!" a member of the group yelled.

Each of the seven members fanned out, something they all had practiced religiously. Each member had their weapon drawn and ready to respond to any hostile encounter. Each member had a death grip on their own weapon but had nothing to fire upon. Since the initial reaction to the Outland Rustler intruder, nothing else had accompanied it.

Straus grabbed the man's arm closest to him. "Follow me. Stay on my hip like we were engaged."

The man nodded in return.

Straus had ventured a long way in his traversing towards and into the Wasteland and his environmental gear, including environmental suit, breathing pack and gloves all appeared to be weathered. Straus could feel the man's body stiffen like a board and didn't care one bit. He looked back at the other five men crouched behind them.

"Stay fast and don't move unless you're engaged with. We don't need to all get lost out here," Straus said. He couldn't tell if the men knew what he was ordering them to do. But none of that mattered at this point. He had to go after the Rustler straggler. Just in case an Outland Rustler security detail was close by.

He nodded to the man beside him, and they briskly moved forward, but with a sense of caution.

The two men moved through the sandy terrain for about fifteen minutes. When Straus looked back, he could only see where they had all stood moments before the straggling Rustler had appeared. Straus took a deep breath and shook off the anxiety. *They all know what to do. They have been expertly trained. There is nothing I can do for them now.*

The leader and his escort moved forward; with his gun pointed out in front of them, he scanned the terrain for any movement. The two men didn't go more than ten paces from their last position when the leader spotted the Rustler knelt in a crouching position, like the outlaw was working diligently on something. The leader couldn't make out what, the Outland Rustler was too far away.

Straus removed his goggles, leaving a dust outline around his eyes; eyes that had seen more than they claimed to have seen. He had grown immensely since the incident in Sonoma and his and his twin sister's rescue from Legion's clutches.

Straus leaned over to his escort and whispered, "A scout."

The escort nodded.

Straus unstrapped his rifle from his shoulder and began to aim it at the struggling Outland Rustler. He tried to get the outlaw in his line of sight. If the Rustler had a way to communicate to a security detail and he told them their location, their element of surprise would be surrendered, and they would all be in danger. None of them knew the Wasteland all that well to flee from a large posse.

"Give me a moment and I'll have this bastard dead in my sight," Straus whispered. Straus's escort shook his shoulder violently.

"Okay. Give me a moment, why don't you. You can't rush me, or I'll miss and the scout will get away."

The next jolt wasn't as gentle. Straus's escort shoved him off his mark, forcing him to tumble away, as his rifle skidded across the sandy ground. All Straus could hear was a sudden, *thump, thump, thump*. The body of his escort fell directly in front of him with five bullet wounds seeping blood. Straus could only stare at his dead escort in horror.

The struggling outlaw was smiling at Straus, like a cat who had sprung its deadly trap. The lone Rustler moved in on the leader; Straus had no way to defend himself. Straus felt his stomach tightening. His eyes began to water, his throat extremely dry and parched. Straus looked for his rifle. Hell if he was going to be killed by this vermin of a human. He would fight to the end, no matter the outcome. His parents would have wanted that.

A whistling sound soared from behind and something flickered past quicker than Straus's eyes could catch. The object that had made the sound sliced through the air, splitting the space between Straus and his approaching attacker. A gasp was heard in the opposite direction and a death-defying cry rent the air. The object struck the approaching Rustler directly in the thorax, creating a gaping wound, expelling the Rustler's blood everywhere.

The body hit the ground without a sound, the Outland Rustler spread out before Straus. At first, he couldn't move a muscle. He was in shock, and he wasn't sure if any of this was real.

A black cloaked figure leaped into view and snapped him out of his temporary trance. The figure retrieved the weapon he had thrown. It all seemed familiar to Straus. A scene from his past, and then it dawned on him.

The cloaked figure turned to him, and Straus knew the figure right away. The nocturnal red eyes, ones that reminded him of a predatory creature. It was Clover! He had returned like he had promised all those years ago.

"Are you hurt?"

Straus felt around and didn't discover any wounds.

He shook his head.

"Good. It's time to go. You have been ambushed." Responded the assassin. "There are Rustlers merging in on your very location as we speak.

A scream came from a distance behind them.

"My men! They are attacking my men!" Straus grabbed his gear and weapon and with Clover by his side, they moved back towards the screams.

†

As Straus returned to the placc he had parted the expedition party, Clover had moved to set his own ambush on the Rustlers. Straus saw the ambushing Rustlers emerge from the darkness. The expedition leader knew the invading outlaws had caught his men off guard, and they were soon too overwhelmed to fend off the invasion. Consternation crept into Straus's mind while anxiety made his heart race, just like when the outlaws had captured him. His heart rate increased, and his hearing semimuted. An echo of his men's voices made it seem like they were in a valley far away. Straus was unsure what to do, the only thing he knew at that moment was that he had blindly led his charges into the ambush.

"I allowed this to happen," said Straus. "Their attention was diverted towards where I had gone. It allowed them to be entrapped." The expedition leader told himself there was absolutely no escape for them; the Outland Rustlers had the upper hand.

A shot echoed, drawing Straus's attention. He snapped towards the sound and one of the members of his party dropped dead. More gunfire sounded all around their set perimeter. Out of the far reaches of the Wasteland, heavily armed Outland Rustlers rushed the group members. One of the expedition team members screamed, but Straus and the other team members couldn't tell which way the member had disappeared—they had been dragged out, into the void of the Wasteland, no trace left for them to follow.

More gunfire rattled in the dry humid air, snapping Straus's attention away from the vanished team member. His heart was still beating rapidly, and the latest shot hadn't done anything to alleviate that.

Out of the corner of his eye he watched one of his people struggle with their weapon. The expedition leader could tell the member's nerves were affecting his ability to retrieve the rifle. Finally, the man got a hold of the rifle, but by this moment the invaders had nearly overwhelmed everyone. Straus saw the weapon shake in the man's grasp as he aimed it at the oncoming Rustler. He released the gun's safety, and the weapon shook even more as the man stared down his attacker. There was determination in the oncoming Rustler's face. The outlaw had a tight grip on the blade he held out in front of him. Straus's group member was going to have to gather himself, or he wouldn't see another voyage into the dreaded wasteland.

Straus held his breath, fearful of what he was about to witness. The Rustler had gotten close enough for Straus to see the Rustler's bloodstained clothing. He could even see the outlaw's dirt-grimed face. It was like the Outland Rustler had thrusted through the sandy ground and crawled his way to them. *This man must have been out here for weeks*, thought Straus.

Right before the expedition traveler was about to be cut down by the blade of his attacker, a whistling sounded; it seemed quite familiar to Straus, a sound he hadn't heard since his teen years. Something struck the Rustler in the back, dropping the attacker dead in his tracks. Straus could only stare at the dead Rustler—he was frozen, shocked and unable to move. The weapon was long and thick, like a humongous claw.

Straus could only shake his head. *That's impossible,* he mumbled.

The expedition leader was breathing heavily and seemed to be in a daze, still in shock from the potential attack. He didn't hear the approach; the man was too mesmerized with the claw protruding from the outlaw's back. It saved his life, and he wasn't sure how to feel afterwards. The more he stared at the claw, the larger it seemed to get.

"I haven't seen such a brutal slaying since . . ."

A large creature had reached the man lying half dazed. It looked down at him with a curious but bewildered expression on its furry, primate face. Straus felt like the primate was either mocking his condition or trying to figure whether to have him for lunch. The creature seemed too surreal for him. The man waved at the creature, confusing it.

"It seems that delusion, along with delirium, has started to set in on this one."

A feline figure reached down and violently pulled the claw from the outlaw's back. She wiped the claw clean, it was one of her deadliest weapons. She possessed catlike reflexes that rendered most victims speechless, especially humans. The feline also possessed tangerine-colored hide that was both mesmerizing and exotic.

She looked down at one of her retractable claws and then gave the humans a serene glance with a wicked smile "He's in shock, Zeus," she responded.

Zeus looked around and let out a grunting noise.

"It seems the humans have a perpetual knack for stumbling over the dead corpses of their own kind, just to fall into the same trap."

"Yes, the humans aren't very aware of their surroundings. Maybe it's the reason they should be allowed to die off. But you know who won't allow that to happen."

Zeus gave her a discouraging look, then took a deep breath.

"I wouldn't say that too loud, Tigerous. He wouldn't want to hear you say such a thing."

Tigerous shook her head. "How does it feel to be back?"

"From what," asked Zeus. "The northern plains? Why did Clover send us there in the first place?"

"Reconnaissance? Or to get us out of his hair, who knows."

From the dark, two more Outland Rustlers charged them.

Zeus grabbed the two outlaws, one in each arm, and slammed them to the ground as Straus watched in astonishment. It was good to see Clover's companions again. It had been a very long time since the battle against Legion and his subordinates.

One of the Rustlers got back up and Zeus struck the individual in the chest, sending him flying through the air to land on his back. He didn't get up again.

Just as Zeus turned away the other outlaw got up and sliced the gorilla with a blade.

Zeus spun, grabbing the man by the throat. Straus could hear the throat of the man breaking, and in moments the outlaw was dead.

Tigerous looked at Zeus calmly. "You're cut, Zeus."

The behemoth looked at his wound, a scrape on his elbow, and shrugged his shoulders. "A battle scar," he returned.

Tigerous spun and threw the same claw she had killed the first Rustler with, then turned back towards Zeus. He had a concerned look on his face, one that read that he wasn't sure she was totally sane.

She shrugged her shoulders. "Target practice."

Suddenly, Clover appeared followed by Straus.

"Boss." Zeus nodded a greeting.

"Clover," Tigerous said. "Its always good to see you, even if you are a tad bit late, per your instructions." She batted her eyes at the assassin. She brushed sand out of her tattered clothes.

Clover's usually stern countenance transformed into a sly, playful expression.

"I thought I smelled something foul over here," Clover said. Changing the tone of his voice, he asked, "Did you find what I asked you to find for me?"

Tigerous nodded.

Zeus sniffed at his armpits and shrugged his shoulders.

Tigerous smiled at the assassin. "Are you sure it isn't your cloak? When was the last time you cleaned it? I bet it smells nasty, doesn't it?"

Chapter 3

Six Weeks Ago

The sun was heading for its peak in the western plains of the Wasteland. A duo of figures moved slowly for this time of day, the immense strength of the sun shining down slowing their progress. Tigerous, followed by the gargantuan Zeus, reached the outskirts of the township of East Sunriot. The pair of travelers halted at the faded sign. Tigerous stared at the makeshift, weather-beaten welcome sign as if it was an estranged lover she was being reunited with. She knew all too well of Sunriot's more-than-infamous reputation in greeting outsiders, especially nonhuman visitors. She glanced over at her brutish friend and understood that no matter what they had done to aid the humans in the Wasteland, it still wouldn't matter. The reception wouldn't be friendly—they might be lucky to get out alive. But Tigerous had to find a specific junk dealer before returning to Clover. The assassin was depending on the intel they would uncover in this town.

Tigerous took a deep breath, set down her pack slung over her right shoulder, and pulled out some human clothes she had procured from a previous town they had visited. Her outfit was slightly worn, but it would conceal her mutant heritage, so long as she kept the underlining hood on to hide her catlike face. The suit was formfitting with an undershirt that had long sleeves which would cover her feline skin. The worn leather pants ran up just below her midsection, hiding underneath the gray tunic. She would let a breathing apparatus dangle from her neck to give the appearance they had been traversing the Wasteland.

Zeus held up the clothing Tigerous had provided and shook his massive primate head. She knew the outfit would be too short, and combined with his titanous frame, they would draw too much unwanted attention; but what could she do? *I can't leave him out on the outskirts of town. That might draw more attention than if he tags along,* she thought.

†

Tigerous sat at the edge of Sunriot waiting for dawn to emerge. The last thing she wanted was to be too conspicuous walking through town, announcing her arrival. She opened the letter she had found attached to the scavenged circuit board that had led her and Zeus to travel Sunriot in the first place. Tigerous scanned the letter.

To whom is letter may concern,

To whom this letter may concern,

My name is Crane Savage and I have uncovered a plot that will wreck life within the Wasteland, as we know it...

Tigerous looked up from the letter and ran the rogue messenger's name through her racing mind. "Crane Savage, where have I heard that name before?"

She focused on a period of her life before she returned to stand beside Clover and reignited their friendship.

Approximately eighteen months ago:

Tigerous had just arrived in the small Wasteland town of Istagard. It was a quaint little town with little vendor activity, the town just didn't have the size or occupant volume to entice many vendors to make shop here. Istagard was out of the way for most travelers since it was positioned in the southwest corner of the Wasteland. The only ones who would stay long were individuals who were fleeing some trouble and wanted to hide. It was difficult to hide away from assassins of all types in the larger communities to the north and central plains of the Wasteland.

Tigerous was merely passing through. Istagard wasn't even a good place to replenish her supplies, so why bother staying? The unpaved streets were narrow and nearly impassable. She couldn't wait to get back on the road. There was something soothing about traversing the open sea of sand dunes and coarse grains of sand.

A crowd had gathered ahead and there seemed to be no way around it. As she approached the mob, yelling came from a centralized location within the ring of Wastelanders. A thin man with a satchel was being harassed by a larger individual, one that was pointing a large dagger in the direction of his victim. The larger man had the appearance of a life-long Wasteland occupant, with worn clothes, tattered pants and faded goggles dangling from his tree-stump-thick neck.

Tigerous couldn't quite make out what the larger fellow was barking, but it seemed to be a threat towards the smaller one. Could this burly human be an assassin, she wondered? If so, he was an amateur trying to draw clientele from the show he was displaying. Or was this a public execution, warning other assassins to stay away from the burly human's contracts? Either way, could she let the smaller human be executed in such a manner? Even if the little one was human, she could never stand for lesser beings suffer at the hand of a superior. Besides, the brute had an arrogance about him that just piqued her curiosity.

Tigerous edged through the crowd, coming a bit closer to the show. Confidence was hers to own and she would have the element of surprise on her side. The brute and his prey were now in striking distance, but she was struggling with whether utilizing her deadly throwing claws were appropriate or if using her bare hands would be more satisfying. There would be a chance the brute had a partner in waiting just for an unlucky soul as herself. She smiled, a solution found. Tigerous would challenge the brute to a brawl.

"Let's see if you are so cocky after I get done with you?"

She looked left and then right, no one seemed to notice she had moved directly behind the two humans. That was good. The brute had returned to pointing the weapon at the scared messenger. The brute let out a cry and lunged towards his victim. The messenger froze, but that was a fortunate thing for Tigerous. She moved to the side of the assassin, retrieved one of her deadly claws, struck the brute's blade end, and guided it off its killing path. Suddenly the crowd finally acknowledged her appearance with a groan.

The brutish assassin stumbled away from the messenger, giving Tigerous an opportunity to survey the motley crowd better. They all seemed appalled and shocked at her sudden arrival. She had to assume that they were less than thrilled by her appearance. She knew her kind was never well received by human communities, even this far out in the Wasteland. Then she heard the small messenger shaking, distracted her for far longer than it should have. The smaller human had a look for fear on him and Tigerous couldn't decide if it was that he had nearly become a human shish kabob or his rescuer wasn't human?

"Get up and get out of here," Tigerous called. "Before it is too late."

The human refused to move.

Then came the sound of the brute grunting as he recovered to his feet. Tigerous looked the larger human's way. The brute didn't seem to be in a particularly good mood, for having his stylistic execution robbed from him. His brow was furrowed, making his forehead appear like a smashed-in pumpkin. He brushed himself off and spat at the ground before him. "You're going to pay for that, bitch!"

She chuckled a little. "Are you sure you are up to the task?" Tigerous readied her fists into an attacking pose with her left slightly more forward than her right, a standard fighting pose for her.

That enraged the titan, and he charged Tigerous with what seemed his best effort. Fortunately, Tigerous was more than a match for any human, especially one with so much bulk slowing him down. She positioned her feet in a balanced position, one foot slightly ahead of the other, ready to pounce into action at any moment. This wouldn't be her first encounter with a human. She placed her claw weapon in a defensive position, ready for action. The brute charged her like an out-of-control freight train, with a full head of steam bearing down on her.

Tigerous steadied her breathing and focused on the madman rushing at her with his blade pointed directly at her. Her confidence never wavered, and a loud gasp echoed all around, as the human crowd waited for the culmination of the events that were now unfolding. The brute let out a massive growl, as if a big cat was about to burst through his human form and pounce on the feline before him. Tigerous could see a rotten tooth or two in the brute's mouth and his fleshy mouth. But none of that would do the brute any good.

The mountainous human lunged his blade at Tigerous and she simply stepped aside his clumsy attack. The brute's momentum had him stumbling past her. To add insult to injury, Tigerous gave the human a kick to his neckline that would eventually leave a nasty bruise. As the human assassin fell to the ground, she launched her poisonous claw at the man, striking just below the shoulder. The beast let out a horrid howl and gripped at his wound. She stood there not sure if the motley crowd would turn on her, since she had just mortally wounded one of their own.

She scanned the crowd, but all she could sense was shock and apprehension in them all. For a split second Tigerous was in a frozen state. What should I do? she wondered. The brute's accusing voice broke her temporary daze.

"Why in the hell did you do that for? Have I wronged you in any way, in the past, is this what this is all about?"

She gave the titan a look of disappointment. This brute is even more dense in the head than I originally thought. "I don't like it when larger beings pick on smaller. I was doing my duty to even the odds."

Tigerous looked back at the messenger with dissatisfaction. "What did you do to make this huge man take out his frustrations on you?" She snapped her attention back to the huge human still gripping at his wound.

"Me? Why nothing at…"

"Pipe down, Crane, you two-faced crony," barked the brute.

Tigerous gave her adversary a disappointed look, as if she was confused by his banter. *This idot thinks I'm the messenger, what a disappointment that will make for him to find out I am not.*

"So much hostility in that brutish form," called Tigerous. "How do you have room for other emotions?" The brute opened his mouth but the only sound came from it was the grinding of the mammoth's teeth that sounded like metal plates grinding down on each other. "Why harass the little man; why not walk away and let him be? Look at him, is the effort worth it? Is he even worth it?"

The mountainous man looked at Crane still lying on the ground and back to Tigerous. She could tell the wheels turning in the large man's brain. Decisions, decisions to make. Then she witnessed the brute relinquish his grasp on the weapon he was holding, drop it to the ground and slowly walk away.

Tigerous relaxed her defensive stance as the crowd began to disburse.

†

Tigerous opened her eyes, wiping away a tear that had formed in her right eye. Remembering Crane in such a manner was difficult, since she had the impression by the way he had written the letter, that it was the one of the last things he had done. Even though she wasn't all that crazy about humans, especially the ones she had encountered here in the Wastelands, Crane had at least changed her perspective on a handful of them.

Tigerous remembered what he asked her right after their introductory encounter. "Why did you do that; save me from surely being killed?"

In a smug tone she'd responded, "I don't like seeing smaller beings being taken advantage of by much larger ones. I have a soft heart for the small guy."

No matter what had happened to Crane Savage, she would do what he asked, even if it slowed her down on her mission for Clover. And by the instructions of Crane's letter and what Clover had asked, the two might aid each other. Tigerous closed the letter, stuck it back into her pack and motioned for Zeus to follow her.

†

East Sunriot was a packed town, maybe the most populated human settlement in the western hemisphere, at least as far as Tigerous knew. The human species was in danger of being annihilated and congregating in one location for too long placed a massive target on every human in that community. That's why most humans either gathered in small communities or had become nomadic.

Tigerous found out quickly that that the outfit she had provided Zeus rode up a portion of his cannon-sized chest, the sleeves pushing their way past his thick forearms. The pants fitted way too tight, riding up on her friend's massive legs and thighs. They were getting some unwanted attention, and Tigerous was becoming worried that at any moment a gang of unruly humans would rush at them. She looked to her right, then to her left. Her gut feeling was they had only a few moments to do something, so the first empty vendor tent they came to she grabbed her friend by his wrist and ducked into it.

Zeus lugged along and she heard him grimace in displeasure. Tigerous pulled him into the shadows of the vendor tent until there was little chance a human could possibly see them. Zeus pulled his arm from Tigerous's grasp as if he had been bitten. He gave her a look that was a mixture of confusion and bitterness. She understood Zeus better than most and knew he didn't like being manhandled.

"Why did you do that?" he questioned in a low, growling tone.

"We can't rampage through Sunriot's streets like this. I need you to stay here out of sight while I search for the junk collector."

Zeus grimaced and moved slowly towards her. "You will be unprotected with me here. I won't be able to come to your aid if something happens. I find it too risky, Tigerous."

She took off the glove she was wearing and massaged an exposed, poisonous claw. "I can take care of myself, and I won't expose myself except to the junk collector. From my understanding the old man is in his eighties; for a human that's quite old." She placed a feline hand on Zeus's shoulder. "I will be fine, my loyal friend."

Zeus growled an agreement, but Tigerous understood he was only doing it to comply to her request and not in agreement. She would take that though, because they didn't have a lot of time to spare. It was only a matter of time before they were exposed in the town and that was a bigger fear than making her friend unhappy. Zeus ducked behind some covered cargo, which only concealed a portion of his bulk. He was still encased in concealing shadows. Tigerous replaced her glove on her hand, pulled up the hood to hide her face once again and swiftly left the vendor tent. She went out into the open air and into the path of the rays of the fiery orb in the sky. The concealed mutant positioned the pack farther up on her shoulders to ease its weight, took one more glance at the sun and proceeded into the town's interior.

The crowded dirt streets hosted frequent travelers that used the town as a rest stop and a way to cut down distances through the Wasteland, but if any of them were smart, they would avoid the sea of sand and debris like the plague, if possible. In her experience with towns like this one, there was one fundamental thing—those types of individuals traversing the Wasteland, whether human or bioengineered, were scarce these days, thanks to the Rustlers. Being a hired killer for any reason just didn't pay. If the Wasteland conditions or the deadly creatures residing in the desert climate didn't kill you, then contract assassins would.

On each corner of East Sunriot were warning signs. Where there might be welcoming signs informing travelers they were entering East Sunriot, population so-and-so, there were warnings telling travelers leaving the township that they were about to enter the Wastelands. East Sunriot was the gateway into the desert sea of nothingness, and travelers who hadn't frequently ventured into the inhospitable climate needed at least this warning to make any traveler second guess his or her decision to venture into the Wasteland.

Rusty pots softly clanged against each other on trade hooks as Tigerous passed by. Tent flaps fluttered wildly in the constant wind gust that never seemed too harsh, especially for a seasoned wasteland adventurer, but the wind never seemed to cease either. The pathways of Sunriot were nearly as sandy as the Wasteland terrain. No roads were ever built, making moving large caravans through town impossible. But caravans never ran through the sea of dunes and sandy terrain, so creating wide roadways in town just didn't seem necessary. If travelers coming from the east drove wagons or mule driven carts, they were usually encouraged to abandon them.

Most of the townspeople were dressed in thick Wasteland gear of all types. But the one thing they all had in common was their breathing apparatuses; no one would ever venture out into the Wastelands without them and some form of protective clothing to keep sand and other Wasteland inhabitants out of their clothing.

Tigerous made her way through the narrow street, towards the eastern-most part of the township. In her mind, she went over the things she would ask the elderly junk collector. *This Crane fellow must really trust the old man, especially as a mentor, maybe enough as a very reliable asset. But would Crane ever doubt anything that came from the old man or any of the contact's agents?*

Tigerous lightly touched the breast pocket with the letter inside, making sure it was secure.

She had seen other scavengers/contract messengers and in her opinion they were all cutthroat types and not to be trusted. Why should she care what the missing messenger thought or did? And why was she getting the sense that this one had everyone's best interest in mind? Was she feeling empathetic to these humans and the way they had been forced to live out their existence in the Wasteland? Had this Crane fellow really uncovered something so vital to everyone's survival that she should follow the trail to were this all was leading?

"Somehow I am receiving the feeling that what this Crane fellow has stumbled upon has more to do with the Outland Rustler elders than it initially appears. If I don't follow through with this task and it somehow ties to what Clover has been searching for, the assassin will never forgive me," she said under her breath.

The farther from the center of the township Tigerous got, the thinner the population became, making her path that much easier. This was the section of the refugee camp town which seemed more a ghost town than a settlement, but the fewer eyes that Tigerous had on her the better. Finally, after what seemed like an eternity, Tigerous came to her destination. She stopped and took in a deep breath; she didn't know what to expect. In her experience, humans were quite impulsive and unpredictable.

She approached the makeshift tent of Cadon Trolotov. An old man of exquisite and bizarre tastes. The only way she knew it was the junk collector's tent was by the description the messenger had provided. The largest vendor tent in East Sunriot with an extra-large flap, always waving in the town's wind. The rust color stuck out against the dirt walkway, and no other vendor tents were even close to it. The top of Cadon's tent had differently colored materials sewn into it, showing the tent's age and how long the collector had lived in the tattered abode. Tigerous even saw some junk items embedded within the shadow of the tent opening. But it was those shadows that kept her from identifying what they were.

The old man collected all sorts of oddities from the lost world of mankind. Trinkets, useless items, but Trolotov's greatest collection of things, according to rumors, was the intel his vast system of spies and agents collected. Intel was like gold to Trolotov, for intel replaced anything of worth outside of clean water.

The wind in this part of East Sunriot had increased, most likely from not having so many tents clustered together. This also provided the old man protection from oncoming attacks. An assassin would come into view long before the attacker could strike the old man. A few mounds stood in Tigerous path. *Most likely booby traps*, she thought. Traps were scattered for fifteen feet in every direction surrounding Trolotov's tent, if the mounds of dirt were indeed security traps. Rumor around the vendor town had it, if Tigerous's prodding had it correct, that before the world was dropped into its current apocalyptic state that Cadon had been trained as a US Marine and could survive under any type of condition including the harsh Wasteland environment.

One of the vendors told her that Trolotov consistently told a story of how he had survived five years out in the Wasteland with no aid and very few supplies. The old man had gained the reputation of being the Old Hermit who resided in the Wasteland.

Tigerous, utilizing her primal instincts, maneuvered through the minefield of traps, adjusted her pack and flipped the tent flap open. The tent seemed to be in disarray, with stuff scattered everywhere. She wondered how Cadon could ever find anything. Tigerous tested the footing inside the vendor's tent by stepping slowly. A tall stack of boxes and junk parts, acting like a set of monoliths guiding into an unfathomable realm, sat to one side of the tent. She was waiting for some madman to come rushing at her in a rage. When no one appeared, she called out. Her voice deadened, hitting the high walls of the tent as if she had suddenly entered a canyon with deep, rocky walls.

Tigerous called for the old man again. "Hey, Trolotov, are you here?" She waited a bit and when no response came, she took another few steps into the tent and called out again. "Where you hiding at, junk collector?"

Some grunting noises followed by the sounds of something being dragged across the sand floor echoed from the rear. It almost sounded as if the old man was dragging a limp body. Whispering emerged from another part of the multiroomed tent, in a place Tigerous's field of vision couldn't penetrate. The dragging noises stopped, and a shadow began to approach.

Cadon Trolotov. The old man was slightly slouched over, but still able to walk under his own power. The old man used a walking cane, with a slow hop to allow the rest of his body to catch up with each step.

Cadon Trolotov seemed to wear fancy clothes even though he was a peddler himself. Tigerous thought the exotic and unusual attire quite out of place.

She decided Cadon Trolotov was truly a man of several skins. More layers than anyone would ever know.

Tigerous and Cadon Trolotov stepped towards one another. A tall lengthy woman turned the corner and took Tigerous off guard. This figure was lean, but athletic, like herself. Deshawna Kreyawn, a former assassin for hire, recently retired and now a Wasteland traveler and agent of the old man's.

Deshawna produced a wicked smile, sending chills down Tigerous's spine. "Well, what do we have here?" The tall ebony-skinned woman gripped her staff a little bit tighter, giving off the impression that she was looking for a fight, but Tigerous understood her tense persona. Tigerous was an intruder, and neither one of the hosts had seen her face yet.

The old man tapped his cane onto the ground, as if to break the electrifying tension in the tent. The two of them snapped out of it and turned their attention towards their host. "Well," said Trolotov. He coughed before continuing. "You're not one of my usual clients but, again, so few people come to see the crazy junk collecting cuckoo these days." The old collector laughed.

"Is there something funny I have missed?" Tigerous lifted her concealment, exposing her face.

The old man pretended to be surprised, but Tigerous knew the old junk collector knew what her purpose was even before she explained herself. Tigerous pulled something from her pack, along with the note she found. The item was a semi-squared mainboard from a military vehicle, one Trolotov recognized.

A gasp came from the woman's throat, "That looks like something Crane would collect," Kreyawn said. The former assassin appeared ready to strike like a viper. "What have you done with him, you wicked beast?"

Tigerous motioned for her to calm down, but that only seemed to enrage Deshawna.

"No, you have me all wrong, my traveling companion and I came across this wreck site and out of curiosity we investigated it," Tigerous began.

The enhanced mutant could sense the dark-skinned human becoming ever so enraged by her story. This wasn't going the way she had hoped. Tigerous needed to redirect the woman's anger to something less tangible. "We found this letter, and I thought you might be able to confirm your messenger friend didn't write it. It seems a little like language of the Wasteland, compared to an individual who lives both out there"—Tigerous points towards the direction of the Wasteland at the other end of town—"and in a settled community such as this one." Tigerous raised the circuit board surrounded by metal flanges and a heat shield so the junk collector and his associate could see it clearly. "The board at the site. I felt that your friend wanted us to take it to you and deliver the letter." Tigerous handed over the board and Crane's letter. "According to the note attached to the board. It had your name," she pointed to the old man, "and after some investigation, I found where you lived."

Both Trolotov and Kreyawn glanced over the rust-filled, torn letter. Tigerous could see trepidation and shock in their expressions.

Deshawna mouthed, *Outlaws*. The agent only stared down Tigerous as if she had just been condemned to die by a jury of her peers. But humans weren't her peers.

"Yes, the infamous outlaws of the Wasteland. About them." The old man gave the athletic woman a look as if he expected her to jump into the new direction their conversation was heading.

"Are you sure they are the guilty ones and not her?" The retired Wasteland assassin nodded towards Tigerous.

Tigerous, now on her heels and ready to slash, gave the rogue agent a half snarl. Kreyawn smiled back, as if to taunt her adversary. "I don't keep track of the Outland Rustler's movements. But if you know of their movements, I think we can make a deal."

The old collector leaned on his walking stick and groaned. "Forgive my weariness, but I must sit down." After Cadon Trolotov found a comfortable resting place, he turned towards Tigerous and gazed at the odd visitor with his old, gray eyes. Tigerous thought those aged orbs had seen a lot and they displayed the old collector's exhausted personality. "So, my friend, let's take a look at what you have brought us and see if we can't properly compensate you in return," the collector said.

Tigerous handed over the electronic device that had been stripped down to its core, but still possessed vital parts, including their silicon main boards, which Cadon could melt down and sell if that's what he decided to do. Two parts had a block shape, stripped wires protruding from empty slots.

Tigerous placed the parts on a cluttered workbench near Trolotov so he could inspect them. The old collector slowly moved to the stack and inspected them all closely. The old man began to hum an unfamiliar song, but Tigerous couldn't be expected to know any of the old collector's tunes.

"That's interesting," Trolotov said, after flipping one of the shorter boards over several times.

Both Deshawna and Tigerous squinted at the old man simultaneously; his eyebrows collided with his forehead, making his entire head look like a wilted brush. His humming became more guttural.

"What is?" asked the two females together.

Cadon Trolotov seemed to ignore them and picked up the second, short, circuit board. The old collector inspected this one in the same manner as the other board. Tigerous occasionally glanced in Deshawna's direction. The woman seemed to be ignoring her. The retired Wasteland assassin was looking over the old collector's shoulder, as if to get a glance at a long-lost artifact. Tigerous wondered what the game these two were playing. She was an agent of information, and Tigerous sensed the assassin was hiding something and was only acting cool for Tigerous's benefit.

The two observers of the artifacts moved to the larger board and that brought even more interest in the old collector's eyes. Cadon took longer inspecting this one.

"Very nice," the old man said as he ran his sandpaperlike hands over the item. It was like Cadon was praying to an unseen deity through a religious icon he had seen maybe once in his life. The collector's mesmerized glare told Tigerous the board was worth much more than she could comprehend. But it was information she was after, not riches. Something told her she would gain a lot in return.

"A good piece?"

Deshawna snapped her head up, venomously glaring at Tigerous. "Where did you find this artifact? I have never seen the likes of it anywhere."

All Tigerous could do was wipe the sand from her feline face.

Without looking up from the artifact, Trolotov said, "It's some type of master controller. From my experience of circuit board collecting, it must control something quite large and mechanical, by all the bus lines and slots for smaller control boards."

Deshawna barked back, "There is no way you found this lying on the side of the road. It would have melted down."

"I discovered it where your messenger friend left it, as I said earlier."

The old collector leaned back into his chair and shook his head. "It's hard to say, but if I had to guess, I would say it's quite a find. I guess we owe you something big in return."

"Worth a good value in exchange, I hope," returned Tigerous.

The old man's sides began to jiggle. "No, my new friend, I think we have something quite worth your scavenging efforts." Trolotov looked at his agent and she nodded back at the collector. "Deshawna has come across some valuable information from reputable sources in the Wasteland."

Tigerous looked at the retired assassin. "If they're Wasteland contacts, I wouldn't call them credible. You know how Wasteland inhabitants lie to get what they need." She glanced back towards the collector's agent. "Deshawna, you didn't kill anyone for this information, did you?"

The human shot back a sinister glare. "I'm not the only dangerous thing out in the Wasteland." She huffed.

Tigerous nodded. "Yes, I am quite aware of what resides in the Wasteland."

"I'm not referring to the predators that live under the surface, even though they are a very formidable obstacle. I'm referring to the two-legged dangers of the Wasteland."

Tigerous began to chuckle, but she was wary not to offend Deshawna too much. The retired assassin had a nasty streak and an ego to accompany it with. "You're referring to the ghost of the Wolf of the Wasteland? Everyone knows the rhyme by heart. But of anyone that I know, I'm surprised you of all people would be afraid of a fable, Deshawna." Tigerous tried not to show she was an associate of Clover.

"Legends are rooted in truths!" barked Deshawna. "I have met those that have witnessed the shadow of the wolf, as human settlements call him, firsthand. Quicker than lighting and agility that would place the most limber human to shame. You wouldn't be so quick to dismiss Clover's mythology if you had seen firsthand the things I've seen. You would respect the fear that the name Clover brings to humans."

To most humans, Clover's mythology had always been secondhand knowledge. Mostly this mythos was developed through word of mouth. Rumors spread fast, especially when the bioengineered assassin left a trail of bodies, mostly Outland Rustlers, in his wake. But since very few humans had ever seen him in person, the rumors that he was a wolf in disguise made the legend even more useful for leaders to keep their flock of followers in line.

"Damn it, Clover," Tigerous said under her breath. "You need to be more careful when slaughtering outlaws."

Tigerous knew how little the mythos was representative of her friend. But uneducated rumors spread like wildfire out here, and even these two individuals, no matter how intelligent they might seem or their ability to cut through the propaganda crap, they couldn't see through their own prodigious biases. If they knew Clover like she did, they would know of his transformation from the assassin he had been designed as to the champion for humanity he had come. *Or is Clover more than that?* Tigerous wondered.

Cadon Trolotov slammed his walking stick to the ground in frustration. "That's enough arguing from the both of you. Quit acting like children and behave."

The old collector struggled to his feet and began to walk into the middle of the room. Trolotov's voice seemed to change, as if something had shaken the old man to his very core. "Ms. Kreyawn has uncovered some vital information that we both feel you need to know. I would highly recommend listening to what she has to say, because it may affect every living soul in the Wastelands."

Tigerous became quite attentive, even though she was unsure how to take whatever the retired assassin had for her. Things seemed to switch gears and Deshawna's antagonistic behavior receded; her demeanor became informant, like a teacher leading a class.

"A few weeks ago, I came across a group of nomads," Deshawna began.

"You mean like those strange nomads that patrol the corners of the Wasteland?"

Deshawna nodded. "Those are the ones." The former assassin paused as if attempting to recollect what had been said between her and the nomads. "Not many trust them, but they see more of the Wasteland and are more connected to its spirit than anyone who resides in the cursed plains."

"One reason many find them weird, like freaks of nature," Tigerous retorted with a snarl.

"Maybe so, but they don't have aptitude to lie or deceive others. According to these nomads, there are rumblings about the Outlaws I think you have the right to know."

"The outlaws of the Wasteland," added the collector.

"The Rustlers?"

Both the old man and the agent nodded.

"Rumor is that something is going on deep into the Wasteland Plains," Deshawna said. "Something that has several inhabitants on edge. We don't have all the details, since the nomads keep to themselves and don't like to get involved in other's business. But it was unnerving enough that they felt it paramount to let someone know about it and thought I could spread the word."

"It seems," added the old collector, "that the outlaw's upper management has been operating a secret project under the noses of the inhabitants of the Wasteland. But no one knows what. Maybe a rogue messenger might be able to sneak in and uncover what the Rustlers are up to."

"The rumor is a great war will come upon those that reside in the Wasteland Plains, one that will rock the foundation of every settlement." Deshawna looked to her boss and received permission to continue. "I know this might sound fishy or far-fetched, but we have uncovered some evidence from a few former corporate facilities to backup what the nomads have told us." Deshawna handed Tigerous a data stick. "Look at it and judge for yourself. But be cautious if you choose to investigate it further. It's our feeling that the Rustler elders may be covering up something that they don't want anyone to discover."

"That means watch your back," barked Cadon Trolotov.

Tigerous looked down at the data stic000k with curiosity, not sure how she would proceed. Then she looked up at the junk collector and the retired assassin. She had seen one place that had a working console, but was it still operational? "I thank you for your warning and for the data you have given me."

✝

Tigerous moved down the dirty, sand-filled pathway; making her way back towards were she left Zeus. She was still thinking about what Trolotov and Deshawna had told her. Would lClover even listen with the information she had? And would it be convincing enough to make him ake action?

Tigerous touched the lump that was the data stick the junk collector gave her. It was there, a lump of plastic reminding her of the transferred responsibility that had been laid upon her. The knowledge she possessed was starting to weigh on her and she had only taken possession of the pending doom moments ago. Tigerous didn't see the two town citizens run into her, nearly sending her tumbling to the ground, her pack acting like an anchor.

Tigerous shook her head to shake off the dizziness; a silhouette swiftly passed by a group of vendor tents. There seemed to be less human traffic than when she arrived. She didn't need to see the second set of watchful eyes tracking her movements, she sensed the figure, the smell of human sweat. The closer to where she left Zeus she came, the closer the shadowy pursuer came.

Fewer tents occupied the space and more open terrain emerged, allowing Tigerous to begin a more intense sweep of the area. "Where are you, little bastard?" she growled.

One last large tent came into view, owned by some major vendor. It was enormous and tan, the size of three vendor tents put together, big enough to conceal a spy or assassin in waiting. She knew it was the last vendor tent before the place she had left her companion.

Tigerous swiftly passed by the only visible flap, which hid receding shadows and just as she passed by the tent opening, the silhouetted figure emerged and raised its arm. By the time the shadowy figure threw whatever was in its clawed hand, something else had leaped from the shadows and embraced the other. There was a struggle and suddenly a cry echoed from the tent's interior. Tigerous watched the dagger pass by, seeing the engravement in the blade; it was too rusted to make out.

Ready to defend herself from her attacker, two silhouetted figures struggled just beyond her field of vision. Tigerous called out, but neither of the shadowy figures responded. The two figures passed by, striking sounds against wet flesh emerged from the shadows. Occasional "uff"'calls followed. The violence was escalating, and a familiar voice whispered in the darkness in a bizarre and unfamiliar language. Tigerous sucked in her nerves and took a step, then another, closer to the opening flap in the tent and threw a claw at the silhouetted figures.

"Deshawna, is that you?"

"Shhhhhh," returned the voice.

Not waiting for a response to a second call, Tigerous pulled out a second claw and rushed into the vendor tent. All Tigerous could make out was a silhouette figure beating on the other. The figure on top was winning, she thought, but not for long. The downed figure got to their feet and fought back. Tigerous threw her claw and retracted another. The farther figure must have heard her coming and just dodged out of the way of Tigerous's claw, being missed by inches. Tigerous moved into part of the vendor tent that possessed the most lighting from a hole at the top where the frame poles penetrated. She could see the retired assassin had her razor-sharp nails into the downed figure's throat. She could only imagine the blood oozing from her victim's wounds.

Deshawna was breathing rapidly; Tigerous could hear her lungs expanding and contracting as air escaped. She could sense the retired assassin staring at her attacker. The look the junk collector's agent possessed was less filled with hatred or malcontent, but more like adrenaline rushing through her veins; it was as if she needed to expel excess energy through her intense gaze. Deshawna could kill him any time she wanted, so why was she here with the man's throat in her deadly grasp?

"Deshawna?" Tigerous said.

The retired assassin pulled her nails from the man's throat and emerged from the shadows, wiping the bloodied fingers off as she approached. Deshawna gave Tigerous a wicked smile. She appeared to not care if the mutant saw what she had done or not.

Tigerous looked into Deshawna's eyes and confidence seemed to radiate from her. "Who was that?"

She looked back at the body she had half covered with an old blanket, but the man's bloodied arm still was uncovered and exposed. Deshawna shrugged her shoulders. "Someone come to eliminate you, I suspect."

"How do you know he was after me?"

"He had been shadowing you ever since you departed Trolotov's tent. Most likely he knew of the data stick and didn't want its contents exposed."

"And how do you know this?" Tigerous said with a stern, unconvinced expression.

"Isn't it obvious? I've followed you ever since you left. You and your traveling partner have a long road ahead of you and I wanted your exit of Sunriot to be unrestricted."

"And why is that?" Tigerous asked.

Deshawna glared at Tigerous. "I can't tell you whether Crane is alive or dead, but I can tell you the first place to look and a place that you can access the information on that data stick with no questions asked, for a price. Also, you're in the position to do something about this coming war." Deshawna sighed. "You can see what the Rustlers think of the service of a messenger." She pointed down at the dead assassin. "They must have thought Crane would gain possession of the information we gave you. The outlaws are up to no good as usual, and this war will devastate life for all that reside in the Wasteland."

Tigerous licked her chapped lips and asked, "And if I do, then what? Do you expect my friend to help?" Tigerous thought Deshawna, and to an extent the old collector, knew Clover was an ally to her; how they knew this, however, wasn't clear.

"Hopefully it will be enough to unite the people of the plains against the outlaws and their allies."

"I understand the dangers that exist in such a venture. The Wasteland, as you well know, is dangerous enough without having a target on my back."

Tigerous nodded her understanding. She would trust the human and uncover what the data revealed. Clover most likely would be more than pleased to take what she could uncover, no matter how little that was. "I'll do the best I can. But I can't promise anything. First, I have to validate the claims before I begin to spread panic across the Wasteland."

The retired assassin nodded her head. "Do what you feel you must."

The two parted ways under the receding sunlight as Tigerous retrieved Zeus and headed west.

Chapter 4

Present Day

The remaining three of Straus's crew gathered next to the campfire. Normally campfires would draw Out-land Rustler attention, but with the events of the day and Clover and his comrades sharing the camp with them, the humans seemed to not possess any doubts about how safe they were. Clover and his comrades sat on one side of the campfire, while the rest of Straus's team sat on the other side. The fire crackled and the camp firelight lit a portion of each member's face.

There was tension in the air, and it wasn't from the ambush laid on the team earlier in the day. Clover and his companions weren't pleased to see the human party out this deep in the Wastelands. A mix of frustration and dis-belief radiated from the glare the bioengineered assassin gave the remains of Straus's party, especially the man he had once saved as an adolescent. It was Outland Rustler territory, and these humans were encroaching on danger-ous ground. Clover and his friends had ventured deep into the Wastelands many times before, but there was a certain unwritten rule between the outlaws and their kind. It was not to say that they hadn't had confrontations ever before, because they had. But each incident was isolated, and the outlaws had never tried to retaliate before.

But the humans invading the Wasteland, when they had never done so before, seemed a little bold. Straus and his team could have easily been eliminated, and no one would have known any different. Clover felt Straus could never comprehend the position he was in, since the human leader didn't live in the Wasteland and could never comprehend the dangers that lurked within. Clover and his comrades didn't have time to babysit the humans and their risk-taking and that's why the camp was silent. The assassin did understand Straus's love for his men, though, since he had led this own team for a while and had experi-ence taking care of himself and others.

Clover shook his head. *No, it doesn't matter*, the assas-sin thought. *No amount of trust between the humans could ever make up for such a reckless act as to lead a group of inexperienced men into such an inhospitable place.*

The sound of the fire popping occasionally broke up the numbing silence. Someone coughed from the far end of the campfire, which gave Straus the opportunity to break the silence. But even such a subtle act could never release the displeased tension, like a dam rupturing and letting forth a flood of emotions.

Straus broke the silence by asking, "Clover, it's been a really long time. How have you been?"

Still more silence from the bioengineered assassin. Clover only gave Straus a dead glare. Straus took a drink of water from his waterskin. When he returned to look at Clover, the assassin hadn't blinked, hadn't shifted his gaze.

"Cat must have his tongue, sir," whispered another of Straus's men. The subordinate leaned in to his boss. "I thought you knew this assassin?"

Straus only gave the man a look, one that told the subordinate to hold his tongue if he didn't want to get them killed.

Tigerous smiled. "We can hear every word you're saying. We aren't as deaf as you humans are." Her smile was one of mockery and distrust.

The man gave her a shocked look.

"Enough of this quarreling. We should be grateful for what you did for us," returned Straus.

Zeus grunted.

Clover still gave Straus a look that said he was about to explode in a mad rage, as if he wanted to kill them, but if that were the case, the assassin could have let the ambushing outlaws do it for them. No, Clover was like a lone wolf sniffing at a new territory to roam and hunt, but instead of curious about the land and what had lived here before, the assassin wanted to discover why Straus and his men had ventured into a place they had no business being in. It didn't take Clover long to begin his inquiry.

"Why are you here, Straus? Why have you led these men deep into Rustler territory? It's a dangerous game you're playing." Clover had his arms folded and he still had the stern look about him.

"Look here," started Straus's subordinate. But he was silenced by Straus as the human leader nearly leaped out of his sitting position to thrash the man.

"Hold your tongue, Johnson. Let me handle this." There was dejection and sorrow in Straus's eyes, as if he was pained by his man's insolent behavior. It was obvious to Clover, and he noticed Tigerous could also feel Straus's inner pain. "Clover," begged the human leader. "I have been leading expeditions into the Wastelands for a while now. We have been raiding Outland Rustler camps and eliminating our biggest foes. We feel we have them on the run. They are a dying breed and they have become desperate to survive. The reason, I suppose, for the ambush."

Zeus snickered at the response. "Is that what you think, human? If so, you have much to learn about the Wastelands, its inhabitants and those that traverse its plains. The ambush happened because of your naïve thinking. Most likely they led you into the ambush, not because of some mythical desperation you seem to believe they are in."

Then Tigerous spoke in a soft and caring manner. "Straus, how is your sister?"

Straus looked away from Tigerous and into the flame as it burned through its fuel. Finally, Straus looked up with a tear in his eye.

"My sister and her husband disappeared for the north two years ago."

The look she gave him was one of shock and heartache. She had helped lead Straus's family to the refugee camp where they had all died, except for Straus and his twin sister. Now she was gone, and he was left all alone.

"They were moving from our settlement and going to the northeastern part of the Wasteland."

"Why would they do such a thing?" questioned Zeus. "That's a dangerous part of the land to settle in."

"That's where her husband came from before getting stranded in our little town," Straus continued.

"It seems her husband was part of this occult group manifesting in the northern plains of the Wastelands," Straus's subordinate interjected. "Their lifestyle is quite bizarre. They use the outline of the Northern Sierra as shelter sometimes, and they claimed to have found a spring of clean water. But not all of us believe it."

Straus nodded his head in agreement.

Tigerous gasped.

Clover shook the information off. "You all are straying off the subject at hand. Why are you hunting down Rustlers in the Wasteland? It seems an unnecessary risk, like walking into the lion's den."

"We already told you," the subordinate snapped.

Straus slapped the man on his chest.

Once again Zeus, interjected. "You have to be a fool to think you're the ones depleting the outlaw's numbers."

Clover didn't release his stern look at the boy-turned-man they all had risked their lives to save. He tried to discern what Straus was really attempting. Was it deception the human leader was using on the assassin and his comrades, or were the humans that naïve to believe their lack of numbers and experience could affect the outlaws who had been terrorizing occupants both in the Wasteland and outside of it?

"I think you have been misled in the information you have been given. The Outland Rustlers' numbers have been depleted, but that's more from the lives they have lived and the many confrontations their leadership have placed the outlaws in, not your sieging their camps at all. Something else must be happening," responded the assassin.

"May I ask why you believe this, Clover?" Straus asked, his tears now wiped away.

"Because I've been roaming the Wasteland for over twenty celestial seasons, and I have learned how they do business. I'm not disagreeing that they have moved deeper into the Wasteland, there are fewer outer-perimeter patrols each season, but they are still stronger than you may believe."

"And why do you think that?" Straus asked.

"Because I've been searching for the Outland Rustler elders for a while now, believing they were up to something." Clover left his comment at this to prevent exposing too much.

My instincts have been warning me, but every time I get close, they seem to move whatever they have been working on right before I arrive. They always seem to leave traceable tracks, dragging something quite heavy with them. But as soon as I track them by the trail they leave, an outlaw ambush impedes my progress, allowing the main group to escape. Something has been aiding in covering their whereabouts.

Clover looked at everyone who gathered around the fire. "I believe that whatever they are planning may very well change everything. How everyone, even themselves, will survive. It needs to be stopped or we could all wind up dead."

Clover watched the occupants all stare at one another, some with at least a hint of fear in their eyes, while others had rage building within them. The assassin stayed calm despite the arrange of emotions buried within everyone.

"I plan to make the trip in search of the elders alone," Clover continued.

"Alone?" Tigerous asked.

Clover nodded. "I can track their movements quicker alone."

"I want to come with you, to aid you," responded Straus, looking at the remainder of his group of men.

"No, I need to do this quickly, before they decide to move again."

Before any of them could object to this, a sound emerged just outside the perimeter of the camp, just outside the campfire's illumination.

Clover sniffed the air.

"Something approaches. One without fear."

Everyone brought their weapons to bear.

Clover held one of his katanas up, in the direction of the noise.

The movement became looser and more casual. Whatever was moving into the camp had no fear of their numbers. Clover sniffed the air a second time and something familiar about the scent had the assassin puzzled.

"Something is unusually familiar with the figure that approaches," Clover whispered to Tigerous.

From out of the shadows and into the illuminated camp approached Preist, one of Clover's allies. His dingy, frayed smock danced from side to side as the scientist walked towards his companions. Preist had his normal somber expression on his all-too-dirty face. Nothing seemed to affect Preist either negatively or positively.

Clover lowered his weapon.

"Preist! Where have you been, old friend?"

Preist nodded his welcome. "I'm sorry, I've been away for a while. But I have returned to you now. Thanks to this beacon I was able to trace you in a minimal timeframe."

"Preist!" Straus shouted. Straus ran over and wrapped his arms around Preist. "It's been such a long time."

Preist allowed the physical contact. "It's good to see you are well, my boy. You have grown so much since our last encounter," responded Preist. The scientist stepped back from Straus. "If you will excuse me, I must talk with Clover. It is vital I speak with him about urgent matters."

Straus stepped back. "Certainly."

Preist and Clover walked out of the campfire light and into the nighttime.

†

Clover stopped directly in front of Preist and waited for him to begin.

"Clover, I believe your destiny is about to be altered." Preist removed the data stick from his smock and displayed it for Clover to see. "I have just come from a place named Dragonaria and I have proof they need your help.

In Dragonaria there is something that requires your immediate attention."

Clover only shook his head. "It's going to have to wait. The Rustler issue has become heightened. I think what ever they have been planning is about to be unleashed and I have to find out what it is and how to stop it before all our lives become at risk."

The tension in Preist's shoulders relaxed, but his voice betrayed his anxiety.

"Yes, I know that. As long as you promise after this thing is over, you and I will have a discussion over this." Preist showed the data stick once again and then replaced it in his smock.

Clover nodded.

"Speaking of this outlaw situation, I met someone on my way to you that should be included in this pursuit."

Clover only gave Preist one of his stern expressions.

"I met Quasar on my way to you." Preist waited to gauge Clover's reaction. Once Clover didn't change his expression, Preist continued. "He was the one Tigerous escaped the moon base with. I feel he has something to offer in this fight."

"An extra ally is always a plus, but the Rustler issue is something I plan on attacking alone," returned Clover. The assassin placed his hand on Preist's shoulder.

"Indeed. I feel he will have more to contribute. But that isn't all. Nikolai Volkov has returned."

"How come that name sounds familiar to me?"

"That's because he is the former CEO of the Corporation and he's one ambitious and dangerous man. You don't understand. He might be involved in what the elders have in store for the humans, as well as our own kind."

"I will deal with him later. The Rustler issue must come first," Clover said.

"I couldn't find proof of it, it's just a feeling I'm getting."

"Well keep your intuitions to yourself, until we have more proof. The CEO will have to wait."

†

The new and improved Nikolai Volkov and Cheeves approached the outskirts of town. A blast-ridden sign hung on its perch for dear life. Black torch-scorched blemishes made it difficult to read the sign that welcomed weary travelers to the former township of Susanville, California. Dried, bloodstained handprints surrounded the blotched scorch marks, only allowing **Wel Su/nv/lle** to be displayed.

The blue light from Cheeves's digital eyes reflected off the scorched sign, as the sun rained down its antagonistic rays. Nikolai glared at the anarchy surrounding the once welcoming road sign. *I wonder if those bloody prints are from death-dealing hands coming to devour the inhabitants of this once quaint township or the result of its habitants going insane. Either way, I'm sure they will welcome me with open arms.*

Nikolai looked at his servant and gave Cheeves a mocking smile. The corner of Nikolai's mouth raised slightly to one side, while the other side stayed perfectly straight; the prosthetics in the other half of his face wouldn't allow muscle movement. It appeared as if his smile started in the middle of his face and like a dammed river was forced to flow only one way.

"Come, Cheeves. Let's introduce ourselves to the nice people of Susanville. I'm sure they will make us feel at home."

Nikolai and Cheeves made their way down the dirt-filled road. The once-paved two-lane entrance into Susanville was cracked and split around the edges of the now dirt road with a few chunks of asphalt making their way to the dusty surface. Many of the town's buildings were bare with several only having their metal structures still standing. Some had even collapsed in on themselves, leaving only a pile of rubble behind.

A few buildings shaded the decimated street with their size, including the old municipal building and the old clock tower, now faceless and starting to deteriorate. The building gave reprieve from the intensity of the sun's rays; the clock tower created sections of shadows on the deserted street. Nikolai thought back to the blast-ridden welcome sign and a smile half-human smile suddenly appeared on his face.

"Cancer is only skin deep, but this cancer is like a plague that has sullied the very human soul. Centuries of human domination have poisoned humanity and corruption has blinded the human soul. Their demise is inevitable, and I cannot save them. But they may be useful to me in taking down the children of Reinhart yet," Nikolai mumbled.

The hybrid man looked up into darkened, glassless windows and with his high-definition eye saw shadowy figures hiding within, like rats keeping to the shadows of an abandoned building or the recess of a sewer. Nikolai slowed down and allowed his assistant to catch up with its lengthy, mechanical strides.

"They hide from us, Cheeves, can't you sense it?" The android made no response. The only sound that came from Nikolai's obedient servant was the squealing of Cheeves's motorized joints and the squishing sound of hydraulic fluid in motion. Nikolai smiled at Cheeves's silence. "They fear what is unique, different from themselves. That's why they hate those that protect them, despite the fact. They are jealous they aren't as unique and guarded in such a manner that Reinhart's children will never be anything but feared. And the humans' hatred will drive them insane. Let's heighten that aversion, shall we?"

Nikolai took a second glance at the hiding figures. Suddenly a scared, suspicious face peered through the darkness at the newcomers. Something inside him began to warm up. Yes, little one, hide. Your kind can only hold off your destruction for so long. Annihilation has arrived at your doorstep. I will enjoy watching your parents and you perish under my leaden foot."

A ruckus began at the far end of town. It sounded like a beached whale crying for help. Nikolai spotted the unruly mob as they approached. The screams became noticeably louder as the mob moved on their location. "Here we go," he mumbled.

Members of the mob wielded archaic weapons like pitchforks and other farm tools in the hope of scaring their new visitors. The mob's leader was a short, bald-headed man who stumbled as he walked but pretended to be in control of his body and the mob he led. The town had bad experiences with outsiders. Several occasions had led to the raping of what few resources the township had possessed from the likes of renegade gangs or invading Outland Rustlers come to steal, rape, and maim the inhabitants of Susanville.

No, uninvited visitors were not very welcome in Susanville and all visitors were considered uninvited.

The mob halted directly in front of them, and Nikolai could sense the hatred coming from the unruly participants. Screams bellowed from the mob as they tried to trample Nikolai, but the bald-headed leader used all his frail might, struggling to keep the mob back. A few members at the rear of the mob threw bits and pieces that bounced off Nikolai and Cheeves harmlessly.

The leader turned back to Nikolai. The man had a scowl on his wretched, oblong face. The man possessed several wrinkles running horizontal to his lemon-shaped mouth, and his eyes were small, dark dots inserted into the recessive crevices that made up his eye sockets. They sank deep into the man's head, making the bald man seem like the living undead. His skin drooped from his neck like a turkey gobbler, and his teeth were rotten as well.

"Who are you, stranger, and what is that thing?" barked the mob leader, pointing at Cheeves.

"My name is Nikolai, and I've come to liberate you from your"—the cyborg looked around as if surveying a disaster site—"obvious horrid living conditions."

"Your kind isn't wanted here!" yelled another mobster.

The leader held up his hands to control the mob. He turned to look at Nikolai with a somber expression. "He is right. We don't take kindly to strangers, especially ones that don't look like the rest of us."

"Please, hear me correctly. I sympathize with you, but don't judge me unkind because of my outer appearance. I'm more like you than you realize, brothers and sisters. I was injured during the war, placing me in this horrendous state. I'm not against you. It's those freaks created by the Corporation that you should be raging against."

"What about that thing?" The leader of the mob pointed at Cheeves.

"Him?" responded Nikolai. "He's just my assistant. A bucket of rust. A worthless trash can."

Nikolai pushed on Cheeves, and the android took a step back as if the strike caught him off guard. The android didn't fight back or object to the unexpected attack. Cheeves just stood there, staring his blue digital eyes at the onlooking humans.

The leader of the mob was still staring at Nikolai, unsure what to say next.

"How do we know what you say is true? Can you prove any of it?"

Nikolai looks back at the metal case. "If it's proof you need, I have all you will need in the case my android holds in his hands." Nikolai looked into the eyes of every mobster. "I have a detailed plan to get all the mutant freaks the Corporation has created and annihilate them. Even though I doubt any of you need motivation to strike out in rage against these monstrosities, I'm here to motivate you into reacting before it's too late.

The mob transformed their aggression from hatred to glee and all rang out a big cheer.

Nikolai looked on with a sense of glee. It was all working according to his plan. He was going to manipulate these poor souls into doing the legwork for him, and they would work as a distraction as well. He looked out among the crowd and was pleased by what he saw.

"Let's not delay, ladies and gentlemen, there is so much work for us to do and so little time to do it in."

Nikolai, Cheeves and the rest of the human mob moved back towards the center of town. It had begun. No matter what attempted to impede their progress, the force of their blow would be too mighty to endure.

The new apocalypse would devour all humanity in its wake.

Chapter 5

Present Day

Tigerous had Clover in a secluded conversation with Preist lending his ear in. Clover had his usual expression, empty of emotion. Tigerous was steaming mad, and Clover watched as her jaw muscles moved rapidly inside her mouth. She was screaming at him, waving her arms around in a wild fashion. Clover could see Tigerous's feline teeth flashing in anger.

"What do you mean you're going alone?" Tigerous demanded.

Clover still didn't respond. He took all her abuse without retaliating. This only fueled her rage.

"You have to be kidding me. I can't believe I'm hearing you correctly."

Tigerous crossed her arms, beginning to pout.

"He won't be alone, Tigerous. He will have me," Preist said.

Tigerous gave Preist a stern look.

"No, Tigerous. This is something I need to do alone. I need the ability move about in Rustler territory unimpeded."

Tigerous can only shake her head. "I just think you don't want me around anymore. Heck, I don't think you want anyone around. You are truly becoming this reclusive mythical individual, the one the humans fear."

"They should."

She didn't know what to say to that. It was something Tigerous never thought she would hear coming from Clover, ever.

"You're not making any sense." She shook her head.

Preist started to fade into the shadows of the campfire.

"Don't you dare disappear on me, Preist. You're just as invested in this as the rest of us," Tigerous snapped.

Tigerous returned her seething gaze to Clover who still hadn't changed his stance. He wasn't backing down from her scolding, and he wasn't going to challenge her either; it would only add more fuel to her rage.

Calmly, Clover responded, "You don't know the truth behind it all. The humans. They can't be trusted anymore."

"What?" Tigerous snarled. "What are you trying to tell me? With all the hard work we have done for the humans and now you're telling me they aren't worth our trust anymore?"

Clover looked directly into Tigerous's eyes without missing a beat. A stone-cold stare that expressed absolutely no emotion. He shook his head in disagreement with Tigerous.

"I was wrong in my assurance of the humans. Since the demise of Legion the humans have become brash, possibly to brash for their own good. You can see that in our recent rescue of Straus and his band of fools. Soon they will become so arrogant that they will be vulnerable. I need someone to watch over them."

"You mean a babysitter for the humans?" asked Tigerous.

Clover nodded. "The humans aren't to be trusted. They are too ego driven. I need you to keep them from doing anything that might endanger themselves or threaten our own kind while I'm away."

Tigerous scowled. "I'm to be their babysitter? Don't you trust me anymore?"

"Don't mistake the request for something it isn't," Clover said.

"And what is that?" she asked.

Clover looked away, not wanting show an entirely different emotion. Addressing Tigerous, he said, "I don't have time to debate any of this." Clover looked over at Preist and nodded then returned his attention to Tigerous. "At least you have Zeus to keep you company."

Tigerous could only watch in a senseless paralysis as Clover and Preist dissolved into the nighttime. It was like a magician had cast a spell over the rest of those left be-hind. Tigerous wasn't the only one feeling rejected, even if Clover hadn't said anything rejective. Her disappoint-ment only mounted as her two comrades were swallowed by the darkness. It wasn't the first time they had left her, and she was sure it wouldn't be the last.

†

In the basement of a desolate building, the cyborg set up shop with tools, scanners, and other devices. Nikolai scanned over charts and ancient maps of an area he had been spying on for a while. He was the only one who knew of this location, and he dared not even let the villag-ers see the charts he was engrossed in.

His digital eye scanned the beaten old map, attempting to refurbish it. The blue tint of the digital eye reflected off the crumply map as if it were an eye in the sky. Nikolai tapped his metal finger on the damaged metal table. The *tap, tap* echo broke the silence.

He stood there for hours. *Where is the weakness of most of the human settlements?* asked Nikolai. He scanned the second, more ancient map that was made before the world was slipped into its apocalyptic tumble. The map's print was faded, but readable, especially for Nikolai's elec-tronic eye. The other map was handwritten and stained, making it much more difficult to read.

Then the cyborg questioned, *And where will you and your mutant friends intervene, assassin? Where can I set my trap for you and deliver the mighty death blow?*

Flashback some ten years ago

Nikolai slowly awoke with a splitting headache and the room spinning faster than he could handle. He felt like a spinning top. The light was a dense gray, but still stung his one good eye. *Wait*, thought Nikolai. *I can only see with one eye? What happened that caused the other to go bad?* "Clover!" he mouthed. *That bastard of an assassin did this to me.* At that moment, if he had the ability to blow a blood vessel, he would have.

Movement was difficult and awkward at best. If Nikolai tried to move his right arm, there was a jerking motion, like the machine portion of the arm wasn't cohesive with his muscles, if in fact he still had muscles left, which the former CEO doubted looking at the crude mechanics of his arm. When he raised it from the lab bed's metal frame, the arm began to jerk chaotically. The portion of shoulder, where mechanics met flesh, sent debilitating pain down his neck that felt as if someone was stabbing him to death; the pain stopped at the mechanical arm.

Suddenly a beeping noise rang in his head and a flashing display grid appeared in Nikolai's left eye. A blue icon flashed at the bottom of the grid—a mechanical arm.

Nikolai began to regain control of the arm and the stabbing pain subsided for the moment. Staring at his metal hand, he wiggled his five alien fingers as if they were new, and in fact, they *were* brand new. *What has happened to me that I am now majority mechanical?*

As if something had read his mind, a digital voice echoed in the room. "You have fallen on hard times, Master Nikolai, and we have reconstructed your body from scratch."

The former CEO turned back around and in a twisting motion saw an android enter the room. The figure was tall and walked with machinelike motion, something Nikolai wasn't used to observing. Nikolai's bionic eye focused on the metal figure now interacting with console, touching holographic images and scanning data Nikolai couldn't see. "Who the hell are—" the former CEO began to say.

"My name is Cheeves, Master Nikolai," the android answered. "I am a helper droid programmed to perform millions of actions, including saving your life." The android continued to observe the console without turning to face its patient. "A tragedy has befallen you, Master Nikolai. We rescued you, aided your fleshy body in its recovery and eventually reconstructed parts of your body that were too devastated to salvage." Cheeves gave him a cold stare with no emotion. It was like the machine wouldn't be there if it hadn't been ordered to do so.

"Reconstructed?" Nikolai mouthed. He looked down at his metal hand and scanned it without even thinking about doing so. Data began to populate the digital grid of his left eye, sending information to his brain and populating the vision grid. How had he done that? Had it been through his subconscious, or something much greater? The former CEO glanced at the android who still hadn't turned to face him.

"I think I can answer that for you," a booming, spine-chilling voice answered.

Nikolai was startled by the voice and looked all over the lab to discover its owner. He even used the scanning tool in his bionic eye without success. Then, out of the corner of his human eye, a shadowy mist appeared and grew quite rapidly. Soon it became large enough to allow a shadowy figure to emerge. The figure was swift and moved like the wind with what appeared to be a dark cloudy cloak whipping behind them, but the CEO understood that couldn't be; there was just enough air for him to intake, not enough to make the cloudy cloak to move in such a manner.

The shadowy figure slowly transformed into a solid figure, taller than the android with clawlike fingers that could rip his head clean off his shoulders. But that wasn't the most daunting thing about the newcomer—it was those sinister red eyes. They were like a predator staring back at him through a dark, wooded area. Nikolai attempted to scan the shadowy figure approaching, but just as he figured, the scans were deflected, and the only thing that displayed in the vision grid was empty space. *Damn it,* Nikolai thought.

By this time, the form of Darkcloak had fully formed and the former CEO fought a shaking fit that disrupted his thinking patterns along with his motor skills. "You have no reason to fear me. I am here to aid in your recovery, Nikolai Volkov."

Nikolai summoned all the strength he could, but he was afraid it wouldn't be enough. Despite his fear and anxiety, the former CEO cried, "What have you done to me?"

"Done? My poor boy, I have resurrected you from the dead," Darkcloak boasted.

Nikolai wanted to scream at the entity before him, but instead demanded, "Who are you and where am I?"

"I am your savior Darkcloak. And for where you are, well, we reside in a phantom realm of my own making far from where we found you. You are safe, my friend."

Nikolai took in slow deep breaths trying to prevent hyperventilation. He had been mutilated by the assassin and now he wasn't even half human any longer. He could only think of his revenge on Clover, no matter what he had to do. That brought a chuckle more sinister than the former CEO had ever heard before. "Put away your retribution, Nicky, I have more far-reaching plans for you." Darkcloak laughed.

That made Nikolai jerk up from the lab bed; a sharp pain ran down his side. He cried out in agony and lay back down again. A buzzing noise echoed from the console Cheeves had been working at. "Master Nikolai, you have pulled a steel rod from your mechanical leg out. Surgery will be needed to correct the malfunction."

"You can't stop me from seeking vengeance on the assassin! I plan on having his head as a trophy, one way or another."

Darkcloak peered down upon Nikolai with his sinister orbs. "Oh, but I plan on doing just that. Tell me, my resurrected friend, wouldn't retribution on what remains of humanity be a more satisfying scheme than a vendetta against one single individual? You could be the instrument of annihilation, destroying every human left on Earth. Doesn't that sound more enticing? Since the human condition no longer applies to you."

Inside, Nikolai wanted to watch Clover flop on the ground like a dying creature taking its last breath. But he was afraid to even think that since it was obvious that this dark figure could sense his deepest thoughts. A smile appeared on the human portion of his face. "Yes. That would be quite pleasurable. But only if in the end, I get to witness Clover's ultimate demise at my feet."

Darkcloak patted Nikolai on his metal shoulder and the former CEO could feel the coldness filling up the metal material that now was his arm and the coldness reached up into the fleshy part of his upper shoulder. He didn't dare cry out but beared the discomforting sensation. He nodded and Darkcloak released him from the deadly touch. Nikolai wanted to close his eyes, but forcefully didn't dare. Would he wake up if he did close his eyes in Darkcloak's presence?

"Good, my new friend. We have much to do before we start our master manipulation of what remains of mankind. Rest, I believe you will need it."

Darkcloak receded into the dark cloud and it vanished as swiftly as it had appeared. Nikolai took that opportunity to take in a deep breath and close his eyes. The madness began quite soon after that, from what his memory would allow him to access.

Present Day

The cyborg shook off the distant memory, knowing he had a task at hand.

Nikolai became immersed once again in the information he was studying, and didn't hear the footsteps approaching. A shadow loomed over Nikolai like an ominous cloud preparing to rain down on its unexpecting victims. The figure's shadow loomed too close, and

Nikolai caught a glimpse of it firsthand. He glanced at the shadow without much expression at all, and when he spoke, his tone was calm and even, not a hint of excitement or fear in it at all.

"Yes, Cheeves, what have you brought to me?"

The android bowed. Only the sound of Cheeves's gears mechanically rotating in their sockets broke the dead silence.

"Sir. A group of humans are coming this way to speak with you."

Without looking into the android's digital face, continuing his own tasks, Nikolai responded, "I didn't summon them. I don't have time for their petty games. Tell them I can't see them at the moment."

"But they are quite insistent, Master. They said the need is urgent and they must speak with you immediately. Shall I terminate them all?" Cheeves asked.

Nikolai finally looked up from the aging maps, now with an expression of irritation that would burn a hole through thick concrete.

"No, that would not serve our purpose. It would only create more problems than it solves. We need seclusion and secrecy to execute our plans. Termination would draw undue attention from those that we are plotting against. I will give them an audience, even with the work still left to do."

Cheeves bowed and left the underground workshop, kicking a broken piece of steel out of its way. Nikolai looked down at his rust-covered, creased maps and began to tap his metal finger on the thin table once again.

"Soon, Clover, we will have you and your allies cornered and there isn't a thing you can do about it." The half cyborg thought about the one-time meeting with Darkcloak that reminded him of the debt he owed that hung over his head. But that alone wouldn't prevent him from seeking retribution on the bioengineered assassin he believed had forced him into his current condition.

Just as Nikolai finished his thought, a group of men came down the debris-filled steps, with Cheeves guiding them down the narrow path. Their shadows exposed the visitors before the townspeople appeared, not that Nikolai's bionic eye would allow them to sneak up on him. Nikolai knew they were there before they were even announced. He looked up just as the leader of the group entered his workshop. Nikolai didn't greet the humans with warmth, but only gave them all a cold, emotionless stare.

Each member of the group bowed to the cyborg as they entered the underground headquarters. Digital illumination lit up part of Nikolai's face.

The leader stepped forward and bowed. The other members of the group followed their leader's actions. Nikolai merely stood there, staring at his visitors. They all made him sick. They were a pathetic excuse of a species, all of them. *Humans have a way of crawling under your skin and making you feel infested with their infectious diseases*, thought Nikolai. The human condition no longer pertained to this version Nikolai. He despised all human life. The taste these individuals left in his mouth made him angered to the point of feeling numb, wanting these insects below his boot.

Nikolai could envision all of them with their heads smashed in or even all their heads on iron posts stuck in the decrepit earth, like human path lights, strung along the main road to the edge of town. It gave him a sense of joy, pleasure beyond any sense of doubt. A partial smile came to Nikolai's face.

Many of the members of the group now standing in Nikolai's presence were clearly anxious, either shaking or overtly sweating. Nikolai could sense their hesitation and thought it a weakness. That also made him gleeful, or the best he could feel, being part machine. Most of the members dared not look him straight in his eyes, for their fear of him was great. It was mostly that glaring bionic eye that the townspeople feared. It seemed to act like an alien artifact, like the Ark of the Covenant. They were afraid it would burn a hole in them from its rage.

"Master," said Cheeves. "These men would like a word with you."

Nikolai looked at the raggedly dressed men without changing his expression.

The leader approached Nikolai cautiously, not wanting to express aggression to their guest, despite Nikolai never being malicious or invective towards the township. It was like they could all feel Nikolai's malcontent, his loathsome nature. The leader was the old man that had greeted them upon arrival in Susanville. The old man looked as if he was approaching death to ask a favor, knowing it would be denied and his life would be snatched from him in the process.

"Sorry to disturb you, master. But we have a problem that needs attending to."

The old man looked back towards his comrades, and they all nervously nodded their heads in agreement.

Nikolai didn't speak right away, but only stared down the old man. He knew this would make the old man crumble before him. The cyborg began to rhythmically rap on the map table. He watched the old man twitch in agony, knowing the silence was making them all uncomfortable, fueling his playful, elated mood. When the humans in his company could take the silence no more, he responded in a low monotone.

"How can I help you, Vespasian Derex?" Nikolai gave the bald-headed man a cold stare, one that didn't dare betray its master's venomous nature.

"Well, master," began the leader, stuttering as he gave his request. "A few weeks back, a small party from town marched out to hunt down some of the last remaining raiders that once ravaged our community. They had been hunting these bandits down for a few years, at this point. The villainous band had raped, murdered, and maimed our kind for a long time. The leader of this search-and-destroy party lead them eastward towards the heart of the Wasteland."

"Outland Rustlers," mumbled Nikolai. Nikolai shot the speaker a deadly gaze.

Nikolai moved around the map table and into the middle of the basement room. He looked directly at each one of his visitors square in the face. Their expressions became tight and hardened. Nikolai gave a wicked smile, none of them knew Nikolai or the plan he was about to unleash, and he wasn't about give anything away, as usual.

He spun around and stood in the center of the room. His metal arms in attack formation and his feet set in a shoulder-length position. His intense digital gaze stared them all down; the cyborg had everything planned and stored in his extensive memory bank.

"The Outland Rustlers, what an unruly gang they have become. Yes, their reputation precedes them. Who hasn't heard of their unthinkable crimes against humanity," Nikolai said.

"Yes," answered Derex. "Well, we haven't heard from them since the group departed. Some have wives and children. They are worried about their loved ones."

Suddenly it dawned on Nikolai what it was they wanted. He gave them all a sinister smile. One that had more meaning than the visitors could ever understand.

"I see what you're asking of me now." Nikolai rubbed his hands together. It sounded like rough sandpaper grinding together and rapidly removing material. It made the cyborg look like a crazed mad scientist.

"Very well, I will aid you in your request, since you have been so courteous to us and have given us anything we have needed for our own tasks at hand. Do you have the group's travel plans on hand? The Wasteland is quite vast, and it would be a hopeless adventure to send Cheeves on, even with his tracking capabilities."

Each one of the group members looked at one another as if they had been punched in the gut. They had confusion written all over their faces—something else that pleased the cyborg.

"Cheeves is a better tracker than I am, and I still have work to do of my own. I will send my assistant in my place to search for your comrades. It's what he really is built for, trust me, friends, your missing comrades will be in capable hands."

The elder group member stepped forward in protest, but Cheeves intercepted him before he could move more than two steps towards its master. The old man couldn't see Nikolai with Cheeves's bulky frame blocking his view.

"But . . ." Vespasian started to say before his windpipe was cut off by a metal hand around his throat.

Without turning around Nikolai began where Vespasian left off.

"I will take something though for our troubles. I hope you can understand that, my friends."

Just then with Cheeves's other metal hand, the android assistant rammed it up through Vespasian's lower jaw and up into his brain. With a loud squishing crunch, the old man was dead. Vespasian hung in Cheeves's grasp like a dead chicken hanging on a barbwire fence. Blood ran from the old man's mouth, ears, and nose cavities. The android could only stare expressionless at the dead man in his grasp.

"Now go, leave me before I change my mind and have you all exterminated for my own pleasure."

The rest of the group's members rushed from the underground room as fast as they all could, nearly knocking each other over in the process.

Nikolai waited until his visitors had all run far enough away before addressing Cheeves. The android servant still had Vespasian in his grasp.

"Go search out what remains of this party and kill anyone left alive, not that I expect any of them to still breathing."

Cheeves nodded its metal head.

"Then seek out the Rustler elders deep in the Wasteland. Inform them of our situation in all its details. Make them understand that our plans have been compromised. Clover will be coming for them all, not that I care if he eliminates every last one of them. But he can't discover what we have planned, or everything will be ruined. The elders must understand the gravity of our desperation. Tell them our timetable has been accelerated, without any more delays."

Cheeves nodded his head again.

"But what about this dead body, master?"

"Dispose of it promptly. Bury it in a shallow grave. The last thing we need is unwanted predators of any kind come snooping around."

A tall thin messenger wrapped from head to toe flew into the Outland Rustler camp, like the wind coming out of the mountains and rushing through the sandy valley below. The messenger was breathing heavily, unable to stop and catch his breath. His chest visibly heaved in and out as he tried to suck in what air that was available to him, despite the thermal gear the messenger wore.

The nearly exhausted Rustler weaved in and out of the multitude of campfires and the Rustlers that occupied them. The messenger's mad dash through the makeshift camp drew all sorts of attention. Outland Rustler officers came out of their tents to see what the commotion was about, just as the fleet-footed messenger passed by in a blink of an eye. The officers weren't the only ones dumbfounded by the messenger sprinting through their camp, Outland Rustler soldiers working throughout the camp were mystified by the messenger's flight as well.

By the time the messenger reached the middle of the camp, a figure appeared out of one of the main officer tents, throwing back its rawhide flap, sending dust skyward. The figure was a wide, broad-shouldered individual wearing a leather pair of field pants. The officer watched the messenger pass through the horrified camp, not one bit amused by the disturbance. Right as the messenger was passing the officer, the officer reached out and snared the messenger by the throat. The officer held the Rustler messenger by the throat with precision that only a seasoned Rustler could have. He brought the insubordinate closer to him. The messenger could feel the roughness of his superior's hands, a field officer for sure.

That's when the messenger pierced into the blue eyes of his commanding officer. Commander Callum Beckett was partially blind in one eye. The eye had turned three-quarters hazed over and surely was dead. A scar ran from the commander's forehead, down across the wounded eye and down to the other side of the man's chin, acting like a dividing line. The commander's large nose surely had been broken more than once, because it was flatter on the scar side than the other side of his face. The officer had a five o'clock shadow that never went away.

The messenger tried to swallow, but it was quite difficult with the commander's grip on his throat.

In a deep, booming tone, Commander Beckett asked, "Where are you off to in such a hurry, soldier?"

The messenger tried to swallow once again and then attempted to explain to his superior officer what he had experienced out in the vast Wasteland.

†

Outside the elders' tent, which was the largest and most fortified in the Rustler camp, was a silhouette of a group of Rustlers arguing. It sounded as if they were attempting not to be heard but doing a poor job of concealing their conversation. A scuffling sound echoed as if some of the guards were forcefully escorting a figure away. One guard halted Commander Beckett, but as soon as the guard recognized the rank insignia and the commander's half-lit face, the guard loosened his stern position.

The leathery tent flap was thrown open violently and the commander dragged the messenger along with him into the elders' tent. The commander threw down the messenger directly in front of the Rustler elders. The elders were mutants that had been around long before any of their human followers. Each had their own abilities, but it was the blind elder who spoke with the commander first.

The blind elder sat to the commander's left. He was sitting cross-legged, much like the three other elders. The blind elder had his hands on his knees and Beckett noticed the odd-looking skin on the elder's hands. He had never noticed how foreign and old the skin looked. It possessed a dark russet color, one that made the commander's skin crawl. *It looks so foreign and demonic,* the commander thought.

Then the commander noticed the elder's extremely long nails; they came to a point like a dagger, razor sharp, and weapons in their own right. The dingy gray smock and hooded cloak that the elder wore looked as if it had never been washed. The ends of the smocklike cloak reached the elder's ankles. It was frayed, and pieces of material seemed to be missing from the bottom of the smock. The soles of the elder's shoes were so worn that Commander Beckett thought he could see right through one of them. It was not a sight he wanted to experience.

Each elder wore an amulet around their neck that Beckett felt signified their own power. The blind elder wore something like a Yin and Yang icon, but instead of having an icon that appeared like two tadpoles chasing one another, it looked as if the top portion of the icon was a ridged icicle with frozen ends and a tale waving chaotically, while the bottom portion of the icon appeared to be a fireball, a flame fleeing from the other symbol. The commander even thought he saw flames falling from the symbol.

The rest of the elders didn't have hazed-over eyes. Each one of the other elders had similar dress, with the same dingy gray smock, but the difference was the cloak portion of their dress each had different shades of color that seemed to match the color of their skin.

"Water," whispered the commander. "And Earth."

Commander Beckett spoke before any of the elders could protest his barging in.

"We have a serious problem." He looked down at the messenger who was still trying to catch his breath and struggling to get to his feet. "Tell them, boy! Tell them what you told me. Tell them what you encountered in the Wasteland!"

The messenger struggled to get it out of his throat. He stuttered but couldn't speak a lick in front of the four elders.

The blind elder leaned forward.

"He is coming. Clover and another approach our camp at a rapid pace."

None of the elders appeared bothered. They stared at the mystical flame of their campfire. The commander burst out in anger at the elders, who seemed to stay calm despite the danger they were in.

"Why are you so calm and nonchalant about this?" Commander Beckett looked madly at each of the four elders. "We need to pack up the camp and flee before it is too late!"

"No," said another elder. This one had full use of his eyes, but his skin was coarse and dry. He appeared to be the oldest of the elders, but it was difficult for the commander to tell. The elders, before they fled their cave dwelling, hadn't been seen for years. Now he was charged with their protection. "Are you even remotely aware of what this assassin is capable of? He could swipe this entire camp away in one attempt. There is a reason the humans—"

A third elder interrupted the commander's explanation.

"We quite understand how dangerous Clover is and what he is capable of, Commander. We are tired of running, and it's time for one last stand."

The commander shook his head slowly. "Obviously not. He has tossed aside many attempts in the past and he has been more than a pain in the Rustlers' side for years." Beckett folded his arms like an angry adolescent. "He will wipe us all out without breathing heavily. It won't stop him from coming for you all."

"Oh, I do miss the confines of our cave dwelling," the fourth elder said.

The blind elder turned to his fellow brethren. "You forget the reason we left, don't you?"

"I do not, brother," the fourth elder said. "Clover had discovered our hideout." Then the elder turned back to Commander Beckett. "You must understand, Commander, that we don't doubt your ability to defend us, but we are old and moving through the rough terrain of the Wasteland has worn us down."

The second elder spoke up. "You will send a mobile party to greet our pursuer."

"That won't stop him!" barked the commander.

"No, it won't," returned the second elder. "But it will act as a roadblock and buy us the time we need." The elder turned to his fellow elders as if addressing an unruly audience. "It is time for our surprise to be unleashed. Someone will have to contact Brother Nikolai and inform him that we have to act now. There is no more time to dance around."

The third elder looked back at Beckett. "After you send a party to impede the assassin, you will send a messenger to our allies to inform them of our latest actions and the reasoning behind them. Nikolai must understand and adjust his plans accordingly. Then send a party of five to these coordinates." The elder handed the commander a set of instructions and Commander Beckett looked down at them with a hard and distrusting expression. His jaw muscles sagged, and he had the look of a defeated man. He looked back at the elder with fury in his eyes.

"This is a hard day and a half away. You'll condemn the men I send out there. It's in the middle of nowhere!"

"We will honor their sacrifice to our cause," The fourth elder responded.

The blind elder leaned over to the second and whispered, "The end is near for us all."

They all agreed.

Chapter 6

Six weeks ago

Tigerous and Zeus's swift departure from Sunriot pushed them towards the northeastern part of the Wasteland. Nothing about the episode on thc cdgc of the village felt right to Tigerous, looked back past her traveling mate, and out towards the west, the direction they had come from. She watched as the sun set, sending purple strands of sunlight over the edge of the sandy dunes from the indigo sun, which had changed colors from the radiation that still lingered high in the atmosphere, giving the skyline and dunes the purple tint they now possessed. It was more than breathtaking, but Tigerous also understood that after dawn set in, it was the nocturnal creatures of the Wasteland's time. She thought of the mythology surrounding her friend Clover. It was funny that the old collector had mentioned that name. Something told Tigerous that the messenger Crane had been holding out on old Cadon Trolotov. In fact, she assumed that the missing messenger had left out a few things. Had Crane seen the legendary assassin at least once in his life?

She thought of the mythology surrounding her friend Clover. It was funny that the old collector had mentioned that name. Something told Tigerous that the messenger Crane had been holding out on old Cadon Trolotov. In fact, she assumed that the missing messenger had left out a few things. Had Crane seen the legendary assassin at least once in his life?

The stigma attached to the legends about Clover was that he was a vicious creature of the night, that the bioengineered assassin prowled the Wasteland of the night. Of course, she knew better, but she or Zeus wouldn't deter the mysticism of his persona. Like most legends there was always some validity to them.

Tigerous took a sip from her waterskin, noticing it was a little on the light side. Their hasty getaway from East Sunriot had ensured she hadn't properly provisioned their supplies. In fact, they were low on a lot of things. Tigerous went digging into her pack, feeling her way through the dense objects that resided in the worn-out pack, until she removed an old, hand-drawn, and weather-beaten map. Electronic maps were useless out in the Wasteland with the unpredictable sandstorms and blistering heat, and since there was no one to maintain the satellites in the sky, they weren't used much in the makeshift villages outside the Wasteland either.

Tigerous thought to herself, as she stared to the east, there was Wallis Adell, a small community, more makeshift township than thriving town, but nowadays only towns sponsored by the Rustlers thrived. Tigerous wondered if the outlaws had a contract on him, and would the messenger be welcomed at any of the Rustler bases? Tigerous pulled out a set of thermal binoculars used during traveling in the heat of daytime. They seemed all fogged up, so she wiped them off and began to scan the eastern portion of the landscape. There would be no reason to travel after the sun disappeared, so she was looking for a safe route in the daytime. Wallis Adell was a long shot at best. It was a two-, maybe three-day hike; would their provisions last that long? Maybe, or maybe not, but the tougher question she asked herself was, traveling under the intense rays of the sun, *Can Zeus and I survive the elongated trip? Even if we make it across the plains, there is no guarantee they will have what we need to resupply ourselves to venture farther onwards, she thought.*

Then there was always Red Rage, but it was a treacherous place, both in legend and reality. The most lethal cutthroats and assassins living within the Wasteland could be found in Red Rage, and that wasn't including the clientele and ruthless vendors trying to slither you out of as much as they could. It wasn't a place Tigerous thought Cane

Savage would choose unless he was forced. So, it was between the distance of Wallis Adell with no guarantee of resupply or the cutthroat nature of Red Rage. She raised the binoculars again and began to look in the direction of Wallis Adell, hoping to see a clear path. Instead, Tigerous saw something moving in the distance.

Readjusting her binoculars to one-thousand times zoom, Tigerous noticed them in one swoop; four Wasteland nomads traveling westwards. *Do the nomads ever travel against the grain?* she wondered. *Could they be heading home? But it could also be they were fleeing a sandstorm approaching from the east.* Not that uncommon for the Wasteland Plains.

She couldn't identify the nomads for the clan they were a part of, but it didn't matter, they were heading in the direction of Red Rage, not the place she wanted to go, but neither would her and her traveling companion march eastwards if the nomads were heading in the opposite direction. Tigerous decided they would camp for the night and set out at dawn.

Tigerous replaced her binoculars back into her pack and began to build a small campfire. They would need to build a makeshift shelter large enough for herself and Zeus's gargantuan body, in case a storm caught them while they slept. None of this was thrilling her at all. She had been sent out to gather intel on the Rustlers' activities, but to do so she had been sent on a wild chase. They had been coaxed into investigating the Wasteland Rustlers' business, a dangerous proposition if they encountered a band too large for Zeus and herself to handle.

Then a contract assassin, supposedly hired by the Rustlers, had come for the messenger or anyone that might possesses damaging evidence of what they were up to, which Clover desired to know. It had to be the information Cadon and Deshawna had given her, didn't it? Then, if all that wasn't enough, Deshawna had implied they were now the outlaws' new target, switching from the missing messenger, whom no one seemed to know where he was, and Zeus and herself roaming the Wasteland Plains. It had always infuriated Tigerous not having the upper hand, let alone being blindsided by unseen assailants.

But it wasn't what Deshawna had said, it was the implication in her voice, in what she hadn't said that put Tigerous on edge. Then the nomads heading in the general direction of Red Rage, a place she had no desire to be. It all was leading to something that would blow up in their faces.

Reading data the collector had given her about a facility up north. *What was the name of the place*, she asked herself while the light-yellow flames flickered? *The Sierra Nevada facility,* Tigerous responded. The name sounded familiar, some old corporate laboratory in the north. That was about all she knew. But knowledge seemed to be a dangerous thing these days. Was that the reason she was being targeted? Was something going on the Rustlers didn't want anyone to uncover?

Maybe going to Red Rage was a good thing after all. They could find someone who knew about the facility and why it was so important. The only issue was that she didn't have contacts in Red Rage, so the price might be more than they could afford. Tigerous sighed, *I could always listen in on conversations at a local watering hole.* It was something, traversing the Wasteland alone, she had done to gain an upper hand. It was how she gained the trust of potential allies and learned about potential adversaries.

Tigerous leaned back and stared at the darkening sky through the paper-thin canvas slapping overhead, while her titanous friend snored away. She utilized Zeus's snoring rhythm to soothe her anxiety. This ordeal was becoming more involved than she liked. Could the data they currently possessed be a bartering tool, or would it get them into deeper trouble? That was something Tigerous couldn't predict. Was this the reason the messenger had vanished, diving too deeply into someone else's affairs? She would just have to see when they reached Red Rage in a day or two.

It had been a hard two-day trek towards Red Rage. They had caught the back end of a sandstorm and were forced to stop and take shelter more than once. The delays were making Tigerous frustrated. She wanted to reach Red Rage swiftly and discover what she might, so a better-focused path might present itself. But the logical side of her brain told her that there would be more challenges in the cutthroat town. After fighting the sandstorm and the blistering heat of the sun overhead, Tigerous and Zeus finally made it to the outskirts of Red Rage.

It was pitch dark out, but luckily Tigerous possessed nocturnal vison which allowed her to see things in silhouette when others couldn't see within an inch of their own hand, like her traveling escort. Her breathing was slow and steady, but Tigerous felt the presence of another, and it wouldn't take long for her calmness to become perturbation. The stale air filled her nostrils, along with sand particles, and was beginning to fill up her lungs, as well. It might not smell all that pleasant, but it was still breathable air. It had the stench of wet, dirty socks.

She didn't sense any airflow. The floor seemed rocky, so she could count out a storage facility or large room. That left really one possibility: she was in some cavern under a mountain range. Then something dawned on Tigerous---*the Sierra Nevada facility!* She gasped and the sound seemed to echo, but her voice's vibration seemed to only travel a short distance then deaden.

Definitely a metal wall structure, but was the Sierra Nevada facility built with a rock-floor base? The sound of whoever it was, was very near; almost close enough to snare the very breath from the feline's lips. Tigerous attempted to adjust her eyes and see if she could see anything moving in front of her, but the place was encased in darkness and not even her nocturnal eyesight was aiding her.

It took her a lot of nerve and time to take a step forward. The sound of rocks kicking out from underneath her was the only sound available, outside of her rapidly beating heart. There was silence, nothing moved, but Tigerous could tell the figure, whatever it was, still shared the place with her. It was like a cat-and-mouse game; but she wasn't sure if whatever it was even thought on an intelligent level.

Maybe it was instinctual and it was doing this out of primordial reflex than out of intelligence. "You don't scare me, whatever you are." Tigerous's voice once again vibrated off the seamless metal walls. She was forced to clear her throat before continuing. "I won't allow you to feast on my weakened state, I will fight you tell the end."

But nothing returned her proclamation, just dead silence as before. Tigerous gripped both hands into fists. Both of her palms were drenched in sweat. Then, as before, she gathered her fading courage and took another step towards where she believed the other occupant's location was.

Slowly she crept along. First one step, then a second, then finally a third. She made her way through the depths of darkness with no sense of direction, but she was now moving, and it was better than standing still, waiting for whatever she sensed would expose itself. A slow and steady sound of breathing nearby emerged from the darkness. At first it made Tigerous pause, but it didn't have an aggressive tone, if breathing ever could, so she continued towards whatever she was approaching.

"I can hear you breathing, so playing the silent game won't work on me." Tigerous's voice echoed.

Tigerous creeped on, beginning to lose her anxiety and growing more confident as she went. One hand scraped the rocky floor to give her some guidance and direction; much like using a rope would. So long as the ground possessed a rocky content, she could continue, but Tigerous knew eventually, unless her progress was halted, she would run into a metal wall at some point. Tigerous needed that guidance until her nocturnal sight returned to aid her.

"Where are you, my friend? Why are we in this place together, and how did we get here in the first place?"

A low guttural growl sounded. It was the same tone as the breathing, not all that menacing, but more threatening, like a dog warning an approaching visitor. The growling became more profound, louder, and now had an aggressive tone to it. Tigerous needed to escape this place, or she feared this would be her burial tomb, she was sure of it.

A final, deep growl sounded directly in front of her, it was no more than five to ten feet from her current location. A dull light came out of nowhere, illuminating a five-square meter area in front of Tigerous. She hadn't seen where the light source was or if it was natural light or artificial; but she doubted she could have deciphered between the two at that moment. The light source was too blinding, shining right at her. Just on the other side of the light, a set of gray and emotionless eyes appeared. Her nemesis had finally come out of hiding.

The being leaned into the light just enough to see a gray, wrinkled skin of a figure that looked to be mal-nourished and disfigured. The creature's head was bald, scarred, and just as disfigured as the rest of its mangled body. The thing had clawlike fingers that seemed to have been shaved down to the bones. Its ears appeared as if acid had eaten away at them until very little was left; they were nearly level with the creature's deformed head.

The creature possessed needle-sharp teeth that looked prone to flesh ripping. They had dull stains on them, and the figure was showing them off clearly. Tigerous cringed as an image of the thing ripping at her own flesh flashed before her eyes. She took a step away from the hungry-looking figure. The creature mirrored her movements and stepped into the light fully, then stopped. The creature, obviously no longer human, still had traits of its human-oid past. It still had ribs, two arms and two legs. It had a prominent forehead and a slightly larger skull, but it still looked human. What seemed to be missing was what you expected to be present in a human being, that emotional expression and life in its eyes, neither of which were displayed in the figure.

The creature leaped at Tigerous with lighting quickness, but Tigerous matched its speed and agility and awaited with her claws, ready for action. The mutated figure and Tigerous's bodies slammed into one another, making a loud thud. As the two struggled in each other's embrace, she could feel no heat coming from the thing—it was cold to the bone. The figure grabbed onto her with its clawlike fingers and dug into Tigerous's flesh. She could feel their flesh-shredding power, and to her surprise the figure was much stronger than even she could have anticipated.

Tigerous cried out in pain as the deformed claws dug in. Blood began to drip from her wounds.

The two of them tumbled to the rocky cavern floor. Rock debris shot everywhere. The jarring effect forced the figure's grip to loosen enough to give Tigerous a shot at retaliation, but she knew she would need to be quick about it. Tigerous ripped the creature's claws from her and motioned outwards with her feline hands, temporarily shoving the figure away from her body. She scooped up a handful of fine rock debris into one hand, then before losing her temporary advantage, she threw the handful into the creature's face.

The mutated creature shielded its face, giving Tigerous a small chance to slither away. She first crawled on all fours, letting the fine rock sediment bite into her hands and knees. She ignored the pain, she could deal with it later. Understanding that crawling would only delay the inevitable, she rose to her feet and ran into the darkness. Her nocturnal eyesight slowly came back to her in the darkness. Tigerous ran hard and fast, quite reckless as well.

Stumbling over a large rock and staggering uncontrollably, Tigerous slammed into a steel bulkhead and fell to the rocky floor. She was dazed and her head was spinning out of control. The mutated figure emerged through the darkness just as the mystical light appeared, but the thing must have not known she could see its approach, or it would have dodged her throwing claws. The ones she had at the ready.

The nemesis had its arms spread out, poised to strike violently. Its rail-thin legs were flailing, as if its leap had sent it into a free fall and out of control. Tigerous could only stare into those gray, lifeless eyes. They were hypnotic, but Tigerous forced herself to snap out of the thing's trance in time to see those needle-sharp teeth bearing down on her. In a desperate move she threw one of her claws and heard a *thud* but never saw it strike home. An uncontrollable fear burst from Tigerous's mouth, a scream louder than she had ever screamed, and the sound reverberated throughout the cavernous structure.

✝

Tigerous snapped out of her nightmare with her heart racing and her chest heaving like a volcano ready to erupt. She was curled up in a thermal sleeping bag, the only thing outside of the dying campfire that would keep the chill of the Wasteland night off her. Zeus was shaking her to wake up and she noticed she was in the behemoth's fantastic grip. She couldn't decipher if it was still dusk or if she had slept through part of the morning. The sky had become gray and there was a low haze looming over the plains. Once she had shaken off her drowsiness, Zeus brushed sand grains off her, and she peeked out from their protective canvas.

Over his massive shoulders, she witnessed sand whirling around everywhere. It was difficult to see anything. Even the thermal binoculars would struggle giving them any sense of what was happening. But she didn't need to see what was happening, she could hear the wind coming in from the east and the storm that would be on them quickly. Tigerous understood if they were going to track the nomads' trail towards Red Rage, they needed to move. If the storm caught them, it would not only make life miserable for them, but make it impossible to pick up the nomads' trail.

✝

They had arrived at Red Rage without being caught by the plains storm. Only the outskirts of the storm had made an appearance. They managed to stay ahead of the sandstorm and arrived in just over a day. The hard pace they had set made them both fatigued, but they weren't out of danger. Tigerous and Zeus had to face the dangers that lurked within Red Rage. With any luck, they would find the information they were seeking, replenish their supplies, and hopefully leave unnoticed. But that, she knew, was a fantasy.

The provisions they gathered in Red Rage would come at a steep price, more expensive than if they had ventured into Wallis Adell, but Tigerous had understood that when she decided to make for Red Rage. It was the trade-off for traveling to the cutthroat township. They both held their packs close, trying not to look too vigilant and hiding their presence. They needed to blend in, like a Red Rage regular, yet as it was in Sunriot, Tigerous's very large companion eliminated any hope to do that.

They lumbered down the town's winding streets going from vendor tent to vendor tent, trying to collect supplies for their continued voyage and asking cautiously about who could supply information about the Sierra Nevada facility as secretive as possible. They didn't ask every vendor, that would have sparked too much curiosity. And the travelers also didn't stick to a pattern of which vendor to approach, just in case someone was watching—in Red Rage, someone always was.

If they were going to have any answers, according to several vendors, it would be at The Vagabond Pub, now that sounded like a place for a bunch of gentlemen if Tigerous ever heard one. They especially would need to watch themselves in that place, because most likely their presence would be noticed. Tigerous, followed by the mountainous Zeus, stepped out into the Red Rage street and began to make their way to the pub.

The way to the weary pub was windy like a maze. The directions they had obtained were about as shaky and un-clear as was the exact location. Several times she had to stop someone in the street to ask the way. Many places in Red Rage were regarded as rough and undesirable to visit, but a place had to be extra dangerous if it was located deep in the lower bowels of the town. That only made Tigerous even more nervous than she already was.

There it was, looking ragged and weathered by the Wasteland. Rotten wood that led to a discolored front door. There was no indication that this was the place they were searching for, but by the description they had received along the way, this was most definitely the place.

Blacked-out windows accounted for a total of two. Rusted and weathered paneling ran all along the sides of the small, rectangular building. In fact, it appeared deserted to Tigerous, but something told her it wasn't.

They set their feet in motion and reached for the pub door. It must have been a place left over from before the world ended. From her understanding, the entire township had been built over an abandoned town, but Tigerous didn't know which town Red Rage had replaced. It was obvious that the township had used some of the old buildings that had been left standing. The door handle was tarnished and made of some type of cheap metal. When Tigerous touched it, the handle felt old, and she feared rust would rub off onto her hand. The door creaked, most likely the door hinges hadn't been lubricated in ages. The door, despite all it must have endured, seemed firm and heavy. Most likely it was made of metal from an older age.

The two weary travelers stepped into the establishment and the dense atmosphere slapped them hard in the face. Neither Tigerous nor Zeus expected the heat from the proximity of bodies to smother them so much. Tigerous had preferred the discomfort of the Wasteland with its dry and uncomfortable climate over taverns with bodies forced so close it could choke a man.

The artificial lighting was dim, but most establishments like this usually had low lighting. It made the shady occupants feel more at home. Taverns, in the post-apocalyptic world, were places where assassins and spies spent their time, and where crooked deals were made. Ones that most readily would be broken at some point, with a rusty dagger in your back or hands around your throat. Only a few bottles of pre-apocalypse whiskey lined the rotting shelves behind the bar on the left. *I guess the supplier hasn't come by yet to refill their inventory*, Tigerous thought.

A few heads turned as they both took their first steps into the room. The floor creaked loudly and Tigerous froze, forcing Zeus to run into her as if something had reached out and bit her suddenly. She was hoping the casual glances were the only attention they would draw from these cutthroats but began to feel something had sensed their presence. But she didn't know what had, or where it was in the dirty pub.

In her extensive experience, humans didn't need assassins to eliminate targets, the harsh and uninviting climate would do it for them. Tigerous took a deep breath and proceeded to walk across the protesting pub floor, which creaked each step she and her companion took. The shadowy figure that had slipped by the metal closing door behind her didn't realize Tigerous had finally tracked their pursuer from her heightened senses.

She walked up to the bar as if nothing was amiss and where it appeared the bartender was doing his best to ignore his new customers. *He must sense I am new to this place.* She tapped on the artificial countertop and waited.

Zeus grunted just in case the human decided to ignore Tigerous. The barkeep turned his head and huffed. Tigerous and Zeus had become accustomed to unfriendly glares.

The barkeep groaned. "What do you want?"

Tigerous leaned on the sticky bar, and looked up and down it as if to make sure no one was listening in. "I need some information and was told I might find it in here."

The barkeep gave a jagged grin. "Everyone is looking for information in here, or making deals. Tell me what you're looking for and I might be able to help, for a price."

Tigerous squinted at the very large man, scrutinizing him. "I . . ." She looked up and down the bar again, then leaned even closer to the barkeep, now able to smell what the big man had for dinner last night, not that she needed to get that close to tell any of that with her feline senses. "I am looking for any information about The Sierra Nevada facility."

The barkeep recoiled as if he had just been bitten. The enormous man jerked his head back and a scowl emerged on the barkeep's face. "Why would someone like yourself need that type of information? Rumors tell that it's a cursed place, where those that venture to its location never return. Not a happy place to go."

"Neither is living off the Wasteland plains these days," returned Tigerous. "Can you help me or not?"

The barkeep smirked, but once the man looked over her shoulder at her beefy companion, she saw his negative attitude lessen. She doubted if it was facetious in nature. "Okay, good point," grunted the large human. The barkeep this time didn't return a sarcastic remark, but only nodded to a corner booth, near the back of the bar. Tigerous gestured her gratitude and tossed the man a coin for payment.

A few of the establishment's patrons observed the two travelers move through the bar, towards its rear, but none with more than a glance and those were seldom. Tigerous hugged her backpack close to her body, knowing at any moment, a pickpocket could strip the contents away without knowing it. She doubted anyone would try to steal from Zeus.

A dark figure was sitting in a shadowy corner in the booth indicated to her by the barkeep. She could tell the figure was watching their approach. The person she had been told had the information they sought didn't move, from what Tigerous could tell. The closer they got, the more apprehensive she became.

Tigerous stepped up to the booth and introduced herself. The aged man's head snapped up with his weary eyes opened. He looked like he was none too happy to be approached in such a fashion. The man wore a tattered, copper-colored top and seemed to be stretched a little thin. His graying hair was thinning out and looked dirty, but that could have been from the dull lighting. The elderly man seemed to be a little on the heavy side, but still trim enough to have traveled the Wasteland Plains recently. Rings encircled his eyes, as if he hadn't slept in a while. Maybe that's why the informant had been half-dozing as they approached.

"My dear man, I believe you have some information in need, so I will have it now!"

The man snarled back at Tigerous. "Piss off, dickhead."

Tigerous smiled at the retort. It was something she had become used to by this point of her life. Mutants weren't very well accepted by humans. "I think you misunderstand me, my good man. I'm just here looking for information on . . ." Tigerous lowered her hands to the wobbly table and leaned in, though not too close to prevent the man from striking out at her. "The Sierra Nevada facility. Do you know of it and its secrets, or not?"

That drew the old man's attention swiftly. He growled at the mention of the place. "You should avoid it like the black plague, my slender feline. In fact, you shouldn't inquire about it at all, especially in this place. Now go away and let me be."

"I can't," Tigerous said. "I was sent on a mission to find out what is going on up there and I see my assignments through to the end. I can compensate you for any trouble it might cause." Tigerous began to reach into her pack for some loose coins. Tigerous didn't think the old man would take anything less than coin for the information.

Suddenly, a rusty knife went into her side.

"So, this was all a sham, the information, the tavern with cutthroats truly lives up to its reputation." Retorted Tigerous. Some cutthroat had slipped by her enormous companion, which was unlike Zeus.

The figure behind her sunk the knife in a little deeper and she got the point.

"Oh, I know more than a care to about The Sierra Nevada facility. I used to work there. And, yes, it was a setup."

Tigerous had to assume Zeus must have been drugged by several tranqulizers, because he hadn't come to her rescue, but she also hadn't heard the behemoth fall to the ground.

The figure behind her began to growl. "Let's move outside, and no funny business."

If Tigerous complied, she felt that she wouldn't see this investigation through, that this was the end of the line. Tigerous and her assailant began to walk backwards, most likely towards a back exit and to her ultimate demise. Tigerous had to be careful not to stumble, she wasn't sure how the man with the knife would respond. Would her detainee slip the rusted knife into her back?

Tigerous listened to the man with the knife's boot heels scrape against the wooden floorboards. She could only imagine, once that sound ceased, that her time would have run out. Tigerous could sense patrons' eyes staring at them as they passed by. But she felt the knife-wielding man wouldn't want to expose his identity, even to these bandits and cutthroats.

They passed through the main section of the tavern into a storage area where old crates and boxes lay everywhere. Something like rotten food seemed to linger in this room, but it fit the aura of The Vagabond Pub. They had gotten what Tigerous thought was halfway through the back room and she saw pincushions of light coming through seams in the wall, telling her that their journey was just about through, when she sensed her captor stiffen. Tigerous could have moved to eliminate her assailant at any time, but she wanted to see where this was heading, and she hoped it might lead to insight on the intel they had come to the shithole of a town for. Then they stopped their descent towards the back door. A second assassin moved behind the first. The second assassin's silhouette half covered the first one, facing her in a threatening manner.

Now she would have to change her approach with *two* skilled human assassins, even though she had no doubt she could handle them both. Taking on one semi-skilled human would be easy enough and allow her to take a straight-forward approach. Having two trained adversaries would need different approach.

A familiar voice came from the other side of the doorway they had passed through just moments ago. "Let her go," the voice said in a guttural groan.

"*Zeus!*" Tigerous yelled.

The man with the knife blade to her throat removed the blade and pointed it at the door. "Be gone with you. This is none of your concern," said the deep and raspy voice of her captor.

"When it comes to this one, it's always my concern," Zeus said in retaliation.

The strong man growled like a predator, but she understood it was this thug that was the prey not the other way around. Tigerous allowed her captor to move another step towards the rear exit, but neither one was swift enough to block the attack coming. Zeus burst through the flimsy door, growling and flashing his teeth in a furious rage, then leaped out without heeding the dangers before them. Zeus slammed into them both with all his might, knocking the three of them out the shabby wooden door and into the dusty alley. The rage-filled attack could have killed them if Zeus so desired, but Tigerous had worked with her companion too often and understood his intent as much as Zeus did.

The thug lost his grip on Tigerous and once the dust settled all three had fallen to opposite sides of the alley. Tigerous got an extremely good look at her detainer at that moment. If it wasn't for the fact she was a little woozy from Zeus's help, she would have slit the thug's throat herself. The figure was a stocky-built normal-height male wearing dark assassin's garb. She couldn't see the insignia on the man's right shoulder, it seemed too small from the distance, but Tigerous assumed it was similar to the one on the assassin from East Sunriot. What did it all mean? The information she had been given, two assassins coming for her, and now this.

The thug rose to a knee with his dagger lying no more than ten feet from him. Zeus had stayed on his feet and Tigerous saw his intent before the assassin did. She could feel the tension as the figures on either side of her were ready to duel; Tigerous was somehow stuck in the middle of it all.

Zeus stood there in a defensive position with his huge thighs spread at shoulder length and his enormous hands out in front of him. Tigerous could sense her companion's rage emanating from the primate's very pores. Zeus's scowl could scare a man to death, but wasn't that why he was originally recruited as Legion's sergeant-at-arms? The human crawled towards his weapon. Once he had the weapon, the man howled at Zeus, but the only reaction was Tigerous's laughing. *Like that is supposed to scare a seasoned warrior like Zeus?* she thought. Zeus's expression never waivered. Tigerous always felt he had ice water in his veins. Now she could confirm it firsthand. She had witnessed the leviathan of a beast tear limbs off larger creatures effortlessly.

The assassin seemed to want to bark at her companion but was too frozen to speak. That was most likely the smartest move he had made in a long time.

Both assailants moved swiftly, but it was Zeus who had the stronger attack, he moved with a genuine purpose, while the other seemed to be taking the confrontation with a little less aggression. Zeus didn't possess a visible weapon, but he didn't need one. His massive strength would be enough to rip the human's head from his shoulders with little effort, even with a knife in the assassin's possession. The assassin did something Tigerous hadn't expected—he went into a sliding motion, sweeping to Zeus's left side. The behemoth swiped at the human and missed. This seemed to temporarily take the male by surprise.

Tigerous had only seen Zeus move with such powerful moves and purpose once, and she understood her companion was about to wreck the human assassin's day with his powerful strength. Before Zeus struck the assailant, the assassin snapped out of his semitrance and lunged at Zeus with his dagger, even though it would have very little effect. Zeus wasn't about to be stopped by something as simple as an assassin's blade, his makeup wouldn't allow it. Zeus snarled at their human adversary, exposing a row of deadly primate teeth.

Tigerous watched as the blade in the male's hand vanished into her companion's tough skin. As expected, it didn't have much effect. Zeus treated the human assassin like a child. With a flip of his enormous hand, the former sergeant-at-arms guided the assault to the side; the sound of breaking bones and a murderous scream came from the now defenseless attacker. With one swift and powerful strike, Zeus struck the assassin's chest with an open palm while swiping the man's legs out from under him. It was like their adversary had been shot out of a cannon.

The assailant tumbled over himself, end over end. Zeus didn't wait for his opponent to gather himself, he pounced over to the man and struck the assassin with both fists, striking the human square in the chest. The man's chest caved in, and Zeus launched him into the air. He picked up the knife with his blood staining the rusted blade and examined it, as if he was shopping and not in a battle.

Zeus, in a mocking gesture, motioned for the assassin to stand up. The male assassin didn't do anything but lay there motionless. Tigerous knew he was down for the count after witnessing what Zeus had done. Zeus growled, "What's wrong, have you finally come to your senses?"

The other kidnapper, who had chosen to stay out of the fight, smiled. "Just the opposite."

Zeus and his new opponent engaged each other. Zeus flipped the male like a toy with his hip, but instead of flying to the ground, the second assailant bounced off the ground and landed somewhat upright, but the human's hip seemed to have become dislocated. The human assassin spun in mid-air and fired an assassin's dagger at Zeus. The needle-thin dagger sliced at the side of Zeus's neck and stuck into his furry flesh. Zeus ripped the blade from his wound and gave out a loud roar as he dropped the dagger to the ground. That pleased the male assassin and he attempted to retrieve his dagger, but a hesitation came over the human's dirty face. In one motion the assassin rolled towards the weapon and snagged it as Zeus was tended to his fresh wound.

The male now had a coy smile on his face, and he was tossing his dagger in the air. "Doesn't feel so good, now does it, asshole?"

"You're going to pay for that with your life, human," boomed Zeus.

Zeus charged full steam ahead. The human assassin went low to swipe at Zeus's powerful thighs, but Tigerous couldn't comprehend the assassin's thinking. *Is he insane?* she thought. The assassin's attack failed miserably, and the powerful primate snagged his attacker by the male's chest with one forearm over his throat and locked to her other arm. Tigerous could see her friend's massive forearms bulging and the human male struggling, waving his arms chaotically with no prevail.

Tigerous cringed at the sound of bones crunching as the assassin's fight diminished and he slowly died. The male assassin fell over dead quickly and Zeus went to one knee, holding his wounded side. Tigerous ran to her brutish companion pulling out a small med kit she always kept for instances such as this and began to provide what medical attention she could, which was minimal at best.

Zeus groaned as Tigerous provided him with aid to his wound and his titanous chest heaved in and out as if the brute had run a hundred miles. Slowly, he recovered.

"Not that I'm upset, but none of this makes any sense at all," said Tigerous.

"Ouch," bellowed Zeus. "Why don't you be careful with that thing." He had a scowl on his face, but he wasn't upset with Tigerous, as she attended to his wounds with some healing ointment she had in her pack that she had recovered after the fight.

"Sorry, I don't really know what I'm doing, but you have a serious wound and without proper attention it will get infected."

Zeus nodded slowly. "Rustler soldiers, I saw two of them watching from across the street."

Tigerous snapped her eyes up from tending to the wounds.

Zeus slowly got up from his knee, groaning as he stood to his over nine-foot-tall frame. He brushed off some dirt from his shoulder and shook his head. To Tigerous it appeared that her comrade would need a little time for recovery before they moved on, but he wouldn't ever admit that to her.

"Must be a cover up. The information, has to be." Tigerous reached down and began to search the assassin. She found a data disk with the Rustler elders' symbol on it.

Chapter 7

Present Day

The sandy plain that spread out in front of the dune hill was full of Outland Rustlers, like ants ravaging an anthill. Clover scanned the area for any potential attack points. He always possessed a plan when invading, especially when outnumbered. Preist waited by the assassin's side, quiet, as Clover scanned the area like a preying cat. In the back of Clover's mind, he wondered what all the activity had to do with the Rustler elders. "Maybe it's all a diversion," the assassin said under his breath. Clover wouldn't put it past them, knowing he was hot on their tails.

"Were they expecting us?" Preist asked softly.

Clover watched the scattered figures below with his heat sensing eyes. Without breaking his concentration, the assassin said, "I anticipated this. It's the reason we paced ourselves in the first place. I wanted the elders to become agitated and nervous, and it seems to have done the job, but I expected them to send more men."

Preist turned to Clover, an astonished expression planted on his face. "You wanted them to come for us?"

"I knew exactly the response I would get. I have been hunting the Rustler elders for a while now. Following their trail in hopes of them leading me to what they have been planning all this time. They seem to pick up and move right before I can discover what they have been hiding. For a while I even thought they might have help, but now it seems that they are tired of running and want to make one last stand before they perish."

An outlaw began to yell at his comrade from a distance that caught the assassin's attention, but Clover saw it was nothing but a drunkard and lost interest fast.

Preist asked, "Is it so wise to take them on in a frontal attack like this? They must have thousands of Rustlers awaiting us."

Clover sensed the scientist's concerns and only shook his head. "It doesn't matter how many they throw at us, they will all die in fiery flame. Their reign of terror ends now, and this is merely a roadblock to buy them more time."

They both returned their attention to a host of about thirty-five to forty Rustlers now scattered before them, while a horde of thousands were just beyond their current position. Neither companion had moved from their current position as they collected intel, but Clover could smell several more within the makeshift camp.

"We should strike now, before they have time to ready themselves."

Preist wasn't sure how to take that comment. Was Clover serious? Or was he on the prowl for more blood?

Clover hesitated for a moment, like he was waiting for something to happen, then the assassin leaped into action. Preist hesitantly followed.

✝

A pair of roving guards patrolled the outer portion of the mobile Outland Rustler camp. All seemed quiet; the sun was now setting in the west and shadows began to creep into the mobile roadblock. None of the rustlers in the patrol unit had been informed about their mission or the reasoning they were forced off their latest patrol sector. Only the leaders of the patrol unit knew what was going on, and even they only had vague instructions about what to do.

One guard looked beyond their patrol station, staring into the oncoming darkness that followed the recession of the sunlight. He saw nothing and returned his gaze towards his patrol partner. The other walked straight with a stern, at-attention stride, like he was a toy soldier. Both Rustler men were grizzled veterans and that was difficult to say in their line of work. Rustler men didn't have a long life expectancy with living in the harsh environment of the Wasteland and doing what they did, especially since the Corporation's prototype assassin had begun hunting them down in their own land.

The Rustler who looked out into the fading ocean of sand started to whistle. It seemed to calm his nerves somewhat.

The other gave him a disturbed look. He stopped the whistling instantly. After looking at his partner, listening to their boots scuff along the surface, the patrol rustler couldn't take it any longer.

"What do you suppose we are out here for, away from our normal patrol sector?"

The other slowly glanced over at him, expressionless. "Beats me," the soldier's deep scratchy voice said. "I don't question orders, I just obey them. I let our superiors think about why they have sent us out here for. You would be better advised to do the same."

The first guard sighed.

"I don't know. It's all so confusing, ever since"—the Rustler looked around to make sure no one else was listening in on their conversation—"*you know who* has been tracking our people, I keep getting the feeling we are being watched." The patrol guard looked behind themself and out into the now darkness of the Wasteland. "Kind of the feeling I'm getting at this moment."

The guard's partner looked over at him with disapproval. "Watch what you say. You never know who's listening these days."

The patrol guards went back to being silent again.

A shadowy figure moved into striking position. Clover could hear the two Rustler guards' entire conversation, while silently moving across the sand. The first patrol guard moved into his line of sight in the assassin's general direction, as if he had picked up a shadow moving farther along the west perimeter of the camp. The first guard tapped his partner's shoulder and unholstered his weapon. Clover froze to see what they were about to do. No matter what that would be, Clover was ready to strike before they could warn the rest of the camp.

"I thought I saw two figures moving within the shadows," the first guard softly said.

The other squinted his eyes in an attempt to see into the darkness. "Your eyes are playing tricks on you. I can't see a damn thing."

"Of course, they are," whispered the assassin.

Then a whistling sound came out of the darkness and the larger patrol guard was struck in the throat by a sharp object. Blood gushed from the guard's wounded throat as he fell to his knees and froze like a statue momentarily, before falling the rest of the way to the ground.

The other guard tried to whip his weapon around and still watch the shadows, the origin of the weapon that had killed his partner. He was shaking immensely now and dropped his weapon. The Rustler guard was standing there, still as a stone statue. All he could do was stare out into the emptiness of the Wasteland, as if he was waiting for something.

The remaining guard didn't hear Preist approaching him from behind. Preist removed a dagger hidden in his smock and sliced the second guard's throat. The Rustler fell to the ground, a lifeless husk.

Clover emerged from the void's darkness and walked to the second dead body. The assassin looked down at the corpse, then back at Preist.

"Preist, I didn't think you were that kind. I am truly impressed."

Preist wiped his hands off and that's when Clover realized his friend was unsettled by what he had just done. "I only did it out of necessity. We have a job to do, and some sacrifices may be necessary, but it doesn't mean I have to enjoy it."

Sounds of soldiers screaming at the top of their lungs echoed. Clover looked up and had a smile perched on his face. Preist looked over at the assassin.

"It appears playtime has arrived," proclaimed Clover.

The assassin picked up his aerial weapon and wiped the blood off.

Several Rustler soldiers came around the bend. Some of them were carrying automatic weapons, while others carried bludgeoning and cutting weapons. The Rustler soldiers all seemed filled with anger and hatred.

✝

Clover held his throwing weapon in one hand and grasped one of his katanas in the other.

It seemed to the assassin that once the Rustlers saw Preist and himself some of their anger disintegrated. Clover wondered what they had thought was attacking their comrades around the bend. Sure, the crowd was still ready to kill them both, but seeing the legend in person made them all take pause, not sure if they were all ready to die for their leadership or if they wanted to flee in fear.

Eventually, the expendable soldiers regained their courage and continued towards their potential doom.

Clover engaged the oncoming Rustlers from his left, and Preist did his disappearing act, leaving no trace of his whereabouts, off to the right.

Clover gauged the distance from himself and the front part of the Rustler attack. It was almost like target practice for him. He carefully aimed and threw the bladed weapon at the middle of the frontal attack to split the group up, giving Clover a chance to slip between his attackers. The weapon was fast and precise, as usual. Its flight was nearly untrackable, a shiny blur passing by. The weapon struck home, dead in the Rustler's forehead, propelling the soldier backwards and knocking a few of his Rustler mates in the process.

Clover leaped into action before his attackers could recover in time. The assassin moved to his left, raised the katana high, as if a guillotine was about to fall and sliced through his first victim. Clover could feel the slight resistance as the katana's blade ripped through the outlaw's flesh, then tendons, muscle and finally bone, before exiting out the outlaw's body. Human blood flung off the blade as a slurping sound rang in the assassin's ear.

Clover didn't hesitate one bit. His blade caught another outlaw off guard and sliced through the outlaw's hand, slicing the assault weapon the man held in half. Without slowing, Clover reached down and retrieved his aerial weapon; the blade end made a *slurp* sound as it was withdrawn from the man's flesh. Clover spun around, utilizing the five-pronged weapon and whipped an attacker from his feet, like a scorpion would use its tail, creating a roadblock against the attackers coming at Clover in full force.

But the bioengineered assassin wasn't about to stop there. He whipped his body around and rammed his katana through a Rustler's eye socket and out the back of his head. Clover's victory was temporary as a sound rattled inside his ears, warning him of potential danger. The assassin moved swiftly away just in time as a dagger nicked Clover's protective armor just above his shoulder blade.

He leaped back, not in pain, but more in shock as he looked at the scratch on the back of the armor plating. Before the Rustler could get another shot in, Clover jammed the aerial weapon through the Rustler's throat and up into his skull, stopping the attack in midair. He pulled out the weapon and the man fell to the ground. The five-prong weapon felt good in Clover's grip as it sliced up his attackers like butcher's meat on a chopping block.

One by one the Rustler attackers died a horrible death, leaving their life force spilled all over the sandy ground. A few Rustlers survive the onslaught, but not very many. Some ran off into the darkness of the Wasteland, while others lay on the ground groaning from severe injuries. The chaos that was just *moments* before now had become a mangled mess of body parts, a landfill of crude weapons atop blood-soaked sand.

The surface that Clover now stood on appeared like small grains of lava without the searing heat or glowing red that normally came from a lava flow. As Clover looked over and through the mass of Rustlers, Preist emerged, blooded like Clover. His smock, his skin, even the knife Preist wielded dripped Rustler blood. The red ground was drenched in blood, a blood-red sea separated by a strand of sandy tan peninsula.

Clover watched Preist look back at him. The assassin thought his friend looked like a child who had just finished finger painting. Clover gave Preist a sly smile and the scientist returned the gesture. "Preist. I didn't think you had it in you, my old friend."

Bloody boot prints followed the scientist out of the carnage that surrounded him and onto the untouched ground. Halfway between Clover and Preist, Preist halted and wiped human blood from his gray cheek. The normally steady, sure-footed scientist began to tremble. Preist observed his hands shaking and couldn't stop them.

"Someone had to assist you in your debauchery."

Clover walked towards his friend and closed his hands around Preist's. "Everything will be all right. We will fix this where everyone is safe, and no one will have to worry about being extinguished. I promise."

"Are you certain of that, Clover? You seem so sure of yourself."

Just then Clover sensed someone far away was in pain, they seemed to call out, even though he doubted it was to him. "Straus! Help me, please." A vision became embedded in the assassin's mind. A woman in her thirties crawling on a rocky ground towards an unknown entity. She physically appeared to be beaten, with wounds every-where, a bloodied lip, and her hair mangled as if she had lost a fight with something ferocious.

Then the assassin felt an uneasy feeling, one that rang out "Death" from a structure from behind. The words, Sierra Nevada Complex forced their way into Clover's mind and that's when he understood who this person was.

"Straus's sister." The assassin snapped out of the vision and looked to his comrade.

Clover nodded his head. "I am very confident in it. But first we must search for answers. First to this facility in the north in the Sierra Nevada, then to Metro City."

Preist sucked in his breath, looked around at the dead bodies surrounding them and exhaled and nodded.

Nightshade, roaming the desolate land near Metro City watched from afar as three anonymous figures sneaked through the darkness of the deserted city. The three figures moved from rusty steel structure to collapsed building as they made their way towards the interior of the once great metropolis. It was a ghost town, with all its secrets hidden underneath the tons of debris left behind.

The once vibrant streets were now littered with fallen material from the now bare metal structures of the high-rise buildings that loomed overhead as phantom relics of a time long passed by. The cloaked Nightshade observed the uninvited figures which were forced to maneuver around obstacles both small and large to get through the now crumbling streets. Metal skeletons of transportation vehicles littered their pathway, but Nightshade didn't bother with traversing the streets, he used the naked buildings like a child would playground equipment. Cracks also littered the pavement with larger crevasses appearing less frequently. Some of these crevasses were large enough to swallow up the remains of the transportation vehicles, with only the rear of the vehicles protruding out of these asphalt mouths.

There were plenty of spaces for the individuals to snake through them. The three uninvited visitors moved silently from demolished vehicle to demolished vehicle, watching the sky and the ground for anything that might impede their progress. The cloaked assassin observed all three figures looking at one another, then the lead figure glanced out over the dark city before moving out behind their cover. *Gutsy little bastard*, Nightshade thought. *I bet you wouldn't even try this in the open daylight. But then again, this sleeping city does come alive at night*, chuckled the assassin.

The second man pulled away from the trailing human and quickly moved to their leader. The first figure had moved to the next metal structure, a turned-over tanker missing its wheels and many other parts. The metal of the floorboard had deteriorated over time and only part of the cab was exposed to the two figures. They both looked around the front of the cab of the tanker, but neither could really see anything.

"Have you located our target?" Nightshade heard the second man ask, as the assassin moved in close to gauge the visitors' intentions.

The first one pointed towards the end of the road, towards a building much higher than the rest. It towered over the entire block, even in the darkness of night. The second figure looked up. Even in the darkness, the building's dark silhouette loomed over the entire block as if it was guarding the street from an unknown threat.

The second figure leaned over and whispered something that Nightshade didn't catch. Their leader returned a nod. By that time, the third comrade had reached their position behind the tanker. Nightshade noticed the figure looking at his comrades and then out in the direction they were previously looking. He was struggling to see out in the darkness like the others had, but he could sense the Corporation building before him.

"Shhhh." Nightshade overheard the other two say to their companion. Then the group leader looked back at the second figure. "It's rumored that it's the home of the one they call the Oracle. That's our target."

These wastes of lives are targeting the Oracle? That made the cloaked assassin enraged, but he understood losing his cool would ruin the fun he had in store for the three of them.

"The prophesized seer?" questioned the second figure.

The first two figures looked at one another, weary-eyed.

"I don't know what's true and what's fiction anymore. I just know we are to take this individual out," responded their leader.

"Impossible. It is said the Oracle has strange and mystical powers."

"Hogwash!" whispered the first.

"Even if that's a myth, it's also said this being is guarded by the dogs of war. The Fucking, Dogs of War! Do you get it? It's a death trap."

"Bullshit, that's all it . . ."

These assholes are going to argue the entire way and awaken the inhabitants of this dead city and take away my fun, thought Nightshade. Suddenly, a sound echoes from down the street, like a glass bottle being kicked around. The sound vibrates throughout the emptiness of the phantom street. The sound was displaced in the silence and the three figures were frozen stiff. None of them was willing to continue onward until they figured out what made the noise.

The scraping of a set of boots across the pavement had the three men moving away from the direction of the noise.

Nightshade squatted on a bare beam on the third floor observing the three shadowy figures traversing the street below. To Nightshade they looked like tiny ants scurrying over a tiled flower. *Interesting. Why are there Rustler scum in this fine town?* Nightshade watched as the three figures stopped at the tanker, just to the right of his current position. His dark eyes gazed through the darkness. The assassin watched with a smile on his face.

"I do believe that there are rat filth in the cellar, and I think that I'm the exterminator to get the job done," mumbled Nightshade.

Nightshade leaped off the building and onto the pavement below. He saw the men running and removed his aerial, five-pronged weapon.

"Now look at that, will you? That is so rude, leaving the party so abruptly and not even saying goodbye."

Nightshade threw the weapon and with his night vision watched the precise flight of it.

The weapon struck the back of the third Rustler who fell to the broken pavement, knocking him semi-unconscious. Nightshade materialized right over the Rustler spy, staring down at the wounded man with interest. The Rustler moaned but couldn't scream out for help. Nightshade was pleased and sad all in one. He would love to have the other men rush up to the aid of their comrade, but he enjoyed the chase, so this was just as satisfying. Nightshade watched the man move around like a fish out of water. The assassin could feel the pain the man was in, and he reveled in it. It was like bathing in a pool of blood for him.

Nightshade jerked the weapon from the back of the Rustler and sniffed the human blood trickling down its razor-sharp blade. It was intoxicating for him, like a drug. He reveled in the cat-and-mouse game, but his claws reached farther than most predators of the Wasteland, and escape was never an option.

Nightshade leaned over and asked the wounded man in a whisper, "Why have you come to this hellhole?"

The wounded Rustler could only grunt and mumble his response.

"Insolent fool!"

Nightshade sliced the man's throat with the bladed edge of the aerial weapon.

✝

The dead Rustler's comrades had reached the south end of the Corporation building. They would have to traverse the side of the building to gain access to it. Nightshade watched the second Rustler glancing back to see what had become of their fallen comrade, but the cloaked assassin knew they were too far away to see anything. Nightshade could hear both men panting from exertion and watched as they bent over, holding their knees.

There was a sound of boots scuffing around the corner. The two remaining intruders had stopped arguing. Everything had gone silent and, the air was still. The Rustler leader went flying against the scorched concrete wall of the building. Hitting the base wall knocked the wind from the spy, leaving the second man alone.

Nightshade materialized directly behind the Rustler, just as the spy turned to face the assassin. The man's eyes grew large, he only saw the silhouette of the assassin's eyes; they were empty voids. Nightshade slashed the Rustler's shoulder and the desperate man dropped to his side, gripping at his fresh wound. Nightshade moved to the Rustler and grabbed his throat, not squeezing it at all, he wanted the man to talk.

The Rustler spy could only mumble something incoherently and was breathing heavier than before.

"What was that? I couldn't hear you."

"The Oracle," mumbled the Rustler.

Nightshade gave the man an aghast expression.

"What do Wasteland Rustlers want with the Oracle? They don't even believe in him or his unique abilities."

In between breaths the Rustler said. "The elders."

"Elders? As in the mythical leaders of the Wasteland Rustlers?"

The spy nodded.

Nightshade began to laugh. "Heck, I thought they were only a rumor that humans made up to explain your people."

"No, they be quite real. Those witches want the Oracle dead. They fear the Oracle and abilities that one has. It aids our enemies and is the reason we are dying off. They have been after him for a long time."

Nightshade looked deep into the man's eyes. They were betraying the spy.

"You're not telling me everything, are you? I can sense it within you, outlaw."

Nightshade placed his hand on the man's temple and closed his eyes. He could feel the rapid beating of the man's heart. The assassin reached into the man's mind and streaks of gray light passed by his eyesight as he searched the outlaw's memories. A library of information. Once Nightshade reached the information he was searching for, he looked up towards the silhouette of the Corporate headquarters.

"That can't be. Nikolai Volkov, the former CEO of the Corporation is alive? It was believed he perished with the rest of the board in the hellfire storm." Nightshade swore he had killed the CEO at his home estate all those years ago. *This does place an interesting twist on things. Unfinished business after all,* he thought. Nightshade reached down and grabbed the spy by the throat again. "What is he up to? What is on this madman's agenda?"

"I don't have this information. It's all between the elders and the CEO."

"A collaboration of minds?" Nightshade mumbled. "If you don't know anything more, then you're useless to me. Not that your life had any worth anyways."

Nightshade slit the spy's throat and walked away.

Chapter 8

Present Day

The campfire blazed before them as the flame slowly dwindled down. The flame's reflection mirrored off Clover's dimly lit face. The yellowish-orange flame seemed as smooth as glass, like a mirror into the bioengineered assassin's mind. The dying flames began to form a scene, one Clover had remembered vividly. The assassin was now in a deep trance, unable to respond to the world around him. It was just him and the image, nothing else.

Within Clover's enhanced memory

The place was pitch dark and possessed an aura of insanity. Evil resided here, but it couldn't harm the assassin, Clover could feel that much. The silhouettes of collapsed buildings littered everywhere, giving off an apocalyptic mood. This place once belonged to an advanced society, one like the one on earth, before it had fallen.

Clover could sense many things that lived in this place, and none of them were good. The air was warm and humid, like a warm summer day. Something else loomed in the atmosphere, something full of damnation, vengeful. The unknown substance acted like a blanket, smothering anything that came too close to its source.

Concrete, asphalt and stone debris littered the ground. Occasionally something would crumble under the assassin's foot as he progressed. Something was drawing Clover in, something invisible, but he couldn't place what it was. The ground was soaked, as if it had just downpoured, marking each of the assassin's footsteps.

The force drawing Clover in seemed alien in content, but also familiar as well. In fact, this entire place seemed all too familiar to the assassin, like he had been here before. A sense of déjà vu. Then a small ruin came into view, or better yet, its darkened silhouette. That's the place he was being drawn towards. The closer Clover came to the run-down place, the more he recognized it. The ruins, the ground surrounding it, the atmosphere, even the strange force drawing him in all seemed too familiar.

"Nightshade," Clover mumbled.

"Welcome, brother. Won't you step inside, we still have a card game to finish?"

He approached a run-down building made of weather-board. At a closer glance, Clover noticed wood rot all over the building. Mud and clay dirt the color of a chocolate Easter bunny covered two-thirds of the walkway and shattered glass littered his path. Clover couldn't remember the reason for the shattered glass or the debilitating condition of the place, but if his senses were correct, it had to do with the immense pressures of the surrounding environment.

Clover attempted to look inside the shack, but all he could see was some old chairs knocked over on the rotten floor. There was no interior light to show the assassin what else resided in the shack, all he could do was use his enhanced senses. Something was drawing him to this place, but he couldn't decide what it was or the reason behind it. This was a different feeling altogether.

The decision is this, the assassin thought. *Stay out here in the gloomy twilight that is making my skin crawl, or enter the establishment with no knowledge of what lies inside.*

He decided to enter the building, despite his better judgment. Clover shook off the euphoric notion, the assassin remembered feeling the same way the first time he had visited. The assassin took several steps toward the run-down building when a centipede moved across his boot. The thing could have been about six inches in length and no more than two inches wide. Clover stopped for a moment to watch the insect scurry away under dead brush ten or so paces from him. *At least this eerie place isn't devoid of life.*

Clover moved onto the first steps and the rotting wood gave a detestable creak in defiance, but Clover refused to allow the noise to break his intense concentration. There was no door, just an opening. Clover hesitated at the opening and sensed something staring back at him from within. The assassin began scan the room for existing life-forms and discovered none, but something was present, just nothing he had ever encountered before. Despite its best efforts, the entity residing in the darkened shack was screaming loud at Clover, even if it wasn't its intention. But despite what Clover's mind was saying, he had doubts that it was a scream, but something the entity was manifesting in the assassin's mind. The sensation was almost as if Clover was looking into a reflection of himself, and he knew from his previous visit who lived here.

Just as Clover crossed the threshold an immense pressure halted him in his tracks, preventing him from proceeding any farther. Something pressed down on his chest, stomach and shoulders all at once. He couldn't sense its origins. He inched his way into the main room of the ruins, still fighting against whatever had halted his progress. Some great force, unknown to him. *What else lives in this place that can prevent me from proceeding forward?*

Finally, he broke free of whatever had stood in his way and fell to one knee, gasping for breath and trying to recover. His lungs flexed in and out rapidly, trying to regain some type of control over his body. Dazed, his mind spun wildly. *Probably from the lack of oxygen*, the assassin thought between long gasping breaths. When his senses returned, Clover sensed a figure in the room with him. This alarmed Clover, because he could sense the figure glaring at him intensely.

A clapping noise sounded in the dark. "Bravo, Clover. That's the spirit I have come to expect from you, brother."

Clover peered into a corner of the room which he had thought was void of life. Something flickered in and out of sight. What little gray light that penetrated this dark place was exposing the figure—now clearer to Clover than before. Clover got up, still with a slight dizziness resonating in his head. He walked over the dusty, sand-covered floor and approached the shadowy figure sitting at a corner table.

Cards were laid out—their unfinished card game. "The game of death," he mumbled under his breath.

The ominous dark figure sat on the other side of a round, decayed wooden table.

"Very good, you remembered our card game. Shall we finish?"

"Very well, Nightshade. I will indulge your curiosity and get you to tell me why you have brought me back to this place."

Clover sat in the chair across from Nightshade. It was like looking in the mirror. Clover and this ominous figure were nearly identical, outside of the dark camouflage color that made the figure's presence ominous and cryptic, and its charcoal-black eyes that refused Clover access.

Clover looked down at the three cards laying face up before him, but the assassin didn't really see the cards, he saw the lives he had taken from his time as a corporate assassin.

"Contemplating the past, brother?" Nightshade asked. Clover's near twin leaned in closer. "We all have our indiscretions. For example, mine are built into this card."

Nightshade flipped a card over from the thick deck and placed it on the rotten card table so that both could see it. The card possessed a pair of scythes made of bone with razor-sharp blades crossing each other as a background. A skeleton creature sat cross-legged in the middle of the card.

"Ah. Our friend, the corporate CEO."

Clover looked up at Nightshade, even more confused now. "What does he have to do with anything? I thought he died along with the rest of the board."

Nightshade sighed, which seemed bizarre coming from him. "One of my rare mistakes. You see I was supposed to knock off the entire board, including Nikolai Volkov. But I got sloppy when Volkov fell down a well. Somehow, he survived the fall into the well, the holocaust that followed, even the thermal winter."

"So, what does the card mean?"

Nightshade tapped the surface of the aged card. "He is our doom. Death of our kind and those humans that remain. The Grim Reaper."

Clover gave the twin a stern look that he refused to waver from. "How do we stop him?"

"It won't be easy; whatever he has planned is tied into the Rustler elders."

Clover developed a dissatisfied expression. "That figures. I knew the elders were up to something, but I never could pinpoint their location to uncover what."

"It is what we both must uncover."

"Us?"

"Yes, Clover. I told you we would need to work as a team, I just didn't know when." Nightshade flipped over a second card. It had a bald man sitting Indian style with his palms facing skywards in a praying position. A blue-tinted orb was oscillating about chest high. "The Oracle card." Nightshade looked intently at Clover. It was enough to make the assassin quite uncomfortable.

Clover was overcome with a series of emotions. He felt dismay; Nightshade baffled him. Anger, because he still hadn't come to realize what he truly needed to do and the version of himself sitting across from him was being serious about them acting together. Fearful, because he didn't know what this figure was capable of. Torment, because he didn't know what to feel, or how to react, or even what to do. Clover was caught in a plethora of confusing emotions he had never felt before.

He attempted to shake the emotions from his mind. "What does that mean?"

The dark figure leaned back into the shadows and laughed. Clover glared at the dark eyes of the shadow figure. For a moment, Clover doubted if the figure was going to respond to him. It was only when Clover thought he might be driven insane by the eerie silence that the dark figure spoke.

"Yes, the Oracle card. It's not a what but a who. The Oracle is a prophet who survived the aftermath, like us. He will be the one to instruct us on how to proceed." He tapped a playing card on the decrepit table. It was as if Nightshade was waiting for Clover to expose something of himself he hadn't yet. "There is something else. You're keeping something from me." Nightshade watched Clover, noticing his attention was locked on his fidgeting with the playing card.

"What are you babbling about?"

Nightshade looked at Clover, with those coal-black voids staring through him. "What are going to do about the Sierra Nevada facility?"

"Wait, how do you know about the facility?"

Nightshade smiled. "Remember, what you know, I know. The Oracle told me about what it used to be. So, what are you going to do about it, brother?"

Clover had to shake his head free from the ache in his skull. He was still confused by the entire encounter.

"I haven't decided whether it's my place to do anything. Most likely it's an abandoned facility with no secrets to give up."

Nightshade shook his head. "No, brother. I believe you're wrong about that. It's a Corporation building, buried underground at that. I'm sure it has more secrets to give up than either of us can comprehend."

Clover looked apprehensively at Nightshade. "Straus's sister and her family."

"Interesting. Definitely secrets lying in the lower chambers of the Sierra Nevada Complex. Ones that might prove fruitful to investigate."

Clover looked worried. "So, is that it? We team up, hunt down the Rustler elders, wreck whatever they are planning, and by doing that we uncover whatever has been happening at the Sierra Nevada facility?"

"For the most part. You forgot the Nikolai Volkov situation, but I have the feeling that he will surface soon."

"Then what? We don't know if he is even human any longer. Anyone that can survive all that he has . . . It won't be an easy solution to handle."

Nightshade shrugged. "We will find out, when we come to it."

Present Day

The elder waited until it was just the five elders left in the cavern room and inserted the data stick into a hologram machine and a holographic image appeared. This technology could play back recording to the user and communicate through it as well, like a holographic communication device. For now, the elders would listen to a recorded message. It was rumored that before the nuclear holocaust, the Corporation had secretly designed the elders from alien DNA and that when all five elders connected, they could do some amazing and dangerous things. One was to predict the future, while another rumor said they could levitate an entire mountain from the earth. In this instance, the elders were simply sharing the data through connective telepathy. All five elders, who weren't human at all, seem to connect to one another with all the members' eyes glazing over.

The hologram was of Major Norman Bishop, the Rustler commander. The hologram hid most of the major's fatigue and age, but even through the blue-tinted holographic image, you could see how tired he was. The major slumped, and even in the image Major Bishop couldn't keep his hands from shaking. Bishop kept repositioning his hands, first in front of him and them behind his back; but none of this mattered to the elders. They only concentrated on the major's message.

Major Bishop coughed and then he began his report. "Distinguished elder members. Let me apologize for disturbing your rest. I know it's quite valuable to you and you need your strength to lead us."

It always annoyed the elders when the major pandered and apologized, but they kept their concentration and let the recorded message continue.

"I have been informed by scouts that the assassin known as Clover has been snooping around several of our abandoned camps in the southwest corner of the Wasteland. All the remaining subjects were found dead, and we found something else." The major collected himself, as if he was fending off a breakdown. Then Bishop recovered and continued his report. "One of the mutant creatures that our men had reported living underneath the Complex's foundations was discovered moving around in several sections of the complex." The major shook his aging head. "What in god's name could have done that to such a colossal thing that size? Nothing to my knowledge has been uncovered, but intel reports denote metal carnage of some lower sections of the complex and a few spies swear hearing an eerie moaning sound coming from the complex's depths."

The major returned to his report, now calm. "I need to know what to do next?"

The hologram dissolved and the flame returned.

All together the elders said, "We must contact Brother Nikolai."

All five elders reached out with their telepathic ability to contact Nikolai Volkov. The electricity in the air seemed strong and made communicating long distances more difficult than normal, but this wasn't the first time they had used their mutation ability and didn't waver when the cyborg didn't answer their first call.

Suddenly a bulky figure appeared through the holographic machine; flickering in blue was the cyborg Nikolai Volkov. Now they were communicating with the cyborg ally and the image of Major Bishop had temporarily vanished. All five elders became stiff, as if they were children caught up to no good. The cyborg didn't look overly pleased, but Nikolai didn't blare out at the elders for disrupting him. But there was a noticeable scowl on the half-machine, half-human's face. "What do you want?"

Tension suddenly filled the room. None of the Rustler Elders wanted to be the first to speak, in fact they all had become apprehensive. Then the elder who had received the message from Major Bishop spoke, still connected with the others.

"Master Nikolai, it alarms us that Clover . . ."

The cyborg hissed at Clover's name even being mentioned. "Don't use that scum's name ever again in my presence."

The elder stuttered his apology. "I didn't . . . mean any harm, Master."

"You were explaining the break-in at the complex, continue."

"The site has been compromised. I and the other elders wanted to know if we should move the others?"

Cyborg Nikolai's image looked at each elder with contempt. "Is this true? Do you all question the plan and its validity?"

Each elder nodded.

"You are all fools!" exclaimed the cyborg. "The plan is perfect, I have planned it for a long time and have covered every corner of it to allow such simple thing such as this to derail it. It's too late for the assassin to stop it now. The assassin is two steps behind and by the time he catches up with us, it will be time to unleash our fury on all of those left behind."

"What about the location of the others? Is it still safe?" questioned another elder.

"They are fine where they are, as long as you did what I told you. But if it will make you feel better, send a few of your elite to throw the assassin and his comrades off the scent. Now, if you're finished wasting my time, I have other things to attend to."

The blue image disappeared. Breaking their telepathic connection, each elder looked at one another, bewildered.

✝

Clover slowly opened his eyes. They were still glazed over, and the nighttime campfire still reflected off his lenses. The assassin's breathing was slightly intensified, which was unusual for the normally calm Clover. It was rare for the assassin to allow his body to show anything but control, a product of his bioengineering. But the image in his head unnerved the assassin enough to get him breathing abnormally.

Preist had just came back from retrieving his waterskin. "Are you okay? You look exhausted and out of sorts."

Clover looked down, as if trying to hide his exhausted emotions from Preist. "I'm fine. The vision was taxing for me, that's all."

"I've never seen you so vexed, what did you see?" probed Preist.

Clover looked up at his traveling companion and his expression only deepened. "The vision in the flame told me our quest's destination and what we will find at its end."

Preist was afraid to ask Clover the burning question aching in his gut. "And where will it lead us?"

"To stop Nikolai Volkov, we must first visit someone known only as the Oracle, which takes us to Metro City—or better yet, its ruins . . ."

"Metro City?"

The assassin nodded.

"Do you know what lives there now? Thugs, mutated monstrosities, and many other undesirable things."

Clover nodded a second time. "I am quite aware of the horrors that reside in the shadows of the fallen metropolis. And that is our path. Once we are finished there, then we must venture to the Sierra Nevada Complex. There have been some rumors of strange things happening around it."

"Odd places to go on a vacation, don't you think? A Necropolis and catacombs to millions of the dead."

Clover didn't bother acknowledging his companion this time, but only stared into the flames. 'If its too much for you or you fear the journey, you don't have to come with me."

Preist mock-laughed. "Oh, I definitely have to come along. Someone has to keep you out of trouble."

"That is for sure," the assassin responded.

"Just out of curiosity, may I guess the source that is guiding you?"

Clover only shrugs his shoulders nonchalantly. "I told you what is guiding me."

"Yes, the visions. But I wonder who is the perpetrator. Nightshade?"

Now it's the assassin's turn to give Preist the evil eye. "You know me all too well, Preist."

"Unfortunately. Why follow your obviously insane brother? The one that lives among mutated and dead things? I thought we agreed he is a bad influence and you and he would never team up."

"Nightshade lives in Metro City, Preist, and he knows his way around. Plus, he has been confiding with the Oracle . . ."

"Someone whom we know absolutely nothing about!" barked the scientist.

Clover pulled out a whetstone and began to meticulously sharpen one of his katanas. The sound of *shhheee, shhhheee* echoed as the whetstone traveled over the surface of the blade and made Preist cringe. Clover understood it unnerved his traveling companion, but the assassin continued to sharpen the blade without hesitating. It was an act that calmed his nerves and he always hated not being ready for the unexpected, especially without a sharp blade. *Who knows what we might run into on our way or within the ruins of Metro City*, thought Clover.

"You do that just to irritate me, don't you?"

Clover stopped sharpening the blade. "The place we are going has many unknown dangers. I want to be prepared."

"You wouldn't need to if you weren't choosing to go on this mindless, crazed crusade into unknown territory," Preist said.

"You don't have to come, as I said before. It's something I have to do. The inhabitants of this time and place need me. They have no one else to defend them."

"You have another place that needs you as well. I have told you that, if you're trying to find a place you fit in. But I understand you know this place and time and feel confident in it. There is more at stake than you can comprehend, maybe the survival of every living species in the cosmos is at stake."

"You would abandon this place, our friends and allies? That doesn't sound like the Preist I know. In fact, he would do everything in his power to save those in need. Isn't that what we were doing in the first place?"

Suddenly, something struck Clover's heightened senses like striking a concrete wall. The assassin tightly grasped the katana he was sharpening. Clover had become as still as a stone statue, waiting to sense what their uninvited guest would do next. The assassin's heart rate had quickened, but that wasn't anything new. Clover understood every time he encountered something that alarmed him, when his adrenaline quickened its pace, his body came alive, and a rush of excitement flowed through his veins.

Preist had turned white with fear. With everything he had done with the assassin, he had never seen Clover become so silent and dedicated to uncovering an intruder in their midst.

"What is it?" Preist questioned.

Clover looked out into the darkness. Despite his night-vision capability, he could only see silhouettes, but his vision wasn't the only thing he could use. Clover sniffed at the nighttime air. It was humid and stale, but a scent was hiding, one that seemed familiar to the assassin. He stood up and placed his katana against a rock; confident he was in no immediate danger. The assassin slowly approached the outskirts of their camp, where the darkness and their campfire illumination touched. It was like Clover was tempting the creature to come closer, to show itself to them.

Preist tensed up even more. "What is it, Clover? What to you sense is out there?" Clover's traveling companion said almost in a whispering tone.

A soft sound came to Clover, one that Preist would never have recognized. The assassin grinned. A set of grayish-tinted eyes appeared in the distance. Their stalker had finally exposed itself to them. Clover turned to Preist. "Hand me our food stores bag. Give me some meat. She's hungry and only searching for food."

Preist frowned at the assassin. "Are you insane? We have a limited amount of food to take us on our journey and you're going to give it away?"

"I thought you were about helping species in need. It's only a plains ginger wolf, and she's only searching for food. I sense she's near starvation and won't last much longer without our help."

The plains ginger wolf is a subspecies of the north-western wolf or timber wolf, forced to migrate into the Wastelands, since most of their homeland was devastated by the nuclear fire. Many of these wolf subspecies have now become Wasteland scavengers that struggle in a hot dry landscape.

Clover unwrapped the raw meat and placed it at the edge of the encampment, just within reach of the camp-fire's illumination. The assassin waited for their stalker to approach, and it didn't take the starving creature long. The four-legged silhouetted creature slowly approached, caution in her movements. Slowly the wolf's snout emerged from the darkness of the night. She inched her way closer towards the prize. Inch by inch, the plains ginger wolf exposed herself, until almost half her lean body was visible.

The hungry wolf stiffed at her dinner and then sniffed at the air towards the assassin, as if to ask permission. "Go ahead, girl, it's yours." The wolf flipped her ears as if to thank her saviors and slowly began to eat the meat. It didn't take the starving wolf long to devour the entire meal. Clover watched in satisfaction. "See, you were right. We *are* here to save other species."

"I sense you are becoming more comfortable with your surroundings, being less the killer they say you are, and more a permanent fixture in this world."

Clover just shrugged.

The ginger wolf looked up at the assassin with a look like they both had found a long lost relative. The wolf stretched out and made herself at home. "Comfy?" Clover asked. The plains ginger wolf merely lay there, staring at the assassin.

Chapter 9

Present Day

Clover, Preist and the timber wolf headed northwest, towards the Sierra Nevada facility. The trek was exhausting and daunting, taking the roving party over five days to travel through the southern portions of the wasteland and reach the Sierra Nevada Complex. The hardest part of their travel was through the southern portion of the Wasteland, since the Wasteland itself stretched from south-central California through the majority of Nevada, their current location, and into parts of Utah, separating the Pacific western coastline and the area of Metro City.

The sun was near its pinnacle, high in the afternoon sky. The reddish-orange tinted orb had been raining down its antagonistic rays for the entire trip, wearing on the weary bunch. The landscape hadn't changed much, even after they had left the Wasteland. The only thing that told Clover and his travel companions they had left the desolation was the deserted building that occasionally popped up along the landscape. Most had been deserted for a while, with their occupants either perishing in the nuclear aftermath or packing what few belongings they had left and moving to safer communities either towards the coast or higher into the mountains.

The mountains provided somewhat more cover for those attempting to hide from hooligans and outlaws, but the few trees that were left standing had become bare and provided little cover. Maybe that's what drew Doria's family to the facility; the idea of safety and shelter. Something inside Clover kept eating away at him. Was this facility a safe heaven, or was it a trap to lure humans to an unknown predator, yet to emerge?

The shells of buildings that had been farmhouses, barns or metal storage buildings that had stood the test of years of nonusage, provided much cover for the travelers. Most of the buildings were shells of their former selves, like someone had gutted them for what little they could provide. Clover understood none of these structures would provide much in the way of shelter, so they kept moving on. It was quite evident that the land had been abandoned for years, a ghostly terrain that only the dead would roam.

The barren landscape began to incline, and the travelers understood they had entered the final leg of their journey. What was once was the Lassen National Forest, was now a barren land of charcoal sticks of wood sticking out of the equally barren landscape. All they had to do was maneuver the naked tree line that outlined the Sierra Nevada Complex. Since they were approaching from the south that wouldn't take but a few hours, unlike traversing through the entire graveyard of trees of the forest.

A broken park sign read: *Welcome to Lassen Volcanic National Park.*

The sign had been severed into two parts and was pockmarked and suffered from heat blast. Another sign that was hanging on its metal post told Clover and his comrades that Redding, California, was forty-seven miles to the west.

The plains ginger wolf sniffed the air. Clover reached down and petted the wolf's soft, grayish head. "I know, girl, this place has an odd aura to it. Doesn't it?"

Clover looked up at the bare rock incline they were about to embark on. The rocky terrain was a grayish-black color as if someone had tried to torch the incline but failed. The surface of the inclining mountain seemed to have a distasteful smile, with the blackened terrain be-ing the mountain's bearded maw; as the mountain rose at a slight incline, the gray surface began to bleach the scorched earth away.

Clover turned to Preist. "Well, I guess we should begin to climb."

Preist sighed. "If your curiosity is aching you that much."

This time Clover didn't look back. "I thought you were a scientist. Isn't exploration what you science types live for?"

"Only if it doesn't lead to our demise," mumbled Clover's companion.

"Well, you had a choice and chose to follow me here, didn't you?"

Clover and his companions began to ascend towards the Sierra Nevada Complex.

The climb wasn't as bad as it looked, even though it could be a bad day for anyone that slipped and fell. They would tumble down the rock-filled landscape, maybe not to their deaths but they would be badly bruised and scarred. It had been only a third up their ascent when Clover stopped and sniffed the air again. The wolf did the same and this time the ginger wolf didn't like what her canine senses were picking up.

The ginger wolf began to whine and back away from the direction of the scent she had discovered. Clover looked back as to console the creature. "I know, I smell it too."

"What is it?" Preist asked.

Clover only shook his head. "A strong scent, possibly an apex predator. Very large if the scent gives any indication."

"How large?"

"Too big for us to tangle with. Something I would recommend avoiding."

"Oh," responded Preist. "What about the human pilgrims, any sign of them?"

Clover took a few small sniffs of the stale, thinning air and turned towards Preist as if confused.

"There might be some humans at the complex, but the predator's scent is so robust that it's masking any other scent. If there are any pilgrims up there its more than likely they are all huddled together in one spot, making their numbers next to impossible to fathom."

It wasn't like Clover to be so edgy and apprehensive, but a tension hovered over this place and none of them knew what to expect or what they might uncover. The travelers began moving towards the daunting complex again, but this time with more caution than before. Slowly, the concealed doorway of the Sierra Nevada Complex came into view.

The Complex's entrance stood a good fifteen to twenty feet tall. The steel blast door was split down the middle and possessed a boxed teethlike design splitting the door in two. The design was meant to mesh the two sides in an airtight seal that could prevent any siege attempt or a thermal blast from penetrating into the Complex's interior. The exterior blast door had to be at least five or ten feet in thickness.

The blast door was showing its age, with rust lining the outer framework and rust stains bleeding from rusted fasteners, making the door look like it was crying rust-colored tears. The travelers moved a little closer. The door was open about six-to-seven feet, letting sunlight into the Complex's interior.

Both the ginger wolf and Clover froze and each alpha hunter sniffed the air. It was becoming far too evident that neither liked what they sensed. The place already had a tomblike feeling. Clover pointed to a wet substance on a nearby rock, and walking over, he touched it.

"Well?" asked Preist.

Clover nodded.

Preist became dejected and sorrowful. His jawline dropped and his skin seemed to sag. They didn't have time to waste, they had to continue. "I can't let Clover down, nor Straus," Preist mumbled.

They were still too far away to see clearly into the mouth of the complex. Preist couldn't tell if there was any illumination within. The companions began to move forward at an even slower pace than before, sliding to the right, then to the left as if attempting to confuse a hidden sniper. Just before the weary travelers reached the mouth of the complex, more blood became evident, this time in larger pools. As with the first sighting, Clover confirmed, "At least ten days, maybe even two weeks old."

Then a stench strong enough to curl your stomach rushed out of the complex. Something rank had died in the Sierra Nevada Complex and left its stench behind. They moved into the facility with grave caution and as the companions passed over the threshold of the opening, Preist noticed a bloody human hand on the frame of the opening.

The wolf began to whine again, like she knew something bad was waiting for them just inside. Inside the Complex's interior, it was a solemn pitch darkness. Clover had the ability to see in darkness, he was a nocturnal creature, as was their wolf companion.

✝

Preist, on the other hand, couldn't see in darkness and was quickly left behind. Feeling for a wall or anything that would guide him, Preist stumbled and nearly fell over. He caught himself and went to a knee. Knowing he couldn't continue at this pace, the scientist searched his robe and after what seemed to be forever, produced an illumination stick. An illumination stick uses concentrated ion particles to create energy in small, contained doses, producing light that will last up to an hour. Preist flicked his wrist, and the stick came to life, providing him with an instant illumination source.

Preist shone the stick in the direction he thought Clover and the wolf had gone, but after scanning the hallway, or what the scientist thought was a hallway, he discovered he had gotten turned around. He had no clue where he was. It was like being trapped in a maze. Without the illumination stick, Preist wouldn't even be able to see his own hand. But even with the device, he had a limited field of vision.

Preist swept the stick to his right and then to his left. All that he could see was a close bulkhead that had seen better days. The Complex walls were rust-stained and gave the impression that the facility hadn't been used since the Corporation's war against society. *But that isn't possible*, thought Preist. *What about the pilgrims, where are they?* A feeling of dread was beginning to creep up on the scientist. This wasn't supposed to be happening. Lights should be powering the complex, even without a true power source. Didn't the pilgrims properly prepare themselves for such a thing? Wouldn't they have packed for such an instance? Even without a power source, wouldn't a section of the complex be lit up? *Well, maybe we haven't gotten that far, they could be deep in the Complex's interior, and we haven't even scratched the surface of this place.*

"Well at least it's cooler inside this place than outside." Preist mumbled. Preist remembered the foul stench radiating down the corridor, the same foul smell that had made Preist and his comrades pause outside the facility doorway. "But then there is that smell. Where was it originating from anyways?" Preist wasn't sure he wanted that answered.

"Clover," called Preist.

His voice seemed to echo down the dark and deserted hallway. But then as if his echoing voice had been swallowed up by the darkness, the echo vanished. That only added to Preist's already high anxiety. He was feeling quite alone, and he didn't care much for this feeling. The scientist began to slowly spin, only adding to the paranoia building inside.

"Clover, where are you?"

No response.

After staring into the darkness and the silence putting Preist on edge, a noise echoed back towards him. At first the noise sounded like razor-sharp claws from a very large predator trying to rip the bulkhead apart to get to him. Then Preist remembered what Clover had said about the original scent of this place. "A large apex predator, Clover said."

The scratching noise stopped suddenly, and footfalls approached Preist. He became paralyzed. What could he do? His body began to perspire, his palms became sweaty, his pulse began to race, and the sound of his heart pounded in his head. His throat became dry, and he had the urge to quench his sudden thirst, but he was too frozen to react. The scientist couldn't even flee, though Preist doubted he could find his way through the multitude of corners and turns it would take to reach the facility's exit.

He was going to have to face whatever was approaching. But just at that moment, the footsteps faded, and he was left alone again. Preist let his heart recover and as he did, a set of red eyes appeared only mere feet from him. His anxiety returned, but then a familiar voice boomed from the same place as the eyes.

"Preist, what is it?"

Preist shone his illumination stick right into Clover's face. The assassin squinted at the sudden brightness, even though the illumination stick didn't produce that much light. "Clover," Preist said between breaths. "I thought you were the predator."

"I heard your loud voice calling, so I came as soon as I could."

With fear in his eyes, Preist asked, "Did you hear that scratching noise?"

Clover nodded. "Something big is moving about. But its movements are too swift for me to pinpoint its location." The ginger wolf appeared in the circle of light, giving the scientist a cocked-head look, asking Preist why he had screamed like a child. "You wouldn't think something apparently as large as . . . well, whatever it is, could move as swiftly as that."

Preist wasn't sure how to take what Clover was telling him. His face became pale, as if he had seen a phantom, and the look in his eyes read that he wasn't sure what his companion was talking about.

Clover grunted. "I can see you haven't the foggiest notion of what I'm talking about. I'll have to show you." Clover looked down at the ginger wolf. "We have found some things that might interest you anyways."

Clover led his companions down a level, through a port hole in the Complex's deck. Preist's illumination stick was becoming less effective than it had in the upper level, and the stench intensified. Luckily, Clover's heightened senses could guide them all through the shadow-filled levels. The shadows deepened and consumed more space down on this level. Even with Clover's predatory red eyes, Preist struggled to see the assassin. Even Clover's silhouette seemed to fade into the darkness.

"What I have to show you is down this hallway," responded Clover.

Clover and his companions walked down the much narrower hallway. The hallway was like climbing a rock terrain with peaks and valleys, most likely from indentions in the metal flooring and open grating. The companions walked a while, with Clover leading the way, their tired legs forcing them to stop several times.

Clover halted them and removed something from his cloak and handed it to Preist. The scientist shook the item and scanned down the metal tubing. "What is this thing?"

"It's an ion flashlight. The Corporation made them before the nuclear war. Turn it on and shine it to your right." Preist searched for an on switch but failed to locate one. Clover grabbed the other end of the cold metal device and twisted the cylinder middle. A clicking sound emerged from within, and the device shot bright light from its round middle. The explosion of light startled Preist and he dropped the flashlight. *Tink, tink* echoed as the ion light struck the deck. Preist took in a deep breath and went to retrieve the light.

"A little perturbed, I see?" Clover asked.

"Sorry about that . . ."

Clover looked over at the object and smiled. "I see you have found what I wanted to show you." Sarcasm reigned in the assassin's voice.

Caught in the illumination field was an incubation chamber, partially embedded into the decking. A single chamber was large enough to fit a full-grown body up to seven feet tall and wide enough to fit a body the size of Zeus in it; quite large indeed. It was reclined, like a hospital bed with two pumps attached to its side. Two lines, one solid metal and the other clear leading from the chamber's side panel and up into the level's ceiling, most likely leading to a master control on the first floor of the facility. The cylinder-shaped device had to be over six feet in length and possessed a curved latch. The material of the device was clearly newer than the decades-old complex. Despite possessing a dull-metal finish, the tube-shaped device was clearly a transplanted piece of equipment. *But how?* Preist wondered.

"What is it?" called out the scientist.

"Apparently, by the equipment surrounding it, it has to be some sort of incubating chamber. But you would know more about that than I."

Preist swung the ion light back on the chamber and the scientist saw the three other chambers lined up next to the first one. Three of the plexiglass that covered the hatches of the tubelike structures had been smashed, like something had broken out in a violent manner. Plexiglass shards were scattered all around the three empty cylinders, so much of it that Preist had to watch were he stepped.

The two men stepped towards one of the incubation chambers and looked inside. Flashing the ion light into the chamber's interior, they could tell whatever had been inside had torn away at any environmental systems, including any cell infusion sensors installed inside. Connection power cables and wires were shredded and dangling at the tube's side, looking like strings of spaghetti. The cylinder was a wreck, and nothing could be deduced from Clover and Preist's inspection.

"What could have done such a thing? If this is an incubation chamber . . ."

"Something that was very desperate to get out," Clover said. "But what got out, and is it roaming the halls of the complex?" barked Clover.

"Could it be human, whatever was in this contraption?" questioned Preist. "Surely any human settlers would have responded to our entering the complex. Speaking of, any sign of Straus's sister or any of the other pilgrims?"

The assassin pulled out a bone and placed it into Preist's open hand. A chill ran down Preist's spine.

"We found a few bone fragments here and there and something that appeared to be a half-eaten torso. Nothing living or anything resembling a full corpse, I'm afraid."

Clover petted the ginger wolf's shaggy head, as if to confirm she'd had a hand in the discovery.

Preist's eyes narrowed and his jaw muscles tightened, as if the scientist had just been given a dire diagnosis. "No traces of the girl or her family then?"

"I'm afraid not. We might have to call this a lost cause. If they had survived the grasp of whatever had killed these poor folks, they would be wise to flee this gargantuan tomb."

Loud scraping noises echoed, along with some banging, as if something was striking the bulkhead up ahead. The shuffling of feet followed, forcing the travel companions to ready themselves. The ginger wolf took a few steps towards the darkness of the end of the hallway. The wolf began to growl and flash its canine teeth.

Clover removed his favorite throwing weapon and cradled it in his hand.

"Is that such a wise weapon to be using inside this place?" questioned Preist.

Without turning back to look at the scientist, the assassin said, "It's a spacious complex and the metal bulkhead might work to our advantage. Well, that's if whatever we're about to face doesn't use the walls to travel by." Clover looked at the wolf and motioned her to lead the way. The ginger wolf vanished into the darkness. "At least we know some of these things roaming around this place, whatever they are, are using the deck stairwells to travel around."

Suddenly, Clover vanished into the pitch darkness as well. Preist flashed the ion flashlight down the hallway, but the assassin had moved way too swiftly and Preist was all alone—except for the moaning echoing from the darkness and the shuffling of feet. The scientist searched his person for something to defend himself but found nothing. He didn't normally possess any weapons, and now he wished he had brought something on the trip.

The moaning and shuffling of feet grew louder.

Preist planted his feet firmly on the deck and prepared for what was to come out of the voidlike darkness. What leaped out at Preist wasn't anything he could have ever dreamed. First the silhouette of the thing swiftly bearing down on the scientist broke through the outlined darkness, like a nocturnal predator with wings, on approach for its lethal strike. Preist's legs began to shake, and he was fearful they may give out on him.

The creature finally emerged from the vale of darkness. It had ashy skin, with bloodstained veins popping out all over its body. It had sharp, clawlike fingers all reaching out for Preist. The thing's eyes were dark and lifeless. Its pupils covered eighty percent of its eyes and at the edge red blood vessels protruded from the orbs' curved surface. Jagged teeth, some fanglike while others seemed to have normal human shape, filled the thing's ridged and peeling maw. Shredded clothing flapped in the air, giving the perception the creature had wings.

The humanoid creature growled in a low monotone, like a predator giving a warning.

Preist moved his heavy feet and stepped away from the flying demon, but he didn't possess Clover's swift agility or innate instincts and moved too slowly to avoid the collision. In a self-defense reaction, Preist raised his right arm and slammed it in the creature's upper chest. The collision sent Preist tumbling down the metal hallway, forcing the attacking thing into the bulkhead wall.

Preist lay there for what seemed to be an eternity, with his head spinning like a merry-go-round, briefly disoriented. The scientist slowly rose from his fetal position, getting to one sore knee. A slight pain was shooting down one side, but Preist chose to ignore it. His blurry vison subsided slowly but made the section of the corridor the ion light he'd dropped, hazy, as if he had walked into a misty cloud.

The scientist could see where the thing that attacked him had landed. Giant steel girders that supported the entire level lined the bulkhead all the way down and made it difficult to see past any of them. He shook his woozy head, trying to think straight. His breathing was deep and accelerated, but that was understandable after what he had just went through. *Where did that venomous creature disappear to?* thought Preist.

Then Preist heard a sound, and the insane, mutated thing was on top of him. The only thing that saved Preist from being mutilated to death by the thing's sharp talons was him striking the thing with his non-bent knee. The strike itself caught the mutated humanoid in the thorax, not doing much damage at all. But it did manage to keep it at bay, though Preist wasn't sure for how long. He struggled to keep his leverage on the creature while it swung wildly, trying to get him. The scientist thought, *Damn this thing is strong. Maybe it's more like one of us than a human.* He wondered if it was possible that someone could have captured some of their brothers and sisters and experimented on them and the result was this abomination, no longer human or bioengineered. Either way, he was appalled.

Preist, with all his might, shoved the creature off him, sending the mutated thing against the opposite bulkhead. Some of the mutated creature's flesh broke off its face and splattered on the steel bulkhead. The gray matter made the steel material sizzle and caused a gaping wound on the mutated creature's face, exposing the rotting insides. Preist understood that had only bought him a minute or two, before his adversary would regain his footing and come at him.

Preist discovered a loose pipe about as thick as his fist. Both ends had rust on them, and one end was jagged, like corrosion had eaten away at it and it had broken off a return pipe. Water lines and other sort of piping littered the corners of the bulkhead on this level. The weight of the pipe was adequate for the job, or at least Preist hoped it was. He moved towards the unmoving body.

"Ha," Preist said. "I thought you were a tough bugger, but I guess the bulkhead won that bout, didn't it?"

The scientist made his way to the body, smacking the pipe in an open hand. His anxiety hadn't faded; in fact, the closer Preist came to his adversary the more his heart raced. But since Clover wasn't nearby to save him, he was going to have to do this alone. Preist swallowed hard and moved in for the kill.

Preist had gotten with striking distance before the creature woke. The mutated creature leaped up and howled at Preist, but this time Preist didn't waver. He swung the heavy pipe with all his strength and as the creature lunged for him, the scientist struck the thing square on the side of its head, forcing his adversary up against the bulkhead once more. It didn't seem to slow its mad rage at all. A piece of the creature's face had been stripped, and now Preist had a good look at the gray membrane beneath. It was decayed and rotten underneath the shattered bone.

"You're nothing but an empty soul underneath, aren't you?"

Preist looked into the creature's dead, black eyes, which seemed to increase in hatred for the scientist. The mutated creature leaped out and grabbed Preist by the throat and his right wrist. The attack knocked the pipe from Preist's hand, leaving him at the mercy of his foe. The grip on him was so great, Preist swore the creature was going to snap his wrist. Preist struggled to keep the crazed creature at bay.

The maw of the abomination came very close to the scientist and the smell of rotten flesh came from the creature's mouth and exposed flesh, making Preist nauseous. Silver saliva, looking much like solder, dripped from the mutation's maw. Preist was being overpowered and his options were dwindling. What would he do to save his life?

A howl emerged from down the corridor, one unlike the one the abomination had made. It reminded him of a wolf.

✝

Clover had chased the pair of incubi down the dark corridor, but he didn't just rely just on his nocturnal vision, he could sense that the two mutations were very close. Their scent was strong, like overcooked meat that hadn't been disposed of properly. Clover heard the patter of four paws approaching, and the ginger wolf appeared out of the darkness, stopping directly in front of the assassin. She tilted her head to one side, as if to ask him a question, but Clover was the one to question her.

"Well," the assassin said, with his arms folded. "Where did they disappear to? Surely they didn't walk through the bulkheads, now did they?"

The ginger wolf yawned and licked her fur.

"Some help you are."

An inhuman growl issued from behind. The assassin slowly removed his throwing weapon from his cloak and waited. Clover didn't have to wait long. With very little brain activity, the "mutties" as Clover called them, were more about aggression than intellectual thought. The mutated creature launched itself towards Clover at less than an ideal speed.

The mutated thing lumbered towards the assassin and compared to Clover's swift agility, it seemed to move in slow motion. The creature extended its sharp claws, ready to thrash at its target. Clover swept to one side as the muttie passed by, like a matador teasing an enraged bull. Before the creature could slow its momentum and reengage Clover, the assassin, with a flick of his wrist, launched the aerial weapon at his target. The razor-sharp blades sliced through the darkness, making a whistling sound. The muttie was too slow, and as the creature began to stop itself and turn towards the assassin, the quad blades of the throwing weapon sliced through its corroded flesh, tendons and bone, severing the muttie's head from its shoulders.

The creature's head rolled in the opposite direction its body fell, splattering its contaminated blood down the corridor. Clover's aerial weapon struck the steel bulkhead and with the strength of its material became imbedded into the bulkhead instead of dropping to the deck. The assassin reached out for the weapon as he approached it. Clover's favorite weapon moved with the magnetic force attempting to draw it from the corridor wall, but the steel bulkhead refused to surrender it.

Clover reached out to the weapon and began to pull at it. The weapon still didn't want to come out of the bulkhead. Clover pulled even harder, and the aerial weapon began to wiggle free, but still it wasn't free of its prison. Clover pulled and pulled, which kept the assassin busy. Something leaped at him from behind and toppled them both, leaving Clover's weapon still lodged in the bulkhead.

The incubus growled at the assassin and pressed itself onto Clover, bringing both of their faces inches apart. Silver saliva dripped from the creature's maw onto the decking below them. The metal began to sizzle. Clover struggled against the mutated abomination with neither winning the bout. *This fucknut is way too vigorous for its own good. Where in the hell did they make this thing?* Clover thought back to incubation chambers, but shooed the image that came to him off.

"So, you like it rough, do you?" barked the assassin.

The mutated incubus only growled and flashed its teeth at Clover.

Clover pulled one of his legs up to the thing's chest cavity without it realizing. It was still too busy trying to take a chunk out of Clover's face. Once the assassin decided he was in position, he focused on that one moment, readying himself to gain control of the situation. "Are we paying attention, my mutated freak? Then you will love how rough I can become." Clover smiled a crooked and demented smile at the creature, which didn't even understand the change in its victim's demeanor.

Clover shoved the incubus off him with a force so great it made an *oof* sound. The creature was propelled across the corridor and slammed hard into the opposite bulkhead. The abomination slapped its head, and a crunching sound came from the thing's neck as it fell to the deck.

The assassin slowly approached the incubus, he wasn't about to be taken by surprise again by the brute. Clover couldn't sense if the creature was alive. Was it unconscious? Or had Clover really forced the mutated incubus to use its last life up? The assassin reached down to check the creature's breathing and the muttie's energy level increased. The incubus growled at Clover and grabbed the assassin with its sharp talonlike claws, drawing blood from Clover.

Clover screamed in agony, but quickly recovered. He had to get those claws out of him. He wasn't sure what that would do to him or what the creature could fill his engineered body with. Clover delivered an uppercut to its cranium. The creature's grasp slackened, then it let it go. It stumbled as if it was piss-drunk. Utilizing his swift reflexes, Clover provided the mutated creature with a roundhouse kick into the chest, forcing the incubus to stumble back on its backside.

Clover then made one last ditch effort and reached out with his hand towards his throwing weapon. The aerial weapon pulled itself free and flew back to its owner. Clover had just enough time to grab the weapon before the incubus was back on top of him. Clover sidestepped the creature's latest attempt to enthrall him and swiped the razor-edge of his weapon at the muttie. The blade sliced through the throat of the creature, and it fell to its knees. The incubus grabbed at its gaping wound.

Clover removed one of his katanas from its sheath and sliced the creature's head clean off its shoulders. The body fell limp and its head rolled into the darkness. The ginger wolf slowly approached, sniffing at the creature and tasting its spilled blood, which it didn't like at all. Clover wiped his katana clean and replaced it in its sheath.

The assassin looked down at his canine friend. "Some help you were." He patted her furry head.

Preist's nemesis reached for the scientist's throat with its talons, snarling at him in the process. Preist struggled against the creature, knowing it would only be a matter of time before he lost the battle. The creature grabbed Preist's throat and leaned back, readying a mortal blow with its claws. *This is it*, thought the scientist. *This is how it will end for me, and no assassin will be coming to rescue my hide.*

Suddenly a whirling, soaring sound came out of the darkness and sliced right through the muttie's neck, severing the creature's head from its shoulders. The aerial weapon struck the bulkhead as before, making an impressionable statement on Preist. He knew it was Clover's favorite weapon, but he didn't expect a rescue from the assassin. Apparently, he had been wrong. But where was the assassin, anyway? Preist looked around, at least in the part of the corridor he could see.

Clover emerged from the dark and reached out with his hand. The aerial weapon snapped back, and Clover caught it with his precision reflexes. Preist's elation quickly vanished and anger replaced it.

Preist pushed the dead creature off his legs.

"Oh, look who decides to show up suddenly? Where the hell have you been?"

Preist clenched his fists and moved towards the assassin.

Clover finished cleaning his throwing blade and replaced it. "Chasing down these crazies, where did you think I went, on vacation?"

Preist was about to explode, but the ginger wolf appeared from behind the assassin and started to lick Preist's wounded hand. The scientist's anger began to abate. He looked at the dead, headless incubus lying on the deck. Its copper-colored blood spilled out of the hole where its head had been attached. Pain mixed with a perplexed emotion filled the scientist. What had caused someone to do this to a person, if it was originally a person at all?

"Who could have done this to these poor souls?"

Clover glared at Preist, one that told Preist the assassin wasn't liking where the conversation was heading. "Do I sense sympathy from you?"

"Yes. Clover, you know me, I am concerned for all life, no matter what they have done."

Clover looked back at the incubation chamber. The two comrades approached the closest tube and began to inspect it closer than they had the first time. For some reason Preist felt that the incubation chamber seemed different, even though he knew that there was no way it had changed since they first discovered it. Both of them looked the cylinder device up and down, trying to uncover any clues.

Clover looked directly at Preist without expressing any emotion, something that always bothered the scientist about his comrade. "You asked me who could do such a thing. If you must know, I think I have a hunch. But it's going to sound crazy."

"I'm listening, Clover."

Preist had a knot form in his gut, and he wasn't sure if he really wanted Clover to disclose who had done this.

He pointed to the bottom of the tubelike device. "If you haven't noticed, the incubation chambers appear to be made of different material than the Complex itself."

Preist nodded.

"Then there are abrasions near the bottom the cylinders, see?" Clover pointed at the deep marks near the bottom of the incubation chamber. "These devices have been moved around constantly."

Preist noticed a faded emblem at the bottom of the incubation chamber. "What's that?"

Both men took a closer look at the emblem and words.

"What is Omnitech?" questioned the assassin.

Preist looked at Clover as if he had just swallowed something he didn't mean to. "Omnitech was a supplier of biotechnology. It's where the inspection tables you saw at the facility in San Francisco were, when we first met."

"And?" Clover said.

"They have been known to do experiments on the bioengineered, but you don't think that's who was doing this, do you?"

"Can't be. I'm sure they're all dead by now. Anyway, I know of only one set of morons who would expose humans or our kind to this type of heresy."

There was that look again. Clover knew something that Preist didn't, but the scientist didn't feel like the assassin was interested in sharing. "I don't suppose your going to divulge your theory to me, are you?"

"Its hunch, but if my instincts are right, and they usually are, we might have a bigger problem on our hands than missing pilgrims."

A colossal roar echoed from deeper in the complex. One that told the companions that whatever had made the sound wasn't something they wanted to trifle with.

"I think we should be heading out. These mutated beings aren't the only thing to inhabit the Complex and whatever made that cry isn't something we want to encounter," Clover said.

✝

Clover, the ginger wolf and Preist made their way back to the surface through a channel of tunnels that was just tall enough for the travelers to pass through, but it was a longer way around.

The drainage trench was dry with a small amount of sludge remaining; Clover and Preist used the trench ledge for balance, while bracing their hands on a lip that seemed to be perfect for the ginger wolf to walk on. The lip was too brittle for either of them to utilize, so both men used it for balance with their hands firmly on the dirt ledge.

A scream like someone was being murdered echoed from down the tunnel. The ginger wolf began to growl, exposing its teeth. Clover already sensed something that seemed out of place, but it was unfamiliar to his senses. The wolf inched its way towards the source of the screams and with caution Clover and Preist followed. Clover removed his throwing weapon and had it ready, not sure what they would find, but the assassin was steady as always, not allowing emotions to overtake him. *My makers made me a well-oiled killer.*

Clover sensed the figure before they came across the moaning individual. The timber wolf stopped suddenly, just as another scream, this one as if someone was calling out in pain. This was followed by soft crying. Clover could tell whatever they were about to come across wasn't in any shape to attack them, but that didn't mean they were safe. They stepped forward, Preist shining the illumination stick they were using towards the silhouetted figure lying on the grated floor.

A figure that was partially shielding the light from their face and grabbing at their leg.

Preist sucked in his breath and said, "Doria, is that really you?"

Clover had to look at the woman's haggard face a little closer before coming to the realization they had found Straus's older sister. "Wouldn't know that would happen," surmised the assassin.

Before the assassin and the scientist could begin to question Doria, a loud thumping noise shook the entire tunnel, as if a massive earthquake was happening. Clover knew what was happening and began to push Preist hurriedly. "No time for one hundred questions, let's move her out of this place." Clover grabbed Doria by the arm and led her out. "Move faster, Preist."

It was obvious that the human woman wouldn't be able to maneuver the broken grate obstacle course before them, so Clover lifted her over his shoulder, and they began to make their way out of danger. The two men began to hurry, abandoning the trench walkway for more substantial footing. Occasionally they even stepped into the sludge, but at that point it didn't matter. The woman would cry out in agony when they occasionally struck a divot or pothole in their path. The wolf didn't have such limitations, weaving in and out of obstacles in their path. Her agility allowed her to go far ahead of the rest, but she was never too far off for Clover to track her. He could sense her pathway through the tunnel and followed suit as best as he could under the conditions Clover and Preist were in.

Clover could sense something large just above them and anticipated whatever was chasing them from the upper level was close. He could hear the metal overhead flexing under something with great weight. The predator seemed to mirror the escaping figures step by step from above.

Suddenly the companions stumbled onto a man covered in a dingy, brown cloak. The man was shivering, and Clover nearly toppled over him. The ginger wolf sniffed at the shaking human and that only seemed to increase the man's anxiety. He was stiff as a statue and wouldn't budge from the gangway. Without the scared human moving, they were trapped.

Suddenly a massive, clawed arm broke through a half-wrecked panel in the ceiling, through concrete, and metal fell on them. Doria cried out in pain as a piece of concrete struck her. All three scrambled from the threat. A mutated snout reached in and snapped at the fleeing people; it possessed humongous teeth that where nearly as long as its victims.

All three managed to wiggle their way through some tight underground tubing and exit the between-level trench through a missing grate in the upper level. The risk was that as soon as they emerged from the sub-level passage, onto the upper-level decking, the predator, might be given a free shot at any of the fleeing morsels.

Each of them moved across the open and spacious corridor, with Clover trailing, being careful not to drop Doria, his precious cargo, just in case the creature did come after them. Sure enough, as soon as all of them men moved out into the open, the predator beast launched itself into a thunderous, ground-shaking pursuit that kept each member of their party stumbling and struggling to keep their balance.

Clover looked back at the creature that was more than fifteen feet tall and as wide as a city bus. *Where does something that huge hide in a place so confined?* Clover wondered.

The creature had a warped, leathery skin that appeared as if it had been burned alive, repeatedly. The creature's head was gargantuan, appearing like it should be on a giant tarantula, not the predator that now chased them. Inside the giant pincers were hundreds of grinding teeth each sharp enough to penetrate any hide. The creature had two sets of beady eyes, one layered above the other, giving the predator dual vision to hunt with.

The predator's skin was rough, like a lizard's, with a hardened shell-like texture. It almost had the appearance of a muscle that had the skin stripped from it, and Clover and his companions could see the red tint, like blood, that was coming off it as it chased them. The predator had four evenly massive legs with razor-sharp claw-filled paws that, along with its six humongous pincers, could rip through the metal hulls, decks and corridors without much effort.

The complex shook and nearly tossed Clover and his comrades around. Clover glanced behind, watching the creature bearing down on them all. *If we don't move quicker, I'm afraid that we won't make it to the Complex's exit.*

The creature opened its outer maw, spread its six large pincers and let out a searing roar. *Oh,* Clover thought. *That thing is definitely a Billy badass and we might be more of a snack than a full meal.* "Okay, everyone, if anyone has a suggestion, I'd love to hear about it."

The predator slammed its mountainous claws down, forcing a section of the deck to break apart and throw Clover and his comrades to one side of the corridor. The collision with the metal bulkhead had rendered Clover half-unconscious, but he still could see a blurred version of the predator stomping its way towards them.

"This is it. I never envisioned this would be the way we all would die," the assassin mumbled.

Preist moaned as the scientist attempted to get up to his feet, but something made him sit back down. Preist mumbled something inaudible.

"This isn't the day you die." Boomed a deep and familiar voice, one Clover couldn't place a face with. "This isn't the day any of you become stardust."

Clover wiped away a trickle of blood that had dripped from an injury from the fall. He still couldn't place a face to the unknown voice. The assassin watched as the titan came closer.

A hooded figure wearing something like a shaman's robe, with the figure's face concealed by the hood, positioned themselves between the predator's targets and the predator itself. The mysterious visitor stood with his feet spread slightly more than shoulder length apart, as if preparing for battle. The figure carried a staff that seemed to be some type of composite material, but with Clover's blurred vision, the assassin wasn't sure what type of material it was made from. The staff possessed a hollow, round tip with a thin ring of material much like a halo surrounding it. The tip of the staff came to a needle point, just touching the thin halo layer.

The figure gripped the staff firmly with his cream-colored hands and that got Clover's mind racing. *That skin tone, where do I know it from?* It wasn't like most of the Corporation's bioengineered beings with gray skin tone; well, most of them anyway.

Without turning around, the hooded figure said, "Don't worry, my friends, I have you covered."

A beam of translucent blue energy shot from the tip of the staff and propelled towards the oncoming behemoth. The blue ionized beam left a trail of smoke in the stale air. The energy beam struck the approaching predator in the chest with such force it lifted the mutated predator off its colossal paws and sent it down the corridor into the dense darkness. The collision between the titan and the high flow of energy had ripped corroded flesh on the deck, still fizzing like steak on an open grill.

Once the attack was over, the hooded figure turned around and bowed.

"Who are you?" asked Preist.

"Let's say I have come to return a debt owed." The hooded figure turned towards Clover and the assassin's heightened senses activated. Clover knew who it was, but it was as if the figure understood that the rest of his audience wasn't as in tune; he reached up and lifted his dingy and tattered hood from his head.

"Quasar!" shouted Preist. "I thought you were . . ."

"Dead?" Quasar started. "Most did, except our friendly assassin here and his female friend, Tigerous. She discovered me living out here alone. She and Clover helped me escape the moon base alive, so I thought it a good time to repay that debt."

Chapter 10

Present Day

Near the outskirts of humanity, in the makeshift town of Holden Crossroads, more an old-fashioned mining camp than a town, the steady *thud, thud, thud* could be heard at the western end. Tigerous continued to throw her detachable claws at a metal target. She had become bored babysitting the humans under her care. She wanted action, not inaction. She wasn't even paying much attention to the target or where her claws were striking the target, despite rarely missing the inner two crudely painted rings.

Zeus approached from behind and slid next to her on the crude bench she was occupying. The makeshift bench dipped downwards, forcing Tigerous next to Zeus's furry frame. She didn't bother acknowledging his arrival, instead she continued throwing her claws. "Something bothering you?" asked Zeus.

Tigerous threw the next claw with a lot more enthusiasm.

Smack, went the claw, nearly severing the target in half.

"I'm tired babysitting these pathetic excuses of life. All they do is gripe and complain. I should have gone with Clover, not be acting as a personal chauffeur."

Zeus sighed. "Another one of Straus's crew disappeared in the night."

Tigerous had stopped throwing at the target. She half giggled. "That's the third in the past five nights."

"Half his crew has left in the last week. Wandering back into the Wasteland is only a death sentence. What do humans think when they do such unconceivable things?" returned Zeus.

"They all are selfish creatures. They should be allowed to curl up and die!" Tigerous retorted.

Zeus looked at his little friend with terror in his primordial eyes. "That doesn't sound like you, Tigerous. You sound way too jaded, even for you."

"I've come to realize that feeling compassion for these creatures is a waste of breath. They definitely would not do the same. I can't see how they have lasted as a species as long as they have."

"Give them a chance, Tigerous. They just survived being annihilated. They must learn to live with others unlike themselves. It's like they have resorted to being children again. Can they be selfish? Sure, what young species can't? You can't hold a grudge against the survivors for what the Corporation did to our kind. To nearly every living creature, that was the corporate nature, to dominate or destroy anything that threatened its power. But they're gone now."

Tigerous got up and began assertively removing her claws from the target surface and replacing them. "I don't think I can ever do that that, Zeus. They only survived because we intervened. What I need to do is get back on the road, even if that means doing it alone."

"Clover asked us to watch them, and you want to abandon them, abandon Clover's trust in us?"

"They have been walking off on their own. How can we stop them? Tie them to a post and stand guard over them? No, I'm ready to move on."

"Fine, Ill tag along with you. Someone needs to watch over you."

Tigerous gave the oversized gorilla a stern look. "Are you sure? I have roamed the Wasteland by myself, I can handle myself."

"Oh yes. I am quite certain. If I don't, Clover won't let me live it down."

She shrugged her orange-colored shoulders. "That's up to you, big guy."

✝

Tigerous and Zeus had packed what few things they had and set out towards the western portion of the skyline. Just as they passed over the third dune, the two looked back, as if saying goodbye. She watched his massive neckline and enormous shoulders move in unison. She knew that she couldn't have a better travel companion, outside of Clover. Zeus was loyal, protective and possessed brute strength. She was in good hands and, in her mind, doing the right thing.

Tigerous took in a deep breath, letting her lungs fill up with air and mumbled under her breath, "Here we go." She pointed due west, but what Zeus didn't know was they were being followed and Tigerous had picked up on it out of the corner of her eye. A shadow loomed just over the next sand dune, well enough back not to be detected by the average eye, but Tigerous wasn't your average person. She had spent years roaming the Wasteland and had taught herself the things to look for. "We will make our way westward and see what it uncovers."

Zeus nodded.

They moved forward with eagerness and purpose.

Their admirer trailed.

Tigerous had gotten far ahead of their pursuer, with Zeus not that far behind. Before the big muscular brute knew it, the feline pulled him behind a receding sand dune that barely hid them both. Zeus possessed a look of confusion, one that screamed at the feline figure "What are you doing?" Tigerous understood Zeus's confusion, but she had a plan, and it involved their little spy, now approaching their hidden location.

The first thing to cross in front of their location was the spy's shadow. It wasn't in any shape Tigerous had ever seen before. It was short and stubby, and it seemed to float in the air. The shadow didn't even touch the ground. Then their pursuer's silhouette emerged from between a pair of dunes. Tigerous couldn't see the spy directly, because of the time of day and the sun's vicious rays keeping the small figure encased under sunlight and causing a shadow. What could be determined was that the spy didn't walk on ground. The figure in shadow had no legs at all and it bounced in midair, as if it was levitating.

"What type of demon are you?" whispered Tigerous. She thought their little intelligencer had heard her, despite being careful. She ducked farther behind the dune, as the shadowy figure began to scan the area. That's when the little thing emerged from the sun's brightness. It was something Tigerous had never seen before, but it did have a sense of déjà vu. The thing looked like a floating tin can, with its dull metal skin reflecting the sun's rays. It had a square head that moved back and forth, making a subdued clicking sound as it did.

Tigerous thought she noticed several marks on the side of the spy's round lower body. *Maybe from too much reconnaissance,* she thought. The automated spy used a blue scanning device that seemed to struggle penetrating the sand dunes. Most likely attempting to uncover their position through some sort of body scan or infrared scanning.

The plump, floating thing had a digital red, blinking eye and Tigerous wondered if that's how the little thing transmitted data to its master. Her legs were beginning to cramp, but she needed to know where it came from and why it was spying on them—and for who. This was Tigerous's adventure; if Clover could have his, why couldn't she have her own?

"What is it doing, Tigerous? Why is it scanning the dunes for us?" whispered Zeus.

Tigerous placed a finger to her feline lips to silence her comrade. The dronelike spy spun in their direction, as if it had heard Zeus's voice. Tigerous eased her big friend lower as the tin can moved closer. It spun its scanning eye all over the dune's surface, but it acted like even that didn't uncover the prize it was searching for. After scanning the entire dune, the metal spy gave up and began to move west in pursuit of its targets.

"That was too close," called Tigerous.

"What was that thing?" questioned Zeus.

Tigerous could only shake her head. "Some sort of intelligence collector. The real question is why was it spying on us and whom does it spy for? I think we will have all those answers if we pursue it."

†

Cheeves walked into his master's workshop and ducked, since his body was too tall for the sagging, low ceiling. Cyborg Nikolai was studiously working on something, soldering away and too busy to notice the *clump, clump* of Cheeves's metallic footsteps. The servant stood there awaiting his master to acknowledge his presence before reporting. The machine wouldn't get frustrated or impatient like most humans might or the insatiable rage of Nikolai. He was a servant machine, and servants weren't programmed with such emotions.

Nikolai finally turned away from what he was working on and acknowledged Cheeves's presence. Nikolai seemed to have a mixed expression on his half-human face. It was a blend of shock and irritation, but Nikolai didn't say anything, that was Cheeves's opportunity to deliver the report.

"Master. The drone has reported in."

The steadfast light flickered over Nikolai's cyborg head, reflecting off the durable metal surface. "And what does the drone report?" he asked in a mechanical monotone.

"Clover and another comrade left several days ago, heading north."

"The Sierra Nevada Complex," mumbled the cyborg. "That's what I was afraid of. Cheeves, we might have to accelerate our timeline."

"Very likely, sir. The drone chose to monitor two other comrades of the assassin." Cheeves motioned to a stool sitting in the middle of the dark and dusty room. An image of Tigerous and Zeus standing near an open flame appeared. It wasn't a live feed or a moving video, just a holographic photo of the two. "The drone thought the assassin might have given these two an alternative directive to follow, but these two seemed to be observing the humans from the search party."

"Observing, maybe; acting like babysitters, more likely. What else does the drone report. Where are these comrades now?"

Cheeves nodded to its master. "Yes, Master. Well, they wouldn't be effective at that, the drone reports many of the human hunters have wandered out into the Wasteland over several nights. No word on what happened to them."

A glow appeared on the human side of Nikolai's face. "Is that so now?"

"The drone," continued Cheeves, "reports that the two Clover allies decided to wander off on their own."

"Did they spot your spy? Possibly looking to find the source of the drone maybe." Nikolai looked away as if he was in a daze. Cheeves had never seen his master look so disappointed. Despite being programmed without emotions, something lingered in the android that could be construed as human emotions. It thought it must be what humans felt when fear had crept in, but he wasn't sure. He was only a machine.

Cheeves puffed his metal chest out and regained his composure. "I would think not, Master. My spies are the best manufactured. Most likely, as you would say, it was a whim of emotion that compelled Clover's comrades to walk away from the human camp."

"And?" questioned the cyborg.

"Sir, the drone followed the two until it lost them about an hour ago, but I surmise that it will re-aquire the subjects, even if I have to find them myself."

"Lost them, how?"

"It's bizarre, it recorded their trace footsteps, but around a dune they both vanished. The drone attempted to calibrate and reacquire the targets, but its efforts were futile." Cheeves's eyes told Nikolai that the android was truly regretful, despite merely being a machine.

"They vanished into thin air, you say?" questioned Nikolai. "Like Houdini. Interesting."

"I do, though, need you to do some preparations," said the cyborg. "We are about to have guests."

"Yes, Master Nikolai."

"Two of them to be exact. We should make them feel welcome, don't you think?"

Cheeves bowed. The servant walked away and prepared for the visitors' arrival, just how his master had instructed. All the servant understood was he was to go visit the other guests they had in their company and make room for two more.

†

Tigerous and Zeus followed the spy drone right up to Sunnyville's outskirts. Tigerous halted their progression, sniffing the air. She had a worried look on her feline face.

"What's the matter?" Zeus asked.

"I only smell the scent of humans, nothing else."

"Okay, and the problem is?" Zeus said.

"I doubt if this makeshift town would have the know-how, let alone the raw materials to build a drone as sophisticated as the spy we followed. Someone else is the spy's master, but they don't have a scent I can pick up on."

"Maybe they left the drone behind, and the villagers found it or lent them the drone."

Tigerous only shook her head. She knew something wasn't right about this human community. Something was hidden under its simplistic façade. "No, I don't think so. We need to be careful in this place. We are strangers with no back-up."

Tigerous began to search in a nearby trash pile for anything that would hide their identities. She didn't know why the people of this run-down place would leave trash—well, not all of it was trash—near the entrance of town, but she wasn't going to look a gift horse in the mouth.

They began searching through the piles, but discovered nothing that would work. Two figures appeared. One was tall and lanky, wearing synthetic pants and a tattered and worn cloak made of artificial wool. The other was a stout human wearing cloth clothing with ripped environmental attire. Zeus stole the short man's khaki pants, and his thermal suit top, which was sealed with rubber sealant around the arms and waist, as if it was still attached to the rest of the environmental suit. Zeus tried to place the man's dusty and worn-out trench coat on, but his massive shoulders and arms bulged, nearly ripping the coat into segments. Zeus also bypassed the man's combat boots, which were never going to fit his colossal gorilla feet. Zeus began to protest, but Tigerous placed a finger to her mouth, as to quiet her escort. He also didn't take the breathing apparatus, but instead found a cloak that partially hid his face.

They began to make their way through the thickening crowd as they moved towards the interior of the town. Zeus's size was drawing some attention, despite their attempt to blend in. No human could match Zeus's bulkiness, let alone how ridicules he appeared in human cloth-ing. It was like parting the red with the town's citizens moving to get out of Zeus's path. The colossal gorilla huffed as he attempted to avoid running into the small human population.

"This isn't going to work," he mumbled.

Tigerous looked over at her large escort and in a low whisper said, "Why didn't you say something before we set out?"

"I tried. You merely ignored me."

"It's too late to back out now," she returned.

Tigerous attempted to hide her anger by pulling down the dusty and beaten cloak hood. She was no longer in the mood to talk, she concentrated on every detail of the town, how it operated, what the people were doing, where they tended to gravitate towards, and she did it in a hurried fashion. She didn't know how much time they would be allotted before the authorities apprehended them, maybe as spies, and then she could only guess what makeshift law they would invoke on her and her mountainous escort.

Tigerous had heard some of the outlandish things some of these makeshift communities had invoked while treading through the Wasteland. Some of the rumors were frightful. Everything from flogging unwanted visitors, to rape and even crucifixion. This horrified her and was a good reason for her distrust of humans. Her fallout and eventual disfavor for the small pockets of human settlements partially came from these horror stories and seeing some of her own kind end up on makeshift crosses and set out to die in the intense sun-filled afternoon.

That's when the vision came to her. Tigerous was marching through a wicked sandstorm and she decided to make for a local shelter spot. The only one she knew that could navigate and utilize a sandstorm to his advantage was Clover. She came across a figure hanging on a crucifix. It was impossible to tell the figure's identity with the storm blowing everywhere. The figure's arms and legs were nailed to the cross that made being impaled a much more appetizing way to go. Later on, she would discover the figure had his tongue removed and his eyes stabbed out without the respect of covering his eyes. A sign read:

I was an unwanted visitor, clearly not human at all. My kind isn't wanted in the township of Las Daycus. Let my death be an example to all those not full-blooded human. I chose to hide my true nature and I deceived the good people of Las Daycus by pretending I was human, in nature, in ritual belief and in my soul. I possessed none of this and denied the good people of this amazing town the truth. Let my sacrifice be an example to all my non-human brothers.

She had heard of towns of extremist views that despised her kind; the measures to rid them of her kind ranged in many forms.

Tigerous returned from her Deja vu daydream with her and Zeus given even more intense glares from Sunnyville citizens. Something inside of her reminded her of that scene in the Wasteland, but something in the back of her mind told her this was totally different, something just wasn't right about the township of Sunnyville. The citizens were no longer just moving past her and Zeus, on their way to wherever they were going; the townspeople were now beginning to encircle the strangers.

"I don't like the feeling I am receiving from this," whispered Tigerous.

"What gives you that feeling? Maybe the fact we stick out like a twig in the middle of a pond. Or is it that it seems we are attracting the attention of the entire town with our ridiculous disguises?" Zeus returned.

Someone began to yell above the crowd. The mob searched for the owner of the voice, then began to separate, letting through four well-armed men. This put the strangers on edge, and Tigerous began to get into a defensive stance; she realized, even if they defeated the armed men rushing in their direction there was still the mob to deal with. Tigerous relaxed a little and attempted to show a less aggressive position. Zeus was tense, but not displaying much aggression. He was either a stone statue or at a loss what to do.

"I don't think we can fight our way out of this," whispered Zeus through his teeth. "It might be wise to use a more diplomatic approach."

"In this case," returned Tigerous, "I tend to agree with you."

The four men moved through the sea of citizens pushing those that were too slow to get out of their way or who refused to make way for them. The leader emerged from the crowd. He was of medium height and weight for a human, and he had a scruffy, unkempt beard. The man's face possessed a scar that ran down one side of his face, which was unwashed, matching his clothes. Most of the clothing the leader wore was worn, tattered or ripped to some degree. The leader refused to smile, his face showing the beginnings of a scowl.

The three other armed men seemed to be dressed in a similar style, each with torn clothing and dirt-covered faces. Unlike their leader, the other men had unslung their shouldered weapons and were pointing them at the town's uninvited guests. Tigerous could tell the men's grips were tight and full of tension. Understandably one false move could set off a maelstrom of fire from the weapons, a deadly domino effect.

The crowd had backed away when the armed men pointed their weapons at Tigerous and Zeus. Now there was space to move, but it would still be a risk attempting to engage the armed assailants. Tigerous thought about it for a moment. What would it matter if a few of the townspeople were injured, so long as she and Zeus could escape? But Zeus wouldn't allow her to put innocent lives at risk, and she knew he would be right not to engage the armed men.

The leader stepped forward, removed a toothpick from his mouth and motioned towards the two strangers. "You two are invited to see our commissioner. Master Nikolai would like to have an audience with you."

The gang leader motioned and the three armed men began to move Tigerous and Zeus with their weapons drawn back into the crowd and towards the middle of town. With each town building they passed, Tigerous understood what poor condition the township of Sunnyville was in. The buildings were run-down with some of the roofs either partially or in some cases totally collapsed in on themselves. Most of the buildings were windowless, but that wasn't surprising in this desolate world. The streets were made of agitated dirt or sand, with no visible vegetation anywhere, much like most of the makeshift communities in the Wasteland.

Tigerous wondered why so many humans stayed in a township that provided so little to them. Her questions would be answered soon. They had arrived at a run-down shop. This was the place the township leader was staying, and they were about to meet him. *Is this the same master that built the drone spy?* she wondered.

Chapter 11

The room was spacious and the ceiling drooped, as if an invisible hand was pressing down on it from the other side. The lighting was dim, and the floor was littered with debris. Whoever lived and worked here hadn't picked up a broom to sweep. There was a light humming sound coming from a room in the rear of the place, and Tigerous assumed there must be a lower level. This couldn't be all that was inside the structure, she sensed it inside her bones. The occupant was hiding something, maybe even hiding it from the townspeople.

There was a metal man standing at the far corner of the room. The figure's blue eyes stared the visitors down and giving Tigerous chills. She had heard of men made of metal, and this one seemed to give her the creeps, but she couldn't explain why. Their escorts were still with them, their weapons drawn and ready. Someone with a heavy foot was moving in the back room, like they weighed more than Zeus, quite a feat.

Suddenly, a creature emerged from the back part of the building. It was bulky and appeared to be made of the same material as the metal man. The difference was this figure was shorter and bulkier. Tigerous could hear the whine of gears, and the sliding of pistons coming from the figure's knees and elbows. It had a stiff, unnatural way about it; as if it wanted to walk like a man, but its body parts refused to cooperate. Then there was the figure's face, it was half machine, half flesh. It even looked human, or what used to be humanoid, with the flesh of its face stretched to the limit.

Their escort leader bowed at the presence of the cyborg. "Master Nikolai." The lead escort finished his bow, military stiff, as if at attention at an instruction by his superior officer. "The unwelcomed guests you requested."

The cyborg smiled a crooked and sinister smile. "Very good, Allen Perez. You may leave our guests under my supervision. You and your men are dismissed."

Allen Perez and the rest of the escorts didn't hesitate and left the shady structure as soon as possible. Nikolai waited for the humans to leave, then moved closer to his guests. Tigerous could feel the rotting floorboards shaking with each step the cyborg took. Nikolai eyed both Tigerous and Zeus from head to foot. It reminded her of the moon prison and Legion gawking at her feminine physique. But this didn't feel like admiration or lust, it felt more like a perusal of his new guests. The cyborg positioned himself in the middle of where Tigerous and Zeus stood and gestured with a metallic hand to relax.

"Welcome to my humble home. I am glad we could meet in person."

Tigerous huffed. She knew this Master Nikolai was hiding something just by the way the cyborg was toying with them, by the way he stood, the way he paced back and forth. Just because the metal man was a mystery didn't mean Tigerous was naïve enough to fall for the good-host game. They had been brought here for a reason and she was determined to discover what that was.

"So, you're the assassin's comrades, are you?" Nikolai looked expectantly from Tigerous to Zeus and back again, waiting for an answer.

That's when Tigerous understood who the machine man really was. *The Corporation CEO, Nikolai Volkov,* Tigerous thought. *That rat bastard.*

"What if we are, what do you want with him? We know the beef you have with Clover and of your detestable ruination of those who were always at your mercy."

Nikolai approached both guests more aggressively, as if he was egging them on. "I'd watch your tongue if I were you, my dear." The cyborg turned to Zeus and smiled. "What about you, my large friend?"

Zeus merely grunted at the cyborg.

"The strong silent type, I see. Well, we will have to cure you of that, won't we, Cheeves?"

Cheeves slapped restraining collars on Tigerous and Zeus. The enormous gorilla lashed out at the machine servant and rammed his bulking shoulder in Cheeves, who stumbled backwards from Zeus's powerful shove, but soon regained his composure without falling over. Zeus's rage wasn't done, he launched his body towards Nikolai, but something beeped and halted Tigerous's colossal escort. The restraining collars zapped the two visitors, temporarily paralyzing them both.

Tigerous and Zeus fell to their knees as the electrical current rushed through their bodies. Nikolai bent down to antagonize his two guests. His digital eye glared at Zeus as if examining the brute as Zeus fought with his restraint. He began to whistle a high-pitched noise, making Tigerous's ears cringe.

"I'll give you one chance to answer this one question. What is the assassin up to, and does he even have a whiff of my plans?"

Neither Tigerous nor Zeus responded. But they both stared back at the cyborg with great intensity. It might have been their loyalty towards Clover or the electricity running through their bodies, but neither one responded.

"Very well. Maybe you would like to stay as my personal guests for a while, won't you? Cheeves, if you would."

The machine servant lifted the controlling device and led the two guests to their new quarters. Tigerous was conscious, even if her head was still spinning out of control, which forced Cheeves to recorrect her steps every so often. Zeus, on the other hand had been drugged to the point of unconsciousness. The brute's pure size forced the android assistant to place Tigerous's friend on a mobile slab.

Tigerous awoke in a dimly lit and dirty cell. It was a large room with restraints holding them to the concrete floor. They must have converted the cell from an unfinished basement where humans might store things like canned goods and other stuff they didn't have room for up on the main floor. Little light was present, and what kept the darkness at bay came through cracks in the foundation.

Zeus sat asleep next to her. She could hear him lightly snoring. They were both chained to the floor and still had the restraint collars around their necks. Hers bit into her orange and black skin, making her uncomfortable. There was no bedding for them to sleep on or a blanket to throw over their bodies when darkness came. Tigerous's eyes adjusted to the dim setting of their prison, but too many shadows existed and prevented her from making out much. Her high-level scent ability took in that their imprisonment was in a mildew-infested place. The basement cell had a moist and dirty scent. She would hate to see it in full daylight.

Very few things were silhouetted down here, but as she was scanning around, Tigerous discovered someone else in the basement cell. A petite figure was curled up no more than eight or ten feet away. The figure was cuddled in a ball with a cloak thrown over her head, in either an attempt to keep warm or to hide where they were imprisoned.

"Pssst. Hey, you." The figure didn't respond. Either the figure hadn't heard her or was ignoring her. Either way she understood. Maybe the person had been down here in isolation for so long that they had gotten used to the solitude. Instead of trying again to communicate, Tigerous began to talk out loud to herself.

"This place is damp and dimly lit. It's the type of place that could drive a normal person insane." Tigerous looked around, despite the inability to see anything in full force. She imagined what everything looked like in daylight, even if nothing down in the basement cell had ever seen any.

Tigerous took a deep breath and a yawn emerged from her feline lips that encouraged her entire body to stretch. Her body was stiff from sitting in the same position for however many hours they had been down here, but her hands were cuffed to the floor, and she could only manage to stretch a portion of the way before having her arms repelled back down. Very little sound surrounded the prisoners. No sound of dripping water, no echoing of the wind blasting away at the aged and decrepit concrete. Not even sounds of feet descending steps into the grave abyss that Tigerous and her comrade now called home.

That's when Tigerous thought she saw a shadow move along the far wall of the cell. It had to be at least twenty feet away, so making out any features was going to be impossible, but it appeared as if whatever was making the shadow, was mobile. The silhouette appeared, moved along the dark concrete structure, and disappeared as swiftly as it had appeared.

"Hello?" Her voice echoed. She waited until the echo died down, then continued with her pleading. "Is anyone there? I can see your shadow; please answer me."

She waited for someone to respond, but nothing came, not even the sound of breathing. Had it been her imagination running wild? Trying to prevent herself from being frustrated, Tigerous called out again. "Hello, can anyone hear me? I can see you moving about."

A knot stuck in Tigerous's throat and Zeus snorted out loud, breaking the silence. It only momentarily distracted her, but then the sound of a boot scraping along the concrete floor broke the silence. Finally, their cellmate had decided to become social. Whether it was from shyness or being scared out of their mind, it didn't matter much to

Tigerous. With Zeus out cold, she would have someone to talk to, to find out what was really going on in this shithole of a town.

The scraping sounded as the owner advanced towards the newcomers, possibly three or four steps, then halted. Tigerous could sense the unseen figure lurking in the shadows, but she couldn't make out the face.

By the sounds of the boots scraping and now Tigerous's ability to hear someone breathing, it was someone with a small set of lungs. It wasn't like the figure was a dwarf, not that small. It was more like a petite figure, somewhat human, but something seemed different about this figure, this unseen and mysterious human. Tigerous just couldn't put her claw on what that might be.

"Are you going to hide forever in the shadows, or are you gonna come out so I can see you?"

The figure hesitated and Tigerous couldn't blame whoever it was. They were strangers and it was better to be cautious than reckless. But then the figure moved slowly towards Tigerous, as if it had been compelled by Tigerous's pleading.

The petite figure slowly sat on an elongated sofa. The figure still wasn't all that visible, her silhouette was still all Tigerous could see, but there was a crack of light, not all that illuminating, that shed some of the shadow. It exposed the young woman, who seemed more like a child, an adolescent, than a woman. At that moment, Tigerous's aggressive, in-your-face personality seemed to dissolve, and her nurturing instincts moved to the forefront.

The figure wore a tan hooded cloak, faded by time spent in the sun's rays. That told Tigerous the young girl had, before her untimely imprisonment, spent a lot of time out under the sun's protection. The petite figure possessed worn-down, tan boots and ragged pantaloons that had surely seen better days, but it was difficult to see them in the shadow the figure sat beneath. It appeared that the frail, tiny figure had her head tucked into her chest, as if praying to an unknown deity. Tigerous could sense the figure sobbing, but the feline couldn't understand why.

"Well maybe I could, if I had been in this frightful place for who knows how long?" whispered Tigerous.

"You have no idea how dreadful or dangerous this place is. You and your mate should have never come to Sunnyville." The young girl took in several deep breaths and then began to cry softly.

"What is your name?" asked Tigerous.

Tigerous moved to console the woman and forgot her restraints. The chain stopped her efforts and threw her back down. The jerking sensation's aftermath nearly shook loose several of Tigerous's teeth and her mouth began to vibrate like an earthquake had just struck inside her mouth.

The adolescent moved towards Tigerous and allowed her golden eyes, now full of tears, to be seen. The girl was breathtaking. She possessed pitch-black hair, a soft, round face and a fairly clear complexion. The girl had a button noise and a mouthful of teeth, which said she had good oral hygiene. The girl had a golden tan that matched her eye color. That's when it dawned on Tigerous who her people were. Only one set of humans had this type of appearance. Most human settlers, either in or out of the Wasteland were pasty white, mostly hiding from the angry sun's rays.

Tigerous was still reeling from her restraints fighting back when the adolescent reached over Tigerous's bound hands and waved her own hand, as if casting a spell on the metal cuffs. The restraints released their grasp on Tigerous and they fell to the floor.

Tigerous gripped her wrists, just to make sure the shackles were gone, then returned her concentration on the girl. "You're a Wasteland Nomad, why are you here?"

The girl hesitated and began to recede back into the shadows, but something made her stop. That's when the nomad girl moved completely into Tigerous's view. "My name is Princess Onaughon, my father is Tyhecu, chief leader of the Western Nomads of the Wasteland. Why am I here, you ask? I'm not quite clear on that, but I think it has something to do with the metal man and his attempt to manipulate my father into doing something he refuses to do."

✝

Princess Onaughon explained to Tigerous about her people and the gift she had been given; despite not ever knowing where it had come from. The princess's tribe had split from the main nomadic tribe nearly a decade ago to become defenders of the western front of the Wasteland. Their goals were to act as responders to settlers living in the western front, which seemed to have increased in Outland Rustler activity ten years ago. The outlaws had not relinquished their control on the region since, forcing the nomads to continuously move around a lot more than they were accustomed to.

Tigerous looked into the princess's golden eyes and listened to every detail the adolescent nomad had to tell her. The princess took a deep breath and began:

"Our tribe had just settled into the region and still struggling to combat the Rustler outlaws in the west region of the Wasteland. At that time, our tribe was losing more men than my father could replace. It was quite stressful for him, considering I had just been born. Directly after setting into the west region, or from what I have been told by my parents, tribal children . . ." The princess squinted and made Tigerous think she was attempting to recall facts that had been handed down to her and not something she had experienced firsthand. "One in every three or four children born in the region develop unique abilities. I know that is bizarre in humans to possess mutations, and the rumor from some of the clansmen were the heavy magnetic properties, including heavier than normal radiation counts in the southernmost part of the region contributed to this anomaly. It was suggested that the rocks possessed heavy amounts of brass and copper elements, and that after the nuclear holocaust, it melted the rock formations and liquefied the copper, brass and other magnetic elements, suppling the region with an overdose of magnetic properties."

The princess stopped to take a drink from a rusty tin can. She also began to sound winded. Tigerous could imagine that these structures still possessed high amounts of radiation, more than even the princess was used to. Tigerous kept her attention on the princess. The story was only getting more interesting, and she was learning a lot about what was happening in the Wasteland since her absence and what might be driving the cyborg that had them captive.

"Once nomad children are discovered to have mutations, they are separated from the rest of the tribe. It isn't meant to isolate them, like an attempt to prevent the spread of some disease; it's so the children can concentrate on their abilities and hone their gifted talents. Some had clairvoyant abilities, while others could develop energy from thin air, but despite all that, no one in our tribe had ever seen what I could do."

Tigerous looked down where the restraints had been. Princess Onaughon touched her lightly on the wrists. "Your ability?" questioned Tigerous.

"Telekinesis."

"Right, telekinesis. So, you can manipulate metal objects, like you did with my restraints?"

The princess nodded. "Among other things. But it doesn't have to be metal, I can move or change things just by thinking about it. But it does seem to be limited. I can't seem to manipulate overly large objects or things that don't have a solidified, physical shape. For example, I can't manipulate weather patterns. I have been told I would need an omniscient ability to do that, and humans aren't gods. But under the right conditions I might be able to manipulate small amounts of earth, but that's only under the right conditions."

"I might know someone that could manipulate weather conditions, but he doesn't, as far as I know, have omniscience."

The princess gave Tigerous a look that reminded the feline that Onaughon was still a child.

"So, the cyborg wants you for your ability?" asked Tigerous.

The princess only shook her head. "I don't think so. I believe he is using me, like I said before, as an insurance policy so my father will keep out of the cyborg's plans in the Wasteland. I think he understands what I can do, but couldn't care less."

"Maybe, or maybe he does and doesn't want to disclose his plans. Either way, I think it might be a good time for a jailbreak," Tigerous whispered.

"How? Even if we could make it out of the basement without the cyborg knowing, there still is Cheeves, the machine servant."

Tigerous looked over at Zeus, who was still fast asleep. "Oh, I think I might know a way to isolate the servant to allow us to escape. But if we stay here, I think we are certainly as good as dead."

Chapter 12

Clover and his merry band had just departed the Sierra Nevada Complex, after battling the monstrosity that Quasar had to save them from. Clover felt that without their emerging ally, Quasar, they all would have been dust in the wind. Normally Clover would be at the point of the group, with his predatory senses, but at the moment he felt more in tune with the timber wolf. She was hanging back a little, as if asking an audience with the assassin.

Clover wasn't about to deny his new companion, the one he seemed to have the closest enthrallment, despite only having been together a short while. She slowly approached the assassin, sniffing the ground and then looked up with curious eyes. What was she thinking? Clover wondered. She sat directly in front of him, and he took a knee to bring their faces close.

Clover looked into the ginger wolf's eyes, seeing his reflection them. He saw not only sadness, which he considered her lonely travels through the burned-out wilderness of the north, but also loyalty to one of her kind. Unlike the rest of their traveling companions Clover and the wolf had a wild predator heritage that the others did not possess. That's what Clover decided drew them to one another, the reason she had traversed the northern United States in search of one of her kind, for companionship.

Clover lightly touched both sides of the ginger wolf's face almost like a parent would a child's face. The ginger wolf sat there allowing Clover to touch her, as if they had known each other for a long time. He gazed deep into her eyes and felt the bond strong and enduring, growing.

A vision set in the Northern Rockies just north of the U.S. and Canadian border.

The scene was somewhat hazy, like a thin fog had rolled in off a lake. Swiftly a current swept in and wisped away the hazy cover, exposing the burned-out wooded area. Clearly the nuclear blast had cleared the forest away, leaving behind only husks of trees and ebony-hued ground that would never return its lively, vegetation growth. Despite having nearly twenty full cycles that had passed, an unnatural warmth lingered, most likely residue from the radiation fallout. A lingering, decaying smell loomed in the air which matched the look of landscape—desolate and uninviting.

Suddenly as the last wisps of haze-cover vanished, a male ginger wolf appeared, staring as if questioning the assassin what he was doing inside the mind of the she-wolf? The male wolf appeared to be strong with thick hind quarters and possessed a dirty, ash-covered coat of fur, as if the ginger wolf hadn't cleaned himself in a long time. The male possessed a healthy-sized snout and a full set of teeth. The male wolf held an aggressive posture, with all four of its legs spread wide enough to pounce in a moment's notice. The assassin noticed an adolescent wolf behind the male, one possessing a grayish-red coat just coming into its own fullness. The adolescent had an unsureness about it, as if it didn't know what to do about the sudden appearance of the stranger.

A string of howls drew the assassin's attention away from the male wolves staring at him and Clover spotted a den, half covered in a small mound. The opening was just big enough to allow the wolves to gain access. It sounded like the wolf pups, which he was sure that's what they were, were hungry.

The vision led the assassin into the wolves' den. He could see clearly despite the dimness of the den. The den's ceiling was low hanging, and it was just enough space for a wolf to move around. The earth-made walls had a wet look to them, mostly likely from a recent rainstorm. The scent of wolf pups lingered in the dense air, telling Clover the litter of wolf pups were close. The vision moved in closer, as if the ginger wolf female was approaching her pups to check on them. Then, around a short corner, there they were, bouncing around and yelping at each other in excitement. That nearly stopped the assassin's heart beating. The pups were quite adorable.

A feminine voice inside his head, one he had never heard before, beckoned him. "Clover, you know my feelings. I know you can sense my fears, my desires, my loyalty to you. You are all I have left. All my pack has been killed."

The assassin nodded. He understood.

Looking into the ginger wolf's eyes, he said, "I understand the kinship we share now. I understand the loyalty that flows between us, and I know you will always be at my side."

Inside the Sunnyville, CA. town limits.

The cyborg made his way down a back stairwell, leading to the farthest corner of the building he was utilizing. Nikolai was going to visit his profound project, the one he had been keeping to himself and not part of Darkcloak's devious plans. The passage was drenched in deep shadows with no lighting, but that's how Nikolai wanted it. The darkness was no issue for his digital optics, he could see as clear as day. There was a damp and musty smell lingering, like the cellar was old, but since the human condition was nearly extinct inside his machine body, it didn't bother him.

The former CEO had made this trip several times since his and Cheeves's arrival in the dreary town. The sound of the energy bars came first, guiding Nikolai to his pet project. Directly after the humming hit his senses, which possessed a rhythm that could thrum a baby to sleep, the orange tent of the bars appeared through the shadows. His digital eye sent back readings, telling Nikolai the radiant temperature. He understood the creature behind those bars sensed he was there. *Hello, my friend, I am back to have another one of our one-way conversations.* The cyborg took another step forward in the hope of enticing it. The sound of scraping feet approached, and Nikolai knew he had the creature.

Nikolai could sense the thing directly in front of him, not more than twenty feet away. Its perturbation made the silhouette creature huff and intense growl announced its agitated state. Nikolai saw the outlines of the creature's red carnivorous eyes filling up the darkness, a contrast to the dark shadows, like a firedrake emerging. The orange glare reflected off the creature's silhouetted form. The human cyborg knew it wasn't possible, but what little lighting did make it into the far reaches of the building basement flickered off the mutant, as if tiny faces were screaming back at Nikolai.

That was ironic, because the creature's purpose would be to annihilate what was left of the human population in western North America. Not that there were many left to die. This beautiful mutant's brethren were hidden in a cargo crate in the Wasteland. Nikolai chuckled. "Hello, my insatiable, flesh-devouring rage monger."

The creature stared back at the cyborg with a condemnation that thrived on violence. It was clearly arrested by a pain that drove it beyond insanity. That's how Nikolai had created the mutant, born from Darkcloak's formula that drove the human condition from the subject and into a droning rageful creature that craved flesh constantly. But these creations weren't totally mindless; well, maybe in a way they were. Darkcloak had devised a substance that would allow scientists to dictate how much individual control the mutants had. The difference was that Nikolai's specimen was customized to the cyborg's tastes; a menace that thrived on one thing, annihilation of the assassin that placed him in the state he now was forced to live with.

A sly smile emerged on the human portion of Nikolai's face. "You can understand me, can't you?"

The mutant growled a little louder and flashed razor-sharp teeth.

"You are going to be the sword of vengeance, aren't you, my deathly friend? They all will perish beneath my mighty boot, and you will be the instrument of that destruction."

The mutant glowered at the half cyborg and its enraged growling had lowered as if it was hoping Nikolai would forget it was there so it might strike its captor down when he wasn't aware. But Nikolai was always aware, sensing the creature's constant rage. Nikolai could see his creation and its comrades on a bloodied field of carnage. The twisted mutant roared out as it ripped another human head from its perch in one clean swipe of its deadly claws.

Blood shot from the headless corpse as it fell to the blood-soaked ground. All around the Darkcloak mutants, the ones that had been created at the Sierra Complex, aided by the Rustler elders, ran all over the desolated field of battle. It wasn't a one-sided battle, it was a bloodthirsty annihilation. Mutants seeking their blood-thirsty teeth into a new victim, making the human feast cry out before their lifeblood drained from their doomed bodies. It didn't take any of the elder mutants long to drain their victims, evident by the corpses littering the ground.

Nikolai's creation thundered through the mass of rabid mutants, slamming into one feeding and bouncing off as if nothing had happened. The creature was more than he could ever imagined it could be. It was a god among flesh-devouring creatures. The cyborg's creation was bloodied from head to toe with human blood on its face, in a thin, ripped shirt and pants. But human blood wasn't the only thing painting the roaming chaos magnet, dark gray mutant blood also stained its skin, more proof to Nikolai he had created a reckless killing machine, with no qualm for what it decimated.

A human had leaped in the mutant's path, and it tore through the man's flesh and bone, flinging it in every direction. It had its fill of human blood, now it was looking for one target, the one figure the cyborg wanted to watch it destroy. His creation moved about like a field general looking for his adversary on the killing field. This mad creature could probably sniff out the assassin in the darkness. Nikolai laughed.

The cyborg remembered the assassin and what he wanted to witness with his one human and one cybernetic eye. "Where are you, you bloody bastard?" He clenched his metal fist in a rage of indignation.

A storm was raging in the distance and moving in on the carnage swiftly. The sturdy wind wiped towards the giant dark cloud, howling like a screaming banshee. The cyclonic action was bringing in anything within its path, shredding tree limbs, body parts and terrain that had been uprooted by the strong gale wind. A lightning bolt rang down without being seen, but the cyborg heard it rip through the air. *It's going to be one powerful storm, just like the doom I want to rain down on the assassin and his comrades.*

The raging storm moved in for the deadly blow as Nikolai looked up and felt the power of the storm. The wind was so strong it could lift a man even as substantial as he was in his cyborg form. It felt as if the wind could strip a mortal of their flesh from their bodies; luckily, Nikolai no longer possessed flesh, outside his partial human face. Looking up into the storm, he could see the eye of the storm; it looked like a primordial predator. Flashes of gray light rang against the menacing dark cloud. "Oh, it's going to be one hell of a show," echoed Nikolai's voice.

Black rain began to fall on the killing field. The dark raindrops splattered like crude oil everywhere. It was like someone had ripped off the top of an oil barrel and tossed it onto the storm cloud. The sludge was filling up the field. The cyborg's attention being drawn towards the black rain prevented him from seeing a figure arriving, but the assassin's appearance didn't go unnoticed.

Nikolai's creation roared at Clover with the assassin's cloak whipping around as if the assassin was flying. Nikolai observed the mutant rushing for Clover as the assassin stood there as still as a statue, refusing to draw his weapon. The cyborg started to worry. He didn't want the creature to tear the assassin apart without a fight—what was Clover's deal? *Come, you chicken shit, pull out your weapon and fight.*

The mutant cut the distance between it and the assassin in no time, but still Clover refused to defend himself. The entire scene seemed to move in slow motion, as Nikolai's creation moved in tune with the pumping of the cyborg's artificial heart. One beat, one footstep. Another beat, the mutant made another step towards the assassin. Now Nikolai clenched both metal fists and ground his artificial teeth. But all of that didn't make the scene speed up or release the tension building within the cyborg.

A flash blinded the cyborg and Nikolai snapped out of the daze. He was frustrated, but he wasn't about to let that control him. Nikolai smiled at the savage mutant as if he were a joyous parent. "Soon, my friend, you will be allowed to release your Jekyll."

Deep within Clover's Dreams

The ground was brittle and arid, you might wait for a tumbleweed to cross your path any any moment. The sky was gray and foreboding. The chill in the air nipped at Clover's neckline. The twin duealing suns had just vanished under the mountainous horizon, creating a purple haze before the darkness took over. The outlining plains that stretched all the way to the mountionous contour of the Shoel Mountains appeared lifeless and matched the mountain's purple and black surface. The mountain's already dark façade made shadows from the fading sunlight seem uncanny without the creeping shadows approaching from them.

Shadowy figures surround Clover like dark, silent assassins creeping in all around. Their crooked forms seemed to stretch far and wide, as an extension of the entire environment itself. His animal instincts told him that these shadow beings were familiar to him, those that he has encountered before. But Clover wasn't for sure how. He grasped his weapon tightly as his grip dug deep into the grainy staff handle. Something was alien to the assassin. The touch wasn't the leather-wrapped katana he was accustomed to. *A woody texture*, Clover thought. *No, there shouldn't be a grainy feel to my...*

Clover looked down and noticed he wasn't gripping one of his katana swords. In his strong, impeccable grasp was an energy staff. This caught the bioengineered assassin by surprise. *How did I come to possess this weapon?* he wondered. The feeling felt foreign to the assassin, bulky but light, still the alien weapon wasn't something he was accustomed to. Then the shadowy figures began to approach, metamorphosing their dark shadowy figures in solid shapes. Many of them were disfigured, some slummed over, while others seemed to have charred armor and crude weaponry. Each had an icon embedded in each figure's breast plate. It was also charred as their armor and crude weapons were, but the ring that echoed from the material as it stuck another weapon rang with a familiar sound. The one dilemma the assassin had was he couldn't place why they seemed familiar or where from.

Then someone gasped at the approaching unruly, disfigured menaces. These shadowy figures now surrounded them in a rush of emotions of chaos and death. The smaller figure now was rubbing up against him. He could feel her slight frail form pressing against his backside, trying to get away from the approaching forms. The assassin had seen Surrora in other dreams before and didn't know why she kept coming back. It was like they had been in a symbiotic relationship from another life, one the assassin couldn't remember, no matter how hard he tried, but she clearly knew him. *What is our connection?* Clover wondered.

Clover took a quick look back. A stranger, who the assassin didn't know, was nestled tightly against his own body. Her eyes were wide and filled with fright. Her normally gray skin was pale and washed out. Clover could sense the fear flowing through her body. She grabbed lightly onto one of Clover's arms.

"Zoran." She whispered into Clover's ear. "What are these things?"

Zoran? Did she just call me that?

Little did Clover realize she saw him in the form of the deceased immortal warrior she had once loved. It was the same DNA used to create the bioengineered assassin, which Clover still hadn't discovered. In the dream Surrora saw him as Zoran the defender of the galaxy and not Clover the assassin.

He didn't have time to ponder on it long because the circle of threatening translucent beings was closing in on them. That didn't make Clover comfortable. Threats from every direction and nowhere for either of them to run. But as usual, Clover had control of his emotions. His heartrate beat a steady rhythm and his cognitive ability was clear and processing everything around their current position. If any one of the beings attacked them, he would be ready. Right on cue, that's when one of the disfigured creatures attacked.

Without time to think, Clover's fighting instincts took a hold. Raising the energy staff towards the attacker, the bioengineered assassin intercepted the attack. The weapon moved with an awkward grace, one that Clover wasn't accustomed to. It was a bit top heavy, but once he got used to it, it became an extension of his own body. Despite Clover's unfamiliarity to the weapon, its perfect balance made wielding the weapon quite easy. The weapon still reached the attacker in time, slicing through the butter-like flesh of the dark, mystic attacker. The creature's arm disintegrated right in front of Clover's eyes and then so did their attacker's body, right before them. It was like some magic trick.

The staff's energy beam hummed as it severed through the pitch-black air. An energy trail billowed from its wake, leaving a reflective orange residue. Clover felt he was always meant to wield the weapon, despite its unfamiliar feel. Clover brought the staff blade to his side perpendicularly in a defensive manner, waiting for the next attack. He didn't have long to wait.

Swiftly, other transparent forms moved in on their position, with their weapons raised. Clover moved to intercept their new attackers. They came from every direction not giving the assassin any time to reposition himself.

Clover stepped forward to meet the closest attacker first and like the first attack, he wielded the energy staff at his adversary. And just as before, the energy beam moved swiftly through the air and sliced right through the assailant, but this time the attacker disintegrated instantly. It was like the dark figures were aspirations with ghostly forms, instead of physical ones. But he had no time to gloat in victory, his instincts took over and quickly took on the next figure directly behind them.

Then a whispering voice came to Clover that introduced the alien woman as, "Surrora."

In an awkward movement, one that nearly took off Surrora's head, making her duck out of the way, Clover stabbed the attacker in the midsection, sending it into a dark cloud of dust. Clover moved with a swiftness that even surprised himself taking on one invader then the next. By the time the first wave of attacks was done, he had eliminated five assailants, gone like the others had. He stood once again at the woman's side readying his defensive strategy. The dark shadowy figures seemed to hesitate as if they were waiting on a signal. Then Surrora let out a gasp and a sharp needle prick pain hit the bioengineered assassin.

He looked at his right shoulder and there was a laceration on it. The cut wasn't a major one, but it was deep enough for the assassin to see it. Clover couldn't see how deep it was, but the slice had gotten in the small area where his armor didn't cover, just below the armpit, though it wasn't low or deep enough to strike a rib. He would have not even noticed if the stinging sensation begun. *Must have happened when I was battling those goons,* thought Clover. He had to brush off the cut. There was no time to soak in sting the laceration had caused. Then he looked up into the dark figure's deadly eyes. He saw darkness and death within them all. That's when it dawned on his. *They must be waiting to see how I will respond to the wound.* The laceration was a mortal wound and Clover knew it. Just a run of the mill laceration, nothing special.

Then Clover looked back into those deadly eyes. He felt they knew something about him that he didn't know himself, but what was it? Now gazing into the dark sockets again he understood. They were there for their own demise, sent to him by some unknown force. Somehow these deformed figures were drawn to him, to his essence, power and very existence.

Five more forms came at him, but in more swifter movements. The figures were gaining confidence and becoming more aggressive. Clover moved as swiftly as before, trying to be more fluid with the energy weapon. He carried the staff low so he could bring the energy weapon upward. Much like the first wave of attackers the siege came from their front position. Clover met the attack head on, slicing through the attacker's blade with ease.

Just like the first wave, Clover dispatched each assailant with little trouble, but this time he dropped to one knee. Blood dripped from a more severe wound. Pain shot through Clover's slowly fatiguing body. The deeper laceration made Clover grip at it. It ran from the middle of his ribcage to where his back began. The pain made Clover grip the staff even tighter. He began to breathe a little heavier. He wasn't exhausted just yet, merely a little winded from all the whirlwind fighting.

Surrora bend down and asked in a soft whisper. "Are you ok? How wounded are you?"

Clover waved her off.

"I'm ok. Its only a superficial wound. I'm merely taking a minute to catch my breath."

He had to lie about the wound. He couldn't let her know how much the last laceration had hurt him. He had to continue, because he wasn't about to let this be his last hurrah. He gripped at the staff a little tighter and prepared to counterattack. This time he wasn't about to be on the defensive. Clover had decided to take the fight to their attackers.

Then the alien woman gasped.

"Zoran." She mumbled.

Clover was getting tired of hearing her call him that name. He stood up and turned to her.

"Look now. I don't have an issue defending you, despite not knowing who you are, but could you…"

Surrora gasped a second time and pointed towards the shadows.

Clover looked in the direction she was pointing and noticed something moving through the darkness. *No, correction*, though Clover. It wasn't moving or at least not like anything normal. It was hovering, that's it! It hovered as it moved through the shadows of the Shoel Mountains. Clover tried to see the figure, but even with his nocturnal eyesight, he still couldn't penetrate the hazy darkness. It lingered like a dark cloud, unable to watch the movements of the, the *whatever it was* that slowly approached them.

Then the ghostly phantasm broke through the hazy façade and glided towards them. The apparition had a halo illuminating all around it and its appearance even made the dark creatures surrounding them take a few steps backwards. The ghostlike figure possessed a light about it, like it was some celestial being with a halo encasing the unknown figure's entire body. Clover noticed it wasn't rushing towards himself and Surrora in a threating manner and the assassin felt that reinforcements had finally come, but Clover didn't know why he felt this way.

The apparition approached the circle of death and right before it reached Clover and Surrora's location it halted right before the dark figures. Both the apparition and the dark figures seem to be transparent, as the remaining light fading quickly exposed the true nature of both. The celestial being pushed back the dark invading figures with shots of laser beam fire from the apperation's hands, vaporizing the dark figures one at a time. Unfortunately, the invaders were appearing so rapidly that for each one the celestial being vaporized three more took their comrade's place.

Surrora mumbled the same words as before. But this time the woman was shaking as if she had seen a corpse rise from the grave.

"Zoran is that you? How can there be two of you?" Surrora turned towards Clover with a look of confusion. Her eyes were like a child's that had witnessed something no adult could ever believe. Tears welled in her eyes and her eyes began to puff, her facial muscles began to shiver.

"You have come home to me after all this time." She barely could say. Her speech was slurred and uneven, unlike it had been before the apparition had shown itself.

Clover looked hard at the glowing figure still hovering over the dark shadows. The apparition seemed to have a calm serenity about it. Its face read of peace and its nature non-threating.

"So, you must be Zoran then." Barked Clover.

The apparition of the immortal warrior and the bioengineered assassin stared at each other for a moment.

The apparition nodded its head to confirm Clover's declaration.

Then it seemed to Clover that the phantasm was smiling a crooked smile at him.

"Come now Clover, I know you are better than this. You're swinging that staff like an old Dragoniran woman. The energy staff is an elegant weapon. You can't use it like any other weapon. Stop wielding the staff in the palm off your hand, it makes the staff unbalanced and awkward to use. Instead, use the upper portion of your hands. Curl the staff into your fingers and balance it as if you mean to perch it in your very fingers. Then you will be an efficient fighter with the staff."

Clover began to balance the staff in his grasp like the apparition had instructed him. He began to whip the staff around like it was merely a stick from a fallen tree. Clover twirled the staff in front of him, at first. He began to gain the elegant feel of the weapon. Then the assassin began to whirl all around him. Over his head, from side to side and then a number of combinations. He was really becoming fluid with it.

Then the apparition bellowed. "You might want to come to grips with the weapon quickly, I don't know how much longer I can keep them at bay."

Clover looked at the dark shadowy figures. He could tell they were becoming restless, and he could feel their anxiety building. Then a handful of them busted through the apparition's grasp, charging Clover in a mad rush. *Time's up*, thought Clover.

Clover stepped towards the sieging figures, but this time wielding the energy staff as the Zoran apparition had instructed him. Swiftly Clover brought the weapon to bear and with his breakneck agility sliced three dark figures at once, sending their ghostly bodies into a whirlwind of dark smoke. Without even realizing it, Clover had whipped the staff over his head and around to take on the rear attack. Three more dark figures ran at him with reckless abandonment.

First Clover swept the energy blade to the left, igniting the dark figure into a cloud of smoke, then swept the middle figure in one fluid motion, not bothering to even slow down. Then Clover spun around to meet the third figure. By now the only remaining dark figure was bearing down on the Dragoniran woman, with its decrepit teeth flashing and a horrendous scream that made Clover's ears ring.

The dark figure raised its cryptic serrated blade towards Surrora, but Clover intercepted the figure and struck it through its darkened chest plate, ending the attack before it rang home. Clover backed his way towards Surrora's location and waited the next attack.

Clapping echoed from the hovering apparition, Zoran said in a mocking gesture. "Very good, my boy. I knew you had it in you."

Then a loud horrific cry and more dark figures appeared.

"Hoe, my boy. It seems they like you," cried the Zoran apparition.

"What do they want?" demanded Clover.

"Who knows, my boy. Maybe they are attracted to your essence. Maybe they seek you out to end them so they may rest in peace," returned Zoran's apparition.

"You don't know?" barked Clover.

The apparition shrugged its shoulders.

Then a loud, ominous cry like a leviathan beast was approaching them shook the entire arid ground before them and echoed throughout the dry plains. All the dark figures turned in fear, and in an instant, they all vanished into thin air. The sky became pitch black, but no stars appeared in the night sky. It was like something had reached up and collected them all.

The Zoran apparition began to float skywards and away from them. Clover could only watch the phantasm fade into the darkness with suspicious eyes.

"Wait!" screamed Surrora. "Don't leave me, my love."

"I see you flee when trouble arises," echoed Clover.

"What approaches, I can't assist you with. It is an abomination and servant of the Darkness."

"So once again I must fight alone?" returned Clover.

"Remember this. What we have started you must finish. The war has only begun and you're the sole key to the Darkness's eventual destruction. Have faith in yourself, my boy, and faith in your comrades."

"Easy for you to say now, you're dead."

As the apparition vanished its slight voice called. "You have more strength than you realize. You can match the Darkness's power—no one else can."

A dark and ominous aura loomed over Clover. It was way too dark to see anything, but he could still feel the evil that approached. Black clouds emerged over the mountain peak. Despite the inability to see through the darkness, Clover sensed a colossal cloud forming, one that slowly materialized into a menacing face that would spread completely across the horizon. Piece by piece the cloud formed collecting other dark cloud formations as it swelled up. The formation of clouds began to mold like clay into a dark face, one that Clover thought was as familiar as the dark figures that had engaged him earlier.

The cloud face moved closer to where the two defenders stood. He was completely alone, not even the Dragoniran woman was with him now. He could feel the evil being's essence bearing down on his location. It was like the evil being was seething mad and it was ready to lash out at the assassin. Flashes of lightning permeated all over the cloud structure, like electrodes sending impulses to one section to another section of the dark cloud. Clover wondered if that's how the being communicated. The only issue was the cloud wasn't raining down moisture at all, it all seemed like a good lightning display, but it appeared to have no bite to its bark.

Then suddenly, the looming cloud made a move towards them and the face cloud, fully formed at this point, peered down at the defenders. It seemed to have a raised forehead, and humongous, pitch-black eyes that seemed like bottomless voids that never had an end. The cloud face had a grilllike face with slits that appeared to envelope a sinister smile. Clover thought it seemed to continuously transform right in front of them, the longer he stared it down. The cloud still collected even more clouds as it hovered over the assassin.

Then a deep and demonic voice, one that seemed to match the cloud face's persona, bellowed out to Clover. "Immortal. Bow before your master. Serve me or perish under my mighty grasp."

Clover looked up at the cloud and gave it a look of derision, as if the spiteful face in the dark cloud had said something that made him laugh. Clover stared back at the cloud.

"I guess you don't know me or my rebellious attitude, very well. Go ask the mighty Corporation how well I take direction." mocked Clover.

First there was a mocking laughter coming from the cloud as if what Clover had just said amused it immensely.

"The Corporation? So, you're the thorn in the side of my pathetic human pawn." The voice in the cloud began to chuckle a devious laugh. "I did what I could to push your human creators in the right direction, but they always seemed to get in their own way."

Then something within the luminous cloud burst, like the being had broken a blood vessel within.

The being within the cloud screamed out and a gust of monstrous wind came out of nowhere nearly knocking the assassin over. Clover grabbed onto the energy staff, buried into the arid ground, and hung on for his life.

"Are mocking me, you pathetic creature?" The voice within the dark looming cloud hesitated for a moment. Then the voice returned but with a steadier, more controlled tone. The being within the dark cloud lowered its voice's level. "Who are you? I sense something vaguely familiar about you."

That's when Clover heard a hissing noise. At first it was a light and a nuisance sound, like a gas bleeding off an open valve. Then Clover saw a blue aura coming towards him and the hissing had increased to a louder level. *That's how this being gets its information.* Soon the mist had passed by Clover's body and now surrounded him entirely.

Clover waved the mist out of his face and away from him.

"Are you done yet? This is becoming quite annoying to tell you the truth."

Silence enveloped Clover's entire location. It seemed the being didn't answer for a long time, but Clover could sense it was taking in the information the mists had collected. Then the sinister voice returned with its booming volume again.

"I thought I was able to sense a familiar aura about you. You and your kind have tried for centuries, and you have failed to destroy me. You will continue to fail, no matter what form you choose to utilize, immortal!" barked the sinister voice.

"Immortal? What the fuck are you talking about, you delusional puff of smoke."

Clover seemed to understand what the voice was implying. He felt something deep within himself reach out when the voice called him an elemental, but Clover wasn't about to admit it to this being. Anyways, it might already know he understood why it had called him that name. Admitting it now might end the game it was playing before Clover had a chance to react.

The demonic cloud face bellowed out sinister, dread laughter.

"Amnesia? That would be a first for your kind."

Then a light flashed far up the face's forehead. It was pondering on something. Maybe something Clover had said. "Where is the shadow assassin, your twin? He hasn't gotten back to us. What have you…"

"You mean Nightshade?" yelled Clover.

"Don't ever yell at me, child. Where have you hidden the traitor?"

"I'll never tell you." Clover yelled back.

The wind had picked up speed and Clover could barely make out the menacing voice. He hung onto the staff to prevent from flying off.

Just then a gigantic burst of wind blew apart the gargantuan cloud and blew Clover's body apart into tiny pieces. Blackness enveloped the scene.

Clover slowly opened his eyes, seeing the dawn just beginning to break; reflecting sunlight off the dimmed campfire. He sighed. Same dream as he had every time he dozed off. He wasn't sure what it all meant or why the woman, Surrora, kept appearing in the dreams. He just knew he was having them over and over again.

Well, no reason to worry about it now, there are other more pressing issues to attend to, the assassin thought.

Chapter 13

The early morning sky had a reddish-orange tint. The temperature was rising rapidly, making the travelers slow down even more than they had. The trek towards Metro City was going to take Clover, Preist, Doria, Quasar and the ginger wolf over rough and treacherous terrain. That didn't include having to gingerly guide the human woman Doria along until she could manage on her own. Doria's elongated time in the Sierra Nevada Complex had forced her to lose a lot of strength and walking long distances was going to be challenging, no matter the shape you were in. The four traveling companions maneuvered over the sea of dunes that stretched for miles. The over three-hundred-and-fifty-mile march would take humans one and a half to two weeks to get from the Sierra Nevada to Metro City, but they could make the trek in under ten days, if it wasn't for their speechless companion.

Clover constantly looked skywards, trying to gauge the time of day. Their traveling party had to conserve energy and pace themselves with the mysterious human traveling with them. He was the few that could do it with his enhanced skills. The bioengineered assassin didn't have to worry about predators hunting in the intense heat of daytime; most of the Wasteland predators hunted after nightfall. The one thing the travelers did have to worry about were rogue Outland Rustlers; they tended to scatter throughout the wasteland.

Slowly Doria's pain seemed to subside, and more color returned to her face. Clover wondered if that was a by-product of leaving the toxic environment that lingered in the Sierra Nevada Complex, or if something else was the ailment. Clover presumed Straus's kin would come around on her own to tell the assassin and his comrades what had happened to the members of her party, including her own family—and how she was the only member who managed to survive. Something didn't sit right with Clover, but being impatient was the last thing the assassin needed at the moment. Pressing her would only lead to more frustration, Clover thought.

A few days had passed, and the travelers had stopped to rest and recharge. A small campfire had been lit and the members were having a meal. Clover kept eyeing Doria, waiting to hear the tale she had to spin. The human female had seemed to recover quicker than the assassin had thought she would. There was a quiet about the temporary camp, set under a dried-out tree that could barely provide them with shelter from the blistering, rising purple orb in the sky. Was everyone waiting for the woman to decide she was ready to tell her tale, no matter how gruesome and horrific it was?

Doria was eating like she had never eaten before, placing another piece of dried food in her mouth before she could swallow what was already there. Then it seemed to the assassin she began to develop stomach aches. Doria began to caress her mid-section and had lost the joy in her face while devouring the meal she ate. In a way, Clover didn't blame the woman; she most likely had suffered for who knew how long in the complex. He was surprised she had the strength and fortitude to make it as long as she had. She dug her piece of dried food into the porridgelike stew to wet the food before ingesting it. Clover thought, *At least she hasn't forgotten some human basics like eating.*

The assassin looked at Preist; should they press her for information? Preist returned an unfamiliar look that Clover had never seen on the scientist's face—uncertainty. Was it time to begin pressing her? Clover returned to the woman, just finishing up her bowl when she looked up, right at the staring assassin. She had an obvious, uneasy look, but, Clover thought, so would anyone if a bioengineered assassin with red eyes was staring at them.

After what seemed like forever, Doria recovered from the stomach ache and swallowed the last bits of her meal and washed it all down with a swig from one of their canteens. She looked back at Preist, and Clover noticed that seemed to make her a little more at ease. She took a deep breath which seemed to hurt far less than when they had found her. Then she returned the assassin's glare with one of her own. "I suppose you all are waiting for a good story?"

Nods returned her probing and Clover could sense Doria's head begin to speed up a bit. "We only want to know what happened. Please, just the bare truth without any sugarcoating."

"Very well, where shall I begin?"

"The beginning is always helpful," returned Preist.

"Right, the beginning," Doria mumbled. The woman began to shake a little and fumbled with her beaten hands. Doria began to unwind her tale, telling her new companions about the journey she and her group had making it to the Sierra Nevada Complex, how excited they were to be setting up a new home and the fairy tales that had been told about the complex. "Boy were those tales farces," Doria said. She described the mutilated animal bodies they found upon their arrival and during several hunts for food. "We didn't expect to find an abundance of food sources, but we wanted to capture enough to survive."

She also told of setting up camp close to the mountainous blast door as a precaution. Clover thought that showed some good leadership skills, not being too bold setting up camp deep into the complex. Clover and Preist's experience inside the complex confirmed the dangers lying within the metal tomb. Clover sensed Doria was holding some of her story back, for what reasons the assassin didn't know, but he could sense her hesitation nonetheless.

Then Doria told of the horrid creature they had discovered in the lower depths of the complex and how finding her dead son frightened her. "That's when several members of my group began to disappear." She told of the bloodcurdling screams coming from every level of the complex, past their living quarters level. She told them that she knew from a mother's intuition that her children had been consumed by this creature and several of her party believed there might be more than one.

Doria told how she waited while sounds of wet sucking, like flesh being devoured, echoed within the lower levels. Her stomach growling nearly gave her away, she told them, but she persevered. She had made her way slowly, crawling on the grated steps back to camp, but everyone had vanished. Bloodstains on housing, near the burned-out campfire—everywhere. She was injured and didn't know what she would do. At the climax of her tale, she told Clover and his comrades that she had eventually crawled into the tunnels they found her in.

Everyone was shocked, except the assassin. He had seen too much of this post-apocalyptic world, and he knew Doria's story was very real. The only question was who was the master that had set loose these monstrosities? Clover doubted that the master was deceased. In fact, his predator senses told him the Rustler elders had something to do with this.

Later that night while everyone slept.
Dream Sequence

Doria was walking through the battlefield full of blood and human bones barefoot. The squishing sound followed each barefoot step, but the blood getting in between each toe didn't bother her. There was a slight breeze and the hot decrepit air made it feel like a humid August summer night in Georgia. A part of the place seemed quite familiar, like what she believed Earth was like before the post-apocalyptic holocaust emerged. Then the other part seemed quite distant from that fictional world, like she was living in her personal hell.

The farther Doria walked the more carnage lay before her, but without the ability to see any familiar faces, she was unmoved by it all—that's what made her the most afraid. She looked skywards and instead of seeing a dark red and purple sky, as Earth had possessed from the poisons of the thermal nuclear explosions contaminating the air and the reduced ozone layer allowing even more sun through; the sky had a dark gray, purple and sinister charcoal color to it.

Suddenly, a sound snapped Doria's attention away from the bizarre skyline, a familiar voice or better a cry, the cry from her youngest, Amelia. Doria began to shake, as she had when her oldest, Noah had died. Doria called for her eight-year-old, then stopped, realizing it wasn't her child's cry at all. How she knew was the same reason she understood the sky wasn't really the color it was, or at least not in the place she lived. There was a sense of a dreamlike persona in this place, a surrealness. It was the same way she understood something or someone was watching her, but who, she didn't know.

A shadow had crept up on her, covering most of the carnage of the battlefield up to a fifteen or twenty-foot perimeter that circled her present position. That's when a shadowy figure moved out of the shadows that had been, to this point, concealing him. His appearance had taken Doria by surprise in a weird way, it had a sense of familiarity to it. She couldn't explain it, but even with the figure's simple dress attire, which was a black cloak that hung to the bloodstained ground and dragged along like a two-foot bride's train and concealed the ominous figure's identity.

The figure might not be winning any fashion awards, but his size was quite imposing. The figure towered over Doria, and its shadow seemed to be one that belonged to a monumental sentinel standing guard to the gates of hell. She also felt a menacing disposition radiating from the unidentified figure. The one thing that seemed familiar about the cloaked man, if it was even a man at all, was his stance; confident and controlling, as if he knew what was going to happen.

Then before she understood what was happening, Doria called out to the beastman, "Darkcloak," as if she knew him even before the cloaked man revealed himself.

The figure began to chuckle a sinister laugh that would make anyone shiver. The hooded individual pulled back his concealment to expose a gray head with thin purple lines that appeared to be veins, leading from his thick neck, and meeting at the top of Darkcloak's head. But since the figure was phantom like or a mistful creature that didn't make any sense to her at all, why would a phantom or mist-like being possess veins at all? The shadow agent also possessed dark, lifeless voids for eyes that only added to the nightmarish appearance. Despite Darkcloak's simple attire, she understood from the dark persona radiating from him that he was far from that, he was a very dangerous being.

"What… what do you want?" Doria asked with a shake in her voice.

Darkcloak only smiled, but that smile sent chills down her spine. It was sinister, like a mad scientist watching his creation come alive. "I think you know exactly what I want, don't you… Doria?"

Something deep within her began to move, like a parasite moving at will. She winced at the pain being executed and she nearly collapsed to the ground. Fortunately, she was able to fight off the weakness within her body and stayed on her feet. But she decided to take a few steps backwards in hopes whatever power Darkcloak had over her would weaken. No such luck would happen. A sharp pain in her mid-section spiked, giving her rubbery legs; Doria went to one knee.

"Are you enjoying the clairvoyance I have gifted you, Doria?"

Doria fought the sharp pain that seemed to be coming and going at will, without any control over it. She knew at that moment that something had been placed within her. She thought back to her blacking out and she touched the bite marks on the top of her shoulder and neckline. "What have you done to me?" She forced herself back to her feet, groaning against the surging pain. "Why have you cursed me and poisoned my body and gave me this wicked insight?"

"My child, this is a gift, can't you see that? Humanity is already on the brink of annihilation and was about to blink out of existence before the assassin intervened. No matter though, I have you as my backup plan." Darkcloak's sinister laugh returned, but it seemed to echo inside her head this time.

Then the voices of her dead children began to blame her for abandoning them.

"Hello, Mother. Where are you?" cried the voice of her son, Noah.

"Help us, Mommy," called Amelia.

"You said nothing would ever harm us, but where are you, Mother?" called Noah.

"No," screamed Doria. "You can't do this to me!"

Darkcloak laughed.

"Mommy? Mommy, is that you?" called both of Doria's children. "Where were you, Mommy? We needed your help."

Doria cried out for both of her deceased children as she began to cry. The faces of both Doria's children invaded her mind.

"Help us, Mother," cried Noah. "Were were you when I needed you?"

Doria cried out for both of her deceased children, as she began to cry.

The faces of both Doria's children invade her head.

"Help us, mother," cried Noah. "Were were you when I needed you?"

An array of faces merged and transformed swiftly. Some of these faces were recognizable, while others were not. All of them from the Sierra Nevada Complex, screaming at the top of their lungs, "You let us die, Doria. You let us die!"

Doria screamed at the top of her lungs, knowing none of the faces of voices were real. "Stop it, get out of my head, you bastard!"

Suddenly all the commotion and visions seized and the only sound she now heard was Darkcloak laughing and applauding. "Good, very good indeed. You are now totally embracing your clairvoyance ability."

Doria froze, with no ability to move a muscle. She began to feel another's presence. Not right there in the same physical area she and Darkcloak occupied, but somewhere far away. But it felt like it was right there, standing next to her. No, in fact it felt as if Doria and this other occupied the same body. She couldn't see what this other looked like, but she could feel this being was familiar, much like the thing that had taken a bite out of her, infected her with the parasite that had her sick and delusional.

The thing attempting to merge with her was full of hate and animosity, she could feel that was what drove it, but she still couldn't quite understand what it was or what it wanted with her. Doria looked over at the smiling Darkcloak, and something dawned on her. The thing inside of her, it had to be a link to this new and disturbing creature. Still, what did it want with her?

A transparent image of the mutant's face came to Doria. It had gray skin, much like Darkcloak, but lighter. It had blood-red eyes that lusted for human blood. Its jaw was misaligned, and its gray flesh seemed to be peeling, because she could see its rotten flesh underneath. Doria began to feel the parasite in her stomach reaching out telepathically towards the horrific mutant figure. Both had a desire to merge, but if they did; what would happen to her. The thought made her skin crawl. That's when Darkcloak's sinister laughter began again.

Doria opened her eyes, less in horror of her nightmare and more in realization that she had once again returned to the living world. *Same nightmare as before*, she thought. Each time she would awaken, so it no longer sent Doria in a state of panic. The only difference from the previous nightmares and this new one had been the presence of the transparent mutant; that was something new.

Doira glanced over to see her comrades asleep. The campfire reflected its luminous light around a ten-foot perimeter, allowing her to see each member of the traveling party. If the days were sultry and hot, the nighttime was cold to the touch. Preist was curled up in his blanket like an infant child. Quasar sat cross-legged on the ground, embracing his staff positioned across his lap. That only left Clover and the timber wolf. The she-wolf was curled up just close enough to the campfire to be visible, but part of her body was covered by darkness. Then there was Clover's predatory eyes scanning the outskirts of their small encampment. It was the only thing Doria could see of the assassin and she thought how creepy he looked at night. But she was glad he kept watch over them all.

She felt safe.

Chapter 14

About a week later, the travelers made it over an extremely steep dune hill and Clover looked out over the vast sea of sand. They were a day from exiting the northern plains of the Wasteland, from there the travelers had another day's hike to Metro City. A sense of urgency had forced Clover to pick up the pace; it was one of the reasons he had chosen to skirt the upper portion of the Wasteland. The vast wilderness of nothingness, sand and dangers living in the desert climate stretched from what used to be Death Valley, California, through much of Utah at its northern peak, while stretching as far south as Nevada, Arizona and New Mexico. That wasn't saying there was much beyond the Wasteland, to the east. Just like the scattered communities littering the western coast, many that had survived still congregated in small communities with very few resources available. Many of the urban and suburban supply lines that formally resided in the larger communities had either dried up, gone rotten with the lack of use, or were annihilated in the nuclear blast.

Whether you were human or bioengineered didn't matter, life was still hard and most of the living didn't last more than a few winter seasons from lack of fresh water and starvation. The Outland Rustlers hadn't helped the situation by coming out of the Wasteland and terrorizing the helpless with their vast numbers. But all that changed after Clover had defeated Legion and weakened the outlaws' grip on the supplies they hoarded.

Now, with the decrease in the outlaws' numbers and their stranglehold on what few supplies were usable, the small human settlements stood a chance.

The assassin stopped, allowing Preist and the others to catch their breath. The extreme heat and long distance they had already traveled was taxing to most, except for someone with Clover's abilities, someone who had adapted to the harsh environmental conditions, to the vastness of the Wasteland. Preist, on the other hand, hadn't traversed the vast Wasteland like the assassin had. The scientist had his hands on his knees and his breathing was quite labored. It was as if Preist had ran a full marathon through the vast sea of sand. Clover had never seen his companion on verge of total exhaustion; but again, it's what the Wasteland did to infrequent visitors.

"Are you okay?" questioned Clover. The assassin reached for his waterskin, but Preist waved him off. The assassin began to check on the others. Quasar was fine. Like Clover, he had walked through the entire Sierra Nevada region, protecting what had been left behind and any settlers that had settled for any length of time, even though Quasar preferred his isolation to cozying up to others. The humanoid mix, on the other hand was in worse shape than Preist, but Clover didn't care about that and didn't check on their mysterious companion.

In between breaths, the scientist said, "I'll . . . make . . . it. Just give . . . me . . . a second."

Clover looked out over the sea of sand like he was visiting a long-lost relative. The assassin was starry-eyed and lost in his train of thought. "The Wasteland is unforgiving, and most don't know how to travel through it in daytime. We should pace ourselves better, it's my own fault for pushing the group so hard. We need to conserve energy, we still have a day or two to travel." The assassin looked at each member of their traveling posse. "Forgive me, I'm used to traveling by myself."

"Thanks for the reminder," responded Doria with both hands on her knees. This time the pain wasn't coming from the parasite living inside of her, but from exhaustion of the trek they had taken and the extreme heat beating down on them from above like an enraged god.

"We all don't have your innate senses and predisposition towards the Wasteland and its extreme conditions."

Preist pulled out his own waterskin and gulped down some water.

"You mean humans roaming the Wasteland, don't you?" Quasar said. He was resting his staff against his broad shoulders.

Clover's expression refused to waver, even if Preist was chiding him.

"Tell me," the scientist said, "is it the outlaws you despise, or all humans?"

The assassin looked back at the scientist, vexed and unable to reconcile the scientist's attitude towards humans. "You saw how they treat one another, how they treat our kind?"

Preist sighed, "Judgmental, aren't we? I know you don't despise all humanity, or why would you have saved those children," Preist gestured in Doria's direction. "In your conflict with Legion and his gang."

"I feel your frustration; my assassin friend is just being cautious," Quasar said. "We all have suffered at the hands of a few tyrannical men. Doesn't make them all bad."

"I have to admit," Clover said, "the Outland Rustlers haven't helped my opinion of humans. Their deceitfulness and hiding like desert rats only fuels my suspicions." His tension had subsided as soon as he remembered he was with allies.

"But they are radicals that don't reflect the whole of their species," returned Preist.

"I'm not so sure I agree. Look what they did to the planet, is that idealism of a small radical faction?" Clover asked.

Preist gave Clover a sad expression. "One man, not the entire species, Clover. You should know better than that. Or have you become so jaded you can't see the lines of separation? In human history, there has always been tyrants. That doesn't make the people they ruled sinister as they were. It makes them victims."

Preist replaced his waterskin under his dingy smock. "I think its time that we move on, the sun isn't getting any less potent, and Metro City is awaiting our arrival."

†

A bright flash, like a small star residing in the middle of a sandy ocean. Preist placed a pair of binoculars over his eyes, but the sun was too bright, and he could see nothing. He looked skywards and smiled. His moved from the bright sky down towards the source.

"There is something out there." The scientist pointed.

Clover sniffed the air and shook his head. "Possibly Wasteland Nomads, nothing more. The wind has increased and picking up any scent is impossible." Clover looked towards his two comrades. "Let's move on."

Preist didn't move. "I want to discover what's out there." He was hesitant, wanting to defer to the assassin's superior instincts. Instead, Doria took up Preist's curiosity and ran off in the direction of the flash.

"Wait!" called Preist, but it was too late. He turned to Clover. "We have to go after her."

Clover wanted to refuse to chase her, but, subconsciously, he would aid Preist. That didn't please him one bit, making the relationship between the human woman they had just rescued and the assassin even less cohesive and strained.

The thick sandy surface wasn't making things easy on any of the travelers. Clover observed the human becoming labored and he still hadn't arrived at the light source. Clover began to wonder if it hadn't all been a mirage, after all. Doria stopped, placed her hands on her knees and took in deep breaths. A shiny object appeared just above the surface of the sand and Clover was the first to see it. It appeared only as a token floating in the sea, and Doria was apparently determined to retrieve the treasure no matter the cost. The item seemed to be a corner of something larger, but from the distance he was at, the assassin couldn't be sure.

A tingling sensation in her abdomen began, like something inside her was trying to warn her, but Doria ignored it.

Doria began to dig. She looked like a dog digging for its bone. The deeper she dug, the more the item she was trying to recover sank. That made the frail humanoid dig even faster. Soon her efforts were rewarded and enough of the object buried under the sand became visible. It was in the shape of a miniature chest that could be held in your arms, or a very large cube—she couldn't decide which. Doria dug with even more verve and energy. Then a flash came across her eyes. Not an entire scene, but she saw a crater with a black hole before her in a blink of an eye. Gurgling sounds were coming from the dark hole, like water was rushing through a vortex or worse, something was attempting to swallow an object.

Then screams echoed in her head. Not the screams from her dream, the screams of her dead children. These screams seemed to be familiar to her as well. *Could they be screams of... No*, she protested. Doria shook off the clairvoyant vision and continued to dig.

Suddenly, an earthshaking sound rumbled. The sandy surface began to recede, and a large craterlike hole began to appear. The woman began to scratch and claw to prevent from falling into the ever-growing vortex below, but the faster she moved the more ground she seemed to lose. Doria couldn't scream for help, the only thing that came out of her mouth was a dry croak. She doubted if anyone cared enough to save her skin, even if she could let out a large enough scream. Out of the depths of the Wasteland sand came a thick and titan-sized tentacle that wrapped around her body and began to drag her towards a dark void that had opened.

Doria slid down the sand embankment towards the darkness below. She thought this was what it felt like if someone had been captured by a black hole's event horizon. She might not be able to see what was coming, but Doria could feel the acceleration of her descent and the wet gurgling of something like a thorax sucking air in, the grinding of *teeth*.

This is it, she thought. *This is how I leave the world, despite all the things I have survived.* Then she thought of her deceased family and began to sob. Suddenly, someone grabbed her arms and her momentum slowed, but didn't stop suddenly, as she still fell towards her eventual doom. Doria could feel someone tugging at her with all their might. Then Preist's voice came to the doomed woman. "Hang on, Doria. We won't let you be taken by this beast."

Clover saw Preist falling towards the pit and noticed the scientist using all his might to save the human woman. *Damn fool*, thought the assassin. *Let the woman go to her death. Hasn't she endured too much already in her life?* Clover reached out and grabbed Preist's dingy robe and used all his might to stop the two figures falling into oblivion. Clover reached with one of his katanas in the hope he could snag a ridged edge, but all he was doing was sand surfing down the open crater. That's when a voice that the assassin couldn't pinpoint echoed through his mind. It seemed vaguely familiar, one he had heard before but never when awake.

"Use your omniscient power. You can strike the creature dead before anyone reaches its mouth."

But before Clover could react, someone had grabbed hold of Clover's waist. When the assassin looked back, he saw Quasar tugging at the falling men, trying to utilize his staff, much like Clover had tried to use his katana, with similar results. The end of the staff merely slid over the surface of the sand, burying the end in a few inches. The staff was leaving a trail behind, as if it were powerful enough to scar the sandy terrain, but not enough to save them. All four of them began to tumble towards the black void at an astronomical rate.

If the situation wasn't desperate enough, as soon as the helpless travelers reached within fifty feet of the pit, its resident appeared. The only thing they could see was the monster's colossal maw, which spread the entire length of the void. Six fanglike teeth, three in its upper mouth region and three in its bottom—Clover could only assume they were for shredding flesh. Then the assassin noticed the rows of smaller pointy teeth that ran across its upper and lower jaw, most likely grinding teeth that would allow the creature to devour its prey.

The gargantuan creature chomped its teeth together several times as if gobbling up an invisible meal. But Clover decided it was more likely done to intimidate its prey than anything else. Clover grabbed both Preist's robe and attempted to reposition his feet, hoping to reduce their fall. But as the assassin figured it had no effect at all.

Then it dawned on him. If he could get a clear shot, he could slice the herculean tentacle and stop their fall towards apparent death. The problem would be that he would have to let go of Preist, and Clover knew it was a one shot—if he missed, his comrades would die. *What other choice do I have?*

Clover released his grip on Preist and signaled to Quasar to take his place behind the scientist. Once Quasar had a hold of their comrade, Clover leaped out of their congo line and used his left hand to glide along with his falling comrades, still giving the assassin a clearer shot at the gripping tentacle on Oracle's waist. The thick and meaty tentacle made for an easy target, but at the speed the group was falling, it made Clover's job that much more difficult. The distance was closing too swiftly for Clover to have more than one shot at it.

Clover concentrated on his target; the meaty portion of the creature's tentacle turned towards the assassin. He took aim with his aerial weapon, gauged the wind direction, and released the weapon. The quad-blade soared through the air, making a whistling noise as it sliced through the hot dense air. The blade rotated end over end and sliced deep through the slimy tentacle flesh and continued on through the air. Instead of getting stuck in the meat of the tentacle, the blade sliced a chunk of the tentacle off.

Unfortunately, the throw didn't sever the tentacle clean-off, it hung there with a portion of the flesh still attached to the rest of the tentacle arm. The creature's grip loosened, but not enough to release its captive. Clover concentrated on the weapon, attempting to reverse its rotation.

Suddenly Clover felt a strong polar force tugging between himself and his favorite weapon. The aerial quad-bladed weapon stopped in midair and reversed its rotation, coming back toward its owner. The weapon finished the job slashing through the rest of the tentacle. Green blood shot out from the exposed flesh and the injured tentacle went flapping away, releasing its dinner.

Clover's comrades slid out of the way of the creature's razor-sharp teeth, now less than fifteen feet away. Clover watched as the gargantuan beast roared its displeasure. The creature swung four more tentacles, each larger than the first, attempting to recapture its meal. Clover knew he couldn't cut down all the tentacles, and he was dumbfounded as to what to do next.

Suddenly, before the pit creature could regain control over Doria, now laying on close to the beast, an ion energy beam struck the corner of the pit and the creature's maw. Particles of green flesh flew in the air, along with the pit creature's slimy blood. Clover attempted to look in the direction of the strike, but the sun kept the assassin blind. Two more blasts emerged from behind the veil of the receding sun. Clover heard a distant screech directly above.

"What do you see?" mumbled Clover.

The additional ion strikes hit the deadly creature directly between its eyes and the other struck the deep within the dark pit below the surface. Suddenly, the pit began to collapse in on itself; a rumbling shook the ground underneath the traveler's feet and Clover knew they needed to run.

"We need to get to the top of the crater," called Quasar.

Clover nodded. Quasar grabbed Doria, while Clover assisted a dazed Preist and ran for the closest sand crater lip. The sandy ground began to fall in towards the collapsing pit, creating a sand slide, which made footing treacherous. Despite all the hazards in the traveler's way, all four reached the edge wall of the crater.

"What now?" a weary Preist asked. "We have no rope to climb with."

Three ropes slid down the side of the crater wall, as if descending from the heavens. Three hooded figures emerged, staring down at them. "Wasteland Nomads," whispered Clover.

After a time-consuming and rigorous climb, all five companions reached the pinnacle of the sand crater. Clover aided Doria first and with the help from the nomads swiftly got his comrades to safety. Clover nodded and thanked the five hooded nomads, one of who was holding the ion launcher gun. After all the travelers had emerged from the new Wasteland crater, a figure approached. It was difficult to distinguish between the nomads with their thick Wasteland dress. The nomads were covered from head to toe, mostly with environmental protective gear, but that made a lot of sense since they spent most of their time out in the open.

The figure seemed to hold himself in a manner that expressed a silent confidence, one that told Clover this was the group's leader. The nomad removed his breathing apparatus, revealing a tan line where the breathing equipment must have spent way too long on the nomad's face. The man was a middle-aged human and wore the stresses of his position. Clover had to assume this man was a high-ranking nomad, possibly a leader of a scouting party or a fighting regime. The man had more than his share of scars and a foggy eye which possessed battle damage, a scar running directly through the eye itself.

"Clover, we have been searching for you for some time. My name is Amasar, and I have come in the name of our aging leader, Chief Tyhecu. The chief is in dire need and requests your assistance; our people and you have had a good working relationship for some time. The chief begs your assistance and asked me to provide you with anything you need if you will come to his aid."

Amasar delivered Chief Tyhecu's plea. "The chief's youngest daughter has vanished. It isn't like her to run off on her own. A few of our scouts saw her being detained by a metal man and a few raggedly dressed humans. They were too far for us to pursue, since the scouting party were heading in the opposite direction. Two nomads could easily take out the band of humans, I have no doubt; it was the metal man that posed the biggest threat."

"Why didn't you gather warriors from your tribe and go after them?" Clover probed.

"Clover, stop that." Preist turned to Amasar with a sorrowful expression. "Do you know where the kidnappers took the chief's daughter?"

The nomad nodded. "According to the advanced scouts, they left the Wasteland and according to the scouts the humans live in a ramshackle community known as Sunnyville."

"I have heard of this town through word-of-mouth. It's a place travelers try to avoid. The inhabitants don't like uninvited visitors much. But that's about all I know," said Quasar.

"Are you certain this is where she was taken?" the scientist asked.

The nomad nodded. "The princess has the ability to telepathically communicate, and even if she doesn't speak to her father or other members of our tribe, her echoing voice is like a beacon; it directs our people towards the town. Before you ask, because I know you will; no, our people don't tend to travel outside of the Wasteland except for roaming scouts and if something draws our attention." The nomad turned to Clover. "You have a respectable reputation throughout the Wasteland, assassin. You defend those that are in need and have been battling the Outlaws for who knows how long. You tend to travel alone, and a small party of individuals would be ideal to rescue her, instead of a vast invasion of nomads."

Clover and his merry band of comrades huddled together. The assassin understood a few of their party would protest his desires, but since he was the one leading them, it would be his ultimate decision. One member of their travel party would want to help the nomads—Preist. The scientist always had a soft heart and always looked to aiding those in need.

"Well, comrades. What does everyone think?" asked Preist.

Clover didn't hesitate one bit. "We don't have time to wander off on a side quest," Clover said. "I don't know about the rest of you, but I have a mission in Metro City to complete."

"You can't surely allow the whatever is going on, including the princess's kidnapping, to manipulate these people. It could eventually affect what the outlaws are doing in the Wasteland. It could benefit us all," Preist returned.

"I would be distraught if my . . ." Doria hesitated. ". . . children had been taken in such a manner. I vote to go after her and aid these people. They did aid us."

"I have an idea, but it requires us to split up," Quasar said.

"No, absolutely not, Quasar!" Preist snapped. "That's what this manipulator wants us to do. We will be easier pickings that way."

Clover stood there, letting his comrades yell at one another. "I still won't waver in my decision. The rest of you can do what you like."

"Let me go alone," Quasar said. "I have my staff and I can sense if anything approaches from a mile away. I can hunt down and uncover the location where the princess is being held, and maybe I will recruit Tigerous to aid me in any rescue attempt, if it presents itself. She has always provided quality support in any endeavours where we have both been involved."

It was agreed that Quasar would move back towards the west, across the Western Plains of the Wasteland in search of the location of Princess Onaughon, while Clover, Preist and Doria made their way towards Metro City. Amasar gestured in the direction Clover should go, that they should continue their journey eastwards. The nomads knew the terrain of the Wastelands better than anyone else, since it was the place they called home. The traveling companions finished their thanks to the nomads, and began the last leg of their journey.

Chapter 15

Deep within The Merciless Reach

Inside the decrepit bastion, secluded underneath the fleshy floor, the most reliable of the Darkness's agents, the Shadow Lord, levitated over the dark ground. The Shadow Lord was in tune with everything associated with the shadows in multitude of realms. The agent of the Darkness also had spies everywhere, and the one focused in the Western Wastelands was setting off alarms in its master. The Shadow Lord sensed the spy crying to its master, a cry no mortal could ever hope to hear.

The agent of shadow stopped in the middle of a spacious, unoccupied room, as if something was in the agent's path. The room was dark and empty of any furniture, not that the Darkness's home possessed any outside of its dark throne. Slowly, a ripple appeared to distort the air, as if the Shadow Lord had ordered a door to another dimension to open. Instead of becoming a tear in space-time, the ripples began to spread in a circular shape, like a pond had appeared before the Shadow Lord. Soon, the ripple effect consumed a space twice as large and just as tall as the agent of shadow.

Its translucent rope moved as the Shadow Lord raised its equally transparent hand. The pool of dark ripples was replaced with a scene, the Wasteland was encased within shadows as the purple sun fell beneath the sandy horizon. The only way to tell the spy was there on the other side of the communication mirror was the creature's blinking eyes. Like most agents of shadow, it had the ability to hide in the shadows and be next to invisible, unless direct sunlight was to shine at—what mortals would call—its two-dimensional existence.

The Shadow waited, but the spy was either reluctant to, or was too subordinate to, speak before being spoken to first. The Shadow Lord was quickly losing patience with the spy. Without moving its lips, because the Shadow Lord had none, the agent of shadow demanded a report. "Well, spy? What is so important that you had me rush to accept your call?"

The minuscule spy flickered in the Wasteland shadows as if balking, but finally spoke. "M-m . . . Master."

"I'm waiting."

"Yes, Master. I have been keeping an eye on the Rustlers like you told me and all I could discover from them was a bunch of moving around. Packing and unpacking their main camp more times than I cared to count."

The Shadow Lord crossed its transparent arms. "This is what you urgently contacted me for?" The Shadow Lord's voice was deep with agitation.

There was a flicker of light as the spy nearly vanished from the communication mirror pool. Then the shadow spy reappeared, as it had left to retrieve something that would help prove his case. The spy bowed and gave its report. It had a raspy voice, almost a collection of buzzes and clicks that only the Shadow Lord could understand.

"Master, I am sorry for the delay, but as I have said, I have learned nothing from the human outlaws, all they do is move from section to section of this place they call the Wasteland."

The Shadow Lord decided to be a little more patient, because the agent of shadow sensed something big was about to be exposed. It felt the pulse that humans would call anxiety from the two-dimensional spy. "What about those called the Rustler elders? Are those devious mutants up to any mischief?"

Inside the head of the Shadow Lord, the spy said, "I was getting to that, Master. After searching for quite a while, I discovered where these elders were residing. There isolation was baffling at first but then after spying on the elders for a while I learned why they had hidden themselves away."

The Shadow Lord sighed which sounded more like a shriek than anything else. "I assume you will be getting to your report soon?"

"Yes," returned the spy. "They are working with a half cyborg named Nikolai Volkov, whom Darkcloak rescued from the protégé Nightshade."

The Shadow Lord growled a deep predatory sound. "That traitor."

"Master, in coordination with the cyborg, the elders are creating a mutant army to invade and wipe out the humans, or at least that's what I took from the elders' conversations with the cyborg."

"Wipe out? That would give Darkcloak the advantage, and I can't allow the rogue shadow agent to gain the upper hand on me." The Shadow Lord looked at the spy's image flickering in the mirror. "How large a force are they building?"

"It's hard to define, Master. I know they have old cargo containers spread throughout the vastness of the Wasteland. It's difficult to determine since those containers are moved constantly."

"We need to get the word out to someone to stop them, but who?" Then it dawned on the Shadow Lord, even though the idea didn't necessarily appeal, it was the only option he had. "Return to your spying, I have something in the works that might counter the elders' plot."

┼

Nightshade stared down at the corpses of the three human invaders to Metro City, his personal playground. *They should have never invaded my stomping grounds*, thought the bioengineered assassin. But something other than the three outlaw thugs was bothering Nightshade. Was he going to join forces with Clover and his twin's comrades as he had promised? He had also promised to kill his twin, but that was more or less an empty threat, wasn't it? There was tension in the air and Nightshade understood something dramatic and big was about to go down, but none of them knew what. He understood that Clover had thought it had something to do with the human child Clover and his mates had saved a while back, but that could be Clover trying to rationalize wiping out the rest of the outlaws. It wasn't all that inconceivable since both Nightshade and his twin were bioengineered assassins, no matter how much Clover tried to refute his design.

Something was eating at Nightshade about the unsettling sensation he and his twin were getting. Whatever it was that was about to happen, he knew they would be caught in its maelstrom. Nightshade didn't like confronting something he couldn't be prepared for. A sensation began, one that he had had a few times near the beginning of his prowling of the dystopian Earth. One he cared not to be having but couldn't ignore.

Nightshade pushed back his sleeve and a tattooed symbol with four linked circles with a dark flame in the middle appeared on the assassin's forearm. Nightshade took a deep breath and exhaled. He motioned his free hand mere inches over the tattoo and the dark hologram of the Shadow Lord appeared. The assassin glared down at the agent of shadow with a sense of foreboding. The assassin didn't have the patience or the time to deal with the Shadow Lord at this time, but he allowed the intrusion anyway.

"Nightshade, my favorite renegade."

"Shadow Lord, I can't say it's a pleasure to hear from you. What is the meaning of this intrusion, may I ask?" Nightshade said.

There was a brief moment of silence, and Nightshade was sure the agent had done this on purpose. In fact, he was sure the Shadow Lord had done it to make him impatient. "Yes, well I have some unfortunate news to convey, and a suggestion as well."

Nightshade made a face that mirrored a wilted prune. "You have some advice for me? That's a new one."

"Don't seem shocked, Nightshade, remember we have been trying to gain control of you for a while without success."

"Yes, Shadow Lord, I do remember. My ignoring the Darkness's beck 'n' call was deliberate, or didn't you understand that?"

The Shadow Lord growled low. "I have something to tell you, Nightshade. It might be a little unbelievable, but I need you to be open to the information."

Okay, thought Nightshade. *Now you have gone crazy if you think I have any inclination to believe anything you tell me.* "What is it? I don't have all day."

A sinister chuckle came from the hologram. "You are aware of Clover's steadfast hunt for what the Outland Rustler elders have been scheming the past three years?"

Nightshade nodded.

"What if you were told that they have been secretly been building a mutant army and plan on unleashing it on the remaining humans? The time is fast approaching, and this attack will wipe all remaining humanoids off the face of the planet for good."

Nightshade couldn't believe what the agent of shadow had just told him, mainly because it was the Darkness's most reliable agent, and no agent of shadow could ever truly be trusted. The assassin shook his head. "I don't believe you. You and your master have tried to deceive everything that follows you, why would this be so different?"

"I was afraid of that and have come prepared to convince you. But, before I do, I will tell you that the human annihilation, even though our master—"

"*Your* master," snapped back Nightshade.

The Shadow Lord didn't change its tone. "Our master would love to see the humans wiped out, but Darkcloak has worked beyond the master's grasp for too long and . . ."

Nightshade stared down at the image of the agent and a sly smile appeared on his gray-skinned face. "I get it now. I knew you had your own angle to this, Shadow Lord. You don't want the elders and Darkcloak to succeed, because it would make you look bad."

Silence filled the air and when Nightshade had enough, he spoke. "I'm still not convinced, and what does this have to do with me?"

"I'll give you proof. If you are convinced after I show you what proof I have, then it is hoped you will recruit your assassin brother to intercept this crazed army."

"If," returned Nightshade.

On a bloody battlefield under darkness.

Through the holograph, a vision came to Nightshade, and he experienced an annihilation on a bloodied field of carnage. A physically twisted mutant roared out as it ripped another human head from its perch in one clean swipe of its deadly claws. Blood shot from the headless corpse as it fell to the blood-soaked ground. The Rustler elder mutants, the ones that had been created at the Sierra Complex, ran all over the desolated field of battle.

It wasn't a one-sided battle. Mutants sank their blood-thirsty teeth into a new victim, making the human cry out before their lifeblood drained from their doomed bodies. It didn't take any of the elder-manipulated mutants long to drain their victims, evident by the corpses littering the ground.

Then the earth split open and began to swallow everything within throwing range. The decrepit ground, the dead corpses and even the gray mutants were devoured by the hungry earth. That's when a cyborg and five Outland Rustler elders appeared on a hilltop. Nightshade could see the crooked smile of the half man, half machine as they observed the devastation. Nightshade could hear demented laughter and he thought it was the cyborg that was laughing at the chaotic scene.

Nightshade clenched his jaw and one fist. He might not have the sympathy for humans that Clover did, but he surely didn't want to see the machine man win the day. If nothing else, Nightshade's ego couldn't concede to Darkcloak's lackey. *We can't let them win, not in this fashion*, thought the assassin. Nightshade snapped out of the hologram's hypnotic trance and his face began to furrow with anger.

"Fine!" snapped Nightshade. "I'll convey your message, but remember this is the *only* time I will comply with a request from the shadows."

Nightshade cut off the transmission before the Shadow Lord could reply, and he took in a deep breath. The hard work would be to convince Clover to listen to any of this, because it was Nightshade giving him the news.

✝

Clover, the ginger wolf, Preist and Doria made their way eastward towards Metro City. I-70 was nearly covered in sand, earth and debris. The difference between walking through the Wasteland and this part of the new continental USA was the number of structural carcasses left behind. Anyone who had lived in the world before it ended would have a flash of déjà vu from the world that had died.

The travelers were consistently dodging burned-out husks of family sedans, eighteen-wheelers and the occasional emergency response vehicles that seemed to be fleeing the wickedness of the colossal storm of fire breathing its cataclysmic radiation onto the land. The highway was cracked in many places and large sinkholes made for more obstacles on their journey.

The wolf moved from one husked vehicle structure to the other, sniffing the charred metal skeletons and quickly turning away. Clover thought the wolf didn't like what she was smelling in each obstacle. *Most likely she smells death imprinted on each one*, the assassin thought.

"Diffident to the end, weren't they?" questioned Doria. "Did they really expect to outrun the holocaust in a vehicle?"

"That is embedded into the human DNA, hope. It's humanity's biggest strength and the one thing that ended their society," Preist said.

They passed the gutted eighteen-wheeler, sitting at an angle like a Prometheus child had tossed the transport vehicle out of its way. No rubber was left of any of its tires on the dual-axle, and only three of the skeletal frames of its trailer still existed, through they barely hung on. When Preist peered into the cab, nothing was left except the massive gear-shift lever. The rest of the interior was gone and there was no sign of the driver's body anywhere. The truck was merely a shell of what it had been.

The same couldn't be said for a family sedan sitting in the middle of what he thought was two interstate lanes, but it was difficult to tell because a portion of the asphalt had been stripped away and sections of the rebar construction were exposed underneath. The car had heat-blast marks covering three-quarters of the vehicle with only the original tan color showing on the last quarter. Half of the metal structure had melted, with the doors and lower frame melting into the broken-up and scorched asphalt. All the vehicle's windows had blown out and wind whipped through the openings creating a hollow noise.

There was a skeleton figure sitting behind the wheel, with its head infused into the half missing steering column. None of the driver's clothing survived.

Doria walked to the half-melted door and stared at the long-deceased skeleton as if she had never seen such horrors in her life. Her eyes had widened, and her body was beginning to shake. It wasn't the first corpse they had come across that appeared to be mummified, instead of completely being vaporized by the nuclear blast. Ninety percent of the interior was gone, only leaving melted springs and the occasional thread of leather stuck to the seat.

There were three other deceased skeletal shapes, all in the same shape as the driver. An entire family that had perished together. One was a small infant tightly wrapped in its mother's arms.

"They must have all died harshly," Quasar said.

"I think they all died poorly, in the end," added Preist. "Let's go before our guide takes off without us."

Clover had stopped at a crater-sized fissure that engulfed the entire freeway and some of the surrounding landscape. It was at least fifty feet to the other side. Not an unreachable distance, but one that would take some maneuvering with the current company included. Preist gestured to the new obstacle. "What do we do know?"

"This doesn't change anything," Clover responded. "We were always going to venture off the road, this only forces us to do it now instead of a couple of miles up the road."

Preist looked out over the desolated landscape. The scientist could see the skyline of Metro City and the monoliths that were once the signature of the city. The sun was now dipping low towards the crest of the horizon, showing the fractured, skeletal remains of the skyscrapers. No longer a thing of beauty, the hollow titans were breathtaking, but in a bad way. The rest of the city was concealed under a blanket of shadow and once the sun went down, the urban graveyard became dangerous.

"Not the sight I expected to witness," mumbled Preist. "The entire landscape acts like a ghost town. The sins of mankind held frozen in time."

"Do you still think humanity is worth fighting for?" Clover glanced over, but never smiled, nor frowned. He was a stoic as ever. "We were never going through the front door. Too many things watching for idiots to arrive. The safer way is through the west side of the city and walk into the corporate district. But I must warn you, Preist. No matter the path we take, it's more likely we will run into a roadblock from something nastier than we have faced, to this point."

Preist shook his head. "Why am I not surprised. It seems like you bring out the worst in everything these days, Clover. You attract bad vibes everywhere you go."

The four travelers began to move off the devastated highway and onto the hardened terrain and made their way to the entombed city. The sun had dipped far enough below the horizon by then that the sunlight reflecting off the bare structures gave the city a purple halo. Clover didn't allow the travelers to travel in a straight line, fearful they would become easy prey to any number of predators lurking close by.

They passed numerous skulls of many types and sizes. Some were baking under the intense sun which had bleached or yellowed the damaged skulls. There were several that had been partially buried under the contaminated surface. The traveling comrades wondered how each victim had perished. Lack of food or water? By death of attack, or something more sinister at work?

Clover stopped them, sniffing the air as if he had gotten wind of something close by. The assassin frowned as if he had just smelled something rotten, and maybe in his own way he had. "We're not alone. He is here, and close."

The assassin only growled and so did his wolf companion. "Come out from your hiding rock, Nightshade."

Clapping suddenly came out of nowhere and a cloaked figure emerged from thin air like a chameleon. "Well, look what the cat dragged in! It took you long enough after my contact. Seeing a lost flame one more time, brother?"

Once uncloaked, Nightshade and Clover stood side by side. Outside of some minor details, it was difficult to tell the two apart. Such things like the weapons each assassin possessed, and that Nightshade was dressed from head to toe in black while Clover wasn't. Clover possessed red nocturnal eyes and Nightshade's was a pair of coal black, each one an abyss. Apart from those minor details, the two assassins were spitting images of one another.

"We made a detour to the Sierra Nevada Complex," Preist said.

Nightshade turned towards the scientist with an unpleasant and disdainful look. "Why in the hell would you go there? It's nothing but catacombs these days." Nightshade turned back towards Clover. "You do have a death wish, don't you? Remember you can't die before we finish our game."

"We went to the complex as a favor for a friend. His sister and her family went missing . . ." Preist's speech trailed off, the scientist too emotional to finish.

Nightshade snickered. "Let me guess. You thought you owed this . . . friend, as you put it. But if your friend's family had family inside the complex, they would be as dead as the rest of the fools that had ventured there. It's a death trap, and now it's the Outland Rustlers' secret laboratory of horrors."

"Now we know," barked Clover. "Thanks for the heads-up, too bad it's a little too late."

"You should've asked me, brother. I could have told you not to go in the first place."

Preist had a concerned look on his face, but one that also expressed his perplexed emotions. Had Nightshade been there at the Sierra Nevada Complex while they were there? Or had the assassin ventured there long before the comrades had arrived? The scientist couldn't get the idea out of his head.

"What could you say that would detour us from the promise we had made?" Preist asked angrily.

Nightshade could only shrug. "If you were that determined to go to your demise, then probably nothing. But I could have warned you what you might run into."

"Like the crazed things living in those tubes? Like the fifteen-foot-tall creature that nearly had us for dinner, if it wasn't for Quasar?" Preist boomed.

"Among other things. Your side trip has cost us valuable time. This issue involves us all and should have been a priority. I thought I had made that clear from the start. The Oracle has been losing patience awaiting your arrival."

Nightshade said, "It's time for us to go. The sunlight is fading, and the Oracle waits impatiently for our arrival."

Doria looked at Preist with a nervous look. "I think I'll wait for you on the outskirts. I can be your eyes, looking out for any unwanted intruders coming into the city."

Nightshade looked back with a smile. "What's wrong, scared of the big city after dusk?"

"The city, from my understanding, isn't very hospitable to humans, from rumors," returned Doria.

Nightshade looked back with a smile. "What's wrong, scared of the big city after dusk?"

"The city, from my understanding isn't very hospitable to humans, from rumors." Returned Doria.

Nightshade laughed at that.

"You have heard right, my little friend." Nightshade looked at Clover, but the assassin was indifferent. "You might be wise to remember," Nightshade said, "that and I am the worst of those nightmares." He gave a sardonic smile to no one in particular.

The three figures made their way through the quiet and shadow-filled city block. To Preist it seemed more like walking into a tomb full of ravaging, hungry, undead creatures, eager to pounce on the living and rip the flesh from their bodies. A less-than-appealing thought. Preist thought he saw movement in the shadowed, empty floors of the looming monoliths of steel that towered over the destroyed streets below, as they made their way up to the Oracle's residence. Nothing came out of the shadows at them or announced their presence beyond what Preist saw. *Could they act as tombs themselves for those who had died during the nuclear holocaust?*

The building on the left side of the street stood erect, with missing windows, walls and some were even bare.

The colossal monoliths reflected sunlight as they approached the city. Cars lay in the street, some melted to the asphalt, others were missing doors, panes of glass, while others were completely gutted. There weren't nearly as many shells of cars on the streets as one would expect. Maybe many the people living in the city had gotten out before the bombs dropped. But Preist didn't think so.

The other side of the street seemed like a flattened field of debris, as if a wrecking crew had demolished the entire side of the street and a bulldozer had pushed the remaining debris somewhere else. The contrast between the two sides of the street seemed like night and day, but the scientist still had no clue what could have done such a thing with so little left behind.

Silhouettes would occasionally appear in upper levels where walls had fallen to expose the interior of the building. These dark figures seemed to stare right at the scientist and then vanish back into the depths of the structure. Preist even caught glimpses of campfires on lower levels, but never at ground level, as if people were living near the surface, but were too afraid to live on ground level. He wondered why.

It was becoming an obsession for Preist, as if he were a child seeing things in his closet or under his bed at night. Suddenly, a scraping of leather on concrete echoed, followed by an eerie laughter. That nearly sent Preist over the edge. He looked to his left and then to his right. The scientist wasn't sure which direction the crazed laughter had come from, and he wasn't sure if he really cared, but it still didn't calm his nerves. He took in a deep breath and discovered his heart was racing a mile a minute. None of his anxiety was aiding him in uncovering who was stalking them.

Nightshade looked back at Preist and smiled. "Reevers," barked the assassin.

Preist snapped out of his anxious state. "Do what?"

"The shadowy figures you're seeing are called Reevers. They are outcasts who act as spies for a ruthless gang called the Phantom Brotherhood."

Clover stared at his twin with intense concentration. "The Phantom Brotherhood, are they dangerous? Something for us to worry about?"

Nightshade giggled. "Scared, brother?" Nightshade said, scrutinizing his twin. "We have nothing to worry about. They're just curious about the newcomers. We have an agreement. The Phantom Brotherhood stays in their territory, which is the innermost part of the city, we stay near its outermost sections."

"What if the Phantom Brotherhood breaks the agreement and ventures into your area?" questioned Clover.

"That's unlikely. Once the Oracle and his followers—"

"Wait. Did you say followers?" Preist asked.

Nightshade nodded. "Like I was saying, once we settled in the city, the Phantom Brotherhood made a move to control this section of town, but with the aid of myself and the essence of the Oracle, we easily defeated the gang and an agreement was settled on."

"And how did this Oracle defeat this gang? It is clear you were outnumbered," Clover said.

Nightshade nodded again. "Your presumptions would be correct, brother." Nightshade motioned to a portion of the street where no buildings, gutted cars and some of the asphalt was missing. It was like an A-bomb had been unleashed, but neither Clover nor Preist could tell if it was the act of nuclear weapons or something more supernatural. "Look around, all this used to be like the rest of the street that stretches for over a mile and a half. Now, as you can plainly see, it's completely leveled."

"And you are telling us this oracle did all of this?"

Nightshade gave Preist a dreadful stare, but with Clover beside him, Preist knew the assassin wouldn't strike him.

"Watch your tongue, scientist," Nightshade growled. "It's the Oracle, you need to show him more respect than that."

Nightshade looked at Clover before he continued more calmly. "Yes. The Oracle has far-reaching cognizance the rest of us don't possesses. It was out of necessity that he displayed his godlike power to the invaders."

The rest was left unsaid, and they continued onwards.

†

Once they arrived at the building where they were to meet the Oracle, Preist looked up; to him it seemed the skyscraper was the tallest in the city. Unfortunately, the scientist couldn't tell since they were directly under the mountainous structure, like a titan guarding the city from this exact location. If Preist's estimation was correct, the structure had to be over two hundred stories tall. Much like the rest of the structures on this block, and the rest of the city, no windows were left untouched. The scientist thought he might have glanced a few broken shards in a windowpane on several levels, but after ten or so floors, his view became blurred and all he could do was envision the rest.

Once they walked into the building's spacious lobby, which could house a small fleet of fishing vessels, Preist began to understand the enormity of the vacant structure. Concrete and dirt debris filled the lobby floor, and there were missing floor tiles that made the lobby flooring seem like a scrabble board. Ceiling tiles were either missing or dangling from their corner slots. The lobby walls were coated in blast stains, and holes, both large and small, seemed to litter the lobby's interior.

Looking up, the ceiling above where the reception or security desk might have been, was an emblem engraved into what was left of the lobby ceiling. A gaping hole seemed to consume three quarters of the lobby ceiling, showcasing the missing emblem. The rest of the emblem, that which remained, was a small planet placed in the forefront with the gaping hole in the shadow, looking like a dark and menacing void slowly beginning to eclipse the planet. The lettering Co . . . tion with the rest consumed by the hole.

"The damn Corporation," mumbled Preist. "This must be its corporate headquarters. From my understanding, it's the tallest building in the city."

"The Oracle is on the fiftieth floor, so we might want to start to make our way up the flight of stairs."

"Why the fiftieth?" questioned Clover.

"There are too many things that roam the night to live on the bottom floor, and beyond the one hundred and seventieth, the winds are too strong. The fiftieth gives him a perfect bird's-eye-view of the city."

The companions began to scale the steep railing steps. It was buried under a ton of debris and Clover, Nightshade, and Preist had to maneuver the obstacle course of concrete and plaster. Doria decided to go to the outskirts of Meto City, she claimed it might be safer for her there and her shaking allowed her to hide the truth of what was coming. Preist was sure there was railing once, but between the elements and the nuclear blasts, the railing must had fallen off and turned into dust. The three figures' boot falls echoed throughout the gargantuan empty structure, giving Preist the chills. The air quality didn't seem to get any better the farther up they journeyed.

The place had a dusty and burnt scent. Preist could only imagine how the scent had been when the building was new. The scientist drew in a breath of stale air that seemed to feel dirty and contaminated. Not like venturing through the Wasteland, which had its own contaminated sensation. This had a confined, concrete-dust feel, like the concrete particles were filling up his bronchi inside his lungs. Unlike some of his kin, Preist was much more like humans genetically. Preist's lungs began to burn, forcing the scientist to stop occasionally to catch his breath.

Since the sun had dipped below the horizon, making their way through the stairway full of debris was becoming harder for Preist. Clover and Nightshade and even the ginger wolf to an extent, had nocturnal vision, and he was quite sure they weren't having the same issues as he was. Clover could feel the ginger wolf's hesitation, but he also understood their deep connection and knew she would follow him to the ends of the planet. Several times the scientist nearly stumbled over some sort of debris that concealed themselves in the darkening shadows.

They finally arrived on the fiftieth floor. It looked like every level they had passed, a cool breeze blew, but more profoundly than the lower levels. Shadows crept all around and with the sun just about dipping below the horizon, the level seemed to be as dark as an unlit cavern. The only way Preist could tell something was on this level was by silhouettes. Even Nightshade, Clover and the ginger wolf appeared to the scientist in silhouette form.

A figure in the far eastern corner of the floor caught Preist's attention.

The figure was enormous, compared to its visitors, at least three to four times their own size. Heck, it most definitely would have made Legion appear like a child. The silhouetted figure seemed to be sitting on a throne of concrete or stone. Most likely it would be concrete, because there was no sign of stones or rocks within the city limits.

The three visitors moved towards the seated behemoth in a slow and subtle manner. The gargantuan figure didn't bother to move, it was like it was a massive statue sitting in the dark shadows. The only way Preist knew the figure was alive was by the reflective properties of its eyes. As they got close the steady in-and-out movement of the sitting figure's chest eased Preist's nerves. That's when the Oracle looked up with his silver orb eyes. It was like seeing yourself through a silver vase. This was more like a clear reflective surface.

Nightshade stopped and whispered to Clover, Remember, the Oracle has had several failed attempts on his life, so he stays in the darkness a lot." That's when Nightshade turned towards the Oracle and announced, "Gentlemen," started Nightshade. The assassin looked down at the ginger wolf and smiled. "May I introduce his greatness, the Oracle."

The Oracle waved off the introduction, as if it embarrassed the humongous figure. The Oracle leaned forward so that his visitors could see him in a more defined light. The Oracle possessed a warm and inviting smile; its shoulders were broad and great muscles rippled beneath the top shirt and robe the being worn. It was difficult to decipher the rest of the Oracle's physical presence, outside of being quite enormous. The Oracle scrutinized his visitors with interest, but without the ability to see beyond those frozen sliver orbs, Preist couldn't begin to tell what the Oracle thought of them.

The ginger wolf moved slowly to the Oracle's concrete throne and sniffed at the figure with caution. The Oracle reached down and began to lightly stroke the wolf's matted coat, only Clover and Nightshade saw this because of their nightvision eyesight. Preist exhaled and everyone was much calmer.

"The infamous Clover in the flesh. My have I anticipated this for a while. I must say, your reputation precedes you."

Preist thought he heard Clover chuckle under his breath. Not noticeable by anyone else in their party and if Nightshade had heard it, the dark assassin hadn't shown any emotion towards Clover.

"Some rep, it's more like a legend or a myth. But humans do have a way with words and imagination," retorted the assassin.

"Don't be so modest. Clover has earned his rep. No matter how mythical it might be," Nightshade said.

The Oracle looked from Clover to Preist and back again. "I can only imagine what you're thinking. Why have I brought you all this way—am I correct?"

"It had crossed my mind," Clover said, impassively.

"Well, I owe you both that much, don't I?"

"There is a war brewing," interjected Nightshade. "One that has been shielding its true nature from us for a while."

"How does that involve me?" Clover asked.

"It involves as all, Clover," the Oracle said.

Preist took a step forward. "May I ask the players in this conflict?"

"There are many moving parts," the Oracle continued. "But there is a hidden agenda underneath it. One driven by an unseen master, until now. The Corporation's CEO Nikolai Volkov has returned, and he has a plan, we fear it is to end all life—not just humans but our kind as well."

"He's the one I thought I had assassinated, but I guess the dead do rise from the grave after all," Nightshade said.

"He's here and plotting against . . . everyone?" Preist questioned. "You have seen this?"

The Oracle nodded.

"You're a seer, then?" Preist stretched his neck, because it had become stiff from standing in the same position too long and coughed.

The Oracle sat on the edge of his throne, allowing the visitors to see what light was present to reflect off his silver orbs. "I'm clairvoyant, I don't see everything that happens. It comes in bits and pieces. But I have seen Nikolai's face as clear as day. He is half cyborg and half man. He is discussing plans of a deviant nature, but I can't see those plans. I do see a great battle with many dead on both sides. I don't see whom he is conspiring with, but I do see Outland Rustler bodies lying on the Wasteland ground, and I feel it in my aging bones that he has something up his sleeve."

"How many men do they have? How many do we have?" questioned Clover.

Suddenly a scraping noise echoed and the three visitors, including the ginger wolf, turned to the stairwell. A shadow appeared to walk towards them, followed by a cautious Reever messenger. He slowly approached and Clover could sense the messenger's hesitation. The messenger stopped and slowly removed a message from his satchel and handed it to Nightshade. The assassin gave the messenger an unsettling glance before the messenger departed.

Nightshade opened the parchment and handed it to the Oracle. The omniscient being read the message and a crooked smile appeared on the Oracle's face. "It is settled. We have enough to take on the CEO's army."

"The Phantom Brotherhood?" Preist said. "How did . . ." The question became stuck in the scientist's throat.

"The Oracle can be quite persuasive when he has to be," boasted Nightshade.

The Oracle grunted. "It's nothing. I just explained it to the human leaders that it was their fight as much as it was ours. If they didn't respond to this threat, we weren't the only ones that would vanish. They also have a duty to their people if they are to survive."

"People?" Preist questioned.

The Oracle nodded once again.

"How do you think they continue to grow their ranks?" asked Nightshade. "So few humans are left and few human refugees tend to gravitate towards gangs like them or Outland Rustlers. They propagate among themselves. Why do you think they use young boys as spies?"

"So they weren't spying on us as we walked down the street, where they?"

"No," Nightshade responded. "I wanted them to see I had brought you to see the Oracle. It was the one thing the Brotherhood required in our agreement. I took you through the heart of the street to show you off. Otherwise we could have come another way, one less obvious. There are things that come out at night that hunt and I'm not referring to assassins, either."

"In that case, I should go check on our human companion." Preist began to make his way down the stairwell.

"I will meet with you in a bit," returned Clover. "We still have some fine details to iron out. The assassin looked down at his ginger wolf companion. "Go see he doesn't run into anything troublesome."

Chapter 16

The sun had nearly disappeared behind the horizon and dusk was taking control. Preist had to maneuver around all the obstacles in his way as he made his way down the street and towards the outskirts of town. The shadows had become more pronounced, and the scientist swore he heard things crying out like signals in the dark warning other predators of his presence. *Nightshade did say no one lived on the bottom floors because of what roamed the city at night, didn't he?*

Preist broke from the city limits and began to rush towards the location they had left Doria. She was nowhere in sight and that made Preist's heart sink. The darkness approaching was making it difficult to see, he could only see anything no more than ten feet from him. Preist searched all around to make sure his charge hadn't ducked behind anything, but there wasn't anything to hide behind, unless the human had made her way back to the highway and that was over a mile and a half away, but Preist doubted that.

Preist heard giggling, a somewhat sinister laugh, like someone was about to do something quite malicious; the sound sent chills up his spine. The scientist looked around, but still, there was no one. *Then who made the giggling sound just a minute ago?* he wondered. He took a deep breath; something bad was about to happen, he could feel it, and he was standing out in the open, most likely with a target on his back.

Doria emerged from out of thin air, clapping in a sarcastic manner. "Are you looking for me?"

Preist spun around to see the human and his breath was sucked from his lungs. Five Outland Rustler commandos accompanied her. All five wore tattered and beaten gear. Their patrolling fatigues showed signs of wear, and a few of the commandos had small cuts throughout their bodies and holes in their commando uniforms that were poorly patched, allowing the harsh environment in. All the men had weather-stained faces, with sand and dirt outlining where their respirators normally sat. A few of the men didn't even possess respirators, and the ones that did had respirators that were broken and dangled from their sides.

One commando carried a rusted rifle, though Preist doubted they had ammo for it. Ammunition was scarce and rarely did the Rustlers possess enough of it to give it to straggling patrols such as this one. But that wasn't the only weapon the Rustler commandos possessed. Preist saw one carrying a machete strapped to his back, while two of them had survival knives. The leader removed his knife and Preist noticed its sharp, serrated blade. The leader made sure Preist saw the knife quite well, holding it a distance from the commando's chest and out in a threatening gesture.

Doria possessed a sorrowful frown, as if she was sorry she had brought what was about to happen down on the scientist's head. A scowl appeared on Preist's face, his gray color beginning to recover.

"What the hell is the meaning of this? How do you become in the company of these scum?"

The lead commando stepped forward. "We have been tracking your little traveling party's movements since you departed the Sierra Nevada Complex. The woman didn't know it, but her mishap with one of the mutants allowed us to keep an eye on your motley crew. I must admit, the assassin can set a horrid pace to track and he's good at hiding his trail. But we found you, and it's time to end his and your existence."

Preist began to back up, now fearing for his life. The Rustlers were backing Preist towards the main city entrance and there was no escape. *I wish Clover and Nightshade were with me now*, he thought.

The Rustler leader began to laugh. In between laughing fits, he said, "What's wrong, are you afraid?"

Preist gave the Rustler a forlorn look which spoke to his displeasure of the Rustler's appearance. A scowl appeared on Preist's face, and his forehead moved down towards his eyeline, making his face appear to have shrunk a great deal. "Let's see if we can pretty up that face of yours. I bet it would make a vast improvement." He smacked a fist into an open palm, making a smacking sound.

The leader stopped approaching Preist, a scowl appearing on the man's face. The other commandos began to laugh, distracting them from moving towards Preist. Their laughter was loud and obnoxious, but Preist thought, *Whatever works that allows me to flee, I'm for it.* He continued to back away from the Rustler commandos.

The leader turned to his commandos. "Shut up! Just shut the fuck up, wont you?"

Preist backed into the front of the rusted and melted vehicle. He bounced back, as if the rusty, metal heap had bitten him. He now had nowhere to flee to. Preist was a rat caught in an alley corner. If the Rustlers hadn't come at him, cutting off the path towards I-70, then the scientist could have made a run for it, but Preist seriously doubted if he would have made it anyways. The Rustlers, lead by the commando leader, holding that threating knife out towards him, approached. The five commandos and the hybrid human were less than ten feet from him, when Doria let out a scream. Preist sensed something standing far above him in the shadow of the city.

Something moved past the scientist, something that flickered and then suddenly vanished. Preist looked up and towering over him was the stripped-down Corporation building and what the scientist thought he saw something, from Preist's perspective, he didn't have Clover's night-vision eyes and whatever it was, it was like a blotch spot on a piece of paper—he couldn't make out any details and was unsure if it was someone on its metal roof or his own imagination.

Clover stood on top of the former Corporation Head-quarters building, letting the gust of wind strike him. The assassin drew strength from the wind whirling all around him. Clover glared down, unable to make out the tiny fig-ures surrounding Preist. The assassin could sense Preist's hysteria and quickly understood his comrade's dire pre-dicament. Even from his perch, Clover could hear the sci-entist's elevated heart rate as the Rustler thugs surrounded the scientist. Clover could see the residue of radiation left behind by the purple sun, despite dawn's continued transformation from dusk into night. It was something the assassin had gotten used to over the multitude of seasons. He was just as comfortable in the darkness of night as he was in his own skin.

The assassin knew he would have to act swiftly if he was going to rescue his friend. Clover closed his eyes, allowing the wind to whip all around his body. Clover felt as if he was part of the environment, then, without thinking on what he was about to do, Clover leaped off the Corporation's HQ building like a diver performing a difficult dive, and propelled his body towards the ground.

Clover's body speared towards the devastated earth at a rapid rate, aided by the surrounding wind current. Clover felt wind whip past his head, making a whistling sound. His body didn't tumble, but performed something that resembled a swan dive, keeping the assassin's body in the right position to land upright when the fall ended.

Clover landed on a demolished vehicle and the assassin's landing sent small shards of burned metal flying. Clover had positioned one leg slightly in front of the other, but he was still squarely on the vehicle. The assassin squatted on the roof of the SUV, facing the five outlaws. He slowly opened his eyes, letting the outlaws all see the pair of red, nocturnal eyes staring vindictively at them. Clover let out a low-sounding growl. At the same time, those outlaws that had dropped their weapons, slowly without taking their eyes off the assassin retrieved those weapons.

"You, assassin," barked the commando leader. "I want a piece of you, but before—"

The outlaw didn't get a chance to finish.

Nightshade had used Clover's explosive entrance as a smokescreen. The invisible assassin had prepared his weapons to strike, targeted a lone Rustler, and made his move.

Meanwhile, Clover, utilizing his lightning-quick reflexes, removed his aerial weapon and threw it at a commando. The weapon soared through the air only making a slight whirling sound. Before the Outland Rustler commando could respond, the quad-blade weapon sliced the outlaw's head from his shoulders and his body fell to the ground. At the same time, a razor-sharp blade rammed into the back of another commando, though no one saw where the weapon had come from, or the assassin who owned it.

Clover retrieved his throwing weapon and came upon a third commando wielding a field knife. The commando had a fearful look sitting on his contorted, dirty face, as if the outlaw wanted to drop his weapon and run. But that would take away Clover's fun, so the assassin, resorting to his base instincts as a predator, used his bloodied aerial weapon to slice the hand that possessed the serrated field knife clean off. The commando was still looking at his hand, shocked, as Clover sliced a katana through the outlaw's chest. The blade swept up, and on its downward pass, with great precision, Clover sliced the outlaw's head free from the man's body.

Clover stared at the corpse a little too long, enjoying the sight of human blood staining the contaminated ground. Once the assassin looked up, he noticed Nightshade wiping his weapon's blade on a dead commando and the ginger wolf tugging at the final outlaw's pant leg. Nightshade, with one of his customary, sinister smiles, replaced his weapon it its sheath. "Nothing better to quench the ground's thirst than by spilling a little blood."

Clover saw Preist approaching cautiously, preventing himself from stepping on a puddle of blood or any of the carnage left behind. "Serves them right. A little vengeance for all the evil they most likely have done." Clover cleaned his katana blade and replaced it in its sheath, then began wiping the two sides of his aerial weapon that had tasted human blood.

"Their corpses will feed the things that come out at night," Nightshade said.

Clover attempted to suppress a smirk but failed miserably. "I thought we were the things that came out at night?"

Nightshade let out a nefarious laugh.

Preist, Clover and Nightshade walked over to the only commando left alive. The shaking human was cringing away from the ginger wolf, who was staying watch over her prisoner. Would the assassins kill him, just as they had his comrades, or would he survive to tell the Outland Rustler leadership about their epic failure? Either way, the commando was good and dead, and both assassins, Clover especially, knew it. They could leave the outlaw commando out here in the open and if the city horrors didn't get to him, a Rustler hit squad team eventually would. The Rustler Elders didn't take kindly to failure, the assassin had seen from a distance a hit squad's ability to kill their own, almost as if they were engineered assassins.

The wide-eyed commando looked from Nightshade to Clover, but the three companions gave the outlaw some space, not wanting to smother the human to death. The commando wasn't any older than an adolescent, not quite an adult, but that wasn't all that shocking to the assassin. Clover had encountered more than his share of Rustler commando units, and more than half were no more than children.

"What do you want with me?" screamed the commando in nervous bursts.

Preist squatted down at eye level, looking to the commando. Clover noticed Preist's calm and nurturing nature, but the scientist had always been that way, no matter the species. "What were your mission objectives?"

The commando looked between the assassins and the bioengineered scientist. He began to stutter, like the commando didn't know what to tell his captors and what not to tell them. Clover could tell the commando would lie to them, at best deceive them with half-truths. "I, I . . ." The young commando swallowed, and it seemed to inflict pain on the human.

"Take it easy, no one will harm you if you aid us and tell us everything you know."

"We were ordered to . . ." The commando looked directly at Clover, and he began to cry. The young commando said, between crying fits, "Detain you."

"Detain us? You mean you weren't ordered to kill us?" questioned Preist. He gave Clover a confused look.

The human shook his head. "Commander Beckett understood we could never kill the assassin, let alone threatened him. He wanted us to impede your travels. It was Serge's idea to kill you, hope to get lucky to get away before the assassin resurfaced from his visit to the city."

"A farce," proclaimed Clover.

The group looked at the shaking human woman who had resurfaced after the blood bath. Both Preist and Clover understood she didn't know she had been marked and had been a liability the entire time she was with them. Clover wanted to do something, but looking at Preist's sorrowful eyes, he quietly agreed she was not at fault. That still wouldn't absolve her from her own guilt.

Preist gently placed a hand on Doria's shoulder and moved her shirt sleeve up to expose the mutant bite mark, just above her bicep. The bite had the appearance that the flesh just underneath the infected skin. It had a grayish, tinted; not the pinkish, fleshy color it should be.

Remembering back to their visit inside the Sierra Nevada Complex and Clover and his encounter with the mutant that tried to end his life. Doria's damaged flesh and the mutant's skin tone nearly matched in color and how they seemed decayed somehow.

Nightshade removed his own throwing weapon and placed it in the general area of the human's ruined skin "What is the Rustler council up to?" barked the assassin. It was clear to Preist that Nightshade didn't care if Doria had meant to betray them or not; the dark shadow assassin wanted answers.

"When did you receive this wound?" Asked Preist.

Doria shook her head in sorrowful dejection. "I don't know!" she said. "All I know is that a voice in my head told me to tag along in silence and allow the commando unit to track you. I never meant for anyone to get hurt or for the Rustlers to threaten anyone. Do I look like an outlaw to you?"

"I have the impression the outlaw brass has something they didn't want us to see," responded Nightshade.

"Oh no," Preist responded with vexation in his voice.

Clover glanced at the scientist "What is it, Preist?"

"Straus and the human settlers. We left him and his family exposed."

Clover's forehead scrunched together, like trying to ring out a sponge full of soap. "Tigerous and Zeus are watching over them."

"Ha!" Responded Nightshade. "You left them in the care of a reckless feline and a former Legion soldier? Ya, they are perfectly safe." Nightshade gave Clover a sarcastic smile, one that the chameleon assassin would use in a card game, when he was about to call a bluff. But Clover didn't think any of this was a bluff. It was more like a nightmare.

Preist turned to Clover. "Tigerous does tend to go off on her own."

"We need to do something! Straus and the humans are in danger," proclaimed Preist.

"I will do anything to redeem my actions," Doria said.

"I think I have an idea," Clover said and looked at Nightshade. Both brothers seemed to be thinking the same thing.

The three companions began to head west to rescue the humans in danger.

✝

After a lengthy conversation following Clover saving them from the Rustler thugs, it had been decided that Doria, through the Oracle's connections to the human inner-city gangs would rouse support for their cause, rescuing the humans and being ready for whatever the Rustler Elders had in store. She didn't understand why she had agreed to this. Maybe Doria meant to honor her deceased family and friends by convincing these gangs to aid them.

Something was bothering her, a lingering fear eating away at Doria's soul. Why had the Phantom Brotherhood accepted her request for an audience with them? The only thing that came to mind was the connection between the Oracle and these band of scavengers and cutthroats. Yes, she was sure that's what they were, at least towards any rival gang. Her two Reever escorts maneuvered them down street corners and through deserted alleyways that were once was the heart of downtown Metro City. Doria hadn't seen the city at its greatest, and she could only imagine what the atmosphere was like before the world ended. She glimpsed small campfires inside of gutted building structures. The gang members not on patrol or posted on a watch detail used the fires to keep warm, since the city was cold at night. Plaster, concrete and at times entire wall structures blocked their path through the alleyways they took, but that didn't deter her escorts. They just found a way around the obstacles.

They made their way into a wide opening that seemed to stretch a good quarter of a mile. Doria had never seen such an arrangement inside a community, but then again, she had never traveled to any other major city before. The Sierra Complex had been the largest place she had ever seen or lived in. Gang member children played around the outskirts of the open space, while adult members worked on weapons and gear and others fixed tents, clothing and cooked large meals in fire pits.

Doria and her escorts moved past the scene and directly to a short, three-story building that still had three-quarters of its walls attached. Two guards halted them, and the escorts explained the situation, but Doria didn't hear anything that was said. Everything seemed to be a blur as she looked back to the open square they had just passed through. She wasn't confident they would be allowed to pass through by the way one of the checkpoint guards had an ugly snarl planted on his face. He was continuously looking back to her as if Doria's very presence was unwelcome and insulting.

The human female could still feel the presence of Darkcloak within her, still could hear the shadow agent's sinister voice taunting her and knew that her unintentional betrayal of her comrades needed atonement.

The escorts halted at the building entrance with a pair of guards talking to Doria's escorts. The guards, who were heavily armed, more armed than Doria's escorts who had small arms always at the ready position, while the guards possessed assault rifles and spiked bats for what had to be close armed combat. She could only see the four men talking and couldn't hear anything said. Doria had to assume they were discussing her sudden appearance, and her escort's, and were justifying letting her pass.

One of the heavily armed guards looked back at her with a look of disapproval; one that made the man appear like he could tear her to shreds in a moment's notice. Doria's heart quickened, faster than it had even as they passed through the deep shadows of the gutted city. His stare didn't take long, and the guard returned his attention back to the two gang escorts. The four men's conversation seemed to continue for what seemed an eternity but was less than five minutes.

They were finally let through, and Doria and her two escorts passed into the three-story building. Rubble, broken shelves and cracked floor tiles littered the spacious room. Candles had been lit and several Brotherhood members occupied the space. Some came and others left, but the one thing that did catch her eye was a corner of the room where no less than five gang members huddled; Doria couldn't tell what they were doing.

One of the escorts walked over and said something to the second escort. Now she was paying full attention. She felt that this is where she was to present what she was here to present. Would what she was about to tell the gang leader affect her as well? Would this get her escorts disciplined from their unit superiors? No, Doria knew there was no turning back, even if she walked out of this building and headed east without divulging what she was here to propose.

Once the five or so gang members parted like the red sea, a middle-aged man, not overly thin but surely not as nourished as he could be, sat on a chair. It was plush and the arms of the chair wide and fluffy. Doria couldn't see the back of the throne-shaped chair, but if the creaking gave any indication, the chair was old and worn. The chair the figure sat on was discolored, a charcoal color that had long lost its original tint.

The man himself wore tattered clothing, not as poorly as some of the other gang members gathering in the room, but it still appeared the figure hadn't changed his clothes in a while. He wore a flannel jacket, most likely to keep warm at night, while a tattered and holey tee was worn underneath. The figure's pants were in similar disarray, stained a dark brown, and his boots had a hole in one sole. Not quite the appearance Doria expected from the leader of such a powerful gang.

The Reever escort motioned for Doria to approach, and she did. The leader had a scar leading from one cheekbone to the back of his neck. The gang leader gave his visitor a stern, unwavering stare, one that didn't tell her whether the gang leader was happy or disappointed to meet her. Doria took a few brave steps closer, even if her instincts were foreboding. The gang leader leaned forward, as if to get a better look at her in the dim candlelight. The Reever escort halted Doria with the guide's weapon.

"Grand Marshal Malahki," barked the other escort.

The Phantom Brotherhood leader sat there staring at her with his stone-cold stare. But then a smirk emerged from the surface of the intimidating man's face. "So, you are the survivor from the death complex, are you?"

Doria didn't know how he knew and then remembered the Oracle's abilities and nodded in a nervous, unsure way. She was starting off giving the gang leader a timid impression.

"Not the brightest of the bunch, are you? I mean, come on, who would dare venture into the depths of the city alone? Rumor has it that the person that could survive in such a mausoleum must possess majestic powers?"

A small amount of laughter surfaced from the gang members in audience.

"I . . . don't know much about that, sir," stuttered Doria.

She looked around the room at all the sets of eyes staring at her. Her nerves began to accelerate and her breathing elevated. Doria took in a deep breath and slowly exhaled. This seemed to calm her nerves, at least for now.

"Have you brought me what you promised?" asked Grand Marshal Malahki.

"I have." Returned Doria. "Rumor has it, the Rustlers are gathering their forces in droves."

"All their forces?" asked a gang member standing next to the grand marshal.

"Yes. Even in the far corners of the Wasteland. As you suggested, Grand Marshal, the Rustler leadership is gear-ing up for something big. A momentous war." She handed the data disk Clover had provided.

"Hum," returned Malahki. "Sounds like the Oracle was right when he sent his lackey to propose an alliance with us."

"There is movement I wasn't able to gather intel on. They are moving large crates, possibly the largest the outlaws have ever moved before," returned Doria.

"What of their complex up north, what is its name?" said the same gang member who had spoken up earlier.

Grand Master Malahki sat back in his cloth chair and looked at Doria, giving her chills down her spine. He looked like he was undressing her before his entire gang, and she didn't like the feeling.

"I'm having quite the dilemma trusting what you have told me, or better yet not mistrusting the intel you have provided, but what's the reasoning behind why you're doing this? I'm not apt to throwing my soldiers into the fire pit without knowing what's on the other side of the fire." He tapped his finger against a metal object, making her squirm.

Doria said, "I have seen some disturbing evidence firsthand, mostly pointing towards these elders, whomever they are. I have seen firsthand or through a reliable network that the elder's actions directly place all that live in their path at risk, living at the complex proved to me what they are capable of. I don't have proof, but what I have been told is the elders are conspiring with an unknown entity, one that could bring the destruction to everything that is left in this world."

The grand marshal nodded. "We have heard that rumor as well. In fact, we have word, from a most reliable source that that is absolutely true. It's the reason we have joined forces with others in the city. A war is definitely on the horizon, little messenger. It is good that you have come to us with this intel. You have done the right thing."

One of the gang members whispered into Malahki's ear. The grand marshal nodded, and the gang member ran off. "We generously accept your intel and offer sanctuary for your cooporation. Benny will show you acceptable accommodations."

"Not to feel ungrateful, Grand Marshal, I have others to warn, because I promised them I wouldn't abandon them in time of need."

"Very well, Benny will show you a way out of the city that may expedite your travels. Good luck."

Chapter 17

D oria and her two escorts take an alternative route towards the city limits. She was told it was a swifter way, and the messenger would be pointed in the direction she desired to go, towards the east. The way they took wound down a nearly deserted street filled with debris, trash and an occasional burning vehicle blocking their path. Smoke billowing from the steadily burning vehicle created a smoglike haze in the air and Doria's lungs began to fill up with the contaminated air.

The lone survivor of the Sierra Nevada Complex began to have a coughing fit, followed by an eerie feeling. Her eyes began to water and made seeing where they were going was next to impossible, so she stayed close to the escort closest to her and followed diligently. Doria thought about asking her guide, but they seemed a little too preoccupied to bother with her anxieties.

A noise reverberated down an alleyway that led to the adjacent street; the escorts stopped dead in their tracks. That's when Doria began to feel a foreboding sensation, as if her entire body was numb and that was a sure sign of death looming. The noise echoed a second time, but Doria wasn't sure what had made the sound. She was almost certain it was something none of them wanted to encounter and noticed the escorts picking up the pace which confirmed her fears. The sound echoed a third time, and it was clear to Doria that it came from something humongous. *Must be one of those things they warned me about. The reason the gang leaves flames of light on around their community along the paths they take.*

A scream followed the roar and both escorts began to run, leaving her to fall farther behind. The closest escort yelled something towards the leader, but the escort only waved the other off. The leader rounded a corner, and standing before them was a massive lizard, something that looked like a Komodo dragon. It stood fifteen feet tall with an enormous swinging tale and an elongated forked tongue splitting the air as it protruded in and out of the colossal creature's maw.

That's when Doria understood the sensation and understood she would most likely die before the end of her journey. *It had to all end sometime, right?* She asked herself.

The enormous thing didn't give the lead escort time to react. Just as the gang member motioned to his partner to run, the lizard creature lunged out and swallowed the man whole. The Komodo dragon lookalike leaned its tank-sized head back and Doria could see a lump sliding down the monster's throat, knowing it was the escort's body being devoured. The sound of bones crunching vibrated through the thick and tough skin of the super reptile.

Doria moved alongside the other escort, away from the feeding monster, still in shock from what had happened. She couldn't take her eyes off the feeding creature that seemed to be enjoying its feast. The beast only stared at them as they fled, as if to say, "I'll be seeing you real soon."

Much to Doria's dismay, the extra commotion had invited the beast's mate to the party. The remaining escort was too busy backtracking to the burning vehicle, retrieving some fire to ward off any other uninvited guests. But Doria saw the mountainous shadow moving at the other end of the street. They were trapped like rats in a cage. The roar of the female beast echoed down the street before the enormous Komodo dragon emerged in view. First its gold-emerald reptilian eyes appeared around the street corner, and Doria realized the enormous size of the creature. The reptile's head was as large as the burning SUV, and it possessed hundreds of razor-sharp teeth in its massive mouth.

Doria observed the reptile take in a deep breath through its nostrils and exhaled, nearly knocking the lone escort over. It was like a small sandstorm coming over the horizon. The Reever escort attempted to reach the burning SUV and Doria realized what the escort was up to, but she was just a step too late. The escort ran for the burning vehicle and the movement drew the female creature's attention. She flashed her rows of teeth and hissed at the fleeing Reever. Then the creature moved in a burst of steps toward her next meal.

The street shook like an earthquake was striking Metro City, and Doria watched as the beast gained on the Reever with each giant step it took. Doria was frozen, unable to flee down the now open street the reptile had just abandoned. Doria felt as if she were the one pursued by the hungry Komodo. Her heartbeat quickened, and her breathing became elevated as if she was climbing a great peak. Her throat became parched and both palms had filled with sweat. Still, nothing could deter Doria from watching the horrible act playing out before her.

The bus-sized beast ripped by a collection of vehicles in its path. One compact car was crushed under the lizard's massive weight and in one motion was kicked out from under the beast's rear legs and into a stripped-down building. A transport van flew in the opposite direction as the Komodo slammed its vast tail into the vehicle, swiping it down the street, as if she was playing a child's game. Doria heard the van crash into the front of the adjacent storefront.

The farther both figures moved down the darkened street, the harder it was to see the action. But Doria could hear the beast's venomous hissing and snapping at the Reever. She could only see the two figures' silhouettes, though she still heard the intense struggle between the reptile and its dinner from the screams and crashing sounds. Doria, sucking up her courage, moved to a better position where she saw the continued struggling between Reever and beast. The Reever reached the blazing vehicle, only to have the tank-sized reptile snap at him. The lone escort pulled back his hand and Doria wasn't sure if the female beast had gotten a piece of him or not.

The echo of the hungry reptile growling at the Reever hung in the air and a sense of death loomed suddenly in the city. The Reever made a move to dodge the reptile's snapping and the beast caught the Reever by his fatigues. The giant lizard lifted the helpless human in the air and shook its dinner. Doria heard the Reever yell out to the beast, despite its inability to understand the escort. "Let me go, you filthy beast!" The female reptile shook the Reever again.

The Reever pulled out something from his fatigue's rear pocket and tossed it at his captor. A small explosion occurred at that moment, one that didn't inflict major damage to the large lizard, but it did startle the beast and it dropped its meal. The female Komodo dragon roared its frustration and Doria felt the earth shake and heard the metal skeleton of the building she was in front of rattle.

The female leaned back to strike the Reever down. But the Reever was a step ahead of the beast and recovered in time to roll out of its bite. Doria witnessed the Reever maneuver himself away from the underneath of the mountain-sized lizard. The escort removed the last weapon he possessed, a field dagger, and threw it at the beast, but it only bounced off the creature's tough and ridged reptilian skin.

The female creature took one step to the defenseless Reever and nearly swallowed the human whole. The Reever was waist-high into the female's mouth and Doria could see the reptilian's throat ripple as its thorax attempted to swallow the escort. Doria snapped out of his intense anxiety and made a move to try and save the Reever, but she was a second too late. Through the smoke of the beached and burning SUV, the male reptile emerged, pushing the SUV out of its way and moved on the feeding female.

The male Komodo dragon lookalike snapped at the female's mid-section as if to tell its mate to share the meal. The female creature stopped trying to swallow the human and looked at her mate. The reflection of fire from the burning SUV reflected off the male's tough hide. The female stared down her mate, leaving half of the Reever exposed. The male lunged at the morsel, snagging the other half with speed Doria never anticipated the beast to possess. The male and female ripped the Reever in half, sending human blood scattering everywhere. The red blood oozed down both reptile's maws.

Without realizing it, Doria let out a loud scream.

Both creatures stopped chewing their food and looked directly at Doria's silhouette. She was now in danger. "Oh shit!" she said. "I'm in for a world of hurt now."

Doria, with her numb limbs and anxiety running through her veins, began to bolt towards the direction the female reptile had vacated, hoping no other reptilian creatures were in the area. Her legs were pumping hard and her arms swinging in tune with each boot fall. The *thump, thump, thump* echoed down the deserted street but at this point she didn't care. Adrenaline rushed through Doria's bloodstream, giving her just that little extra energy in her flight. Finally, she had to stop, nearly out of breath.

She took in several deep breaths of the stale air. There was less smoke in the air, the farther away from the burning vehicles she got. But Doria also understood that that meant she had a better chance of becoming lost. The fire acted like a deterrent towards anything roaming the streets at night. But she thought of the reptilians she was now fleeing from and wondered, *If the burning vehicles act as a deterrent, then why did the enormous reptile couple come after us?*

That thought seemed to fog Doria's mind, even after several noises seemed to emerge from the darkened vacant street. A loud bang sounded no more than twenty-five feet from her location, but after Doria tried to investigate by walking in the general direction the noise had come from, she found nothing. In the darkness, that wasn't all that surprising. Doria wondered where the feasting reptiles had gone. Had they eaten their fill and returned to whatever location they had emerged from? Or were the creatures toying with her and waiting until she reemerged to make a run for it?

The street had become still and quiet—a very eerie quiet. It wasn't like the street was busy with life, but it seemed that the distant noises had hushed and that sent chills up Doria's spine. This type of quiet in the Wasteland was natural, even though Doria didn't have much experience in the heart of the Wasteland, but her brother Straus did. It was something Doria wasn't sure she could live with, but in the busy nighttime of Metro City, that was something that set off warnings: It was time to run. Doria set off, away from the direction she had been facing. Her arms pumped hard and she lifted her tired legs as much as she could.

A roar penetrated the nighttime air and Doria knew both reptiles were coming for her. She headed farther down the darkened street not wanting to see the gargantuan creatures with salivating mouths racing after her. She felt the rumble of the broken pavement as the mountainous beasts pursued. Neither creature needed to see her. She only anticipated their heightened sense of smell, the reason the giant reptiles had found them in the first place. They were the type of creatures that hunted by smell and the fleeing woman was sure she smelled like a top sirloin hanging over a fire pit.

The sound of something giant huffed not too far from her and Doria could hear the two behemoths fighting over position as they chased her down the dark street. The pavement shook quite steadily, and she nearly fell over during her sprint. It wasn't too long now before the hungry reptiles would catch her. Doria didn't think about the pain she would feel when that happened. The only regret was not seeing friends again, but her family and those under her charge were all deceased anyways, except for her brother.

A premonition came of the colossal lizards taking turns tearing her flesh and insides apart, feasting on her corpse. Life just didn't seem fair.

Something tugged at her mind and without slowing down, Doria dove down an alleyway. She didn't relent her fleeing pace, but something inside told her to look back after about twenty paces. All Doria could see was the silhouette forms of both reptilian creatures. Their heads appeared in the alley entrance and the naked frame of the building to her right shook as both massive bodies collided with the structure.

The building frame began to bend as both gargantuan heads pushed on the metal structure. It was like the pair of lizards were trapped by an invisible web. The more the two reptiles pushed on the metal obstacle, the more entangled they became. Doria couldn't take her eyes off the two struggling behemoths. Just like when the female was chasing down the Reever, Doria seemed to be stuck in a time loop. But instead of being frozen in place, her body was still in full motion, heading down the dark alley.

Doria nearly stumbled over debris lying in her path several times, but that didn't stop her from fleeing. The shadowy figure moved with stealth and purpose, stalking Doria through the internal framework of the adjacent building, then leaping into the next structure. Normally bricks, plaster, wiring and other internal material that made up the building would have impeded the night stalker, but this was Metro City in its post-apocalyptic state and large creatures had become customary residents in the semi-humanless metropolis.

The shadow creature began to become entangled in the metal jigsaw puzzle that was the towering building frame. It blew through the rusted metal framework of the building. The creature's attack forces Doria to collide with the hard pavement, scraping her back, shoulders and arms.

When Doria came to, she noticed the massive thing that had been stalking her on top of her chest. A powerful set of paws held her down with superior force, making it difficult to breathe, let alone move. Doria felt the flesh-tearing claws penetrating through her torn clothes, but not enough to puncture the flesh. The creature that had her pinned down hadn't decided to devour her just yet. She had no delusions about it; this beast meant to have her for dinner. Just like the two reptiles that had tried, which still struggled down the end of the alley.

Doria felt a rough and large tongue running over her body, but she couldn't decide if the beast was licking her wounds or tasting her exposed flesh. Her adversary was too fuzzy to tell what it looked like underneath. The creature was still encased in the shadows of the night. The only other thing Doria could tell was those enormous golden-hue nocturnal eyes that unnerved her, but they weren't giving Doria much attention at the moment. The shadow creature seemed too intent on licking its prey's wounds.

What should she do in her current predicament? She needed to act and quickly. Her anticipated end was creeping up and if this was going to be how her life ended, she wanted to give this nemesis all it could handle, but by the feel of the predator it might not amount to much at all. Doria attempted to move her right arm, but the paws of the predator had it pinned down at her shoulders and wouldn't budge an inch. So, she tried her left, with the same result. Doria took a deep breath and pushed up with all her might, lifting herself up a few inches off the ground.

The beast leaned back and in between shadows Doria saw the creature's enormous maw. It had a heart-shaped mouth, a fierce-looking muzzle, one that made her think it could take half of her body in one bite. The look on her adversary was one of shock and anger, if a creature like it could ever have human expressions. It possessed elongated whiskers, longer than she had ever seen before. She had seen something similar in a zoology book she extracted from a devastated building once in Somona as a young girl. What did her mother call it? *Yes, a library,* she thought, but she wasn't quite sure. Doria looked deep into the big cat's eyes. It looked like one of those from the zoology book's pages. Doria could barely read the book, it had a language that she had never seen before.

Despite the inability to comprehend the Zoology textbook she remembered the many classifications of the big cats by photographs that seemed to litter the pages of the aged and weather-beaten book.

The huge cat had a purplish-black coat and powerful paws that seemed they could rip a man to shreds. *Was it a tiger? No,* she thought. *That isn't it at all.* What about a lion? No, the predator seemed to have a different disposition than a lion, but either species had similar likenesses. Then it dawned on her the black fur coat, the enlarged whisker length, the paws that seemed to be able to ascend any type of structure. Doria's adversary was an oversized panther!

Doria involuntarily gasped at the revelation and suddenly jerked upwards. That drew a deep growl from the panther. She knew she was in trouble and didn't know what to do; she was trapped under the cat's strength and weight. Doria raised her left arm to defend herself from any retaliation. That action alone caused the enormous cat to strike.

The black panther swallowed a portion of Doria's arm.

Doria let out an ear-shattering scream that shook her to her core. Without thinking about what she was doing, Doria lunged at the muzzle of the beast and struck it square, forcing the large panther to jerk its head back in shock. A numbing sensation, one that felt as if her swallowed arm had turned to dead flesh and poison seeped from her veins. The big cat seemed to stop chewing on her flesh. Doria was no longer pinned down. Without thinking, she removed her arm from the beast's mouth and ran for her life. She didn't know in what direction she was heading, so long as it was away from the thing that had tormented her. Doria ran through alleyways, over trash heaps and burning debris.

Once the fleeing woman felt she was free of the panther's deathly reach, she slowed down and stopped in the middle of an adjacent street from one of the giant reptiles that had pursued her. A puddle of blood was at her feet, but she still had the upper portion of her arm, though it was extremely mauled. Doria followed the carnage up to where her arm was still attached, despite the mutilation of her arm. The arm's flesh was now a dull gray color and that brought back images of the mutant creature that attacked her in the Sierra Nevada Complex. No pain had surfaced, and even now she didn't feel any, just the numbness of her arm. *What did you do to me, you mutant abomination?*

The panther appeared through an alley entrance, staring at her with hungry eyes. *At least a portion of its jaw couldn't be used now*, she thought. Doria froze, not knowing where else to run to. She was out in the open and exposed but felt as if she was trapped in a no-exit alley. The big cat shook off some disonitation, as the creature took a step backwards and shook its head, it temporarly wasn't able to attack her. A feeling rushed over her, as if this was all some crazy dream, as if the huge panther was too surreal and nothing but a nightmare. This whole place, the scenario Doria found herself in, everything. She would awake up at the Sierra Complex with her family close by, safe. But all she had to do was look down at her mautlated arm to know it was all real. But in the back of Doria's mind, she knew that to be a lie. That part of her life had passed into history.

The panther moved out of the darkness and towards a burning vehicle, turned over on its roof. The orangish-yellow illumination lit up half of the big cat's face, while half its body was still consumed by the darkness. It appeared more as an anomaly than something real. The panther leaped out into the middle of the street. Doria would have never seen its swift approach if it wasn't for the burning vehicle lying in the middle of the street. Doria could feel the motion of the pavement below her feet, but it all seemed like a distant disturbance with her numbness. She was a still target.

Doria anticipated the killing strike, not afraid to die; now wishing for death instead of fleeing from it. She had no more desire to run. Doria had seen more than her share of death to last her several lifetimes and her own didn't seem nearly as scary. The beast moved in slow motion, taking one giant step at a time towards its victim. Doria watched the panther's muzzle open, with the beast still over twenty feet from its prey and saw the orangish-yellow illumination flicker off a gray tooth inside the creature.

Doria took a deep breath, preparing for her final moments in life. That's when an adolescent reptile, most likely the child of the two that had devoured the two Reever escorts, plowed into the panther, forcing the big cat to cry out in pain. The big cat's adversary used the crown of its head to push the cat from Doria. At first her heart beat faster than it had when the adolescent's parents had feasted on the Reevers, she was still mesmerized by the two titans combating.

Even though she was no longer able to see the two creatures fight one another, Doria could still see their silhouettes entangled. The panther had contorted its body enough so it could claw and bite the adolescent's large head. Cries of pain and vicious calls emerged from the darkness. Doria could only imagine the big cat gnawing at the reptile's scaled forehead, with green blood dripping from a wound. The ramming reptile slammed the contorted cat into a naked building front and the big cat let out a roar; the force was so immense it shook the entire block, and with her still standing stiff, the force nearly knocking Doria to the pavement.

Doria snapped out of her dazed and confused state. She decided it was as good a time to flee. She ran off towards the eastern part of town, in the opposite direction to what she had originally planned to go, but at this juncture any place away from the battling beasts was better than just standing in the same place.

Doria ran as fast as she could, but it didn't take her long before she reached a low plain of concrete, asphalt and twisted metal. It was like several meteorites had struck down onto the eastern portion of the city, creating deepened crevices. It appeared that several somethings had struck throughout the several blocks of the commercial and residential districts of the once proud city. The momentum seemed to have made the buildings, already in dismal shape, collapse under the force of the fallen objects and bury the culprits under heavy amounts of debris.

Doria weaved her way in and out of the minefield of craters. She thought this might be where the creatures that roamed the city at night made their homes, since none of them seemed to appear during daylight. A few times Doria had to leap over a crater or two, nearly falling in one when she lost her footing on a broken piece of asphalt. Once Doria saved herself from falling into the massive crater, she scrambled back and watched broken shards of asphalt descend into the darkness.

This entire night had been one gigantic horrorfest and Doria's body was wearing down from fatigue. She wiped her face off and removed the canteen that had been given to her by the Reever escorts before exiting the gang camp. She was astonished she still had possession of it. After taking down a few swallows of refreshing water, a heart-stopping scream came out of the darkness. It sounded like its owner was quite large and very close to her position. The prospect didn't thrill Doria. She got to one knee and a set of massive red eyes appeared before her, but she couldn't tell how far away the owner of the eyes were.

Neither the heart-stopping scream nor the eerie set of eyes made her feel safe. Doria replaced her canteen and began to run in the general direction she had been before stopping. The problem was she was still watching the red eyes staring back at her and not watching where she was heading. Before Doria was aware of it, she nearly slipped into a second crater. This time a piece of rebar jabbed into her shin. Doria began to hobble, and she could feel the blood streaming from her wound, but the wounded woman didn't have time to stop and tend to it. Even if she could have seen to nurse her injury; she had no way of cleaning it or wrapping the wound.

Doria hobbled a little way and the crazed scream that had scared her earlier into running as fast as she could have echoed again. Doria looked back in the direction of the sound, and where she had seen those red eyes, saw nothing. She began to hobble even more, the wound slowing her down as she imagined the shattered leg bone rubbing like flint to a match. Then a sound echoed she hadn't ever heard before. It sounded no more than ten feet behind her, nearly giving her a heart attack. She turned towards the eerie sound, which seemed more like sadistic laughter than a cackle or a scream. Doria's attention was drawn a second longer than it should have been, and the wounded woman fell into an open crevasse and tumbled head over heel, not sure which direction she was headed.

Doria stopped, and a searing pain shot from her chest. Blood began to gush from a chest wound, making her look at the steel beam protruding through her chest cavity. Doria's mouth became dry and parched; she had the urge to reach for her canteen to quench the thirst, but her remaining arm wouldn't move, she had lost all feeling in her body except the excruciating pain in her chest. Doria looked up to the nighttime sky in wonderment as the sky filled with tiny little specks of light. Stars coming on to light the night sky.

She attempted to laugh, but the beam protruding through her made that impossible. It was ironic, if only the stars hadn't been shielded by the smoke covering the city from the burning cars, she might have seen the crater. But, fortunately for her, the burning cars kept the creatures at bay. The light show above was a warm and settling sight as she slowly drifted into oblivion.

One by one the lights began to fade as Doria drifted into a permanent sleep. The last thing the wounded woman thought of was all those that she had known, her family, those under her protection, even her younger brother Straus. She would miss them all. But a sensation came to her before the lights dimmed from her life. The gray mutant, the one from her dreams; the one that she seemed to have a strong connection to, the image of its face suddenly appeared to her. It snarled at her and a broken voice said, "You will rise again as something else." Doria focused on a bright star in the sky that had caught her attention, as she lost consciousness. His vison blackened, and Doria died still impaled on the steel beam.

Chapter 18

Quasar had made the long trip to Sunnyville and at the township's outskirts he still hadn't encountered anyone, which seemed odd to him. He removed the amulet the nomads had offered him from beneath the mantle he wore. They must have thought it would guide him to the nomad princess's whereabouts and it had brought him here. Whenever Quasar went on long voyages, he was never going to take chances with the people he met, and he kept his distance. Usually, humans would never know he was even there, Quasar was that elusive. Only enhanced individuals could sense the power within him and these days he didn't run into very many of those either. Quasar never knew what individuals might think of him, being an outsider and his seething energy residing within. Most humans would consider him a weapon either to murder them or utilize for their own diabolical whims. "A ticking time bomb," Quasar used to call himself.

There was no use in taking chances. Quasar flipped the hood attached to his mantle to become incognito, to blend in. He had done this before, before making his home in the mountains. Quasar had even blended into human society just as he was about to do in Sunnyville, until Legion had forced his army of followers to eradicate what was left of human society. The former Corporation weapon moved towards the interior of the town with the grace of a ballet dancer.

The township was in shambles, Quasar realized, but like most of the former human settlements like Sunnyville and Sonoma; the war had broken every foundation, forced the remaining buildings to settle in the sandy surface and he had noticed several buildings beginning to collapse in on themselves. The humans that lived in these shells of a distant past weren't intelligent enough to reconstruct, repair or demolish and then rebuild the crumbling buildings.

As Quasar made his way towards the interior of the township, he began to glance at the silent skeletal structures; some though still possessed some sort of exterior, but most had blast marks painting their outsides; all that told the history of Sunnyville's past. Broken concrete debris occasionally lay scattered in the sandy walkway. Some of the houses and the tiny shops seemed to be carcasses with shingles dangling from their rusty hinges; paint long stripped from their exteriors, missing gutters and even large holes in the roofs. Quasar sensed that some of these buildings lay unoccupied, while others he had the feeling were crowded with families, most likely gathered in the structures' dark basements.

He pulled out the nomad amulet, exposing just enough of it to get a read on the princess's whereabouts. He felt a pulse in the trinket. It was leading him through the heart of the township to the western portion. As Quasar got closer to the center of town, the streets began to fill with towns-people. Some glanced at the visitor, while others were too immersed in their daily routines to bother. That was all fine by him, the least amount of attention the better.

Soon Quasar came across what seemed to be a main square with a demolished fountain; only its base remained. *This must have been the central gathering spot for the town, when it was a thriving community*, he thought. Quasar sank his head deeper into the mantle's hood, try-ing to hide his identity. That only seemed to draw a few strange looks. Was his attire that different, was his overly tall physique creating some suspicion?

All he could do was keep moving on and hope for the best.

Once Quasar made it past the center of town, traffic began to thin and once again not many of the townsfolk roamed about. It was almost like humans were forbidden on this side of town. Out of his peripheral vision, four stout men began to follow Quasar. *I must have drawn more attention than I was hoping for.* The four men didn't seem to be armed, but he understood that didn't mean they weren't. With the men's demeanor and the pace, they had set tailing him, Quasar received the impression these men were either sentries ordered to follow him or some form of authority. That didn't surprise the stranger, knowing humans as he did.

"Nikolai Volkov must have this town under lock and key. It's surprising I haven't encountered more security. But what does he have that keeps these people in obedient or fearful of him?"

Quasar ducked behind a mound of sand and debris to conceal himself and waited, despite his large frame. It didn't take long for the hoodlums to reach his location. In fact, the four of them stopped right in front of his hiding location. Quasar crouched even more trying to do a better job hiding. He gripped the amulet tight in his hand, attempting to stave off any anxiety that might surface. He could feel the blood in his body racing despite his heart rate being steady and his being in control of his emotions.

He overheard a few of the thugs speaking about him.

"Where in the hell did that hooded freak disappear to?" asked one of Quasar's pursuers.

"He is somewhere around here. He couldn't have vanished into thin air, now could he?" said another.

"You are assuming that the freak is human. Maybe he is one of those Corporation freaks," barked the first.

"Quiet, both of you," ordered the leader. "Search every building on this block. Every nook and cranny, if you must. Master Nikolai will have our hides if we don't find him and fast."

Now I do need to see what is really happening here. But first I must complete this mission, I gave my word I would rescue the princess. Then I will find Tigerous and maybe she will aid me in uncovering what really is going on in this town.

Quasar waited until the thugs began searching building to building and exposing a sliver of an opening for him to slip by them. With a burst of energy, Quasar dashed down an adjacent alley. In his wake, his hasty departure left a cloud of dust that drew one of the thug's attention because he heard the thug screaming for his comrades. Four sets of footsteps began from behind. The thugs were in pursuit, and Quasar was sure that more would join in not too long after.

He continued his flight from the humans, when he noticed the crumbling alleyway was getting narrow and he could see a dead end—not that it would stop Quasar. It was a question of how he would continue. He could blast a hole right through the building's rear wall, but would the building collapse on itself, blocking his escape or, worse yet, killing anyone residing within the building?

No, Quasar decided that would be a horrific chain of events and still wouldn't get him any closer to his mission goals. He would discover a way to distract his pursuers, then run out of the alley. He halted and searched for a solution to his dilemma. There on one side was a pile of concrete, sand and other debris. *Perfect*, he thought.

Quasar removed his staff from his mantle, making the Corporation weapon look like some aged wizard from a fantasy novel and waited for the thugs to come into sight. It didn't take the humans long to appear, with two close by and the others not far behind. Quasar aimed his staff at the pile, hoping the display might react like a firework display. Then he let the energy loose. The pulse energy beam rushed from Quasar's staff's head and ignited the pile. The explosion rocked the alley and sent the debris, or what was left after the pulse energy ignited much of the pile into dust, towards his pursuers.

The two closest thugs had to duck to avoid the enflamed debris, but that didn't protect them from the rushing cloud of dust. The two men slowed their pursuit and covered their faces. Quasar took that opportunity to flee. Even though the first two thugs were less than fifteen feet from him, he rushed by without incident, leaving the thugs coughing and blinded. He hadn't had to kill anyone, but how long would Quasar's luck last?

The thick cloud of dust blanketed the alley and even Quasar wasn't immune to its blinding effects. He was going to have to hope he was fleeing in the right direction. As his flight took him away from the thugs, he thought about how he would find the nomad princess. Where was she? What was her condition, and would she need medical attention? Was the former corporate CEO performing tests on her? Was that the reason behind her abduction? That's when Quasar remembered the nomad amulet and he reached into his pocket and removed the item.

He emerged from the alley as the dust cloud dissipated. Quasar looked down at the rust-colored trinket with its sky-blue face. The amulet sent Quasar into a brief trance. It searched all the structures in Sunnyville, searching for Princess Onaughon. "Where are you, Princess?"

Quasar was too distracted by the nomad amulet to notice a small group of Sunnyville's finest citizens until some shouts emerged. A mob was moving in his direction. There were no pitchforks or torches ablaze, but Quasar knew the electric atmosphere that surrounded these men. They didn't like his kind, and with the orders from Nikolai Volkov, it gave the mob fuel to hunt him down. He didn't know what to do, but Quasar understood this wasn't a battle he wanted to fight.

He had absolutely no desire to kill every mob member if he could help it. Most of them were likely only following orders of their master and once he went down the path Legion had chosen before his own demise, then Quasar would be hunted down by every human with any thought of retribution. Let alone Clover and the rest of his allies.

Luckily enough, the nomad amulet was taking him in the opposite direction of the rapidly advancing mob.

Quasar felt an ever-stronger pulse of the nomad princess; it was at the far end of the street. The only question was could he break into the building she was being held in and rescue her before the mob caught up. Then he would have to decide between the princess's and his own well-being and the lives of their adversaries. Quasar picked up his pace and started to run. His lean legs tossed up sand in his wake, and his body moved like a gazelle in full flight from a predator.

His respiration and heart rate worked in harmony; neither overpowering the other. His emotions stayed calm despite the situation and kept his body from overtaxing itself. The closer he came to the nomad princess's beacon the stronger Quasar felt.

Through the air a torch was launched, flying end over end, sending sparks flying off the torch base. It was no way a human should have been able to throw with such strength and accuracy, but the situation was perfect, the planets must have been aligned and it could never happen ever again. The torch struck Quasar on his side and his momentum sent him falling. The fall sent pain throughout his entire body. It took Quasar a while before he could move, and the shouts had grown louder. He knew the mob had gotten very close and he needed to move.

Quasar shook off the wooziness he felt. As he looked to his right, the half burning torch that had struck him was blurred. He thought caked blood coated his shoulder and pain made it difficult to lift his right arm. The screams of the mob reached him and by the sounds they were too close to run again. Quasar doubted with the impact of the ground he could even return to the swift running he had been doing. He would have to fight his way out this time.

Once his vision returned, Quasar realized any escape routes had been blocked off. Enraged villagers raised their torches and other assortments of weapons. Nothing compared to his own, but the decision had to be made to kill or be killed. Then something came to him. *What if I use my pulse energy to create another diversion?* He understood this one would have to be much larger than the last one to provide time to get to the princess and flee. But he decided it was doable and his only choice outside of killing villagers.

Quasar once again removed his staff and that alone made the village mobsters gasp in fear; several of them moved back. There was a two-story building that would be Quasar's target. He gripped his staff firmly. The energy rushed through his body like a weapon charging up. That's how things worked. He utilized the staff to generate the pulse power in his body and a as way to discharge it without destroying everything within an earshot.

As the pulse energy began to dwell and build within him, Quasar began to perspire. He felt like an overheating engine ready to explode. To contain the energy and not let it go before he was ready, Quasar slammed the staff's butt flat on the ground. That created a shockwave that shook the ground like a seven-point-five earthquake. Buildings began to shake on their foundations, and some of these structures already on the fringe of collapse, fell.

Quasar's hands began to burn from the staff's intensified energy. He wasn't sure how long he could contain it. The surrounding mob was becoming restless, but the quake and the anticipation of what might come next was keeping them at bay. By this time, the energy was too much to contain. Quasar aimed the head of his staff at its target, held it steady and fired. The pulse energy released from the staff and raced towards the two-story building faster than the villagers had ever seen anything move. The energy scorched the air and an acrid taste filled everyone's throat, even Quasar's, that forced the mob to their knees, coughing and begging for mercy.

The energy beam struck its target a split-second after it had been released. First there was a flash of light so bright that it might seem like the sun had exploded. The building, which was already fragile, disintegrated under the immense power. The ground below it collapsed at the same time, making an impact crater nearly twenty feet in diameter. Some of mob members fell into the crater while others were forced back by the intense wind that had been created by the collision.

The hurricane-strength wind made it seem like the pulse energy had ripped a hole in space-time and was attempting to suck the entire block into a colossal vortex. Quasar knew it was time to leave; he wasn't sure how long the spectacle he had created would last. He tucked his staff away and hobbled down the road, away from the mob and the damage he had unleashed.

✝

The last explosion rocked their underground prison. Tigerous glanced over at her companion. The aftershocks seemed to be even more intense than the quakes. With each shockwave, what made for lighting in their dungeon prison flickered and a few times they had even gone out, temporarily. Zeus wasn't taking the quakes well at all. The burly creature had his head between his knees, and she thought she heard him mumbling some type of prayer. Had she ever heard the former sergeant-at-arms praying? No, she didn't think so.

Tigerous searched for Princess Onaughon, the nomad princess had retreated into the prison's shadows, but Tigerous could still see her silhouetted figure hiding in the same corner Tigerous had first found her. She could sense the princess's anxiety and fear. *I bet she has never seen war before.* The only nomads who had seen battle were those nomad scouts who watched over the Wasteland. They weren't a warrior clan and never chose sides, even when Legion had forced all humans to scurry like gutter rats.

Tigerous took a deep breath, then exhaled a lungful of air. In a way, she was curious what was going on up there, but she wasn't an oracle able to see past, present or future events. Nor could she see through walls. She was just going to have to trust they would be safe where they were, even though something inside her doubted that. She took another elongated breath.

Then she heard the princess ask in a dreary tone, "What's going on up there?"

"I wish I knew, Princess. Maybe they are killing one another and soon we will be free."

"Do you believe that?" Princess Onaughon asked in a not-so-convinced voice.

"No, I suppose I don't," returned Tigerous.

Then a blast that sounded like it came from just above them rained down debris from the ceiling. Screams followed the incendiary blasts, like their captors were being torn to pieces. *Good,* thought Tigerous. *Let them feel some misery for a change.* The building shook violently and the lights went out for good. Luckily, Tigerous could see in the dark, her companions, on the other hand, weren't so lucky.

Tigerous had picked the energy restraining mechanism with a point from one of her claws. It took some time, but the work wasn't nearly as difficult as she had anticipated. Then once she was done with her restraints, she worked on Zeus's and the nomad princess.

Then a blast severed the energy connection and the door that separated the prisoners from the upper floor dissipated without warning. The captives' energy restraints shut down as well. They were no longer prisoners. But another dilemma replaced their captivity, a dark and looming figure appeared at the edge of the stairs. Was it friend or foe? Either way Tigerous wasn't taking any chances. She prepared to defend herself and the lives of her companions from whatever might be out of her sight.

At first, the silhouetted figure just stood there. Was it having second thoughts about approaching them, or was it just toying with their unstable emotional state? Tigerous looked over at the princess and knew she was just as much on edge as Tigerous was. Tigerous clenched her jaw and readied her claws into a fighting position. By that time, their looming guest had begun to make its way down the old, creaking steps, one step at a time. The sound of the figure's massive weight made it sound as if the old wood steps would collapse under the approaching figure at any moment.

Tigerous's heart rate had increased. She felt the blood pumping through her veins, giving her an adrenaline rush and increased strength. That wouldn't be a good combo for their visitor if he proved to be an adversary, especially with her ability to throw poison-tipped claws. Tigerous looked over at Zeus, he was still in his prayer pose; she didn't think he would be much help. What a pity, with Zeus's strength, he was a formidable opponent for anyone or anything they might encounter.

Tigerous looked for the princess, who she had decided to be protector of. As she figured, the nomad princess was huddled deep into a corner and Tigerous thought she heard the nomad softly crying. She was alone in this fight, making her chances that much slimmer. But Tigerous was used to that. She had never relied on anyone, not even Clover, who always had an ulterior agenda that she never could figure out. *Damn him*, she thought. Tigerous quickly shook off the thought; she didn't need any distractions, at the moment. She needed all her concentration on their unannounced guest.

Finally, the shadowy figure reached the bottom of the steps. Tigerous took a fighter's stance with her body as low as she could get it. Her claws out ready to attack or be used as aerial weapons and prepared for the worst. But then something caught her off guard, something or someone she hadn't seen in a long while. The voice of an old friend, someone she could always count on, even in hard times. The voice of Quasar. When her friend's voice echoed in the cellar she nearly began to weep in joy. Her muscles relaxed and her anxiety dissipated.

"Princess Onaughon," called out the voice.

Wait, what did he say? Was he searching for the nomad princess and not here to rescue her? She shook the thought off. They had an ally and whatever the reason for his appearance she was welcoming it.

She could see the outlines of stains on his mantle and Tigerous could only ascertain who the blood belonged to. But there wasn't time to question her friend. Tigerous turned towards the princess with an offering hand. "It's okay, he is a friend, come to rescue us." She slapped Zeus and the behemoth snapped out of his praying trance. Princess Onaughon cautiously, but with renewed confidence, stepped towards their visitor.

Quasar asked in an inquisitive tone, "Tigerous, is that you?"

Even though his face was drenched in darkness, Tigerous could see the surprise on her old friend's face. "Yes, Quasar, it is I."

She could hear the confusion in his voice and understood why. If it was her come to rescue the princess and an old friend was there, she would have a million questions to ask. She wanted to reach out and hold him, but they were still in Sunnyville, and they didn't know what Nikolai Volkov's reaction would be once he discovered they were no longer his prisoners.

"I am confused. I was sent by Clover to rescue the princess." Quasar reached out to hand the nomad amulet to his rescue. "Princess, this is yours."

Slowly, with guidance from Tigerous, the nomad princess took possession of her people's most prized symbol. Princess Onaughon hugged it to her chest like a lost babe who had been suddenly found.

"We don't have time for drawn-out stories, maybe a later time would be more appropriate. For now, can you guide us from this place? From the clutches of this madman and this corrupted town?"

"I believe so but do have the question. I overheard the villagers talk about some of their comrades disappearing. Is that tied to this place?"

Tigerous could only shake her head. "Now isn't the time to dive into that."

Quasar nodded and the four of them began to ascend the cellar stairs.

✝

The upper floor was brighter than the darkness of their cellar prison by far. But being that, the lighting was a dull gray with a tint of yellow highlights, just providing the fugitives enough light to make their way through the empty building—was it completely empty?

Once the four fugitives emerged from the cellar prison, they were met with a scene of carnage; blood splatter decorated the faded walls. Three corpses lay lifeless and apparently not going to cause them any issues. One of the dead men was missing his head, but when she tried to look at her friend to see if his gaze would give away why he had chosen to decapitate the villager, Tigerous just couldn't bear to see the guilty look on Quasar's face. It was better to believe he had done this in self-defense and knowing his personality, it most likely had been.

Pot holes littered the floor, making maneuvering through the upper level difficult, but not impossible. They all followed Quasar in single file. One wrong step could send them tumbling back to their dark prison. The floor creaked, making Tigerous cringe. She didn't know which she feared most, the floor collapsing before them or the creaking sound bringing in a host of Nikolai's trance-induced thugs.

Tigerous refused to look at the bodies acting like obstacles in their path for too long. She needed to keep her focus on the living and not the deceased. Suddenly something passed by the entranceway to the back door, temporarily blocking their light. But as soon as the thing had appeared, it was gone; too swift for even her catlike eyes. *Did Quasar see it?* she wondered. Most likely not, but she never knew what other abilities he had inherited once his twin had perished in the weapon's experiment.

She had her answer in a split second. Quasar had stopped, forcing the rest of them to halt. That made Zeus groan in frustration. He saw why they had stopped so suddenly, they all did. Standing in their path, halfway across the pitted linoleum floor, was a monstrous metal thing. It was nearly as tall as Quasar and as girthy as Zeus, if that was possible. Instead of fur and muscle, the thing was solid metal, with piston gears and turning sprockets that created the creature's outer parts. Those blue eyes were the scariest thing about it; they were ice-cold blue and calculating. They only made their adversary even more menacing with the whining of its hydraulic gears.

The mechanical man stood there like a western gun-fighter ready for a gunfight. The android was motionless and refused to fall into their coy means of persuasion. He had one job, and he wasn't about to be scrap metal for failing. Neither the fugitives nor the android made the first move—it was a standoff.

"Master Nikolai isn't quite finished with the detainees. If you would be so kind as to return them to their cell, it would be much appreciated. No blood will be spilled that doesn't have to be," the machine said.

Zeus growled at their adversary and before anyone had time react, the burly beast launched itself at Cheeves. That seemed like a mistake in judgement. As Zeus reached out for the metal limbs of the android, the swifter and more mobile machine evaded Zeus's weary grasp and snagged the former sergeant-at-arms by his wrists and maneuvered him in any fashion the android chose. Those cold blue eyes didn't waver at all, not even the one in its metal eye socket.

"You are an unruly creature, aren't you?" bellowed Cheeves.

Zeus responded by growling at his adversary even louder, exposing his mouth full of primate teeth. The servant android shoved Zeus, forcing the behemoth to collide with the adjacent wall. Then the machine turned on the rest of Tigerous's comrades. Quasar hadn't waited to see the results of the fight between Zeus and the machine. He had removed his staff, gripping it firmly in his extra strong grasp.

Cheeves gave Quasar a cold stare, as if inviting him to come at the android. Quasar had other plans, it was as if he was pondering choices or maybe using an old chess tactic, waiting out his opponent. Either way, it made the machine impatient, and Cheeves was the one that attacked first. Quasar raised his staff in defense and the android's elongated arms slammed into the staff, stopping the machine's momentum dead in its tracks. Both adversaries struggled against each other. The machine pushed against Quasar, then Tigerous's friend pushed back. Neither adversary could gain any momentum.

Cheeves's digital eyes reflected off the head of Quasar's staff.

The android pushed down on the staff, attempting to force it against Quasar's chest, but the former corporate weapon locked his elbows and refused to budge. It was like the immovable force versus the unstoppable object.

That wouldn't suffice for Cheeves, the android reached for the staff head.

"You don't want to do that," warned Quasar.

The android didn't heed Quasar's warning.

Quasar built up his energy staff and launched his pulse energy, incinerating Cheeves's metal hand and sending the android off in the opposite direction. While Cheeves recovered without one of his hands, Quasar moved in to finish his adversary. He sent his pulse energy through the staff, making the shabby building shake. The head of the staff glowed purple as the energy embedded in the staff grew. The light emanating from the staff head grew ever more intense. When the staff maxed out, Quasar lifted the staff over his head and brought it crashing to the floor. The pulse energy erupted from the staff head like a volcano erupting. The purple beam ripped through the air, leaving a singed vapor trail in its wake. The energy attack was quicker than the android could react, and the beam of energy incinerated the arm missing the hand, forcing Cheeves to the ground. That shook the entire structure and rubble began to fall as the structure began to collapse.

Quasar retrieved the semi-unconscious Zeus, and the four companions ran out the building to safety, leaving the wounded android behind.

Cheeves hobbled into Nikolai's workshop, worse than he had been before he had left to reacquire the prisoners. The android fell to one knee before his master and began to beg for the cyborg's forgiveness. "Master, forgive me my transgressions. I have failed you. The prisoners have escaped."

Without turning around, Nikolai said, "I know."

"Shall I gather a posse to go after them, my master?"

"No, their capture would no longer serve our purposes. But I do believe it's time to unleash our project. Time to inform the elders that the hourglass sand has just about run out. But first go get yourself cleaned up, I feel we may have visitors coming."

Chapter 19

The Rustler leader ordered his men to line up the humans they had been ordered to capture. Straus and his human comrades stood before him. The captives were forced to their knees and their wrists bound, like a hog prepared for the slaughter before they were thrown onto the pit fire. Straus had begun to shake, right before the Rustler soldiers had placed them all in a circle and onto their knees. The group had been traveling for what seemed like weeks, but in reality, it had been only five days' hike from where they had been captured.

Straus's heart was racing a mile a minute and his throat was dry and parched from the heat. His hands were perspiring, making his restraints rub against his bare skin. The traveling party had been stripped of all their possessions except for walking attire. His biggest fear was they had been brought to this place to be systematically eliminated, but Straus still didn't know why. Had it anything to do with his sister's family's disappearance? Had Clover and his companions discovered anything at the Sierra Nevada Complex? He hadn't heard anything from Clover and his companions since they had departed. *How long ago was that?* questioned Straus. He wasn't sure he knew a lot of things, including why they had been captured by the Wasteland Rustler band.

Straus didn't know any of these things, but what he was certain of was the very muscular Rustler that was slapping the rusted machete blade in his bare hand was igniting his anxiety. It surely didn't help that the thug was walking around the circle, coming quite close to Straus. Was this it? Was the slaughter about to begin? He couldn't bare to watch the executions, so he closed his eyes and waited for death to come.

The Rustler leader was barking out details to his men, but with how rapidly Straus's heart was pounding, he couldn't make out a single word. That Rustler leader was definitely the scariest thing Straus had ever seen. Straus wasn't sure what was the most intimidating for him. Was it the leader's square, iron-jaw appearance, the bloodstained, sleeveless fatigue jacket or the scars that littered the leader's arms, neck and face that turned his emotions sour?

Then it began.

First it was the sound that appeared to mimic wet vomit striking pavement, but Straus knew it wasn't vomit that he was hearing, it was the first of his groupmates being executed. That sound was followed by a muzzled cry from the man being slaughtered. The metal blade diving through the man's flesh and devastating his insides was what Straus was hearing. Then the slushing sound as the blade rapidly was removed from the victim. The body hit the ground with a muffled thud.

Straus knew he had to turn away from the carnage about to erupt or he would vomit. A sinister chuckle echoed in his ear, as one of the Rustlers taunted him. The soldier leaned down and whispered, "Doesn't that sound excite you? Imagine each one of your companions dying at the end of my blade, boy. Since you're not man enough to watch them die, I guess the knowledge of your fear is good enough for me."

The Rustler thug strolled away whistling, as the sound of another of Straus's group dying struck the humid air. Straus grew angry and began to grind his teeth to prevent a scream. It would only satisfy the soldiers surrounding his companions. A third death reached his ears and that was more than he could bear. Straus let out a scream that echoed for miles. That seemed to stir the soldiers' amusement as all of them within Straus's proximity began to laugh.

That enraged Straus even more, he let out a curse he had never uttered in his life. "Damn you all to hell, you nefarious Neanderthals. You are very wicked men."

That seemed to strike a nerve in the Rustler soldiers. It shut them up, only briefly, as they tried to process the insult. Then once the moment had passed, they all began to bellow laughter louder than before. That only enraged Straus more, but he didn't allow the heathens to know that.

The carnage continued.

✝

From a short distance away, Clover and his allies watched. In a way, the bioengineered assassin felt responsible for this, despite his warnings to Straus and his men. Humans just had an ego that reeked of invincibleness that always, in Clover's opinion, got them into more trouble than it was worth. Then why was he doing this? Why risk his life and the lives of his companions?

Thanks to Nightshade's reluctant conversation with the Shadow Lord, Clover, Preist, Nightshade and the timber wolf knew the approximate location of where the mutant army would emerge, and the Oracle confirmed that approximation through the vision it had explained to them. It wasn't a perfect science, the Oracle's foresight, but like the information the Shadow Lord had given to Nightshade, it placed Clover's motley gang of would-be heroes close. Nightshade went to scout the area and promised to return. The information that Nightshade had brought back was both disturbing and insightful. Clover felt he knew how to attack the Rustler gang and save as many humans as possible, including Straus.

The bioengineered assassin wondered, *Should I inform Straus that his sister is alive, or should I wait to see if she made it to the gangs and survived that encounter?*

Clover scanned the scene, counting the number of Rustlers, the entry and exit points that the soldiers could use. He also evaluated the number of hostages they were going to have to rescue. The place was nothing but an open field of dried-up land, nowhere to hide, nowhere to run. The soldiers would see them coming from a mile away, but the Rustlers had nowhere to run off to, making their slaughter a free-for-all.

Then Clover thought about his aerial weapon. It could be used to distract the rest of the thugs, allowing Clover's comrades time to save the hostages. Clover touched the weapon hidden beneath his cloak and a smile came to his face. He and the weapon had been loyal comrades for a long time. It had aided him every time he was in need of a long-distance kill or bailing him out of a hairy situation. But as his mind drifted to the weapon, Clover could sense his twin very close and slowly approaching his position. Even if Nightshade was in his cloaked mode, the sound of an occasional dry branch snapping and the steady rhythm of the other assassin's heat beat exposed Nightshade's position. Clover had learned how to keep his twin from sneaking up on him unannounced. It was one of the advantages of spending too much time around Nightshade.

Nightshade's sinister voice whispered into Clover's ear. "Naughty, naughty, brother. I thought you cherished the humans."

Clover grunted. "Only the ones that don't systematically kill others for sport."

Nightshade snorted at that response. "Come now, if you expect me to believe that killer instinct isn't still within you, then you take me for a fool, which I am not."

Clover ignored his twin and looked back down on the scene. Two more of Straus's comrades had gone down. Clover whistled and his brother and Preist, from their set positions, both in striking distance of individual Rustler positions a few yards away, nodded. Even if the Rustlers had heard, which Clover severely doubted, they wouldn't have time to react. Clover removed his throwing weapon and cradled it at each of its four razor-sharp edges in his throwing hand. Nightshade wasn't done taunting his kin, so Clover was just going to have to ignore him.

"What is my part in this masterful rescue plan of yours, brother?"

"Stay out the way and don't injure any of my allies." Clover gave the fading assassin a stern glance. "Can you handle that?"

Another bloodcurdling scream appeared on cue.

Clover aimed and threw his attack weapon with precision.

A whistling sound shattered the air as each blade ripped through the dense humid air on its way to its intended target. The executioner stood over his next victim, with the rusty machete blade held out in a striking arc. The whistling noise distracted the Rustler who looked to his right, then to his left—nothing. But the thug didn't look in the one place he should have, to the southwest.

The blade of Clover's aerial weapon sliced through the Rustler's muscled neck and bone in the snap of a finger. The blade cleared the target as swiftly as it had struck, not allowing any of the Rustlers to see the weapon's flight. At first the behemoth only stared at his victim, as if nothing had happened. Then the thug smiled a shit-eating grin at his victim, but still didn't move a muscle. Next, a blood line appeared on the thug's neckline, which grew to a substantial size and the skin separated swiftly, exposing the inner flesh beneath the skin.

The executioner's head slowly rolled off his shoulders and hit the ground right before the victim. The man was in total shock; he didn't know whether to scream out or run. The executioner's head proceeded to roll away, as the thug's body collapsed to the ground. That drew the attention of the rest of the Rustler soldiers. Some panicked, trying to decide whether to discover what was happening or flee, while others scanned the area for the attackers.

Clover's allies rushed in and aided the assassin's efforts to save the human prisoners. Preist snuck up and stabbed the tall thin Rustler before the thug even knew what happened. Once the Rustler fell from the scientist's grasp, Preist slipped back into his camouflaged state. Nightshade, on the other hand, preferred his cloak of invisibility. Clover slipped between two disoriented Rustlers, pulled a dagger from beneath his cloaked cloak, slit a Rustler's throat then removed his katana, and with lightning quick reflexes, he chopped the thug's head off. Nightshade admired his handiwork a moment or two too long before moving off to his next victim.

Clover moved through the ranks as he always did, with precision, skill and dominance. No human could ever hope to match the assassin's swift speed and agility and no human had the instinct to stay one to two steps ahead of his opponent. With a slice from Clover's aerial weapon and a slash from a katana, Clover mowed through Rustlers like a gardener displeased by the weeds that had sprouted in his garden.

The bioengineered assassin tossed his throwing weapon through one Rustler, it bounced off another's skull, sending bone fragments into the thug's brain cavity, then reached out as the weapon returned to its owner. One by one, the Rustler soldiers fell, not even getting a chance to fight back. Clover and his allies were that proficient and swift that the chaos they had administered in the beginning of the attack left the humans at a constant disadvantage throughout the slaughter.

The Rustler numbers dwindled down to a handful before the thugs could mount a stand. One of the Rustlers grabbed a hostage and threatened to slice the man's throat if Clover and his comrades didn't relent. Nightshade was the closest to the thug. He had uncloaked himself and approached the Rustler, slow, but with extreme confidence as always. You never knew when the dark assassin would strike, what weapon the assassin would use and the manner he would do it in. That is what made Nightshade so dangerous, his unpredictability, which was opposite of Clover.

The differences, at times, between the nearly identical twins seemed like night and day. Clover may have been swift, cunning and next to unstoppable at times; Nightshade was a loose cannon, holding no loyalties and never restraining his actions. Those were the differences between them. Unluckily for the thug, he knew none of this and only assumed this was another dangerous assassin. Where Clover's reputation preceded him in the Wasteland and especially with the Wasteland Rustlers, the soldier thought there would be a line Nightshade would also never cross.

"Stand back!" barked the Rustler. "I'll slice this man's throat if you provoke me. I'll do it, so don't push me, man."

Nightshade began to laugh a skin-curling laugh, one that seemed to come from the depths of a dark pit. His sinister smile was even more intimidating than his laugh. "You assume that I really care, my friend." The dark assassin only shrugged his shoulders. "Be my guest and kill away, if you like. It makes no difference to me."

The Rustler's dirt-filled face filled with shock.

Nightshade went for a throwing dagger, his signature weapon; much like Clover's four-bladed circular throwing weapon. With reflexes only matched by the dark assassin's twin, he threw the dagger, and it struck its target before the thug could retaliate. The problem was the muscle reflex still made the blade held to the prisoner's neck slice the jugular, killing the man. Both the Rustler and Straus's dead companion fell to the earth.

Clover watched with interest as the dark assassin walked over to admire his handiwork. Clover disapproved as his brother inspected both corpses, seeing that the dark assassin wasn't sure which death pleased him more, with his smug smile planted on his face, as the dark assassin, kicked first the Rustler assassination, then the human prisoner. This action made Clover's skin crawl. Clover could tell from the intense stare of Nightshade that he took too much pleasure in killing, even though Clover understood they both were designed for that very thing. The difference between them both was Clover knew killing without meaning was vile, but Nightshade took way too much pleasure in it.

In fact, all human existence made Nightshade supercilious. Maybe that's why, Clover thought his brother, Nightshade, enjoyed killing as much as he did, no matter the target.

Clover was engaged with three Rustlers. The thugs, quite aware of the assassin's reputation, used their numbers to their advantage. They did not realize the assassin was merely toying with them. He could have systematically illuminated his targets with ease, but Clover was in the mood to punish each individual thug for torturing and killing Straus's friends. He held one thug at a distance with the blade tip of his katana, while slicing the clothing of another. The third seemed to be a loss of what to do. Clover sensed the thug's desire to rush him, but that was Clover's plan all along.

His design was to use false hope as a dangling piece of meat to lure in his target. Clover had learned while being the Corporation's favorite assassin, that human beings tended to seek out hope, whether false or not, and cling to it like a fly on flypaper. Clover smiled at the Rustler to his right, stepping towards the thug like he was fencing. Then he took a step towards the thug to his left and swiped at that one.

Finally, the third Rustler drew up enough confidence to attack. The thug lunged at the assassin with a knife. To the thug's surprise, Clover wasn't there any longer, forcing the thug to lose his so-called advantage. All the third thug managed was to slice the arm of his compadre. The injured Rustler and the surprised attacker were about to duel each other for the confusion, but neither one had the time to spare. Clover spun around and kicked the second thug in the chest, sending the Rustler off his feet. The assassin then kicked the first Rustler's weapon from the thug's grasp and, disarming him, sliced the thug's throat, forcing the Rustler to his knees. The knife-wielding thug was bewildered by the move; it had happened so fast it had been a blur. The Rustler watched his comrade bleed out.

Clover wasn't finished. He took a katana and pointed it at the downed thug he had kicked in the chest. The Rustler appeared panicked and unsure of himself. The human refused to get up, so the assassin decided to end the confrontation.

"Any last words, Rustler?"

Cat had the thug's tongue, but he still refused to speak. The two adversaries stared one another down. Without any remorse, the assassin inserted the tip of his katana into the man, and with a swift and violent thrust, the thug died instantly. The assassin spun around and intercepted the final Rustler. Clover slapped the knife out of his opponent's hand, making the thug weaponless, then grabbed the man's collar and drew the human closer. The assassin's red eyes gazed down onto the thug with hatred and contempt, but something made the assassin hesitate, when it would have been so easy just to snap the Rustler's neck and move on.

Clover pressed his thumb against the thug's throat just hard enough to make the human uncomfortable. The assassin whispered, "You have taken a hazardous profession, one that places me at odds with myself. I highly suggest you find a new way to make a living before you find yourself face down like your comrades. Do you understand me?"

The scared thug nodded, and Clover released him with a shove.

Straus found his restraints cut and he was free.

He tripped over a corpse and stumbled backwards into the arms of the burly Rustler leader. The muscled brute wrapped his tree-trunk sized arms around Straus in a bear hug.

Clover sensed Straus's anxious emotions and searched out the boy. It was difficult hunting, even for the bioengineered assassin with all the slaughter and chaos consuming the area. But that didn't deter Clover. Suddenly, the assassin spotted the Rustler leader holding onto the man that Clover had once rescued as a teenager from the clutches of his insane nemesis, Legion. The brute gave Clover an ugly grin as the assassin slowly approached.

"So, we finally meet at last, assassin. Your reputation does proceed you. I am not disappointed in the least," barked the Rustler leader.

"And whom might you be?" returned Clover.

The thug chuckled, a deep burly sound that would scare anyone, but not an assassin designed to kill without remorse or fear. "They call me Trapjaw, but my mother named me Lucius."

Fitting, thought Clover. The assassin gripped his throwing weapon, ready to strike at any moment. But with the hold the thug leader had on Straus, one wrong move would mean the end of the boy who had grown into a righteous leader of men. The assassin took a slow step towards them. He kept the aerial weapon in plain view to show the thug he was armed and could pounce at any moment.

"Aww, not so hasty, assassin. We wouldn't want me to overreact and crush our friend."

Clover gave the Rustler a low growl. "No, we wouldn't want that."

The thug smiled. "Good. As long as we are on the same page, now ditch the weapon."

"Why would I do something like that? Then you would have the advantage over me. How do I know if I comply, you still won't crush him?"

"Faith, assassin. You just have to have a little faith."

"Not in humans that murder, rape and kill their own kind."

The burly Rustler laughed. "Just as I expected. I guess we will have a game of chess after all."

The assassin nodded. "I guess we will."

Clover gripped his aerial weapon firmly; despite his superior reflexes, he would only get one shot. Clover eased his breathing and concentrated on the Rustler thug. His adversary didn't know it yet, but the thug was about to receive a schooling on what it was to tangle with a bioengineered weapon. He nodded to Straus, hoping the human would understand what he wanted. As the Rustler had said, he would have to have a little faith in humans for this to work.

With one swift reaction, Clover threw his weapon with a precision only he could provide. Nearly at the same time the thug began to tense up and squeeze Straus, but the human had a few tricks up his sleeve. The smaller human pulled out a knife from his boot and stabbed the thug in the inner thigh. That's all that was needed. Trapjaw loosened his grip on Straus and the smaller human wiggled out of the brute's grasp.

Clover's weapon was right on target, as always. It struck Trapjaw directly in the right shoulder with such a force it not only stunned the brute but forced him to stumble a few paces back. Clover leaped into action and pounced on the thug. The assassin gripped the man and kept him upright. Clover pressed on the wounded shoulder, making the Rustler cry out in agony before backhanding the thug, forcing Trapjaw's head to snap backwards ferociously.

Lucius seemed quite dazed by Clover's attack; his eyes rolled to the back of his head, and he was barely conscious at all. Blood trickled from the man's nose and his mouth quivered like he was scared. Clover knew the thug could still hear him, even if Clover's victim couldn't respond. The assassin forced Lucius to stare into Clover's fiery-red eyes.

Clover grasped the Outland Rustler operative around his thick neck, like a clamp holding down, and began to squeeze. Despite Trapjaw's half-unconscious state, the thug's face began to turn blue, as he struggled to breath. Clover was wary of squeezing too hard, he had no desire of letting the Rustler's life extinguish that quickly. He was looking for the thug's punishment to linger long enough to taunt him. But in the man's condition, the assassin wasn't sure any of it mattered. A quick or prolonged death may result in nothing but a waste of the assassin's time and breath.

"I don't know if you can hear me, or if you are playing dead like a wild dog, but the time of the Outlaws time has ended. Hear the death of your gang, the one that is supposed to send fear into the hearts of every human in the Wasteland; it's fading like the light. Your kind was right when you made those legendary stories, ones that made me out to be a monster. Heck, maybe I am the horror in the darkness, but if I am that predator in the Wasteland night, it's what the Corporation made me and none of my choosing."

Clover waited to see if Lucius would bite at his mimicking and taunting. All the Wasteland thug could do was moan incoherently. It didn't satisfy the assassin one bit, but he guessed it would have to be enough, he and his comrades had too many fish to fry, and time was growing short. Clover took one last look at his victim. *Pathetic thing, isn't he? In the end your kind can't survive. Your kind isn't strong enough.* Then the assassin looked over at the ginger wolf that had been his and Preist's companion since they started this journey. She had a sad look on her snout, if a wolf could have one. He got the sense she wasn't pleased with his actions.

"Girl, what should I do with him?" the assassin whispered. "Should I give him and all like him mercy?"

Clover looked back at the nearly dead thug, shook his head and snapped the human's neck. The dead thug slumped over in the assassin's grasp and Clover released the man, letting Lucius fall to the ground. Clover stepped over the dead man's body, noticing the ginger wolf's gaze still on him. "What now?" Clover exclaimed calmly. "Do I need to bury the pompous jerk as well?"

The ginger wolf slowly spun on her heels and moved back across the bloodied killing field, waiting for the business to be finished.

Clover spun in Straus's direction. The young man had a horrific stare on his face, as if he had just witnessed Death on a Harley run over an unexpecting old woman, and in a way he had—witnessed Death, that is. Clover felt for the boy that the young man used to be. He could never get the adolescent out of his mind, the horrors he had endured, the loss. Heck, if Clover thought hard enough; the tragedy Straus had endured superseded his own.

"I'm sorry you had to see that. It's men like this that return me to my killing days. The time I was a corporate assassin." Clover shook his head. "I'm never proud of those times, never proud when I have to do something so sinister."

Clover had a sad look when looking down at the dead Rustler.

Panic slowly dissipated from Straus's face and Clover saw the young man's breathing had return to normal. He would be just fine. "No. You did what you were designed for. What that man forced you to do, much like your . . ." Straus froze. "Thank you."

Then the revelation soon left them both when an individual walked onto the bloodied field. Not the four Clover was expecting, Tigerous, Zeus, the nomad princess and the one he sent to rescue them, Quasar, Clover watched the haggard Quasar approach. To the assassin, his comrade had the appearance that the mutant weapon had endured a hard road.

"We have returned with the princess."

Clover remembered Quasar's task and the initial shock of his friend's sudden appearance wore off. The assassin nodded. "The Nomads will be pleased," was all he said.

There was an errie silence for what seemed like eternity, then the assassin spoke up, "The Rustler Council has been raising an army of hybrid mutants. Humanity's last fall," spoke Clover.

"You learned that all from visiting the Nevada facility?" questioned Straus.

"That and a trip to Metro City," returned Preist.

Nightshade walked over to the comrades and smiled. He nodded to his twin, then interjected, "We are ready. The gangs of Metro City have united to fight this new threat."

✝

The Wasteland Rustler elders were gathered around the brightly projected image of Nikolai Volkov. It was never something they relished, but it was something they had agreed upon. Despite not confiding in one another, each elder could sense the others' anxiety. Each felt something different when the cyborg addressed them.

It, the former CEO of The Corporation, treated the elders like adolescents, or even worse, less than equals in their arrangement.

Unfortunately, the one responsibility the cyborg had promised the elders had still yet to pass. Clover, the elders' biggest adversary, was still walking around and breathing. But none of the six elders dared to accuse the cyborg of his lack of diligence. There were two individuals the elders would never challenge, the bioengineered assassin that had been making their lives a living hell, and the former CEO, both associated with the entity known as the Corporation.

The deep and growly voice echoed in the dimly lit place the elders called home. Each Rustler elder sank deeper into their hiding, concealing the terror cemented onto their decrepit old faces. One or two of the elders were shaking profusely and no matter how hard they concealed their abrasive, pale-skinned hands in their cloaks, it was impossible to hide their fear. The cyborg seemed to take pleasure in this.

"It's time, gentlemen." Nikolai Volkov taunted the elders with the gesture of equality. His half-machine, half-human face possessed a wicked smile taunting them even more and usual.

A sense of urgency filled the room. The elders began to whisper to one another, but despite their farce-played confusion, each knew what the cyborg was referring to.

Nikolai waited until the elders got their anxieties out of their system. Then he continued. "Our hard work has paid off. Our adversaries have been kept out of our plans and now it's time to reap the rewards of our labor. Release the subjects in the Wasteland."

There was a gasp of surprise—the elders knew this was the endgame for everybody who stood in their path. Still, it was sudden, and the mutants weren't ready. Then one of the elders stood up abruptly, allowing his gown to fall back to its normal resting state.

"Why, comrade, you look unwell," mocked Nikolai. "Have you been eating well?" The cyborg let out a dark and wicked laugh.

"You have deceived us," barked out the elder. "You promised to dispose the assassin, but he still lives."

The rest of the elders were stone-still, not moving a muscle.

Nikolai Volkov began to chuckle, a deep and heinous sound. "My friend, you mistake me for a riverboat gambler. I have yet to show all my cards. The elders aren't the only ones that want Clover dead. While our mutations keep the assassin's comrades busy, I have laid a surprise for the assassin. Trust me, it will work out Clover in the end."

Suddenly all the other elders were looking at the outspoken one, giving death stares. The elder was caught between looking like a fool and being forced to defend his outrage. Nikolai's image stood there awaiting a response that never arrived. Slowly the elder sat back down, giving the rest a chance to express through telepathic wavelengths their sorrow for their brother's outburst.

"So, if no one else has anything to get off their chest, shall we let the festivities begin?"

The blue image evaporated.

Chapter 20

The town of Sunnyville was quiet, but as Tigerous and Zeus had already discovered, appearances could be deceiving. The sun had a purple haze to it this day. Was that a sign that things were going to become messy? The magnificent orb faced towards the western portion of the town, like an anxious spectator waiting for the gladiatorial match to begin. The township was still as an underground necropolis, but how long would it be until the dead awakened to feast on their flesh?

It was like Sunnyville was a ghost town, and Tigerous didn't like the feelings it was emanating. Chills ran down her spine and an eerie sense loomed over the town. "Nothing good could come to them today" was the sensation Tigerous was getting. She needed to focus on the task at hand or risk losing her marbles to the unknown. What might or might not happen in the coming hours. As a trained warrior, she had the ability to silence her emotions and concentrate on the here and now. And she would need that ability more than she realized.

Tigerous wasn't sure how the mutant zombies would react to their presence and wasn't wanting to find out. Would they move fast? Would they fumble over one another to get to the township and their unassuming prey? Were they already too late and the mutants had slaughtered everyone? Tigerous wished her and her traveling companion had stayed with their comrades.

Still, Tigerous had wished that Quasar had accompanied them. She wasn't sure if just the two of them could fend off a horde of crazed zombies on their own. She wondered how Preist was doing. He had been sent to escort the nomad princess back home, not that she thought the scientist would be all that useful in this conflict. Preist had played his part against the defeat of Legion and his vast knowledge always seemed to come in handy, but this was something totally different. A war against humanity with Tigerous, Clover and their allies stuck in the middle once again.

Well, here we go again, Tigerous announced to herself. *Once again we leap from the firepot into the flames.* She looked over at Zeus, possessing a tempered, but defined scowl. Tigerous knew that when the chips were down, she could count on her companion. She had seen it firsthand in the final battle against Legion's goons. "Ready?" she asked.

The mammoth primate merely grunted and nodded his head.

†

As they made their way through the sand-covered streets, Tigerous and Zeus noticed one thing in particular; there wasn't anyone roaming the streets—consistent with the feeling of a ghost town. They didn't even hear towns-people crying out for help, which triggered their worst fears. They had been too late after all. Zeus knocked on door after door, but there was no response. It was like the town had become deserted, but neither of them believed they were alone. Tigerous sensed dark and hungry eyes watching them, but she couldn't be sure from where.

Once Tigerous thought her companion had seen some-thing in the deep shadows of a crumbling drugstore. The former sergeant-at-arms stopped and stared into the shop's broken windows. The building had a look of old, decrepit stone with a weathered tint of gray, making it seem even the creepier. Zeus clenched his burly fists and that's when Tigerous thought she had seen a pair or red eyes peering out through the heavy shadowed front window, or was she hallucinating?

Her companion must have seen it as well, or were they both caught up in entranced emotions? But Tigerous didn't think so. No! She was sure something had stared right at them, and they had seen its hungry eyes. Their time was going to be short for sure. They were on borrowed time.

Zeus wasn't taking any chances. The behemoth made a move towards the run-down building, but at a methodical, slow pace. Tigerous thought it was deliberate and more strategic than being worn out from all their traveling. She could only guess how much energy her companion expended from traveling back and forth and what type of stress his joints took just supporting him. Tigerous had no clue because Zeus didn't talk about anything much; maybe at most to complain about some ache or pain or how hot it was, but that was it.

Zeus had made it a quarter of the way to the building when a heart-stopping scream pierced the humid air. It froze them dead in their tracks. At first neither Tigerous nor Zeus knew which direction it came from. Zeus looked back and hesitated for a moment, as if the scream had made him debilitated and unable to respond as swiftly as Tigerous knew him always to, mouthing, "Where did that come from?" All she could do was shake her head, confirming she had no clue.

Then the scream came again, but this time it seemed to come from a few blocks over. It was clear, unlike the first scream that someone was in despair and needed their help. This time Zeus didn't need conformation or direction from Tigerous. The primate shot straight for the source of the screams. Zeus made a path through debris and broken concrete, even smashing a few holes in the side of buildings in their path, making them a little wider.

She had never seen her companion move so swiftly. She had never seen anything so vast move with urgency and swiftness. Even with her grace and stamina, Tigerous struggled to keep up. But she shouldn't have been so surprised. She had been traveling with the primate for a while now and he always seemed to amaze her with something new. Zeus passed by the first block, kicking up dust, as he rushed down the makeshift path on all fours; dragging his knuckles as he went. Tigerous leaped over a half-broken polymer bathtub like a plains deer. *It must have fallen out of a home during the devastating quakes directly after the post-apocalyptic war*, thought Tigerous.

A third scream that seemed much more muffled than the first two echoed only a few houses away. That got both comrades moving even faster. Tigerous's heart was racing a mile a minute, from both running as fast as she could and the adrenaline pumping through her veins. Before she knew it, their destination was right before them, making Tigerous even more anxious. Was there a mutant devouring a family? Were there several of them inside? Had they arrived too late to provide any type of aid to those in need? All these questions rushed through her mind in a split second.

The house was a bi-level, and it was apparent that the second floor was sagging. The cellar door was broken off its hinges, and if it were her guess, that's where the screams had originated from. Before she could call out to him, Zeus rushed through the doorless cellar and into its dark interior. She wished he hadn't barreled right into the unknown; they didn't know what or who was down there. What situation were they blindly rushing into?

First, she didn't hear anything as she approached the cellar entrance. Tigerous approached a little more cautiously than her comrade, slowing her approach without stopping as she creeped up to the doorway. Zeus was engaging something, and her burly companion was mad as hell. Tigerous began to panic; her heart raced even faster than when she was sprinting.

Without any hesitation, the feline rushed into the cellar. The place was encased with shadows and had a mildew aroma. The only lighting besides what could penetrate the doorless entrance was a forty-watt light swaying back and forth. Once Tigerous forced her senses past the smell, she saw two dead human forms lying on the ground in the middle of the cellar floor. Blood trickled from their lifeless bodies, and she could see what appeared to be bulges protruding from their necks. Most likely their necks had been snapped and their deaths were instantaneous.

She doubted the adults were the ones that had made all the fuss that brought them here. She sighed a sorrowful sigh, knowing their efforts were in vain. But they weren't alone in the place. Tigerous saw Zeus battling a mutant zombie away from another form, one that seemed to have put up a struggle. Another mutant was chewing on flesh from its victim, a young girl with fresh blood staining her tattered dress. The mutant must have been yellow at one time, thought Tigerous. But now the only color existing was her blood splatter. The girl showed no signs of life and Tigerous wasn't sure, but she thought the little girl's lips had turned purple; but it was difficult to say since the lighting was inconsistent throughout the cellar.

The mutant who had taken a chunk out of the little girl still cradled the child's lifeless body. All the thing could do was stare at its uninvited guest with a cold, dead stare. The mutant had gray, wrinkled skin and clawlike fingers that seemed to be more knife-shaped than human fingers. The creature had drool dripping from its razor-sharp teeth and part of the child's flesh it had been chewing on could be seen in the thing's rotten mouth. Tigerous had a distaste in her throat, one that was like swallowing a finger or another small body part that did set well with her and hatred for the thing in her heart.

It seemed that the creature was losing interest in its victim and its recent interest in the new guest. Slowly the creature released the limp body of the dead girl and began to lunge for Tigerous. Sensing the thing's intentions, she drew herself into a defensive crouch with her claws raised to eye level and ready for battle. All it would take was one clean shot to take the mutant's head clean off. But with the poor lighting, that would provide a challenge for the seasoned warrior. The gray-skinned mutant ducked back into the receding shadows and growled at its target. That was the only way Tigerous knew where the monstrosity was hiding.

Tigerous was just going to have to estimate where to attack and hope for the best. The one advantage she had was the ability to see in darkness, and that she could see the silhouette of the mutant would aid her immensely. With a great amount of energy built up, Tigerous leaped towards her adversary, with claws drawn ready for the kill. She temporarily soared through the air into the shadowy part of the cellar, where her adversary awaited.

Tigerous roared as she approached her adversary.

As the darkness unveiled her target, she could see its intense red eyes that displayed nothing but purpose, no emotion whatsoever. Tigerous didn't wonder whether that was a good thing or not, because she had a single-minded purpose, but vengeance for the little girl and her family. Nothing would waver her from that purpose. As soon as the shadow veil receded, her and her adversary were less than a foot apart and adrenaline began to pump through her veins once again.

She drew back and propelled one of her many retractable claws at the mutant, but she was too slow to defend herself while attacking at the same time. In fact, the mutant's speed surprised her, and its needlelike claws raked her side, forcing Tigerous to ricochet from the mutant's thrust and tumble to the floor. Before she lost her bearings, she witnessed her claw strike the mutant as it was recovering from its off-balanced attack, not directly in its head, as intended, but slicing through the mutant's right shoulder.

The mutant cried out a ghastly sound as it too stumbled off in the direction Tigerous had first entered. She had become dazed by the stumble and needed to collect herself. She noticed two silhouetted figures fighting in the far corner of the cellar. She recognized Zeus's grunts and assumed the smaller figure was the other mutant. What she could see was her companion was winning the battle, but it seemed Zeus was having more trouble than he should have, for the size difference.

Despite her companion's struggles, Tigerous didn't have time to dwell on Zeus's issues, she had issues of her own. The mutant she was entangled with came rushing at her and this time her adversary got on her a lot sooner than she would have liked. The mutant launched itself at her and despite the obvious size difference, Tigerous being much taller than the mutant, her adversary forced her off her feet again. Unlike the last time, Tigerous had the mutant on top of her with no separation. They both fell to the cold, hard floor together. Tigerous felt the impact in her back and shoulders as pain shot up her spine.

The mutant growled and snapped at her, while its slimy drool fell onto her face. Tigerous held the mutant at arm's length, but that was a struggle. The mutant was definitely stronger than it looked, and that might explain her companion's struggles with his own mutant. The mutant swung wildly at Tigerous and clawed her right shoulder. The injury stung, but she didn't believe any poisonous toxin had entered her body—it was difficult to tell with almost all her attention drawn to her attacker.

The mutant forced all its weight down on her and holding the mutant at bay was taxing. She wasn't sure how long she could hold out. Her arms shook and Tigerous's arms were wavering. By this point the mutant's face was inches from hers, and she could smell the rotten stench coming from its decrepit mouth. Tigerous gave the mutant zombie a sour face, as if she had just swallowed something horrible.

"You have breath like a decaying corpse."

All the mutant did was growl at Tigerous.

She wasn't sure if that was its way to answer her sarcastic remark or if that was a way to intimidate her. She would need a way to turn the tide of this battle or risk losing and giving the mutant its chance to do to her what it had done to the human girl. It was not an image that sat well with her. Tigerous forced the mutant with all her remaining strength to one side of her, despite the mutant still clinging to her. At least the thing was no longer raking her with its claws.

Once Tigerous had her adversary in position, she took a swipe at it with her tail. At first, her tail only managed to whip past the mutant's prunelike head. She felt the stale air as it rotated around her tail. She tried again, and this time her striking tail managed to graze the thing's back. It felt rigid and deformed, like the rest of her adversary's body.

The third try hit its mark, smacking the creature square in the face, but that only seemed to enrage the mutant. It gave out a monstrous cry, exposing a mouthful of flesh-shredding teeth. The thing lunged at Tigerous with all its might and ripped some flesh from her tangerine-colored hide. She let out a scream as pain shot down one side. Tigerous rolled over to face the cold concrete floor. That didn't stop her nemesis from pursuing her. It was like the taste of her flesh had been intoxicating and it needed more.

The mutant leaped at her from its current position, temporarily leaving the floor. Tigerous had enough awareness and energy to utilize her catlike reflexes and kick the mutant in midair. She heard the air escape the mutant as it was propelled backwards, still airborne, to where it had come from. That would only give her a short reprieve, since she had yet to see this thing be killed—or wounded, for that matter. But she hadn't had the chance to use her deadliest weapon. Tigerous looked down at one of her retractable claws and smiled.

"It's time to come out to play," she said to the claw.

Tigerous rolled over and to a knee, ready to go on the offensive. With the shadows being deep, she couldn't rely on her instincts as she normally did. She would need to get much closer to the mutant, something she wasn't really relishing. But instead of allowing fear to overtake her, Tigerous used her training and calmed herself, allowing her heart to beat a calm and consistent rhythm.

She heard the low guttural growl of her opponent. She knew the time had come. Tigerous began to charge the mutant, only seeing its silhouette. It was waiting for her with those red, demonic eyes. Tigerous blasted into the cloud of darkness and saw the mutant make its move. If Tigerous had stayed upright, she would surely have been dead. The creature reached for where it must have thought she should be; that was the difference between a drooling mindless creature and a seasoned warrior.

Tigerous went into a slide, allowing the mutant zombie to pass over her, then she kicked out a leg to one side and whipped her tail at the thing's throat. Her tail wrapped around the mutant's throat and Tigerous tightened the grip on the creature. The sudden momentum change forced the mutant to snap back and slam hard to the floor. With the creature still dazed from its collision, Tigerous tightened her grip on the thing, and she sensed it was struggling for air. The mutant clawed and reached for her, but her grip on the thing was too superior to allow it to escape. The creature flailed back and forth, attempting to escape Tigerous's grasp. None of it mattered, her adversary was caught in her trap, giving her the chance to strike it down.

Tigerous reared back and with precise aim, rammed her claw through the creature's skull, up through the back of its head. The mutant didn't retaliate, despite having a claw rammed through its skull, it didn't even bother to growl back at her. The mutant's muscles didn't even twitch from the wound of her attack. It was finally dead. She sat back and took in a deep breath. *If that is what it takes to kill one of those things, we might be in serious trouble*, thought Tigerous.

Then a scuffing noise snapped her from her temporary rest. "Zeus?" She had forgotten about her companion. Tigerous stood up gingerly and looked for the enormous primate. In the far corner, he and the mutant he was fighting continued their dance, but it appeared to Tigerous that Zeus was wearing the mutant down. The primate held the zombie out by one arm, with the mutant's throat consumed by Zeus's enormous hand. Tigerous could hear the bones snapping in the mutant's neck as Zeus bore down with all his might. Soon after, the mutant fell limp and Zeus tossed the body like a rag doll to the side.

Zeus noticed Tigerous watching and pounded on his chest, but when he walked towards her, she could see him slump in pain and grab his right shoulder. His fur was matted with his own blood. The mutant must somehow have taken a chunk out of her companion, but she really couldn't see how. Unlike herself, Zeus was a hunk of a beast with thick muscles, a barrel chest and enormous forearms.

Zeus hobbled towards Tigerous and fell to one knee once he got to her. She could feel his heart pounding. He was exhausted and wounded, something they would have to contend with if they encountered more of these zombies. Tigerous still couldn't fathom how these monstrosities had gotten into town. Neither her nor her companion had seen any signs of the mutants on their way to Sunnyville. Had they snuck past them? Not likely, since the two they had battled seem more like brutes, not philosophers.

"Are you all right? Can you stand on your own?" Tigerous asked.

Zeus nodded, but she was still not convinced. Her companion still had a grimace planted on his apelike features. He also still appeared to have lots of pain coming from his wound. They would have to take it slow.

"We must bury them," Zeus proclaimed.

Tigerous looked down at the half-mauled little girl and the corpses of her parents. Tigerous agreed with her companion but understood there may be more pressing issues in town. They still hadn't discovered if there was anyone else left in Sunnyville or if there were any more zombies. Tigerous caressed Zeus's head. "I know, but we have more pressing issues to—"

Suddenly, out of the shadows of the cellar, a third mutant rushed by the companions and up the cellar stairs like the wind. The mutant's appearance and sudden disappearance startled the two companions. Neither would have time to dwell on the recent events. They might uncover what happened to the rest of the township by pursuing the fleeing mutant. Even with Zeus's condition, Tigerous would need his assistance, even if he trailed her.

She patted the behemoth on the back. "Come, my friend. We still have work to do. Paying our respects will have to wait."

Zeus groaned, but reluctantly stood. Tigerous smiled at him, then tore off after the fleeing zombie. Zeus slowly moved after her.

Tigerous realized the zombie was making its way, even if it was carelessly, back towards the town square. There, they would be exposed. Out in the open were too many ways they could be attacked; much like the last time they had been captured. Tigerous couldn't help that at this point. She needed answers, and following the mutant was their only option at this point.

The closer towards the center of town and the town square they came, the more devastation the companions encountered. Roofs had collapsed in on foundations, debris scattered everywhere, even entire foundations had fallen in, leaving gaping holes on the surface. It made the town look like a true apocalyptic settlement, a place nothing could live in.

Tigerous entered Sunnyville's town square with Zeus laboring behind her. The place was nearly leveled, like a flat plane of concrete and sand. Nothing had changed except there were no Sunnyville patrons scurrying about. It was just her and the mutant. Or was it? Something told her that several sets of hungry eyes were watching. She gasped at the realization. They had been led into a trap. *But how can that be? These creatures are mindless brutes!*

Zeus had caught up with her at the center of an oval circle that once had a wall marking a fountain structure that no longer existed. Suddenly the mutant zombies came out of their hiding spots and began to surround them in every direction. Tigerous thought there were thousands of them, but that couldn't be right, there weren't that many citizens of Sunnyville. Then the thought dawned on Tigerous, *Now I know why we never seen any evidence of the mutants*. She turned to her companion.

"Zeus, the zombies are all the remaining people in town. That's why we never saw any footprints in the terrain. No evidence whatsoever. This whole mess was a trap."

Zeus grunted.

"How can that be? Aren't zombies mindless walking corpses?"

Their question was soon answered by a digital voice.

"So perceptive you are."

Tigerous gasped as the voice's owner exposed himself.

The zombie horde split and Cheeves's metal body appeared. The machine's body was partially mangled, but still functional enough to move on its own. The damage was mostly from having the house structure fall on him. Luckily the machine man played his Houdini act and escaped through a secret exit Cheeves's master had installed to allow them to move throughout the town undetected. Cheeves had welding scars from where the android had been broken but repaired quite crudely. There hadn't been time to fix the android properly. The machine had a considerable limp, dragging a leg behind it. An awful screeching sound came from its leg where a hydraulic piston had been but now was visibly absent.

One of the android's blue digital eyes was hazy and dim, much like a dead eye that has been damaged. Even with these ailments, Cheeves was a formidable foe. The android stood at least as tall as Zeus, and Tigerous had seen firsthand, how tough the machine's metal body was. *How could that thing survive an entire house falling on top of it?* she wondered.

The android stopped less than eight feet from Zeus and Tigerous and stared at them for what seemed to be an eternity.

Tigerous snapped back to reality and remembered the predicament she and her companion were in.

The voice of their adversary drew Tigerous's attention. The android seemed to be staring at them with a gleam in its android eye.

"Cat got your tongue?" teased the android.

It seemed, to Tigerous, that the machine was attempting a joke, or at least oozing with overconfidence for something that had nearly died, if machines could die. In fact, she was confused, because she didn't think androids, not that she had seen a lot in her time, were capable of any emotions. Wasn't pride and egocentric behavior a human trait? There was something amiss here, and the pieces weren't adding up.

"I bet you are wondering why I am here instructing these mutants."

"The thought didn't even cross our minds," retorted Tigerous. That took Cheeves by surprise. Once again, the android was acting too much like a human, and that puzzled her. "Where is your boss?"

That seemed to get the android going like a chatterbox you couldn't turn off.

"Master Nikolai had a previous engagement that he didn't want to break. He ordered me to greet you upon your return to Sunnyville."

"You knew we would return?" questioned Zeus.

"Master Nikolai anticipated it, yes. He wanted me to introduce you both to our new friends." The android motioned towards the zombie horde that had become restless and were starting to creep in. "Speaking of friends, I notice you're a little light on numbers. Where is your tall, lanky friend? The one that decided to drop the house on top of me."

Was he talking about Quasar? Was the android looking for a little revenge? Another human trait. Impossible. Tigerous could only look at the machine with disdain. What had happened to it to have such a vendetta? Did it matter? They were surrounded by a hungry horde of mutant zombies, possibly the remaining residents of Sunnyville with a deranged android hell bent on retribution.

"Pity," retorted Cheeves. "It would have been a joy going another round with him. But since he isn't present, I guess I'll have to do with you."

Suddenly the android's good arm transformed into a metal pipe with a sharp point at the end. Cheeves pointed it at them both. Tigerous gave the android a death stare that would have chased any attacker away. But she didn't think Cheeves was going to be intimidated by her or her burly companion, especially with the horde of zombies waiting to attack.

"Barbarians," Tigerous whispered. *Death by beatdown by a mad machine or being mauled by crazed zombies, what choices we have.*

Cheeves smacked his good arm into the metal palm of his bad arm, taunting them.

Zeus looked back to Tigerous. "Keep them off me."

She wasn't sure who her companion was referring to until one of the mutants howled. Some of the zombies were disfigured and several had a serious drooling problem. Many were ready to charge in and feast on their flesh. Tigerous doubted if either her or her companion would make it back to bury the little girl and her family. The family would just have to forgive them for that transgression.

Zeus and Cheeves circled each other, sizing each other up. Tigerous looked around nervously, as she tried to keep an eye on the fight. She realized the machine man had placed the horde of mutants in a temporary trance with a radiowave silently keeping them at bay somehow. The android's significant limp allowed Zeus to lap the machine one-and-a-half turns to the machine's one. That didn't seem to effect Cheeves.

The android still mocked the gargantuan Zeus through a crackling digital voice. Cheeves began to cackle. "I will savior this victory, rejoicing my victory over your dead body, before allowing the mutants to devour your corpse." Zeus, on the other hand, was becoming enraged by the machine and the combination of Zeus's wound and fighting angry, might spell disaster. Their circular pattern got tighter as both combatants prepared to engage.

Tigerous's nerves were kicking in at a high level. Her anxiety was already dangerously high, and this confrontation wasn't helping. But her emotions alone kept her in a frozen trance.

The two adversaries engaged one another with an explosion of energy. Both grabbed their opponent with great strength. The two danced around, as if at a ballroom dance, attempting to get the upper hand as they struggled to find proper footing in the dense white sand that covered the town's center. Zeus grunted and pushed hard against Cheeves and vice versa. Tigerous could see the alloy the android was made from wasn't easy to grab a hold of, and the enormous primate nearly lost his grip several times.

Frustrated with the results, both combatants disengaged with a push against their opponent. The android took a swipe at Zeus with its metal weapon, but only grazed Zeus's wound. That made the nearly seven-foot-tall and over five-hundred-pound Zeus groan in pain as he grabbed the wound the mutant zombie had created. It threw the gargantuan creature off balance and kept Cheeves a step ahead of Zeus.

Zeus took the android by surprise, vaulting at his adversary and grabbing its metal neck and with all his strength began to shake Cheeves. But Cheeves's construction was of a stellar mold, and the material it was designed from unearthly strong.

Suddenly, Cheeves, without Zeus noticing, struck the behemoth with its metal weapon right in his wound. Zeus let out a tremendous roar, his head tilted back in agony. Blood stained the dull metal weapon as the android ground it inside the wound. Zeus built up enough strength, stealing some from other parts of his body, which hadn't depleted from the attack, and shoved Cheeves off. Even that movement brought a grimace to Tigerous's companion.

Cheeves tumbled backwards and fell to the earth, but that didn't seem to sway the android, or even faze it one bit. The machine looked down at the stained weapon and seemed to be smiling inside as it taunted Zeus some more. "Your blood looks good on my metal surface, creature. Consider it war paint for a warrior that is about to kill you."

Zeus, still holding his wounded arm, roared ferociously, an echo that seemed to travel miles. Before her companion could leap at the android and certain death, she got his attention. "Zeus, you might need this."

Zeus turned to face Tigerous with a painful and sad look, as if he had already seen what was coming. Tigerous removed one of her throwing claws and tossed it to the behemoth. Zeus caught it in his massive hand and the claw only consumed a quarter of his hand. That would make for a great concealed weapon, if Zeus chose to use it. Tigerous hoped he would, because she wasn't sure if he could defeat the android in his condition. Maybe not even if he was in pristine health.

Zeus closed his hand over the gift.

The machine man saw the exchange and still refused to stop his attack. Confidence was high with Cheeves—or was it arrogance, a new trait from a tin man.

Cheeves stood. "Are you ready to end this, beasty? I know I am, despite how enjoyable this has been."

All Zeus did was growl.

The two combatants charged each other, kicking up plumes of sand and dust in their wake. Neither one made a sound this time, until the collision that seemed monumental. The two combatants struggled for what seemed to Tigerous to be forever, but she knew it was only a few moments. Her heart began to race. Both adversaries struck one another. Cheeves struck Zeus dead in the chest with its metal weapon, but in a surprise move, the behemoth rammed Tigerous's claw through the android's metal head, devastating its central processor.

Cheeves's digital eyes flickered and dimmed, like someone had shut down his power grid. There was no movement from the machine, no retaliation. Cheeves was dead. Zeus wasn't in any better condition. Tigerous ran to her companion's side and the behemoth rolled over into her waiting arms. The rod was still protruding through his chest. It had snapped off when the two combatants had fallen on each other.

Zeus's breathing was labored, with quick breaths as his burly chest rose and fell like the ocean during a violent storm. Blood poured from his chest wound and he was struggling to speak. Blood slowly trickled from the corner of Zeus's mouth. "Did I win?"

Tigerous looked at the unmoving android and nodded. "Yes, you won. Now relax, you have taken a bad fall and need your rest."

"Nonsense, girl. You can't lie—" Zeus coughed up some blood. "—for shit. You never were a good card player."

Tigerous only caressed Zeus's head. She could sense the mutants getting restless again and creeping in on them. She noticed Zeus try to look over. *He must hear them as well*, she thought. "Shshsh. You need your rest for the trip home," she lied.

Zeus chuckled in between coughing fits. "You must be delirious, girl. You know as well as I do, neither one of us will be leaving this hellhole alive."

Then Zeus closed his eyes, stretched one last time and died in her arms.

That wasn't the last of her problems. She knew there was still the horde of zombies no longer controlled by Cheeves. She was on her own.

Do I stand and fight until my last breath, or do I kill myself, preventing myself from being mutilated before I leave this place? She looked up at the reddening sky as she closed her eyes.

A feline scream filled the humid air drifting out towards the edge of the Wasteland.

Chapter 21

Their long journey had taken them to the westernmost edge of the Wasteland. Clover, Quasar and Nightshade stood on a sand dune bank overlooking the ocean of sand that stretched as far as the eye could see. The only thing visible outside of the sandy surface was the top of a large shipping container that only exposed one side to the surface, while the rest seemed buried under sand drift. The metal shipping container was so rusted it was impossible to decipher what the container's actual color had been.

There was a mild wind gust blowing out of the east and heading westerly, making Clover and Nightshade's cloaks whip around the two assassins. Clover was staring just beyond the desert horizon, as if he was waiting on the arrival of something. In fact, he was waiting for the arrival of the promised multi-platooned gang army that had been promised by the Oracle. Still no signs of the Metro thugs, but that didn't surprise the assassin at all. Humans had let him down before, and he wasn't expecting much from them in such dire times.

Clover just didn't know how they would fight a mob of crazed mutants without support. It was highly unlikely the three of them could hold the zombies at bay, despite their unique talents. If this was the right place, and according to several sources it was, this is where the great conflict between the living and the elder's chosen army would be. But Clover didn't say a word, all he did was stare.

"Penny for your thoughts, brother?"

Clover grunted. "Wondering when our new allies will arrive."

"Is that all, brother? I sense there is something more on your mind. Maybe you seek the crazed CEO and the trinkets it covets."

Clover only stared at Nightshade, refusing to give in to his brother's usual games.

Nightshade laughed. "You're not the only one seeking vengeance on the cyborg CEO."

"I seek to stop this war that will wipe out all who stand in its wake. I want to end the suffering of all who didn't ask to be thrown into this oblivion. I want to save those who remain and give them a chance to start over."

Nightshade placed a hand on his brother's shoulder.

"You want to be free of the burden that is the human's savior and discover your real destiny."

Clover gave Nightshade a look that made the shadow assassin step back.

"What do you know of my destiny?"

"I have seen it. Both of our destinies."

"Through whom?" Questioned Clover.

"The dark lord. The shadow entity, known as the Darkness."

As the assassin pondered on this, he sensed a figure appearing on the next dune mound. Nightshade sensed it as well, and both assassins looked at the figure in the distance. The sun shone brightly over the figure, but there was something about this figure that was both imposing and familiar to both assassins. It was the former corporate CEO.

Then, out of the western plains, emerged a collection of nomads, the same ones for who Quasar had rescued their chief's daughter. A nomad dressed in simple garb—a leather breech, a bare torso with a light knapsack, most likely to carry his courier messages—slowly approached Clover and his allies. Clover noticed the nomad possessed a confident and prideful walk, as did most of his kind. The nomad had dark skin, more like a tan than possessing a naturally dark skin tone. Sweat poured down his back as if the young nomad had run a mile, but he seemed full of energy and didn't seem breathless from the short jog across the sea of sand.

The young nomad nodded as a greeting. "My chief will be honored to fight at your side. Your rescue of his daughter has pleased him, and he sees benefit to continue the friendship bond." The young nomad bowed.

Clover wasn't sure that a few hundred Wasteland nomads would be sufficient support, but he wasn't going to look a gift horse in the mouth. He nodded towards the messenger and then turned his attention back to the cyborg CEO.

The figure raised his arms to the sky.

Despite the distance, both assassins could hear what the figure was saying with their keen hearing. "Welcome, distinguished guests to the end of everything. Today, I will be introducing the project I have labored at for years. Today I will be providing the vehicle of your destruction. Allow me to present the mutant zombie horde."

Suddenly the enormous rusty cargo container's side fell off its welded hinges like a drawbridge, exposing the container's internals. Through the new opening rushed a legion of mutants. Several other shipping crates had crazed mutants emerging from them, a few dozen from each. Several fell over each other to reach the outside of the container, while those that rushed out of their confinement from the corner of the opening made it through with ease. A roar that sounded like a legendary creature from the underworld emerged from the sandy surface.

It was the horde of zombies crying out all at once. The sound echoed for miles.

Once the mutant zombies made it out of the container, they began to rush towards the nomads awaiting their arrival. The horde covered the distance much more swiftly than Clover or Nightshade thought they should have, but neither assassin had a way to gauge what should or shouldn't be occurring in Nikolai Volkov's experimental army.

"They don't have a clue what they are about to encounter down there do they?" questioned Nightshade.

"I'm afraid not. Even aid from us three won't turn the tide with so many crazed maniacs," said Quasar. He gripped his energy staff firmly.

Clover was the only member of their posse who didn't say anything. All the bioengineered assassin did was watch as the two sides came together in a cataclysmic explosion. There was tension in the assassin's eyes, like a parent watching their child go into battle, fearing the worst outcome.

Then, over the horizon, coming from the eastern plains of the Wasteland, a flock of humans appeared. There were arranged by different colored dress, some with decorative leather outfits, while others wore rags for clothes, displaying their low rankings. The line stretched as far as the eye could see. It was like a desert mirage; thousands of gang members from Metro City had arrived.

"The Rustler Platoon from their main campsite," whispered Nightshade.

"So, reinforcements have arrived," Clover said.

"It appears so," returned Quasar.

"What are we waiting for?" Nightshade removed one of his black steel katanas. "Let's get our asses off the bench."

†

The horde of mutants reached the approaching nomads in full force, while the platoon of humans from Metro City was raging from the eastern front, not far away. Nomads were resilient and unwavering fighters, but they had never experienced anything such as the horde before. Despite the nomads' experience and fighting prowess, the nature of the mutant zombies made dueling with them a challenge that only Clover and his comrades understood, because they were derived from a similar creation process. The mutant zombies were created from existing humans, not designed from scratch; even if the mutants were a physical match for Clover's comrades, the zombies didn't possess the designed intellect.

Humans were physically inferior to those bioengineered by the Corporation and Nikolai Volkov's mutant army. The question was, how would they fight the mutants on the battlefield, once they discovered this?

The gruesome sight of the mutant horde alone made the nomads nearly falter. The carnage was worse than anyone could have imagined. Once the mutants engaged the nomads, the zombies began to tear them limb from limb, leaving a trail of blood and body parts scattered all over.

The noises of mauling and flesh eating filled the battlefield. It wasn't taking the mutants long to devour the nomads. The nomads just didn't have the ability to take down crazed zombies like Clover and his comrades. Cries for mercy filled the battlefield, along with the carnage. One zombie still had a nomad's stripped flesh dangling from it's mouthful of flesh-shredding teeth when a Metro City gang member approached with his spiked weapon.

Clover observed the crazed mutant from afar as it devoured the human flesh, still with the piece of flesh dangling as it let out an eardrum-bursting cry, like some wild beast. The mutant was faster than the Metro City gang member, but Clover knew he was swifter than the mutant had anticipated and stumbled as the mutant finally dropped the flesh it had gnawing on just a minute ago. The mutant reached out with its clawlike hands and sliced the gang member as the human struck the ground hard. The collision with the ground forced the gang member to lose his weapon. The man shook like a tree under gale-force winds, attempting to keep the mutant and its acid drool from getting all over him. The only thing that kept the mutant at bay and devouring the gang member's flesh was a spiked baseball bat to thing's throat, which was stuck in the mutant's meaty neck. It couldn't hold it off long.

The mutant's sharp teeth snapped as it tried to take a bite out of the gang member.

In a mad panic, the man stretched out for the weapon he had dropped in the collision. The human could only reach a finger on the weapon's cold steel handle. It had been forged through a recycled fence post cleaned of its thirty-year rust so the gang member could hold onto the crudely constructed weapon. He reached and reached for the weapon, but like a prize just out of reach, he just couldn't grab hold of the weapon.

The human had the mutant to deal with, snapping and drooling on him every chance it could. Clover could tell keeping the creature at bay was hard enough and the only way the gang member would be able to grip the weapon handle in his shaking hand would be to allow the mutant to come at him with no resistance. That wasn't the human's only problem; Clover could tell the human was beginning to tire and that would compound the issue even more.

"Come on, you stupid beast. Give a reprieve, so I may retrieve my weapon," said the gang member.

All the mutant did in return was growl.

In a last-ditch effort, realizing the mutant zombie was about to overtake him, the human reached for his weapon handle with both hands. With no way to protect himself, the mutant lunged in for the kill.

As the mutant reached inches from the human's flesh, opening its mouthful of razor-sharp teeth, the mutant stopped. Its facial expression transformed from raging and lustful, to pain and agony. The Metro City gang member, with his spiked weapon in hand and ready for a killing strike of his own, also hesitated. Clover sensed that all the human could do was stare at the ugly mutant's strange facial expressions.

Then gray blood seeped from the creature's mouth, first slowly, but then as if someone had turned on a faucet to full blast. Blood flowed from every orifice the mutant possessed. Suddenly the mutant wore a shocked mask, right before a blade sliced off the mutant's head from behind, spraying the creature's blood all over the gang member's clothes. Some of the mutant's poisonous blood went up the human's nose and into his mouth. Trying to keep himself from swallowing it down, the human spit it out and wiped his face clean.

The mutant's head had rolled several feet away. Clover said, "Are you going to lay there while the rest of us have all the fun? Or are you going to join the fight?"

The human looked up and saw Clover wiping the mutant's blood from his katana. Then the bioengineered assassin rejoined his comrades. Clover stood with his back to his twin, Nightshade, who was barely visible to the naked eye. If it wasn't for the flickering of the shadow assassin's outlined aura, he wouldn't be seen at all. But that was Nightshade's uniqueness. Standing directly to

Clover's right was Quasar with his energy staff at the ready. The three of them appeared godlike among mortals.

Clover and his friends sliced through the mutants as if the flocks of the zombies were playthings. When a flock of the creatures came at them, the closeness the allies used kept the mutants from cornering or isolating any one of them and they fought as if they had battled together a million times. Their unison in fighting techniques was flawless, well timed and coordinated. Quasar would keep the mutties, as they called them, from coming at them in hordes, blasting away any group of mutants that attempted to rush them.

Nightshade would taunt the scattering individuals to come at them. The shadow assassin would whisper taunting phrases, such as, "Aren't you hungry, muttie? There is fresh meat over there," directing them towards Clover. It wasn't that Nightshade expected the mutant zombies to understand what he was saying, because they couldn't comprehend any language at all. But the noise was enough to enrage a hungry zombie into attacking without its friends.

The ruse worked. Single mutants charged the bioengineered assassin and Clover more than kindly sliced the mutties into pieces. One after the other, the mutants who rushed the comrades ended all the same; sliced into pieces. Mutant arms flew in one direction, while legs went another and shoulders and heads of the unfortunate usually flew in the direction their owners had came from. Gray blood covered the battlefield and Clover's killing blade.

The three comrades were enjoying themselves. Clover got a rare chance to activate his pure assassin instincts. He hadn't enjoyed killing this much since he walked away from the assassin game. And Clover was certain Nightshade was enjoying the carnage unfolding before them. It was the game the shadow assassin was designed for. Clover remembered his dark twin claiming the Game of Death was his favorite and constantly trying to urge Clover to embrace his assassin instincts.

Clover couldn't see Nightshade, since the shadow assassin was currently in his cloaked state, but Clover thought he sensed his twin smiling as he taunted the crazed mutants, but the bioengineered assassin couldn't be too upset with his twin; they were eliminating a threat to humanity's very existence—even if what was left of humanity didn't deserve the effort they were exerting.

The sound of a razor-sharp blade slicing through flesh echoed. That was followed by wet sounds of flesh falling off limbs, striking the ground and ejecting liquids of all types as Clover swung his katana first in one direction, then back the other way. None of the slaughter was difficult, but there was one zombie Clover took an interest in, though the assassin couldn't explain why. The mutant was like all the other zombies they had slaughtered, but for one thing; the mutant had a familiar look in its dark crimson eyes. Instead of looking like the eyes were on fire inside the eye sockets, a softer and more human look, a look that read "I know you" called out to the assassin.

Clover hesitated cleaving this one's limbs off. Instead, the assassin went for the thing's head. He slid his katana under its chin and up through the head, a mutant kabob. Instead of lopping off the thing's head, Clover stood there staring into the thing's saddened eyes. It was like it was begging Clover for mercy. The eyes seemed like they were in pain, but that was impossible; zombies didn't feel anything but the hunger for flesh. That's what had the assassin so hypnotized. How could he be so transfixed by such a creature? How could a crazed zombie be calling out for mercy?

Clover shook his head.

"Clover, are you alright?" called Quasar.

The assassin didn't respond.

Then a voice, one he was familiar with or at least in his dreams of late. "Clover, we need your help. Please come and rescue us from certain doom."

The eyes of the zombie became even sadder than before. The voice whispered over and over in Clover's head. It was consuming the assassin's attention. Who owned that voice? Then he thought back to the bizarre dreams he had been having. The one with the strange setting, the wild adversaries and the woman that he didn't know—but in a way did, not that he could explain any of it. It was a dream, and dreams usually didn't make sense, but Clover had never dreamed anything before. *Aren't dreams a human trait?* he wondered.

Then at the tip of his tongue Clover whispered to only himself, "Surrora."

A pang in his heart awoke his heroic side. "Don't worry. I will save you and salvage Zoran's honor."

Announcing her name seemed to wash away the creature's pain and sadness from its red eyes. It was no longer something that was familiar, or as familiar to Clover as anything could get without knowing someone from a dream that didn't even seem like his own. The thing growled at the assassin and displayed its mouthful of needle teeth. It waved its claws at its captor, but Clover was too fast for that.

Clover removed his katana with a wet, sucking sound that followed, reared back in one smooth motion, and lopped off the thing's grotesque head. He didn't bother to stare at the head as it rolled off into the middle of a crowded battlefield of slaughter.

Suddenly, a throng of mutants broke for an area on the battlefield were a mixture of nomad warriors and Metro City coalition members were dueling individual mutants. The nomads, who generally kept to themselves, seemed ill-prepared for such a devastating attack. A peaceful people who had experienced several horrific things in the Wasteland, they had never experienced such brutality in a species. Clover had encountered the mutants in the Sierra Nevada Complex, the nomads, on the other hand, had not. The three comrades noticed the influx of mutants instantly, since their position overlooked a valley, where the three human groups were located. Not one of them knew what to do. The area that the throng of zombies were focused on was too far for them to make it in time, even if they allowed a portion of the human population in that area to die, they still wouldn't make it in time.

"We have to warn them," Clover said.

"How? There isn't time," Nightshade said. "The horde is moving too fast and the area they are headed is too far to reach; even with our enhanced reflexes." Nightshade shook his head. "I'm sorry, brother. Those humans are beyond our aid."

Despite not wanting to concede that his dark twin was right, Clover knew deep inside that Nightshade was correct in his assumptions. The groups of humans were doomed—or were they? There was one thing none of the comrades had thought of up to this point. The one thing that may backfire, but was worth a try.

Quasar spoke up. "No, there is a way to reach the throng of mutants before they arrive at the humans' position."

Both assassins were puzzled by their friend's declaration and perplexed at the same time. Neither one knew what Quasar was referring to, but they were all ears. When Quasar had their full attention, he continued.

"I can concentrate a focused energy beam at an acute point that would disintegrate the zombies without affecting the humans within the locality of the approaching throng. As long as I can strike them far enough from the blast sector."

"Can you really do that, Quasar?" questioned Nightshade. "Is your weaponized energy that precise, I mean."

Quasar nodded.

The three comrades looked carefully at one another, but they knew they didn't have time to debate it. Clover took a deep breath and both assassins said together, "What are we waiting for?"

Clover knew to give Quasar some extra space, as he didn't know if there would be any residual backlash from the staff their comrade wielded. Quasar had informed the assassin that normally there wasn't, but there had been a few instances where even Quasar was taken by surprise by his power; Clover could only imagine the devastation that had been caused. He thought back to when his friend had rescued them from, well, whatever had lived inside the complex. Once Quasar blew a hole inside his cavern home, according to his legendary tales, when practicing close by. Even by being careful the pulse energy was too much for him to control, but that had been a while ago. He had learned how to harness his power much more since.

The former corporate weapon stood downwind from Clover and his comrades to prevent any energy seepage from heading towards the two assassins. Clover observed Quasar gripping his energy staff straight up, ensuring the head of the staff faced in the direction he wanted the energy to go. Then Quasar focused on the throng of demented mutants now within a quarter of a mile from the human fighters, battling the other mutants.

Clover watched Quasar's eyes which were calm and ready for his mission. A humming noise began, and the energy began to dwell inside the staff. The assassin understood Quasar needed to concentrate to keep control of the powerful energy building up within him. Clover could feel the pulse energy building inside his friend, flowing through his entire body, like blood rushing through his veins. Clover felt as if the energy was rushing through his own veins and not Quasar's. Quasar's face was beginning to become flush and sweat began to tumble from his forehead.

The steady humming became intense and grew louder by the second as the dwell of energy intensified. Quasar's staff began to glow a red hue and pulse energy swirled around their comrade. The former corporate weapon had his eyes closed, concentrating on the increasing energy. The earth shook beneath their feet as the sandy hilltop started to give a little to the building well of energy.

An avalanche of sand fell inwards as if the Apocalyptic Earth had opened and began to swallow anything in the proximity.

Quasar began to whisper, "Allow the power that flows through me to become an extension of my will. Allow the pulse energy to reach out and annihilate our enemies, and our enemies only. Bring our adversaries a doom that they deserve, bring them the death blow I have witnessed."

Quasar's pulse energy had culminated and was ready. The staff was next to unbearable to hold on to with all the energy that had been transferred from Quasar's body into the staff. Clover felt the power build to an almost explosive point. The corporate weapon opened his eyes, but instead of the purple orbs they usually were, they were now chrome moons. The head of his staff rang out deafeningly, a consistent ringing that wouldn't stop.

Quasar released the power from his staff.

The immense pulse energy soared at a tremendous speed, leaving a comet trail of energy as it seared the air. The energy moved swift enough it sent distortions in the air, creating small tears in space and time that lasted milliseconds before dissolving back into nothing. The pulse energy made up the distance between the place it had been launched and the mutant throng had reached, making point of impact merely seconds.

Both assassins held their breath in anticipation. Would their attempt work? Or would it be in vain, causing more damage than it might if they had done nothing? Quasar had sunk to one knee from the effort. The attack had drained him of all his energy, and he barely had enough to keep him upright. Clover wondered if their comrade would be alright, but there wasn't anything he or Nightshade could do. Maybe if the Oracle was present, the seer could utilize his psychic kinetic abilities to aid Quasar in his recovery.

The throng of mutants moved towards their target with ambition and purpose, but they didn't see the pulse beam bear down on them, and when the energy struck their horde their mindless, mutilated bodies instantly evaporated as if they were steam rolling from a cooking pot, without any awareness of what had happened. But out of the flash mob emerged a mutant that drew Clover's undivided attention. Nikolai's mutant had a different heartbeat, a different mannerism than the other crazed mutants. Clover sensed the creature had a single purpose and it had spotted its target and was moving in on Clover.

The pulse energy ignited in a flash, then the sector where the charging mutants had been an instant before was flooded by an extreme rush of energy. The shock-wave shook the entire battlefield. Cascades of sand hills collapsed instantaneously as the shockwave blanketed the area. The devastation was severe, and the mutant horde wasn't the only thing that were devastated by the blast. A handful of nomads who had been too close to the horde had perished in the blast and a few small groups of platoon members from Metro City had also died.

The collateral damage was unavoidable, but that wouldn't make Quasar or the two assassins feel any better. The sector was cleansed of any life and the energy had even created a crater in the earth, exposing the rotten soil beneath the sandy surface. If anything had dwelled in that spot, it didn't survive.

Nikolai's pet mutant rushed through the smoke-filled battlefield, the only creature to have survived the surge of energy. Clover and this raging creature would swiftly be face to face and the confrontation would commence. Clover wasn't sure why this thing had its sight on him, but he could sense the rage that lived within this beast was only increasing, and he was the source. There was nothing the assassin could do but take this challenge head-on. Clover charged the approaching mutant at three-quarters speed. Going all out would only aid his nemesis and allow for mistakes to happen.

Clover concentrated on the creature with his in-tune senses, but unusually Clover couldn't anticipate the mutant's moves or its motivation. It possessed one sole purpose, his destruction. The mutant was still a bit away; in fact, it would take twenty steps for Clover's adversary to reach him, and he still had no clue how to attack the thing. Still running at three-quarters speed, the assassin removed his throwing weapon; it was the best thing he could come up with. He pulled his weapon from its hiding place, all while keeping a steady pace towards the charging mutant.

The bioengineered assassin released the throwing weapon, watching it glide through the air as if it were in its natural environment. The weapon weaved its way through the cascade of mutants, missing one by the thinnest hair length that could have decapitated the mutant in an instant. The razor-sharp blades rotated in the air, guiding the weapon back to the right, just missing a mutant devouring its prey.

Still, despite Clover's weapon cutting the distance between both combatants, the crazed mutant didn't waver from its path. Clover leaped over a corpse lying on the ground. He couldn't tell if it was human or mutant, and he didn't care either way. The assassin's focus was strictly on the wrinkled forehead, dark-gray-skinned mutant heading directly for him. Without breaking stride, Clover observed the whirling weapon make its killing approach. The death blow played over and over in the assassin's mind.

Clover could imagine brain matter exploding from the mutant as his weapon sliced the creature's head in two, exiting from the other side. In his mind, the mutant would stumble directly after its head became a bowl of slush and gray matter falling from decayed flesh. Then the mutant would fall to the ground, a slaughtered creature after a hunter had killed it.

Clover snapped out of his semihypnotic trance to watch his weapon miss its mark. The mutant seemed to know when to move out of the weapon's path, but Clover sensed it was more an instinct than something the mutant had contemplated. Either way, Clover nearly went into a rage, because he rarely missed a target, and most of the time when he did it was certainly on purpose. Clover didn't have time to stop and contemplate his failure, though that didn't mean he was indifferent about it.

"Shit, I missed," the assassin mumbled.

Finally, both combatants came within striking distance of each other. The rageful mutant took a swipe at Clover, but Clover's swift reflexes allowed him to dodge the sharp claws. As both adversaries passed each other, Clover performed a left-handed roundhouse, smacking the mutant in the upper back and sending decayed skin flying off its back and temporarily sending the mutant off balance. Not a major victory for the assassin, but since he had missed from a distance away, Clover would take any victory he could manage.

The mutant recovered quickly and stared at the assassin with hellfire in its eyes. It growled at Clover. The assassin had removed both katanas and began to swing each one from one side to the other in an almost mini figure eight. Both combatants proceeded to stare the other down, but this wasn't Clover's first confrontation, so it wasn't like the creature would be able to intimidate him. *Come on, you bastard, give me your best shot*, thought the assassin.

Quasar mumbled a prayer or incantation, most likely it was to clear his mind and reset the high levels of energy from continuing to flood his body to the point of overload. Either way, the former corporate weapon had several emotions to deal with and neither assassin was going to step in and awaken their comrade from clearing his conscience. Clover looked from the mutant's heaving chest to its daggerlike claws trying to discover a weakness.

The cyborg must have placed all his best into it, because it matched Clover blow for blow. The assassin made the first move, went to his left, purposely trying to force his adversary to commit. Clover thought he had the mutant off guard, leaning away from the assassin to Clover's left. Clover went to strike at the mutant, but the single-minded creature had fooled the assassin and swiped back to Clover's right, raking Clover's torso protector. Sparks flew from the assassin's armor and the attack placed Clover off balance, temporarily on the defensive.

The mutant reached back with its claws, readying for another round of attacks, but as Clover watched the creature's claws begin to move towards him, something smacked the mutant's head. The mutant's head swiftly moved to one side, as if a mighty blow had just occurred. The creature's attack stopped as quickly as it had begun, and the mutant staggered to one side of the assassin. Clover hadn't seen anything, and it took a concentrated effort before Clover recognized distortions in the surrounding environment, like something was cloaked under an invisible veil.

Clover knew exactly who had come to his rescue. The figure uncloaked and Nightshade gave Clover a sly grin. "Looks like you can't manage without me after all," boasted the dark assassin.

"Better late than never," mocked Clover.

Neither bioengineered assassin had time to celebrate. The mutant recovered and seemed to be turning its head from Clover to Nightshade, trying to decide which one had struck it from behind. Before either assassin could get the creature's attention, the mutant chose a new target. Clover saw the swift movements of the mutant towards his brother and knew no matter how fast he moved he would never reach Nightshade's side in time.

The mutant swiped at Nightshade's head, just missing it by inches, as the dark assassin deflected the mutant's claws with one of his swords. Clover knew Nightshade would never have enough time to reach his own throwing weapon and the only reaction Nightshade would have been to continuously deflect one attack after another. At this point, Clover learned that this mutant creature was relentless, and without aid Nightshade might be done for.

The mutant's claws clanged against Nightshade's lone drawn blade, as the dark assassin moved his katana from one side of his body to the other in self-defense. The only advantage Nightshade had that Clover didn't, was his ability to cloak himself, but Clover wasn't sure if that would be enough to evade Nightshade's potential doom. Swiftly, Clover moved in to give his brother aid. The question that floated around in Clover's head was if he would make it in time before the mutant disposed of Nightshade. Then the bioengineered assassin remembered who Nightshade was and knew his brother would be alright until he arrived. Clover hoped, at least.

Clover felt an echo with each step he took. The pounding in his head made a thunderous *stomp, stomp* sound. The only thing that seemed to compete with Clover's footfalls inside his head was the beating of his heart. Normally he had complete control of his breathing and heart rate, but in this moment the assassin couldn't anticipate what would happen next, which made the outcome of this encounter, or what Clover would do to save his brother, unpredictable.

Nightshade had been forced into a defensive position with the crazed mutant slashing at the dark assassin with its claws. Continuous scrapes against his katana prevented Nightshade from countering the threat before him. Everything seemed to be moving in slow motion for Clover, making the tension in his muscles increase. Clover raised one of his swords in one hand, and after retrieving his aerial weapon, gripped the weapon tightly in the other.

I can't afford missing this time, Clover thought. He was running out of time to aid Nightshade and that would result in taking on the thing single handedly, and the first encounter wasn't successful; Clover had failed to uncover the creature's weakness or who had sent it after him.

As Clover came closer to the two combatants, Nightshade had temporarily made a short recovery and was now on the offensive. Clover understood that might not last long and decided to act. He reached back with good ol' faithful and let his aerial weapon go. The weapon's four-pronged blades rotated at hyperspeed as it made its way towards the mutant. Even with his last miss, Clover had confidence the whirling blades would find their target. Both Nightshade and the mutant had no clue what was approaching, but no matter the results of this attack, Clover's intention was to continue towards the dark assassin and the one-track-minded mutant.

The mutant pushed Nightshade off it, giving the weapon a clear shot at its upper body, and Clover saw Nightshade spot the approaching doom. The mutant lunged forward, claws ready to dig into the dark assassin, that's when Clover's weapon struck the mutant's upper back, straight in its shoulder blade. The attack threw off the mutant's engagement of Nightshade and allowed the dark assassin to perform an attack of his own. Nightshade sliced at the mutant in a hurried fashion, not one of his precision attacks, and cut the mutant's face. Gray blood began to dribble from the wound, but that's all the weapon managed to do. As soon as the weapon had landed and cut the creature, it began to heal. Clover noticed the expression on Nightshade's face and knew something was wrong.

"This thing can heal instantly," Clover heard his brother's voice say inside his head. "We need a new plan of attack."

"I have it. We need a two-pronged attack," returned Clover.

"What do you mean?" asked Nightshade.

"You distract it and I'll provide the mortal blow."

"What do you think I have been doing, surely not giving it a massage," Nightshade growled.

"Just keep it busy and I'll handle the rest." Clover moved off to the combatants' left wing, hoping the creature didn't sense his presence. He would have to be swift in his movements and hoped he could kill the mutant before it had a chance to heal.

Clover moved swifter than he ever had, pumping his arms and legs in perpetual motion, cutting the distance between he and the two combatants rapidly. In one fluid motion, Clover flung his aerial weapon, then gripped one of his katanas in both hands firmly. This was going to be the final blow, one way or another. The bioengineered assassin was focused on just one thing, much like the crazed mutant.

Nightshade was still in his defensive position with the mutant raking its claws against the dark assassin's katana.

Clover asked his brother, "Nod if you can understand me," said Clover inside the dark assassin's head. Still in his defensive stance, Nightshade nodded.

"Good. I want you to strike the mutant in the shoulder, where its neckline meets the shoulder. Nod if you understand." Once again Nightshade nodded his understanding. "On three—one, two, *three*!" yelled Clover.

Nightshade used the flat part of his katana and pushed the mutant off, temporarily putting the creature off balance. With some distance between the dark assassin and the mutant, Nightshade lunged forward and struck the creature directly where Clover had asked his brother to strike. The blade sunk into the gray, decayed flesh and gray blood began to spill on the katana. Acid began to smolder on the sword blade. Luckily for Nightshade the construction of the blade was from an alien ore from Dragonaria, so no acid would rust or eat through its construction.

Clover arrived just as the mutant noticed Nightshade's blade in its neckline. The mutant growled at the dark assassin, but Clover swung his own katana towards its neck. "Now force you weapon to your right, making a circular motion." At first Nightshade seemed confused at Clover's instructions, giving Clover a lemon face, but soon understood.

The dark assassin flicked his wrist, and without much resistance, the katana blade sliced through the mutant's flesh, cutting tendons and muscle towards the back of the mutant's neck. Clover swung around the back of the mutant and sliced through the creature's neck, like he was butchering a turkey for thanksgiving dinner. The neck ripped from the creature's shoulders but didn't completely fall from its shoulders. A small strand of flesh still hung to the gray flesh and both assassins were afraid the flesh might start to repair itself.

"Die, you dirty monster!" shouted Nightshade. He kicked the mutant dead in the chest and the violent attack made the mutant's body jerk backwards. The sudden jerking of its body made the head rip from the mutant's body. The head rolled around the two assassins, like the mutant wanted to get one last look at its adversaries.

"Let's see you recover from that, asshole!" mocked Nightshade.

Clover scanned the horizon from his left to right and finally settled his vision to the west, towards the figure they had first spotted and who had unleashed the horde of zombies onto them all. Then looked down at the mutant Nightshade and he had defeated. Something greater was awaiting them all, the assassin could feel it.

"Come," beckoned Clover. "We have a crazy CEO to kill."

Chapter 22

The three comrades crossed the battlefield carnage as swiftly as possible. They were more than eager to finish this encounter and reunite with their other comrades. The cyborg stood there awaiting their arrival. Clover could tell the reception would not be joyous, but the assassin didn't really expect a cozy one. The atmosphere between the comrades and the former CEO was electric.

Clover turned towards Quasar, knowing their comrade was still both physically and mentally drained from the attack. "I think we have this. You can sit this one out."

Quasar raised his weary head, but still had a glare of determination in his gray eyes. "Are you sure about that?"

Both assassins looked at one another, then nodded.

As the assassins approached, the Nikolai Volkov stood there still as a stone statue. The cyborg didn't flinch or move one ounce, not even to exhale at their approach. The cyborg, much like the machine he was, showed no emotion. The two assassins stopped far enough from the cyborg to prevent their adversary from getting too easy a shot on them. Then a half-machine, half-human face peered at them both.

"So, we finally meet face to face, assassin. This time you won't get the drop on me." Nikolai Volkov squeezed his mechanical hand, and it made a semi-squeaking nose in a show of strength.

Clover looked at Nightshade then back towards the cyborg. "I think you have it all wrong, Volkov; we have never met before."

"Liar!" shouted Nikolai. "You attempted to assassinate me, but you failed. What's wrong, Clover, too afraid to admit to your failures?"

Clover looked once again to his brother.

Nightshade burst out laughing. "Oh, this is too hilarious."

The cyborg turned on Nightshade with clenched fists and his human eye focused with hatred on the shadow assassin. "What seems to be so funny to you, assassin? Is your death some punchline?" The cyborg clenched his fists as if he wanted to strike down Nightshade, but couldn't. Nikolai still was confused by the presence of both Clover and Nightshade, he had no clue who was there that day to assinate him.

Nightshade couldn't help shaking his head. "It's that the last time I saw your scrawny ass, you were too busy running for your life. How could you know who was coming for you? Unfortunately, I assumed you dead when you fell in the well. A mistake I will not make again, I guarantee you."

The cyborg's human portion of his face began to turn a sun-red texture.

"You will pay for the insolent remark, assassin. I may have mistaken the identity of my would-be killer, that doesn't mean I still won't seek vengeance on your bioengineered ass!"

With that taunt, Nikolai reached into his armored body and threw a sharp, round object, similar to a saw blade, at Nightshade. The attack came from out of nowhere, and if it had been anyone else besides the shadow assassin, it might have killed him. But with the ability to anticipate actions, much like his twin Clover, Nightshade was a step ahead of his adversary.

The shadow assassin, in a simultaneous move, went into his cloaking mode, blending in with the desert climate and with his inherited swiftness, eluded the attack. Both assassins, one visible and one now incognito, drew their katanas from their sheaths. Both assassins began to circle their adversary.

"Do you think me a fool, assassin?" taunted the cyborg. "I know where you are, despite your chameleon ability."

Simultaneously, both assassins came at their target. Nikolai raised one arm to deflect Clover's blade, but the cyborg's heavy and bulky metal body made him too slow to avoid Nightshade's blow. Both katanas scraped over the metal surface of the cyborg, igniting sparks from their sword's contact and merely scraping the surface of Nikolai's body. Deciding it was foolish to attack from the same position twice, both Clover and Nightshade kept moving around their target.

"What's wrong, assassins? Am I tougher than several of your previous victims?"

Nikolai watched Clover move away but targeted the shadow assassin. Without looking for the cloaked target, Nikolai Volkov raised his arm, and a miniature weapon came out of a side panel of his arm—an ionized cannon. With precise aim, he fired. It barely touched the shadow assassin, but the shot did manage to graze Nightshade's shoulder. The shot also shattered the sword Nightshade wielded; leaving him with one weapon left. The attack caused his cloaking ability to falter, and Nightshade emerged right behind the cyborg.

"Not so cocky without your ability to hide, are you, assassin?"

Nightshade grabbed at his wounded shoulder, and then at the shattered sword he still had a grip of. "You will pay for that insult, cyborg."

Nightshade took a step back and retrieved his second katana.

The cyborg's attention was temporarily diverted by Nightshade being behind the half man, half machine.

Without making any sound, Clover sent a telepathic message to his twin, "You go low and knock the cyborg off balance; I'll go high."

Nightshade nodded.

Carefully not allowing their adversary into their plot, the shadow assassin got into position. He was going to love sweeping the former CEO off his feet. Nightshade glanced down at the cyborg's legs. Without hesitation, he rushed for the cyborg. The shadow assassin stayed low, not giving Nikolai a clear shot at him. Another one of those shots might just end the shadow assassin for good. When the cyborg tried to force Nightshade to one side, and to his advantage, the shadow assassin moved back the other way.

Nightshade's antics were making Clover impatient and timing his own moves was nearly impossible. Clover would just have to improvise when the time came. He watched Nightshade's little dance routine and even though he understood what the shadow assassin was doing, all Clover could think was *Show off!*

Nightshade made the cyborg believe he was going to attack from his left, forcing the former CEO to expose a portion of his left side, then Nightshade dove for the cyborg's legs in such a swift movement that it surprised even Clover. Nightshade passed through the cyborg CEO's lack of defenses and kicked out the Nikolai's legs, forcing the top-heavy machine to become off balanced. That gave Clover the opening he needed.

The bioengineered assassin launched his body into the air, soaring towards the dazed and unaware cyborg. Clover struck Nikolai square in the chest plate, not with one kick, but two. The first thrust forced the CEO to lose control of his ability to stay upright, but it didn't complete the job. Nikolai was too sturdy for that. But Clover's second kick, which came directly after the first, finished the job. Nikolai wasn't prepared to take two blows from the assassin, and even if he was prepared, it would have been unlikely his top-heavy construction could have sustained both as swiftly as the kicks came.

Clover watched the former CEO crash to the ground, sending sandy debris up into the air. The cyborg landed on his side, but it was apparent that Nikolai would be having issues getting back on his feet. The former CEO waved his metal arms wildly but still couldn't get his heavy body to roll upright. Clover heard a winding noise, like something was attempting to turn inside the CEO's body but couldn't. Clover had broken something inside the cyborg and knowing that, gave him the knowledge Nikolai Volkov could be beaten.

A clapping noise, sounding more like metal against metal, but in a rhythmic tone came from the topsy-turvy cyborg. The cyborg's cybernetic eye looked at the assassin. "Ha, ha, ha. Very good assassin. You caught me by surprise. But tell me, is that the best you can do?"

Slowly the cyborg had gotten to a knee somehow but was still unbalanced. Clover, in his fit of rage, swiftly moved towards the cyborg. Trying to find a weakness, Clover struck the CEO numerous times. Each time sent sparks flying, just as the last time the assassins attacked the cyborg's protective outer casing. But no matter how many times the assassin tried to discover a weakness in Volkov's armor, he failed.

The CEO began to laugh. "You fool, my metal casing is made of metal one hundred times tougher than your sword. You wont ever penetrate it."

Just then, Nightshade shoved the former CEO on his back and rammed his remaining katana through the CEO's cybernetic eye. Electrodes exploded and sparks shot out of the hole that was the cyborg eye. Nikolai cried out in pain. He slapped the shadow assassin away and pulled out the assassin's katana. Nikolai was panting, as if a vital organ had been struck.

"You idiot!" barked the former CEO. "Do you know what you have done? Who I work for or who built me?"

The shadow assassin didn't respond. In fact, Nightshade wasn't sure how to take Nikolai's banter. He looked at Clover, confused. "What is this psycho babbling about?" he mouthed.

Nikolai got to one knee and opened a compartment in his arm. Then the cyborg began to press something on the display screen that lit up a portion of the cyborg's face. The stern face of Nikolai Volkov concentrated on what he was doing. Neither assassin made a move to finish off the cyborg, fearing whatever he was up to might ignite with the cyborg's death. Once he was finished, Volkov looked up with his ruined cybernetic eye piece and sneered at both assassins.

"You have both spoiled my plans, defeated my mutant army and ruined my master's plot. Now you will experience one last torment. Your end is at hand, and I will be there to watch it firsthand."

Both Clover and Nightshade gave each other a perplexed look. Neither one knew what was about to unfold.

Suddenly the ground beneath their feet shook. It nearly wiped them all out, but Clover and Nightshade saved some grace and recovered in time not to fall flat on their backsides. A few smaller quakes followed. Another large quake emerged that sent both assassins and the cyborg CEO tumbling through a vortex of sand and earth as the dune collapsed. All three figures found the bottom after falling for what seemed forever.

Clover was the first to recover. The bioengineered assassin shook of his wooziness as his vision slowly corrected itself. He was no longer seeing double nor was his head spinning. Clover's first action was to search out

Nightshade and their adversary. Clover's dark twin lay some distance, possibly twenty or so steps from him. Nightshade seemed to be only semiconscious, but at least the shadow assassin was breathing normally.

The assassin searched for their adversary. At first Clover couldn't spot the cyborg, but that was because the thing that once was Nikolai Volkov was half buried under sand. Clover noticed instantly when the cyborg started to rise. The dull shine of cyborg Nikolai's body was unmistakable against the sandy landscape. The cyborg shook off the sand dust and appeared to stare at Clover. If the two adversaries hadn't been so far apart, Clover would have said the cyborg was smiling its half-human, half-machine smile at him. And boy was that crooked and deformed smile something that would send chills up your spine.

There didn't seem to be any way out of the dish-shaped hole they were currently in. The smooth, curved edges looked like a death sentence if either one of them attempted to climb out. Plus, they would be an easy target for the others. Clover couldn't put it past Nightshade to take a shot at him with his back turned. It wasn't his dark twin's fault, it was just the way he had been made.

Then another large quake shook and some debris from the rim's edge tumbled down the curved sides and towards the crater bottom. Clover had lost eye contact with Nikolai Volkov for just a moment during the quake, and when Clover looked back the cyborg had vanished. By that time, Nightshade was on one knee shaking his own wooziness off. Clover went to Nightshade's position and aided his brother slowly to his feet.

"Where is the cyborg?" Nightshade asked.

Clover shook his head.

That's when they heard a heckling laugh, one that both assassins could equate with Nikolai Volkov—the cyborg had used it before the quake had upended their encounter. "Well, assassins, it's about time you meet her."

Clover thought, *Time to meet who?*

The floor of the crater split open from the last quake, and from the depths of the Wasteland underground appeared a humongous creature. The beast ripped through the sandy depths with two large pincers protruding through the cracked earth. The pincers were the size of a commuter bus and supported an even more mountainous body. Each pincer slammed into the earth, creating a hold for the body to emerge.

From the Wasteland depths appeared an enormous arachnoid with three pairs of massive cybernetic legs that had the appearance they could crush an oil tanker. With each movement of the mechanical legs, Clover could hear gears rotating in the arachnoid's joints. The sound went *tick, tick, crunch*. The body the legs supported was a titian-sized metal scorpion, one that towered high above the two assassins like a leviathan. The machine scorpion whipped her gargantuan tail in the air, leaving remnants of static electricity in its wake. Her beady red eyes searching for her master. Then at the last moment a thick and even more massive tail ripped through the earth, tossing sand everywhere.

"What the hell is . . ." started Nightshade. "Am I still knocked out and dreaming?"

"Gentlemen. I would like to introduce you to Charlene, my pet scorpion. She has an affection for human blood, but I think substituting your blood for human will do nicely." The cyborg touched something on the panel of his arm. "Go get them, girl."

The leviathan spun towards the assassins. It seemed like it had hatred in its memory banks and hunger in its circuits. It lunged forward with large, crushing steps that would make up the distance in no time. The thirty-five-foot-tall scorpion slammed its deadly stinger tail where the two assassins had been only seconds prior. The collision punched a hole in the ground and sent debris into the air. The tail created cracks in the crater floor that ruptured and spread out across the crater bottom, causing their own ripple effects. The ground began to have aftershocks that made it nearly impossible to maneuver.

Her missed attack enraged Charlene and she gave out a robotic cry as she ripped her tail out of the earth. Clover had moved to the left, away from the attacking scorpion, and Nightshade to her right. Splitting up seemed the most logical thing, but it also left each assassin isolated.

Charlene danced to her right, and then back to her left. Reaching with a pincer at one assassin, then whipping her tail at the other. Each attack a near miss for each assassin.

Clover could feel the air pass by as the scorpion tail just missed his head, nearly decapitating him. He struck the ground hard, and his aerial weapon popped out of his cloak. That gave the assassin an idea. Clover retrieved the weapon and aimed it at the tip of the scorpion's tail. While Charlene's attention was diverted on his brother, Clover aimed the weapon, and took in a deep breath. With his usual precision accuracy, Clover threw the weapon and watched it slice the humid air like warm butter. With all the commotion, neither Nightshade nor the titan saw the weapon's approach.

At the last moment, when it appeared that Clover's aerial weapon would hit its mark, the titan scorpion whipped its tail out of the path of destruction. The weapon missed its target by inches as it flew past. Clover gasped, he had missed and that was uncommon for the assassin. Now Nightshade was truly exposed without any backup and his brother had no clue what to do next.

Clover wasn't the only one to notice his missed attempt, Charlene had as well. The scorpion turned and faced the assassin. She glared down with her red digital eyes and Clover understood she was determined to make him her next meal. In the distance, the assassin heard the cyborg cackling. Charlene lunged forward and tried to slice Clover in half with a pincer. Only his swift movements kept the scorpion from succeeding.

Charlene slammed the pincer into the ruined earth, sending sand, rotten soil and other things into the air. It rained irradiated earth all around and Clover was just nimble and swift enough to avoid the fallout. Then the titan scorpion slammed her second pincer into the ground, with similar effects, except this time she got the pincer stuck in the ground. It was the break Clover needed.

The assassin reached out with one hand and concentrated. Before he could take a deep breath, the assassin felt a tug, like an invisible force was tugging back. With his superior hearing, he heard a faint whistle and that's when his aerial weapon struck Charlene's unprotected tail. The impact was significant, but it acted as a distractor long enough for Clover to run towards his unconscious brother.

When the scorpion's attention returned to where Clover had been, he had passed her and was a quarter of the way across the crater floor. Clover was sprinting at top speed, his legs churning up sand and earth, but it wouldn't be enough. Charlene, now cognitive of where her victim was, swung her injured tail one hundred and eighty degrees from where it had been struck, towards the assassin's getaway path.

The might of her tail sent a vortex of debris into the air and in its wake as it made its way towards Clover. The strong wind began to build, and soon a tsunami of wind and sand engulfed the assassin, making it difficult to see, let alone find his way to his downed twin. The mighty tail slammed into Clover, knocking him unconscious for a moment and sending his body flying. There was no pain, but that could have been from the instant concussion his head suffered, or maybe something was looking out for the assassin.

A sensation began to pull at Clover, something very foreign; a sensation he had never experienced before. Then an image of an enormous warrior, one decked out in fine armor and the crest of a dragon. It was clear to the assassin the being wasn't human or his own kind, or better yet, not *quite* his kind, because there was some familiarity with the figure, something Clover just couldn't pinpoint. This new figure had a broad chest, thick shoulders and was very muscular. If Clover knew what a god might look like, then he assumed this is what one might appear as. The being's armor was draped in crimson with silver borders.

The godlike figure spoke to Clover in a soothing monotone, like a gentle parent consoling a child. "My dear Clover, you don't know me, but my name is Jetsuenete. I am the leader of an elite group of defenders known as the Elementals. As you will discover, you have elemental blood in you, even though you're not a direct descendent of us. Your purpose is much more than you realize, and you have abilities that reach farther than you can ever imagine."

The godlike warrior gave Clover a gentle smile.

"I don't have time to tell you everything, that will be later since you have met Surrora; things will be a little easier for you to swallow when the time comes. For now, I will lend you my power to aid you in your current condition. Just remember one thing, there are greater forces at work and deeper meaning for yourself and your twin. I can't foresee your twin's role quite yet. All you have to do is reach out with your mind and touch the sensation that has already called out to you."

The vision vanished as suddenly as it had appeared. Clover slowly awakened from his concussed condition and realized Charlene was nearly on top of him. He would need to act swiftly to save himself and his brother. Clover did what the vision told him, even though he didn't know why he was compelled to comply. It was just a feeling inside him that told the assassin the image could be trusted.

Clover closed his eyes and reached out to the sensation that had been beckoning his attention for the past five or six minutes, but it seemed like eternity to the assassin. At first the sensation was like a conversation coming from a long way away, faint and weak. But the more he focused on the sensation, the stronger it became. The sensation quickly changed from a whisper to something like a beating heart drawing ever so close. The *thump, thump* seemed to mimic Clover's own heartbeat. The rhythm drew nearer with each passing moment until it seemed that the foreign sensation was inside the assassin.

Then Clover sensed his blood was on fire, like lava rushing through his veins. He began to shake uncontrollably and he had no way to make it stop. A gigantic eye, like a colossal reptilian one, had come into the assassin's mind. Clover was sensing something grandeur than either himself or Nightsahde and it was rampaging through his mind, blood, his entire being. But it wasn't a lizard's eye at all, it was the eye of a leviathan beckoning him to call for its aid. But it wasn't a thing at all but an idea, a collection of beings currently living within him, a celestial collective, an ancient and long deceased essence. He was now part of a collective mind wave, a celestial force like no other.

The assassin's body suddenly froze and the fiery sensation now filling his entire body felt as it would burst. Then the thing spoke. "I will do as you command me." That took Clover's breath away. He hadn't expected the sensation to have a voice, let alone speak to him. "All you have to do is think, and I will obey."

Clover thought about the fiery sensation flowing through his body and that sparked an idea. He reached out and instructed the thing to do his bidding. Then the earth shook beneath Clover's feet.

The hourglass had run out of sand.

Clover had a sensation that some great power was building in the distance, somewhere far off, but it also felt so close. Inside the assassin's mind a vision appeared as if he was viewing through a fog; the events that were about to unfold were directly tied to him somehow.

One hundred miles away, at the outskirts of the abandoned town of Demure, right at the spot Clover had ended the reign of his most hated adversary Legion, a crimson and golden glow began to illuminate under the surface. The sandy earth began to shake, and the glow became more prominent, as if giving birth to a monumental being of immense power and size. Then, below the sandy surface, cracks began to form, an egg preparing for the birth of the thing the assassin was conjuring. The earth shook and caused numerous sand slides and collapsed several dunes and hills nearby.

From under the collapsing surface came the elemental to its new master's call. An elemental dragon, with a wingspan as large as a bomber aircraft. The creature launched towards the sky, leaving behind a trail of sand and terrain. Clover watched the elemental soar high into the red sky at enormous speed. Inside his mind, the post-apocalyptic terrain flew by in a blink of an eye. The creature would make the one-hundred-mile journey in very little time; but would it be in time?

The assassin snapped out of his visionary dreamscape to see Charlene hovering over him. There was no time to think of what was heading for them. Even if the soaring elemental came to their rescue, Clover couldn't just sit by, or he and his twin would be roasted along with the titan scorpion. Clover stood up and quickly scanned the crater from horizon to crater floor as swiftly as he could. Distracting the scorpion from Nightshade and buying his new ally time would be his best bet.

Then a colossal shadow passed overhead, the cavalry had arrived; it was time to leap into action. Clover jumped to his feet and ran in the opposite direction. It seemed to take Charlene by surprise and for a moment the creature was bewildered by the assassin's jailbreak. But it didn't take her long to find Clover; she spun as quickly as a titan could and targeted him.

Right before she could attack, a rain of ionized fire covered the scorpion, stopping any attack momentum. The elemental's first attack didn't stop Charlene, and she spun on her new assailant. The titan whipped her great metal tail around, the same one Clover had struck with his weapon, and posed to strike back. She swung her tail at the elemental with great force that brought on another round of profound wind currents.

The elemental dragon wasn't about to be swatted like a fly; the massive beast swung its own thick, muscular tail at the scorpion's. The dragon's tail stopped the scorpion's in midair and shattered the upper half, sending metal shards and pieces all along the crater floor. Then the airborne elemental swooped down and grabbed Charlene by the bulk of her body with its enormous talons and punctured the metal flesh. Charlene tried to fight back, swinging her deadly pincers in every direction, but it only made her look like a chaotic and out-of-control beast.

The elemental began to fly, flapping its wings furiously and taking the scorpion with it. Clover never thought he would ever see two leviathans airborne, but there he was, watching the two leave the crater and fly towards the scorching sunlit sky. Higher and higher the titans flew and soon they became one giant shadow. Clover was having issues, even with his enhanced eyesight, seeing the titans anymore. It dawned on him that he had the chance to check on Nightshade.

Clover reached his twin just as Nightshade was recovering. The shadow assassin shook his head, but his eyes were still glossed over. It would take a while for him to come fully to his senses. Clover lifted Nightshade up by the shadow assassin's shoulders and began walking towards the curved crater edge. Clover continuously looked skyward to see what was happening, but still nothing but dark shadows hovered overhead.

Then Charlene fell back to earth. The elemental had let her go, but not before ripping some of her metal hide from her backside. The titan arachnoid waved her six massive arms in the hopes to slow her death fall. Nothing was going to save the scorpion from her doom. Once she struck the crater floor, her body gave, and the floor bottom nearly collapsed. The elemental swooped down and shot her with more ion fire. Clover could smell metal burning and the assassin could only imagine the scorpion's body slowly disintegrating into nothing.

The shockwave of Charlene's fall reached the two brothers. The crater floor disappeared and sent Clover and Nightshade into a headlong fall. Clover tried to reach for Nightshade, and vice versa, without any success. Then Clover tried to flap his arms, more in an automatic reflex than in any hope to stop his falling. Clover began to become dizzy; it would be his and his brother's death if he didn't do something quick. The assassin closed his eyes and reached out to the elemental dragon one more time.

At first, he couldn't sense the beast like before and the assassin had to assume the thing had done its duty and fled. But then the same dual heartbeat began again and before Clover was aware, a pair of enormous talons had him and he became airborne, no longer falling to his death. In one grip Clover rested, while in the other his twin rested comfortably. They would be rescued one last time, but what would be next? *How will this all resolve itself?* Clover wondered.

The confrontation site, which now was a devastated crater, now ran a few miles across and several hundred feet deep. Both assassins dug through the sand and rotten earth but after searching for what seemed like hours, couldn't find the cyborg anywhere.

"Do you think the CEO survived?" questioned Nightshade.

Clover took a deep breath, trying to collect his thoughts. "I don't know. This place has changed since we last encountered him."

They performed some more digging and at last discovered something reflective half buried in the sand. Clover picked their discovery up and both assassins inspected it thoroughly. The thing had taken on more than its share of damage and sand filled every crevasse of its design. The cybernetic eye no longer had its luster, its eerie life, like it had as part of the cyborg that was Nikolai Volkov. The metal casing holding the eye was dull and beaten up. No circuitry ran from the back of the eye, only sockets to plug into the cyborg.

Clover offered the souvenir to Nightshade. "Want it?"

Nightshade didn't bother to respond.

"Suit yourself." Clover tossed the eye in the direction they had found it. "I say, if Nikolai Volkov is still alive, he is buried deep under a sea of sand and not worth the effort to uncover. In my book, he is dead."

Epilogue

Somewhere within the Merciless Reach

Somewhere hidden in the Merciless Reach, a dimension where things become corrupted, decayed, weathered and die; far from the residence of the entity known as the Darkness, creeped an arachnoid thing. It possessed thousands of eyes, the ability to blend in with shadows, and possessed infinite amount of memory, a perfect spy for its master. The six-legged creature had been in reconnaissance in the Donix, which was better known by its common name, the Vision Realm. It is the place where the shadow spy could see in dimensions closed even to the Darkness's own spies. Then it had taken the long journey home, across the desolate Merciless Reach, if home is what this place was.

The creature made its way inside the cave's structure—cold, desolate and lonely—but it's just what the creature's master liked. The thing utilized its ability to see in the shadows to search out its master and report what it had found. Each of its thousand eyes looked in a different direction, while its pointed, hardened legs danced in its unnerved state. The creature's master made all his spies nervous. The master of spies had the habit of killing spies who brought bad news.

The creature used its telepathic wavelength to call out to its master. The spy couldn't speak, and its only form of communication was telepathic. It's how the master of spies had created the creature and prevented any would-be agent of shadow from discovering his new creation, manipulating it before Darkcloak had a chance to insert his own malice into it. A sound came from the far-left corner and the arachnoid spun to speak to its master. But once the creature peered into the darkness, it found it empty. Had some invader infiltrated their cold and comfortable accommodations?

The spy danced around in a circle, stopping ever so often, calling out to its master with no reply. Then another sound forced the spy to spin around one hundred and eighty degrees. Still nothing! The short shadow spy was becoming paranoid, if such a creature could ever be.

Then, through the shadows a dark and less-than-friendly voice emerged. "What have you to report, spy?"

The six-legged spy spun around to face its master. Darkcloak stood tall for a Merciless Reach occupant, with the immense pressures constricting growth, but unlike his spy, Darkcloak and several of the Darkness's agents were less physical in presence and more specterlike. Darkcloak, like most of his shadow agent counterparts, could merge into and utilize shadows as a way of transporting himself from one place or dimension to another through a dark portal. Darkcloak was also the biggest adversary to the Darkness's greatest agent, the Shadow Lord—keeper of all the shadow entity's secrets. The two agents had never gotten along, and in fact, a few times Darkcloak and the Shadow Lord had nearly annihilated one another. But it would be highly unlikely if either agent would be gone for long, since they were tied to the Darkness's own destructive power.

The arachnoid spy took a few steps away from its master, with its thousands of eyes looking directly at its master yet avoiding eye contact. That only prolonged its unfavorable report. Darkcloak spoke again, only this time it was in a sinister and more demanding tone. "I order you to report what you have uncovered, spy! Don't make your master ask again. That would make for an unpleasant experience for you."

This time, the arachnoid used all its eyes, but still refused to look directly at its master. Through its telepathic ability, it reported. "I have returned from the Donix, and I possess the knowledge you desire, Master."

Darkcloak let out an impatient grunt. "And?"

The spy still hesitated, and the agent of shadows had his answer, but the agent still wanted to see it for himself. Darkcloak reached out and through the spy's multitude of eyes saw the devastation for himself. The battlefield of corpses of humans and mutant bodies lying in their sandy graves. Darkcloak hadn't seen the handful of zombies scattered to the east and west racing for cover. Only what remained of the mutant throng. A smile penetrated Darkcloak's sinister, shadowy face.

He snickered.

Then Darkcloak saw the devastation of the dune crater all leveled. He felt a significance to this spot and their plans. The agent of shadows searched the wrecked site carefully until he came across the half-buried cybernetic eye. That drew Darkcloak's undivided attention. "Well," he said with a hint of amusement, "what do we have here, little one? It seems the cyborg has failed in a monumental effort. I did warn Shadow Lord that his pet would fail, but his hard-headedness got the better of him. The Darkness won't be all that happy with this."

The little spy gave out a whimper at the mention of the Darkness.

Then the shadow agent found the trace that showed him what had transpired that led to the dune crater's destruction. First Darkcloak saw the battle between the cyborg, Nikolai Volkov and the two assassins, then the dune collapse and the assassin's encounter with Charlene.

Then what seemed to astonish the agent even further was the arrival of the elemental dragon and the metal scorpion, which was another of Shadow Lord's favorite pets. Once the scene went airborne and the two behemoths dueled in the air, Darkcloak only could shake his head. He mumbled to himself, "This isn't going to end well, is it?" He glanced at the arachnoid spy, but didn't wait for an answer. Then Charlene dropped and he watched her enflamed body crash.

"Elementals emerging, have they risen from their lengthy slumber finally? The Darkness won't be pleased by that revelation and it's something to distract the dark master. Another adversary it will have to kill."

Darkcloak snapped away from the image and spun on the little spy.

"And what of our own agent, why hasn't he answered any of my calls? Has Nightshade fallen under the influence of the human savior, Clover, and gone rogue?"

Darkcloak searched the arachnoid's memory banks. Darkcloak searched and searched but couldn't find his creation anywhere. It was frustrating the shadow agent. He was a different creature, not like Shadow Lord, who only existed to serve the Darkness. No, Darkcloak had his own purpose and the only reason he stuck around the horridness of the Merciless Reach was his attachment to the Darkness and his master's insidious will. That's the reason Darkcloak had stolen some of the DNA from the vial that had been used to create the bioengineered assassin, Nightshade. Darkcloak didn't necessarily need Nightshade to do anything on Earth, he needed the shadow assassin's physical body to inject his own malevolence and allow the shadow agent to venture away from the Merciless Reach without being detected.

Before Darkcloak could accomplish this, Nightshade had gone rogue. Now the shadow agent was out an asset and the means to oppose the Darkness's will from another dimension. Darkcloak witnessed Nightshade talking to Clover and Preist in the presence of the Oracle and afterwards outside of Metro City intervening against the cyborg and the outlaws. That was the last image Darkcloak had of the assassin. Darkcloak clenched a fist that sent shadow smoke flying from his translucent hand. The agent would have a lot to uncover before his own plans could proceed, but for now finding Nightshade and separating the twin assassins was top priority.

Sierra Nevada Facility

Deep within the depths of the Sierra Nevada Facility, a calm quietness resided. An transdimensional portal emerges. Out of this unidentified portal two figures emerge. One had a dark persona that moved in and out of shadows like a second skin and the other, a short and nervous subservient creature. The two figures had emerged deep in the facility's subterranean levels, where no one since the nuclear devastation destroyed this world, had been.

There was a smell of what could only smell like rotting corpses, despite no one having been down to this level in decades. It seemed to stain the metal material of the level. This didn't seem to deter either one of the guests. This must be something they were used to, if they had the capacity to smell at all. The only sound audible down in this subterranean world was the occasional settling of rusted metal braces and the cracking noises coming from the hidden bulkhead supports.

The smaller creature stepped forward, towards the end of the dark hallway, but that didn't bother the figure with the ominous aura. The smaller creature looked up at what would have to be its master, and the taller figure nodded. The dwarf-sized being made its way down the somewhat extensive hallway. It floated inches from the rusted metal flooring like a balloon in the Macy's Thanksgiving Day Parade.

At the end of the dark hallway there was a thick blast door that would take a missile strike to knock down and that was what it was built to withstand. That wouldn't matter the individual with the sinister aura. The shorter being glanced back to its master and the master raised its hand and grabbed the subservient creature in the other.

"Are you ready, Edogan?" asked the creature with the sinister persona.

The dwarf-sized creature nodded. "Yes, Master Darkcloak, I am."

The two figures slipped through the thick metal door as if it was a curtain of water. On the other side rows of storage tanks were lined up and filled with emerald-colored liquid. More storage tanks lined up above the ones closest to the visitors. The shadow spy was in shock by the discovery, but his master was acting as if this was a normal sight for the shadow agent.

A digital light was the only thing that lit up the space before the shadow beings, which covered a three-by-three square foot area before them.

Edogan turned to his partially translucent master in what had to be shock for the being, but it would be difficult to tell since it had no way to express itself without facial muscles. "Master Darkcloak, what is this place?"

"This, my little spy, is what I have been working on for a long time. It was meant to be the endgame for humanity. Little did the CEO and its scientists realize I was orchestrating this from behind the scenes and they were doing the dirty work for me." The shadow agent looked down on the spy.

Nikolai Volkov had no idea his company was being manipulated into creating the serum for Darkcloak's diabolical plans. It was Darkcloak's plan all along to use the cyborg to accelerate its mutation population to rise against the Darkness and the Shadow Lord's own plans for the destruction of what was left of humanity.

"Unbeknown to my nemesis, I inserted the idea into the cyborg's hard drive brain to pursue the creation of the mutant army, for my own purposes. When the half-cyborg thought, he was being directed by the Shadow Lord and given a new lease on life, in reality the resurrected CEO was doing my own bidding."

"I played each and every one of them as a disposable pawn in my own game of chess. Obviously, I am the queen piece on the board." The shadow agent smiled.

Darkcloak touched the nearest tank with his translucent hand and an air pocket suddenly formed and released its contents, as the bubble burst. That placed a smile on the shadow agent's face, now illuminated from the light reflecting off the tank's glass exterior. The bubble was like a metaphor for what was about to transpire for the remaining members of humanity. The image of thousands of crazed super mutants running over the Wasteland, invading every township and makeshift settlement, tearing limb from limb, devouring human blood and doing what the Darkness failed to do: end the human race on Earth.

Still touching the tank full of serum, Darkcloak said to no one in particular, "Soon my army of super mutants will wreak havoc upon this land like a plague of locusts. And it will be I who is triumphant, not the Shadow Lord.

It will be I who can boast of finally conquering this land. My finest masterpiece yet."

Edogan cringed as its master fluttered away from Darkcloak.

"What is it, you fool? Why do you dare trample on my glory?

The small spy hesitated and possessed fear reaping from its mouth. "But Master Darkcloak, forgive my impertinence, but didn't that fail miserably with the cyborg CEO and his own army of mutants?"

Darkcloak's smirk vanished, and it appeared if the shadow agent would lash out a venomous furry upon the spy. "Their attempt wasn't a failure, but even if you have to see it as such, what do you expect from a group of morons?"

The little spy fluttered backwards a bit, as if its master slapped it with a backhand. "I . . . I don't understand."

"You're not supposed to. I am the brains of the operation and you're my gofer. Cyborg Nikolai's mission was meant as a test run, and now I know what errors to avoid so I may create the perfect army of mutants."

Darkcloak peers down the row of serum-filled tanks with a smile of delight, even though it was pitch black in the room.

"Then you would want to know when any asset goes rouge?" questioned Edogan.

Darkcloak didn't have to respond to that, the shadow spy received a telepathic tingling, as if its master had reached inside the spy's head and was attempting to rip its mind from its head. Not a pleasant feeling at all. There was some information that Edogan had, and the spy wondered if its master already knew what it was. Would Darkcloak be upset at another failure and finally take it out on the spy? Or would the shadow agent revel in his adversary's failure?

Master, do you know about Nikolai Volkov's mutant creation?"

Darkcloak possessed absolutely no emotions on his face, but that wasn't anything new to the spy. Very rarely did the shadow agent show any emotions, outside of pure joy when the Shadow Lord was proven wrong or had a setback. The shadow agent wasn't expressing anything such as that now; he was a poker player with a stone face.

"Yes," responded Darkcloak. "Why wouldn't I know anything the cyborg Volkov did? Didn't I just tell you my gift to the cyborg was the concept of a mutant army to manipulate the foolish elders."

"Then you know the bioengineered assassins killed Volkov's pet mutant, the one he built for his own amusement."

Darkcloak nodded.

"Then I must tell you our own experiment . . ."

Darkcloak straightened and glared at the spy. "You're referring to the human woman that fled the Sierra Nevada Complex with Clover and his comrades?"

The spy acknowledged the shadow spy's rhetorical question. "The human woman known as Doria, who was killed in a pit, has arisen as your experiment."

Edogan raised its hand and an image broke the dark void of the serum chamber.

Inside the Metro City limits

Within the crater that Doria fell into, fleeing the monsters of the inner city, something awakened. Under the whirling of the wind a sudden cry, like something was both dying and being born at the same time. No one heard the scream, so no one could attest to how horrifying the bone-chilling cry really was. It was pitch-black so the movement inside the pit couldn't be seen by anything that didn't have thermal vision. Whatever it was at the bottom of the crater, it started to move at a snail's pace, first crawling in a circle, repeatedly. Then it began to discover its way and began to ascend the crater.

Inch-by-inch, the figure crawled. It was a slow process, but what had emerged in the reserected corpse of Doria now determined to crawl its way out of the crater. Primal growling echoed and slight huffing was made by the determined thing. The Doria mutant grabbed at the scorched earth in an attempt to gain a grip, as the creature moved towards the top of the crater. Earth fell to the bottom of the pit, as the creature's feet propelled its body slowly.

"Food, food," the beast that once was Doria cried out. "Hungry," it called out.

She was quite determined in getting to the top of the crater. With every fiber of its body, the unseen creature struggled. Darkcloak watched in anticipation as the thing reached the top. Gray talonlike hands gripped the soil, digging discolored fingers into the soil. Then the beast, with an energy-filled lunge, lifted itself out of the pit. A gasp, followed by a sinister cackle came from the shadow agent, as he witnessed his new creation emerge as if it was the Kraken itself surfacing and ready to devour sailors whole.

"Oh, what a delightful sight this is," proclaimed Darkcloak.

Doria stared at the shadow agent, as if she could see her master even though the shadow agent was thousands of miles away and underground. Her fair skin had transformed into the traditional mutant gray color, with spots of rotting flesh here and there. Her eyes had filled with a red tint that would allow her to see in infrared, quite helpful when hunting at night. Darkcloak also knew that she could sense other mutants, even the assassins and their comrades. He knew this because he had designed the serum for this, adding a bit of DNA from each of the remaining of the Corporation's misfits. The shadow agent had made sure of that during manufacturing before Nikolai Volkov ended the world.

Darkcloak also knew that the new Doria would not stop until she had hunted down all of them, until she killed them all. That thought made Darkcloak laugh even louder. "Soon, my sweet investment, you will make me the victor and destroyer of this retched place. Let us see the Shadow Lord dispute my blindsiding victory."